CHRISTMAS OFF SCRIPT

EVIE ALEXANDER

First Published in Great Britain 2024 by Emlin Press

ISBN (eBook) 978-1-914473-34-0

ISBN (Print) 978-1-914473-35-7

ISBN (Audiobook) 978-1-914473-47-0

A CIP catalogue record for this book is available from the British Library.

www.emlinpress.com

For my husband, the original Mr Christmas

ALSO BY EVIE ALEXANDER

THE KINLOCH SERIES

Highland Games

Hollywood Games

Kissing Games

Musical Games

Wedding Games

Christmas Games

THE FOXBROOKE SERIES

One Night in Foxbrooke

Love ad Lib

An Unholy Affair

The Upper Crush

The Love Position

Christmas off Script

One Night Only

Righting Mr Wrong

Under the Influencer

Foxbrooke Extras

By Evie Alexander and Kelly Kay

EVIE & KELLY'S HOLIDAY DISASTERS SERIES

Cupid Calamity

Cookout Carnage

Christmas Chaos

Get Evie's books in all formats as well as special offers, early releases, and exclusive deals direct from her website:

www.eviealexanderbooks.com

EMLIN
PRESS

WHAT IS A PANTOMIME?

Hello, lovely reader!

If you're not from the UK, then PLEASE read this foreword! It's vital for you to understand what a 'panto' is and why it's synonymous with Christmas. Otherwise, you may find large portions of this story rather odd.

A 'pantomime,' also known as a 'panto' or 'the Christmas panto,' is a particularly British cultural phenomenon and theatrical tradition dating back hundreds of years. Pantos are ONLY ever performed at Christmas, though the stories are never *about* Christmas. They blend comedy, music, dancing, slapstick, fairy tales, audience participation, and can be enjoyed by everyone from the youngest of children to the oldest of grandparents.

Pantomime has its roots in ancient Roman theatre, where 'pantomimus' was a form of entertainment that combined dance, music, and mime. However, the British pantomime, as described in *Christmas off Script*, began to take shape in the eighteenth century. It evolved from the Italian *commedia dell'arte*, which featured stock characters such as Harlequin and Pantaloon, into a uniquely British theatrical tradition.

In the Victorian era, pantomimes became hugely popular as Christmas entertainment. They began incorporating well-known fairy tales and folklore, which provided a familiar framework for the comic and musical performances. Over time, pantomime has become synonymous with the festive season in the UK, to the point where many Brits, including myself, cannot imagine Christmas without it.

One of the most distinctive features of a panto is the level of audience participation. The fourth wall is not just broken, it doesn't exist. Audiences are encouraged to engage with the performers throughout the show, and often unwitting audience members are drawn into the action. Some of the most famous interactions include:

• **'He's behind you!'** - This is shouted by the audience when the villain sneaks up on the hero, who seems oblivious.
• **'Oh, yes, it is!' / 'Oh, no, it isn't!'** - This call-and-response occurs when characters argue over something obvious to the audience but disputed on stage.
• **Booing the baddies and cheering the good guys** - Audiences are invited to boo and hiss whenever the villain appears and to cheer for the hero.

A central figure in any panto is the **Pantomime Dame**, a comedic, exaggerated character played by a man in insanely bizarre women's clothing that no woman would ever wear. The Dame is usually played by an older man, and they are usually large, with enormous breasts.

It's important to understand that a Pantomime Dame is not the same as a drag queen. Drag queens are beautiful and often perform to celebrate and explore gender identity and expression. The Pantomime Dame is about broad comedy.

The Dame is usually a maternal or comic character, such as Widow Twankey in *Aladdin* or the Ugly Sisters in *Cinderella*. The humor is more about the absurdity and larger-than-life personality rather than any commentary on gender.

Another quirk of pantomime casting is that the 'Principal Boy' — the hero of the story, like Aladdin or Prince Charming — is traditionally played by a woman. This dates back to the nineteenth century and though less common today, this tradition still holds in many pantomimes, adding to the playful and topsy-turvy nature of the performance.

In recent decades, pantomimes have become big business (most professional pantos run for at least a month and end in mid-to-late January), and it's expected that TV stars and celebrities play major roles. You might find a popular soap opera actor playing the villain or a well-known comedian taking on the role of the Dame. This blending of familiar faces from television and the panto tradition helps make the shows appealing to audiences of all ages. Amateur productions, on the other hand, usually run for only a handful of performances in the run-up to Christmas and are put on by local communities.

Pantomimes are also famous for their mix of humor that caters to the whole family. There's slapstick and visual comedy alongside puns, wordplay, and innuendo that go over children's heads but give the adults a good laugh. Additionally, pantos always include topical jokes, political satire, and jokes at the expense of local areas or sports teams.

Despite its association with Christmas, the stories told in pantomimes — such as *Cinderella*, *Snow White*, *Jack and the Beanstalk*, and *Puss in Boots* — are not Christmas tales. These are classic fairy tales and folk stories, but in Britain, they are exclusively performed during the festive season. The reason for this is more about tradition and the festive spirit than any connection to the holiday itself, although the performances usually end with the cast wishing the audience a merry Christmas and a happy New Year.

In pantomime performances of Cinderella there are characters and places that will be unfamiliar to people who have never seen this version of the story. Cinderella has a loyal best friend, Buttons (often played by a woman), a servant at Hardup Hall (where Cinderella and the ugly sisters live) who's secretly in love with Cinderella. Prince Charming also has an equerry/servant/friend named Dandini, and a central part of the plot in the first act revolves around the two of them changing places so Prince Charming can experience life as a commoner.

At its core, a pantomime is a bonkers and bizarre celebration of fun, community, and a shared experience. It's a genre that refuses to take itself seriously, embraces silliness, and revels in the interaction between audience and performers. For many Brits, Christmas wouldn't be the same without the laughter, the cheers, the terrible jokes, and the slapstick of a good panto. It's a tradition that brings people together, young and old, in a uniquely British way, and if you ever get the chance to see a panto, then do!

❧ I ❧

Should I be worried?

Huddled under the narrow concrete overhang, her brolly facing the biting November rain, Ella waited for her stepmother to come to the front door.

She might be still asleep?

You told her you'd be earlier today.

Yes, but she's not great at remembering things.

Or listening.

And if she's in bed, then she's got to get down the stairs.

Which is difficult because of—

Wrenching her gaze from the peeling paint of the door, Ella stared at the broken paving slabs beneath her Converse trainers. Despite being the beginning of winter, weeds still shoved their way through the cracks, pushing the weight of the concrete aside.

It's not your fault. It's not your fault. It's not your fault.

How many times had she said those words to herself? Almost enough for her heart to believe it. Yet lurking behind the blame for her stepmother's injury lay a truth she could never rationalise away.

She's on her own because of me.

Holding her breath, Ella tensed, fighting down the nausea in her stomach. Even after nine years, the anxiety hadn't lessened.

Come on. Make yourself useful.

Pressing the doorbell for the third time, she took her phone from her bag and stared at the screen, her thumb hovering over the 'call' icon.

What's the point?

Communication with her stepmother was only ever one way. Michelle rang Ella whenever she wanted anything. However, if Ella rang *her*, the call wouldn't be answered.

Opening her message app, Ella gazed at the last texts she'd sent Oliver, her boyfriend of six years.

> Ella: Do you know yet if you're coming back this weekend? Last month you said you'd try to but you haven't confirmed yet. I can't believe it's been ten weeks since we've seen each other! Miss you xxx

> Ella: Don't forget I'm making limoncello and lebkuchen with Leo this afternoon. He's bringing extra ingredients in case you change your mind about joining in xxx

> Ella: Oh, and the read-through for the panto has been moved to Sunday morning, but it shouldn't take more than a couple of hours. Maybe you could visit your parents then? Although you're more than welcome to come along. Last I heard, they still don't have a Prince Charming, and you'd be perfect for the role! Xxx

> Ella: Sorry the weekend's got so busy and I know it's a really long journey for such a short time… If you want me to rearrange Leo on Sat then just say. He'll totally understand xxx

> Ella: Every time I've called you this week, it's rung out. Is everything okay? Xxx

> Ella: I know you're super busy, but please let me know if you're coming later and if you'd rather I put Leo off for another time. Miss you xxxxx

Just over a year ago, Oliver got a new job teaching history at a private school in the north. He taught on Saturday mornings, so only came back home during the holidays or on the occasional weekend. Over the long summer break, he'd spent most of it running a summer school, and had spent the October half-term skiing with year nine students.

His communication had become increasingly sporadic, but Ella refused to worry. If she allowed even a drop of doubt to rain on her love parade, she'd be drowning in it.

The front door opened and Michelle's puffy face scowled at her. 'What are you doing here?'

Seeing her stepmother without make-up was always a shock and it took Ella a second to reply. 'I messaged yesterday to remind you I was coming earlier this morning.'

Michelle tugged the sides of her grubby fleece dressing gown closer, protecting herself from the rain blowing into the house. 'Why?'

'I'm making lebkuchen and limoncello with Leo later.'

'So, you're putting that posh twat before your own family?'

Ella bit the inside of her cheek as she internally screamed that Leo's parents and siblings were more of a family to her than Michelle and her two daughters had ever been.

Taking a deep breath, she forced her voice to stay level. 'I wrote in the calendar on the fridge that I would be here at eight, rather than eleven.'

Michelle sniffed. 'I never look at that. Don't know why you got it.'

The back of Ella's jeans were now wet and clinging to her calves. At times like this, it felt like the last straws were being chucked casually onto her back.

'I can come back next week if that's better for you?'

Her stepmother's bloodshot eyes flared with a brief look of panic. Then she smiled and tugged on Ella's arm to bring her into the house. 'No, my love. Now's fine.' Closing the door behind them, Michelle led Ella into the living room, her limp less pronounced than usual. 'You get started and I'll make you a cup of tea. Piece of cake?'

A lump formed in Ella's throat at the unexpected kindness and she nodded, her heart grasping for the crumbs of affection. No matter how secure she was in her relationship with Oliver, nor how close she was to her best friend, Leo, and his family, inside she was still a little girl craving love from parents who rarely gave her any.

Michelle squeezed Ella's arm. 'You're a good girl. You look after me, don't you?'

Ella nodded again, all the earlier anger at her stepmother dissolving into guilt and compassion.

'Okay, I'll leave you to it.' Michelle limped towards the door, her breath shortening each time she put weight on her right leg.

Grabbing one of the many walking sticks that littered the house, Ella dashed forward to pass it to her.

'Thanks.' Her stepmother paused, now breathing heavily. 'I think I'd better get back upstairs. I ran for the door when you rang and my leg's now screaming at me.'

A fresh wave of guilt rolled through Ella, washing away any

doubts or questions about the truth of her stepmother's statement. 'Can I get you anything?'

'No. Bastard GP won't give me any decent painkillers. He doesn't understand,' she replied bitterly. 'Nobody does.'

'Can I at least help you back upstairs?'

Michelle shook her head. 'I need you down here. I'll be okay.'

Ella moved forward, wanting to assist.

Her stepmother scowled. 'Leave it. I'm fine.' Hobbling from the room, she made her way up the stairs, each thump of the stick on the tread feeling like a blow to Ella's stomach.

Hearing the bathroom door close, Ella let out a held breath, quickly checked her phone to see if Oliver had been in touch, then surveyed the living room. It had only been a week since she'd last cleaned, but she couldn't tell.

Overflowing ashtrays, discarded single-use vapes, glasses greasy with fingerprints, mugs with dirt-brown coffee dregs, half-empty takeaway boxes, and copies of *Soap First* magazine littered every available surface. The room smelled of vegetable oil, cigarette smoke, and chemical fruit. It made Ella's skin itch.

Retying her long black hair into a bun, she took a pair of rubber gloves from her bag and went to work. She'd been cleaning for her stepmother since she was a teenager and was fast and efficient. If she wasn't, then it would take all day to get the job done. Several times a year, Michelle went abroad on holiday, and Ella always took those opportunities to spend a weekend doing a deep clean. Her half-sisters never lifted a manicured finger to help their mother, so Ella did.

Oliver despised her family and resented the fact she spent every Saturday cleaning for Michelle. But it made sense to do it then, when she wasn't working and he was teaching until early afternoon.

Wiping a strand of hair from her sweaty forehead, Ella pulled out her phone and stared once more at the string of unanswered messages she'd sent Oliver, her nerves jangling.

Don't go there. Don't go there.

Oliver *was* her happy-ever-after. He was proof she'd dragged herself up two social classes and broken the familial cycle of entitled poverty. It didn't matter what he or his parents thought of Ella's family. With her politeness, kindness, and respectable job as an art teacher at Foxbrooke Secondary, she'd proven she was nothing like her mum, dad, or stepmother and half-sisters.

Then why don't they ever invite you for Christmas?

Stop it!

Why are they so patronising and condescending and think you're too thick to notice?

Shut up!

Perching on the edge of the sofa, Ella scrunched up her face, fighting the internal monologue as it picked away at the created fantasies of her life, trying to unravel them. If she was in her own home now, she would have grabbed a pen and started drawing, soothing away her stress by creating fairytale worlds with handsome princes and happy princesses, butterflies big enough to ride, and castles in the clouds. A place where every magical day was either midsummer or a perfect Christmas.

Her phone buzzed.

> Leo: Would you consider playing Cinderella this year? Summer is such an insufferable flake now she's an 'influencer' and I don't want her to bail at the last minute and leave us without the eponymous star x

> Leo: Look at me with my big words. I'm so audacious x

Ella grinned, her heart immediately lifting. Leo knew her better than anyone else. He may have disliked her family even more than Oliver did, but he hardly ever let it show and was the one person who truly understood why she spent so much time helping her stepmother.

Ella: U R sew smarrt x

Leo: Dear god. You just made me throw up in my mouth. Don't do that to your BFF. He's too much of a posh twat

Ella: OMG have you been listening outside the window?

Leo: Lol, no way. Michelle's just boringly predictable, and I know what she thinks of me. Did she forget you were coming early today?

Ella: Yeah

Leo: Sorry x

Ella: Not your fault. I've got to get back to it. I'll see you later x

Pocketing her phone, she took a deep breath and went back to sorting out the living room.

TWO HOURS LATER, THE THREE ROOMS DOWNSTAIRS WERE clean and tidy and Ella had moved to the upstairs bathroom. Brown smears of foundation and the chalky remains of toothpaste coated the sink, a film of oil and strands of bleached hair lined the inside of the bath, and the toilet was unflushed.

Could she at least attempt *to clean up after herself?*

She can't bend down easily and it's a small space. You know *this!*

Dropping to her hands and knees, Ella scrubbed the toilet bowl, daydreaming about the hot shower she would have when she got home, followed by a relaxed and fun afternoon with Leo, baking Christmas cookies and making limoncello together.

The bathroom door opened and Michelle appeared. On her bottom half was a pair of stained jogging bottoms, grubby socks and dirty sliders. From the waist up, though, she was camera-ready.

Dressed in a voluminous black blouse and a heavy diamante necklace, her make-up was artfully contoured to give the impression of cheekbones, big doe eyes, and a narrow nose. Her lips, already plumped with fillers, now appeared so huge it was as if two lilos were stuck together. Aided by Botox and the filters on her phone, by the time Michelle posted to social media, she was every inch the influencer she aspired to be, and utterly unrecognisable from the real person underneath the façade.

She peered around the bathroom. 'You doing my bedroom next?'

Ella nodded. 'And I'll make sure I don't touch your lights or the bed.'

'You'd better not. The last time you moved them, it took forever to fix.'

Michelle had social media accounts under the name 'Chelle Shops'. Every video was the same: her dressed in black against the backdrop of her frilly pink bed, showing her audience everything she'd been buying.

Posting for the past four years and against all odds, Michelle had built up a sizeable audience of people who loved shopping, and wanted to know what she'd bought and what she thought of it.

Nobody seemed to realise they never actually saw her

wearing any of what she presented, nor the items for a second time. Another one of Ella's jobs for her stepmother was returning every item Michelle had bought for a full refund. And if Michelle got anything for free, then the moment she'd posted about it, she sold it online.

'I've already sorted the packages downstairs and I'll take them to the post office when I'm done here,' Ella said. 'Is there anything else I can help you with today?'

'Yeah, can you go to the shops and get me a few things?'

Alarm flashed across Ella's skin. Michelle seemed to think she was a walking cash machine, but her teacher's salary was modest and she was perpetually short of money. This was mainly because of the extortionate rent she paid to Oliver's parents for the privilege of living with their son in the house they'd bought for him.

'Er...'

Michelle's eyes narrowed. 'You won't help your own family? When you know my disability payments don't cover shit? You think you're better than us?'

Despite the adrenaline pulsing in her veins, Ella was tempted to point out she was the one cleaning a toilet, and Michelle not only possessed the funds to eat takeout for every meal and have cosmetic procedures, but also go on expensive foreign holidays many times a year.

The sound of the front door opening saved her from replying, as Michelle's attention was drawn to the excited screeches of her daughters.

'Mum! Oh my God!' Kyla-Marie yelled.

'Freaking out!' shrieked Billie-Mai as she thundered after her elder sister up the stairs.

Giving a cursory glance at Ella kneeling next to the toilet as if to acknowledge her place in the family pecking order, they hugged their mother.

'I couldn't believe it. I was like, "no way, Kyla-Marie".'

'And I was like, "it's the truth, Billie-Mai".'

'What are we going to do? Something special?'

Ella tuned her half-sisters out. Aged twenty-two and twenty, respectively, Kyla-Marie and Billie-Mai were slimmer and younger versions of their mother. They were trophy girlfriends for the kind of man Ella crossed the street to avoid, and were building their own social media followings instead of seeking a more traditional form of employment.

'Ells, you excited?' Billie-Mai asked.

Ella glanced up. 'About what?'

'Dad coming out.'

Raw fear shot through her and the scrubbing brush fell out of her hands, clanking on the inside of the toilet bowl. Her mouth fell open, but nothing came out.

'Shut your pie hole, Ella,' Kyla-Marie said disdainfully. 'You look right thick. Are you going to do something about yourself?'

'Wha—'

'For when he comes out. You need to make an effort. Don't you care?'

'We can help,' Billie-Mai chimed in. 'I can do your nails.'

'No, you can't,' said Kyla-Marie. 'You won't have time. She needs to learn how to help herself.'

Ella's gaze went to her stepmother. 'When's he coming out? Why didn't you tell me?'

'Don't take that tone with me,' Michelle snapped.

'God, Ella! Don't be such a bitch!' Kyla-Marie added.

'He'll be out in time for Christmas,' Billie-Mai said.

'And I *did* tell you,' Michelle continued. 'It's not my fault you don't listen.'

Ella's knees gave way and her backside hit the floor. She thought she had at least four more years until her dad was released from prison. Memories churned inside her stomach, as fresh and putrid as when they'd been formed, nine years ago.

Her stepmother and half-sisters had already turned away, making their way down the stairs, Michelle keeping pace with her daughters.

'It's going to be the perfect Christmas!' Billie-Mai said excitedly. 'Has Dad told you what he wants to do as soon as he gets out?'

'Not yet, but I'm sure he's got a few ideas,' her mum replied, then turned her head to eyeball Ella. 'And some scores to settle.'

As her stepmother continued down the stairs, Ella closed her eyes. What should she do?

Talk to Leo this afternoon.

Hands shaking, she finished cleaning the bathroom, then vacuumed, tidied, and dusted the rest of the upstairs as quickly as she could. The rooms seemed smaller, the walls closer, as if they were inexorably turning into her own tomb. Her heart hadn't slowed since the bombshell about her father. She needed to get out of the house so she could breathe properly and organise her thoughts.

Downstairs, she collected all the purchases her stepmother was returning, as well as the gifted items she was selling online, yelled an unanswered goodbye and ran from the house.

Now she welcomed the wet weather. It was cleansing after the suffocating negativity of Michelle's home. Running along the pavement, her trainers slapped through the puddles and she squinted to protect her face from the sharp stabs of icy rain. Hands full with her stepmother's packages, she couldn't hold a brolly, but right now she didn't care. She just wanted to get home and wash everything about the day from her skin.

. . .

'YOU'RE EARLY TODAY,' THE POSTMASTER SAID WITH A SMILE as Ella got to the front of the queue. With budget cuts over the years, Foxbrooke's post office had gone from being in a large building to one counter in a newsagent. It was currently packed with people getting the Saturday papers, sweets, or taking refuge from the rain. Ella was now soaked to the skin and beginning to shiver.

'I've got plans for this afternoon,' she replied, lifting the first parcel from her bag.

There was a collective groan behind her as the rest of the queue clocked just how long Ella was going to take, followed by the kind of passive-aggressive tuts and huffs Brits excelled at.

'I'm making lebkuchen for Christmas,' she continued.

The postmaster's eyebrows raised as he scanned the returns label. 'Won't they get stale?'

'No, the flavours need to develop and mingle. Leaving them for a few weeks also improves the texture.'

'I'll take your word for it.'

As soon as he lifted the first package off the scales, Ella replaced it with the next one. She usually visited the post office later when it was quieter. Now the back of her body prickled with the mental daggers being thrown her way by the people behind her.

Her phone rang and she pulled it out while manipulating an unwieldy parcel onto the scales.

Oliver!

Wedging the phone between her ear and shoulder, she took the call. 'Hey! How are you? I—'

Slipping out of place, the phone crashed to the floor.

'Can't it wait?' a man grumbled behind her.

'Sorry, sorry.' She retrieved it, taking out another parcel. 'Are you coming back today?' she asked Oliver.

'No.'

'Why not? What's—hang on.' Feeling the phone slipping again, Ella put it on the counter and turned on the speaker, mouthing '*sorry*' at the cashier. 'Sorry, Oli, I'm back. What's going on? Is everything okay?'

He sighed. 'No, it's not.'

Already wired from the morning and the news about her father, Ella's nervous system ramped up a gear. 'What's happened?'

The hubbub of the crowd in the post office disappeared as everyone listened in. The only noise was the beep from the scanner and the pattering of rain on the windows.

Ella placed another parcel on the scales, trying to pretend everything was normal even as each cell in her body was freaking out.

'Nothing's happened, but we need to talk.'

Her mouth went bone dry. 'About what?'

'Us. I don't want to be in a relationship with you anymore. I want to break up.'

Ella listened to the ring tone, grief clawing at her heart, waiting for Oliver to answer as she ran from the post office.

Come on! Come on! Pick up! We can make this work!

After Oliver's statement had broken her world apart, Ella had cut the call, finished processing her stepmother's parcels in silence, then left, not meeting the gaze of anyone around her.

Everyone in Foxbrooke knew who Ella was. She was the teen pregnancy accident of chavvy Nadine Butcher and drug dealer Ronnie Chamberlain. Damned before she was even born, and bearing the brunt of every bad decision made by her family, it would only be a matter of minutes before everyone knew she'd been publicly dumped by the upper-middle-class Oliver Fitzcannon. Ella Chamberlain and her family didn't deserve nice things, and she'd got what was coming to her for thinking she could aspire to more.

'Hey,' Oliver sighed down the line. 'Look, I'm sorry. I—'

'We can fix this,' she interrupted breathlessly. 'We can't just throw away six years without a fight.'

Silence.

'I know it's been tough spending so much time apart,' she continued. 'But I won't have to look after my step-mother forever, and then I can move to wherever you are.'

'Ella, Michelle's forty. She's only eleven years older than I am.'

'But...' When her dad came out of prison, would the burden of looking after Michelle pass to him? Or would he simply expect Ella to carry on being a skivvy like she'd been before he was sent down?

What do you think's going to happen? It's not like he's turned over a new leaf when he's been inside.

'We barely see each other and I'm building a life up here now,' Oliver continued.

'What do you mean? You said this was a career step. That you'd move back in a year.'

Ella reached the front door of the modern house Oliver's parents had bought for him in an attempt to keep their son closer to them, and fumbled to insert the key.

'They've offered me the Head of Department position.'

'W-what? When?' Pushing the door shut behind her, she leaned against the hall radiator.

Oliver didn't reply.

Ella shrugged off her coat and frantically tugged at the laces of her Converse. 'What about your parents?'

'They're happy for me,' was Oliver's eventual reply.

'What? They already know? When did this happen? Why didn't you tell me?'

First the news about her dad, and now this? Why was she the last to know about the most important things in her life?

Oliver cleared his throat. 'It was offered to me after the ski trip.'

Weeks ago. 'And you didn't think to discuss it with me before making a decision?'

More silence.

Padding in her wet socks through into the living room, Ella turned in a circle. On every wall she'd hung canvases printed with photos of her and Oliver. 'Look at us!' they proclaimed. 'Look how happy we are together!'

She'd spent so long creating her happy-ever-after, and now Oliver was ripping the fairytale apart and changing the ending.

This was it. The chance to do what she should have done years ago. She wasn't even Michelle's kid. Kyla-Marie and Billie-Mai would finally have to step up. Oliver had to come first.

'I'll hand in my notice on Monday. You get three and a half weeks off for Christmas. We can spend it together, then I'll come back with you up north and look for work nearby.'

The line remained silent. Had they been cut off?

'Oliver?'

She heard him sigh.

'I'm making it happen, Oli. Did you hear what I just said? I'm putting us first.'

'Ella, it's not going to work. You're too tied to Michelle. You—'

'I'm not. I'm walking away. Anyway, Dad's coming out next month, and—'

'What?'

'I found out this morning. He's got early parole, so—'

'Great,' Oliver interrupted sarcastically. 'Just what Foxbrooke needs. Ronnie Chamberlain at large again.'

Ella bit her lip. She knew Oliver was right, but Ronnie was her dad, and a part of her was still the little girl who hero-worshipped her father and had once believed he could do no wrong.

'Look. This isn't some spur-of-the-moment thing, Ella. I've been thinking about it for a while now.'

She collapsed with a thump to the floor, her fingers picking at the rug. 'Why didn't you tell me?'

'I don't know. I...' He took a big breath. 'I've made my decision, and it's final. Mum and Dad are putting the house on the market next week so you'll need to take down the pictures of— any personal pictures and tidy it up ready for the estate agent to take photos on Monday. Mum will use her key to let them in so you don't need to take time off work.'

He sounded so matter-of-fact, as if he was delivering a well-practised speech.

'The estate agents already have clients lined up to view and expect an offer by the middle of the week. It's tight, but any buyer is likely to want to be in for Christmas, so we're giving you plenty of time to find somewhere else to live.'

All the oxygen had been sucked from the room. Ella was dreaming. Hallucinating. These words couldn't be coming out of the mouth of the man she'd given her heart and soul to for the past six years. The man she presumed she would marry.

'Ella?'

'Yes?' she eventually managed.

'Did you hear what I just said?'

She shook her head as if that would shake Oliver's words away and everything would go back to normal.

'Ella, it's important you understand what this means. Do you want to—' He let out a heavy breath. 'Do you have anything you want to say?'

'Like what?' she replied dully. 'Out of the blue, you're dumping me and making me homeless just before Christmas.'

'Oh, come on, Ella, don't be like that. You sound just like Michelle.'

'Well, how do you want me to sound?' Her voice rose with

anger. 'Ecstatic? How the fuck would *you* feel if you were me right now?'

'Okay, okay. I get that you're upset.'

Fighting to breathe as grief crushed her ribs, she made a keening sound of pain that didn't seem to belong to her.

'We can speak again when you've calmed down. I'm sorry, Ella. Really, I am.'

Then he was gone.

Curling into a foetal position, Ella howled like an animal in pain. The seismic shock to her system split her in two. Half of her was detached, gazing down at her screaming form and frightened by the noise she was making. The other half was battered by a storm of grief so powerful it was tearing her apart.

Please stop making that sound. It's scaring me.

But she couldn't stop.

There was the sound of the front door opening and closing, then someone entered the room.

'Ella! Jesus Christ! Are you hurt? What's happened?'

The part of her soul that was hovering outside her body like a frantic parent cried with relief.

Leo. It's Leo.

She watched him fall to the floor beside her, his gaze darting around the room for danger, as the shopping bags he'd brought with him were discarded, spilling their contents.

'I've got you. I'm here.' His strong arms held her tightly and she fought to control her cries.

You're safe. It's okay. Leo's here. He won't let anything bad happen to you.

'You don't have to say anything. Just nod if you're hurt, okay?'

She shook her head. Then her howls turned into wracking

sobs, and the external part of her that had been hovering above the two of them slipped back into her body.

Leo held her to his chest, gently rocking as he soothed her. 'Shhh... It's going to be alright. I promise. You don't need to talk. Take your time. I'm here.'

Ella's cries intensified with the love she felt from Leo. He was always there for her and had never let her down. He comforted her with the ease and familiarity of a favourite soft toy.

Time passed, and so too did her tears, but Leo didn't let go until she moved, uncurling her stiff limbs and shuffling out of his warm embrace.

She shivered, suddenly freezing.

He caught one of her icy hands. 'Your jeans are soaked through. Can I run you a bath? I think you've still got some of those aromatherapy salts Willow gave you for your birthday. I could chuck them in?'

Nodding, she closed her fingers around his, worried about falling back into the chasm of grief if he left the room.

'Come with me?' he suggested. 'Sit on the landing and order me about?'

Ella nodded again, and Leo helped her to her feet, not letting go of her hand as he led her up the stairs. In the bathroom, he sat her on the closed lid of the toilet and turned the bath taps on with his free hand. Seeming to understand instinctively that she needed physical touch to ground her, he kept hold of her hand as he emptied the container of fragrant salts into the tub.

'Don't forget that Mammy and Willow harvested the lavender and chamomile at the right phase of the moon according to biodynamic principles, so the salts are infused with—' He paused and pulled a face as if trying to find the right words, then grinned. 'Hippy magic?'

The corners of Ella's mouth tried to move, and Leo squeezed her hand a little tighter. The bath was filling quickly, but she couldn't bear the idea of him leaving.

Again, he seemed to read her mind. 'Why don't you get in it fully clothed?' he suggested. 'Then, when you've warmed up enough, I can sit outside and you can get undressed.'

Tears springing to her eyes, she nodded.

Leo helped her stand as if she was an invalid, then held onto her as she stepped into the water and sat down.

The relief was immediate, soaking through her jeans, then working its way under her sweatshirt and t-shirt.

He perched on the edge of the bath, still holding her hand. He was smiling at her achievement, but she could see the concern behind it.

'Thank you,' she whispered.

His smile grew until it lit up his face. 'Anytime! It's one of my duties as your BFFF.'

She raised an eyebrow.

'Your Best Fantastic Friend Forever. Although, as it's me, I could probably add Funny and Fandsome to the list.'

A spark of happiness flashed briefly inside her. 'Fandsome?'

He wiggled his eyebrows. 'Most definitely. And many ladies would also describe me as "Fexy".'

She snorted. 'Don't forget to add "Full of it" to your list.'

He gave a theatrical sigh. 'It's a hard cross to bear, being the best-looking Foxbrooke.'

'Didn't Henry model for *Vogue*?'

Leo pursed his lips and sucked in his cheekbones. 'I could do that any day of the week.'

Ella smirked. 'You look deranged.'

'And very fexy.'

'Er...'

'Oh, come on. You're my BFFF, you've got to take my side.'

'Okay, you're better-looking than Henry.'

Leo looked as happy as a little boy who'd accidentally guessed how many sweets were in a jar and was now attempting to eat them all.

'Although... Connor is incredibly handsome. That black hair and blue eye combination?'

'I've got blue eyes!' he replied indignantly. 'You're being blond-hairist.'

'Is that a thing?'

'Course it is. Why do all romance heroes have to be "tall, dark and handsome"? Why can't they be "tall, blonde and fexy"?'

Ella giggled.

'And why are the dudes with blond hair always the best friend?'

She squeezed his hand. 'Because they make the best, *best* friends.'

'Humph. So, do you think Connor's better-looking than me?'

Ella tilted her head and narrowed her eyes as she gazed at him critically. 'Objectively, you're both above average in the looks department, but you'll always win because I'm biassed.'

Leo appeared sufficiently mollified.

'Although,' she continued, 'Estelle, Willow and Summer are very beautiful.'

'I'll give you that. But if they were men, I'd still be fexier.'

'If you say so.'

'Oh, I do. All the time.'

Ella fell silent, thinking of Leo's unconventional family. Leo's father, Arthur, was the Duke of Somerset and had two wives, who were also in a relationship with each other as well as with him. His official wife, Vivienne, was a Black American model and movie star and the mother of twins, Estelle and

Henry. When the twins were two, Vivienne had met and fallen in love with an Irish single mum, Dervla, who had Connor at the time. After Dervla had been introduced to Arthur, she had three more children with him: Leo, Willow, and Summer.

Leo's parents were blissfully happy in their three-way relationship and loved every one of their children equally. The media may have portrayed them as morally corrupt and destroying traditional family values, but Ella received more attention and affection from them than she'd ever had from her own parents and stepmother.

'Ella,' Leo began hesitantly.

She gazed at his face, almost as familiar to her as her own, seeing uncertainty and worry in his expression.

'You don't have to tell me what's happened, but I need to know if you're safe,' he continued. 'And I want to help.'

Tears sprang again to prick her eyes. 'You can't,' she whispered.

He rubbed his thumb across the back of her hand as he held it. 'I'd like to try,' he said softly. 'Seeing you this upset makes my heart hurt. It's a physical pain and one I've never— haven't had for a really long time.'

Ella knew what he was thinking about. Or rather, *who*. When they'd started sixth form, a new girl, Lila, had arrived. In that first week, she'd decided that she and Ella were going to be best friends and that Leo was going to be her boyfriend. But Lila's feelings for Leo never ran as deep as Leo's feelings for her. She kept breaking up with him, then changing her mind. This went on for four years until Lila left for the States to do an MBA and never came back.

Leo and Ella had only briefly talked about how Lila had affected him, but he hadn't had a girlfriend since, and Ella suspected it was because he still hoped his first love would return to Foxbrooke. And him.

'Oliver dumped me,' she said in a rush.

'Huh?' Leo appeared utterly bewildered by her statement.

'He's staying up north and his parents are selling the house. I have to be out by Christmas.'

A pause followed as her words hit home. Then Leo's expression went from confused to furious.

'WHAT?'

Ella felt the tension running from his hand into hers.

'He—he can't be serious!'

'He is,' she whispered.

'But I don't understand. How long have you known about this?'

'An hour.'

Leo stood, letting go of her hand and running his fingers through his tousled blond hair. The bathroom was small, but he still managed to pace, taking two small steps, then whirling around to start again.

'I... Jesus Christ! He's lost his fucking mind.' Leo's cheeks were dark red, his sapphire eyes burning. 'He can't do this,' he said decisively, as if his word was law, then turned to Ella, staring at her with furious intensity. 'Is he doing drugs?'

'What?'

'Has his behaviour changed since he started that job? Has he been hiding things from you? Does he seem different?'

Oh god. Has Oliver fallen in love with someone else?

'He's been really distant for a while, and we haven't seen each other for weeks, but I thought it was because of how busy the job was.'

'I'll speak to him. Put him straight.'

'No—'

'But none of this makes any sense!'

'Why not?'

Leo returned to sitting on the edge of the bath and took

her hand again. 'Because you're the best, Ella. You're funny, kind, smart, gifted, caring, thoughtful, not to mention stunningly beautiful. If Oliver is serious about breaking up with you, then he's either gone insane, or he's on drugs. There's no other option.'

'He might have found someone else?' She bit the inside of her cheek to stop more tears from spilling out.

'Impossible. There's no-one better than you.'

She let out a bitter laugh. 'You're very sweet, but most people in Foxbrooke think I'm scum.'

'They don't. And even if they did, they're fucking idiots.'

'It's breaking news to me, but Oliver said he's been thinking about us splitting up for a while now. And he's been offered the job of head of the history department, so I really don't think he'll change his mind. His mum is letting the estate agent in on Monday to take photos.'

'You're joking.'

'Apparently they've already got bookings lined up and expect an offer by midweek, with completion before Christmas. That's why they want me out.'

'Jesus!' Leo stood again and resumed pacing. 'They can't. What about the rental agreement you signed? Surely they have to give you three months' notice?'

Ella shook her head. 'I didn't sign anything. I just paid a deposit and the first month's rent into his parents' bank account, then set up a standing order.'

Leo stared at her in shock, his hands flexing, then forming into fists.

'They—' He shook his head. 'Those tight bastards made their son's girlfriend pay a *deposit*? When's the next payment going out?'

'At the end of the month.'

'Cancel it. You can't trust those fuckers to give you back your deposit. They can use it in lieu of your last month's rent.'

'I can't do that.'

'Yes, you can.' He paused, his body now as still as a big cat, preparing to pounce. 'How much rent have you been paying them?'

What's the point of covering for them anymore? Ella told him.

'Fuck!' Leo yelled to the ceiling, the tendons in his neck taut and a pulse beating wildly under his skin. He took a deep breath, then sat on the edge of the bath, his hands interlocked and his knuckles white.

'Ella.' His voice thrummed with anger. 'That figure is way above the market average and should have been paid by you *and* Oliver.'

She nodded, the lump in her throat too big to let any words out.

'Please. *Please* cancel your next payment.'

Ella didn't want to. To do so was to admit defeat. But what choice did she have? Oliver had made up his mind and his parents had never liked her, no matter how hard she tried to win them over. No doubt they were breathing a sigh of relief that their beloved son had finally ended his relationship with her.

'I've got to take all the pictures of us down by Monday,' she choked out. 'So they aren't in the estate agent's photos.'

'Oh, mate...' Leo's hand reached forward and took hers again. 'I'm so fucking sorry.'

'Me too,' she whispered, tears falling from her cheeks into the bath.

'You don't deserve this. It's not fair.'

Ella shrugged, her eyes on the surface of the water and her jeans underneath.

'Come and live at the manor. You know there is masses of space and my folks would be over the moon if you moved in.'

She glanced up at him. Surely he couldn't be serious?

His expression brightened. 'It's the perfect solution. My family adores you, it's closer to your work than here, and you've stayed over so often you know what it's like. And don't even *think* of offering to pay rent, or my parents will be horrified. Please?'

Ella remembered the first time she'd ever slept at the manor. It was Christmas, and she was only fifteen. Her mum had gone away with a new boyfriend, and her dad and Michelle had taken Kyla-Marie and Billie-Mai to Disneyland. With her only living grandparent suffering from dementia in Foxbrooke Haven, Ella had nowhere to go. The Foxbrookes had taken her in and she'd spent the happiest two weeks of her life with them. She'd fallen in love with Christmas as well as with Leo's family, and they'd treated her as one of their own ever since, standing by her when everything went wrong with her dad.

The thought of staying there again, even for a few weeks until she found somewhere else, filled her with hope. Foxbrooke Manor was a fairytale, and where her heart felt safest.

Really? You felt safer there than with Oli?

The answer came back without hesitation. *Yes.*

She'd trusted Oliver to never leave her, but he'd discarded her more quickly and efficiently than the weekly recycling.

'Ella?' Leo squeezed her hand. 'Please say yes?'

As she gazed at his anguished face, her heart grew too big for her chest. Leo loved her as much as she loved him. He was the truest of friends. Someone who took on her pain as if it was his own. If she turned down his offer, she'd hurt him as much as herself. She knew Oliver and his parents well enough to know there was no going back. And the longer she stayed in this house, the more miserable she would be.

Sniffing loudly, she braved a smile. 'Thank you.'

His eyes widened. 'You'll stay?'

She nodded. 'Christmas with you and your family sounds like my idea of heaven.'

❧ 3 ❧

Leo glanced around the kitchen of Ella and Oliver's house. It was like a show home, with none of Ella's personality to be seen. The only art Oliver or his parents had allowed on the walls were blown-up photos of the two of them in the living room. Had they wanted it pristine so they could sell it the moment their son finally finished with his unsuitable girlfriend? Or did they just want to pretend Ella was the kind of woman they thought their son should be with?

His phone pinged and he looked at the group chat with his brothers and sisters. They'd been as shocked as he was when he'd messaged them with the news.

> Henry: I've been googling and I think Ella should go to Citizen's Advice

> Estelle: Leave it, Henry. She won't have a leg to stand on, and that house probably has far too many memories

Leo: Estelle's right. Thanks for trying to help, but I want her around people who care about her

Estelle: She's not still skivvying for Michelle, is she?

Leo: What do you think?

Estelle: FFS!

Henry: Just tell us if we can do anything to help

Leo: Thanks. Depending on how much stuff she's got, we might need a hand moving her out of the house. I'll take as much as I can later this afternoon. His folks have arranged for the estate agent to come in on Monday to take photos

Estelle: Jesus! They must have known for ages! WANKERS!!!!!

Leo: Yeah. I don't think I've ever been this angry before

Willow: Where's Ella now?

Leo: Upstairs having a bath

Willow: I'm so sorry he's done this. She was really pinning her hopes on Oliver being the one

Estelle: But he was a fucking donkey from the start

Summer: OMG drama!!! Poor Ella. She's a sweetie. I never liked Oli either. He was such a condescending prick and creepily smarmy at the Christmas quiz last year

Estelle: I'm going to get him barred from the Horse and Hounds

Summer: She's better off without him. Should we start looking for a replacement?

Leo: Jesus, Summer, NO! She's absolutely devastated. We CANNOT tell her we hated him and we CANNOT try to fix her up with anyone else. She's way too fragile and 100% not ready to rebound

Summer: But she's so lovely! She needs to be with someone who appreciates her!

Connor: Summer, Leo's right. She needs our support right now. Hopefully, the panto will give her something to focus on, and we've also got the Winter Ball coming up. In the run-up to Christmas there's so much to distract her, and she'll be surrounded by people who love her

Summer: #TeamElla

Leo: Estelle, are Oli's folks likely to be coming to the Winter Ball?

Estelle: No. They hate our family, but I'll double check with Jack and make sure

Leo: Thanks X

Willow: I feel awful for her. And right before Christmas as well

Leo: Yeah, it's shit. Gotta go. I think she's
finishing up in the bath XXX

Putting his phone in his back pocket, Leo stared at the bags of ingredients he'd brought with him, his heart still thudding loudly in his chest.

Thank god I had a key.

Ella had one cut for him in case of emergencies, but he'd never needed to use it before. Today *had* been an emergency, just not one he'd ever anticipated.

He rubbed the centre of his chest. Was Ella still crying? Her tears had felt like knives to his heart. No-one was allowed to hurt her like that. *No-one.*

Ella had been doing her PGCE in Bristol when she'd met Oliver, and seemed so excited when she'd introduced him to Leo and Lila one Christmas in the Horse and Hounds. Almost as if she couldn't believe Oliver had been interested in her.

It was the night of the Christmas quiz, something Leo and Ella took very seriously. They'd been reigning champions for the past five years, under the name the Noel it Alls, and were wearing costumes for the occasion. This December, they were both dressed as reindeer, with enormous antlers that Ella had made from papier mâché.

Lila had rolled her eyes at the two of them good-naturedly, but still wore an elf hat and tried her best to contribute to the team. Oliver, on the other hand, made jokes about their outfits that were more like sneering than humour. Leo and Lila had pretended not to notice, but Ella was clearly thrown off-kilter, and they'd lost to the Beardy Boys, who were all in Santa suits.

Oliver never took Ella seriously. Or Christmas.

Since that night, Leo had made a Herculean effort to get on with Oliver, but it was hard work. After everything she went through with her first boyfriend, Zach, Ella deserved the moon on a stick. Instead, she'd got a snobby arsehole who thought he was better than she was.

Hearing Ella's footsteps on the stairs, Leo straightened his shoulders and smiled.

Don't think about him now. Just focus on her.

She entered the kitchen, her face pink from the heat of the bath, but her eyes still puffy and red.

Without thinking, he opened his arms. 'Hug?'

Chin wobbling, she nodded and crossed the room towards him.

Leo held tightly to her. Ella was the perfect height, with the top of her head resting just below his chin. *It's going to be alright. I'll make sure it's alright.*

'Thank you,' she mumbled into his chest.

'Anytime,' he murmured.

She pulled away and gazed at the shopping bags. 'Are we still making lebkuchen and limoncello?'

'Entirely up to you. I just thought it might be nice to pretend everything was okay for a bit?'

She nodded. 'And I'd like my last memory of this house to be a happy one.'

'Well, we're making two things, and it's also our official start to Christmas, so we can make more than one happy memory today.'

'Our fourth official start to Christmas.'

'That's true.' After Christmas pudding making in March, Christmas cake baking and mincemeat preparation in August, then batch-cooking and freezing mince pies in October, it was their fourth official start. 'But the first to involve Mariah.'

Ella brought her hands together into a prayer position, and Leo copied her. Taking a deep breath, they lifted their gazes to the ceiling, then bowed their heads in reverence.

'To Saint Mariah,' they said in unison. 'May she grant us another win in the Christmas quiz.'

They grinned at each other and Leo took out his phone. 'Are we ready to break her out?'

Ella hesitated. 'Would you be able to do something for me first?'

'Of course. As your BFFFF friend, I cannot refuse.'

'What's the extra F for?'

He put a hand on his heart. 'Faithful. As long as we both shall live, I swear I will never let you down.'

She smiled, but her eyes were liquid with unshed tears. 'Thank you, Leo.'

The silence was painful and his chest hurt again. 'What can I do to help?'

'Please, can you take down the canvases in the living room so I don't have to see them again, and change the lock screen image on my phone?' Ella swallowed. 'In the bath, after you left, I forced myself to look honestly at my relationship with Oliver, and...' She took a deep breath. 'It always felt a bit one-sided. Like I made more of an effort than he ever did. On the phone to him earlier, I offered to give up helping Michelle, quit my job and move up north to be with him. But it would have been yet another way I did things to make his life better, not the other way around.'

Leo was silent, keeping perfectly still as his pulse quickened in panic at the thought of Ella leaving Foxbrooke.

'I haven't seen Oliver since the end of the summer holidays and even before that he'd been distant,' she said quietly. 'I was so desperate to make it work, I didn't allow myself to contemplate that our relationship had already been broken for a very long time.' Taking out her phone, she unlocked it and passed it to him. 'Use any other photo, just delete the one of him, please.'

Leo did, inserting a photo Ella had taken of one of her line drawings, this one featuring a princess with long black hair, her arm around a lion, the two of them facing forward as if posing for a portrait. He handed the phone back to her.

'Thank you. I love that picture.'

'So do I. It's of us.'

'Us?'

'She looks like you, and my star sign's Leo as well as my name.'

Ella gave him a watery smile. 'She looks *nothing* like me and that's not what I was thinking about when I drew it.'

'Ah, but your subconscious *definitely* was.'

She rolled her eyes, but her smile was less tentative. 'If you say so.'

'Oh, I do.' He moved to the kitchen door. 'Anything else you want me to get rid of?'

'Yes, please. There's a picture in our bedroom of me and him. I don't want to see it again.'

He saluted. 'Consider it done. Why don't you get the ingredients sorted out? I'll be back in a bit.'

She nodded, and he left the room.

Leo collected the canvas prints and the picture of Oliver and Ella from their room that he remembered taking, and hid them outside behind the garden waste bin. He would collect them and take them to the recycling centre when she wasn't around.

Taking out his phone, his finger hovered over Oliver's number. He desperately wanted to ring him up and tear him a new one, but what was the point? Even if Oliver *did* take Leo's call, he'd no doubt hang up again halfway through Leo's first 'you fucking arsehole'.

Shoving his phone in the pocket of his jeans, he went back in the house. In the kitchen, Ella had lined up all the ingredients he'd brought, including eight bottles of vodka.

He clapped his hands. 'Now, this looks like a party!'

She smiled. 'I've still got the Mason jars from last year to pour it into.'

'Cool. Are we starting with limoncello?'

'Yes, but if your pieces of peel have any pith on them, we're making separate batches. And I'll make sure to write "made by Ella" on my bottles so your family doesn't think my standards have slipped.'

Leo clapped the back of his hand to his forehead. 'Madam, you wound me with your aspersions!'

She threw him a potato peeler. 'Prove me wrong.'

He flexed. 'Get ready to swoon at my lemon-peeling skills.'

That comment earned him a belly laugh from Ella that made his soul sing.

They stood side-by-side at the counter, peeling the zest from the unwaxed organic lemons he'd brought, and he internally breathed a sigh of relief. Ella's world may have been crumbling around her, but here they were, bringing a bit of normality back into her life.

'Are mine up to scratch?' he asked when they were done.

She peered at them. 'Not bad, Foxbrooke. You've upped your game.' She pulled a face as she looked at the sixty-five lemons he'd brought. 'Do you think we've gone overboard this year?'

'Go big or go home? And no-one complains when they get it as a Christmas present.'

'True. Oh! I almost forgot!' She went to a high cupboard and reached for the top shelf. 'Can you give me a hand?'

'Sure.' He pulled down a bottle of limoncello they'd made the previous year. 'You've still got some!'

She shrugged. 'I gave it to Oliver, but he didn't want it.'

Leo popped the stopper. 'Well, as ever, he can't see gold when it's right under his bloody nose.'

Ella grabbed a couple of glasses, and he poured the bright liquid out.

'It's not cold,' she fretted.

'It's still going to taste amazing. Got any ice cubes?'

'Yep, good idea.' She added ice to the tumblers, then held her glass to Leo's. 'Happy official start to Christmas, number four.'

He clinked his glass against hers. 'Chin-chin, down the hatch, bottoms up, and cheers, me dear.'

'Same to you with knobs on.'

They downed their drinks, then shook their heads like wet dogs at the sudden alcohol hit.

'Again?' Leo asked.

Ella nodded. 'But this time we have to savour it with Mariah.'

He refilled their glasses, then took out his phone and cued up the track. This was the moment that happened only once a year. The moment when they knew they were on the candy-cane superhighway to Christmas town.

He paused. 'You ready, my BFFFFF?'

'Another F? What's that one for?'

'Festive!' he cried, then started the song.

Holding their glasses high, they followed Mariah's voice as she began singing. Leo held Ella's gaze, happiness expanding inside him as they sang along, reaching the end of the intro and the words 'all I want for Christmas... is you...'

There was a brief moment of magical silence, then the piano and sleigh bells kicked in and they were off, dancing around the kitchen like drunken elves and shouting along to the song like football supporters after their team had won the FA Cup.

Ella's hair had come loose from her bun and was flying wildly around her head, her face lit up brighter than a Christmas tree. She paused briefly to drink her second limoncello and Leo did the same. Then she grabbed his hands, and they bopped around the kitchen, both of them hitting the high note at the end of the song with the accuracy of a teenage boy whose voice was breaking, but with the confidence of adults who didn't give a fuck.

As the track faded out, they collapsed against each other, out of breath and laughing.

'That never gets old,' Ella said. 'Although I think I am.'

'Nonsense,' Leo wheezed. 'We're in the prime of our lives.'

She snorted. 'We both sound like we've run the Bath half marathon.'

'We sprinted it in four minutes.'

Ella pulled back and lifted the bottle of limoncello that was now two-thirds empty. 'We might as well finish it.'

'We'd be offending Saint Mariah if we didn't.'

She poured the rest of the liquid out. 'And this will only help us make lebkuchen.'

'Exactly.' Leo took his glass and held it up for another toast. 'To the best Christmas ever.'

Ella clinked her glass against his, a beaming smile on her face. 'My first one back at the manor since—' She broke off, her happy expression cracking. 'Oh, god.'

Ice-cold panic stabbed Leo's heart. 'What is it? What's happened?'

She stared at him, ghost-white, her eyes wide and fearful. 'Dad's coming out of prison early.'

$$\text{❧}\ \ 4\ \ \text{❧}$$

Leo's mouth hung open as he stared at her.

Ella's heart thumped painfully hard and fast against her ribs. 'I only found out this morning when I was at Michelle's, then I totally forgot after Oliver... when he...'

Leo's shocked expression quickly changed to a reassuring one. 'This must mean the parole board think he's changed?'

She shook her head. 'It's been a long time since I've spoken to him, but when I last did, he sounded exactly the same as he's always done.'

'How do you feel about him coming out?'

Ella swallowed. 'Terrified he's going to find out what we did.'

Leo took her hand. 'He won't. It was an anonymous call.' He paused. 'Did you ever tell Oliver?'

'No way. He couldn't stand me even mentioning my family. The only people who know are us. But I'm not just worried about him finding out. Michelle thinks he "has a few scores to settle".'

'With the Prices?'

'Who else?'

'Honestly? He's probably got beef with half the crims in the West Country, not to mention the family of the kid who died after taking the drugs he'd supplied. And he'll be coming out on licence, so if he went after anyone, he'd be insane.'

Ella raised both eyebrows and gave him a look. 'Since when has Ronnie Chamberlain ever made sensible decisions?'

Leo pulled a face, acknowledging the truth of her words. 'But Kurt lives in Australia now, and...'

Ella squeezed his hand, even though an old hurt needled her belly. 'It's okay. You can say his name.'

'Zach is in Yorkshire on *Swallowdale*. Their parents are still in Foxbrooke, but they're in their eighties. You don't think he'd blame *them*, do you?'

'I don't know, but we have to let them know.'

'The police or probation service will have done that, along with his other victims and their families.'

'Yes, I suppose so.'

'Ella,' Leo said gently. 'You don't owe him or Michelle anything.'

She shook her head, guilt hard-wired into her brain.

'The accident wasn't your fault and if we hadn't told the police where Ronnie's lock-up was, someone else would have, or the police would have eventually worked it out. We just sped the process up.'

'But if they'd found it later, most of the drugs would have been gone and he might not have had the gun there. His sentence would have been much shorter.'

'You don't know that. And if Kurt *had* died, it could have been even longer. We can't play the "what if" game. Ronnie did what he did, not us, and it was only a matter of time before it all caught up with him.'

Ella knew everything Leo said was true, but worry and doubt still rolled in her stomach.

'You told Oliver you'd give up Michelle for him,' Leo continued. 'Now your dad's coming out, do you think you could give up Michelle for you?'

Biting the inside of her cheek to keep her tears in check, Ella accepted the enormity of his question. She'd been willing to make that decision for Oliver, but she couldn't summon the strength to do it for herself.

A fresh tear rolled down her cheek. 'You must think I'm pathetic.'

'No! Never!' Leo tugged on her hand and drew her in for a hug. 'You're the loveliest person in the whole world and I'm so lucky to be your BFFFFFF.'

'Is that another F?' she mumbled into his chest.

'Yes. It stands for fortunate.'

ELLA AND LEO MADE LEBKUCHEN FOR THE REST OF THE afternoon and listened to their favourite Christmas songs as they sobered up from drinking an entire bottle of limoncello. Leo then helped her pack as many of her belongings into his car as would fit, and they set off through the village towards the manor.

As they drove through the massive stone pillars that flanked the entrance, Ella gazed in awe at the building waiting for them at the end of the long drive. Originally built in the sixteen hundreds, Foxbrooke Manor was now a double-fronted, three-storey building with two large wings projecting from the front. Ella had taken years to get used to the fact she was welcome here more than anywhere else she'd ever lived or visited.

'I know I should take the piss about you being twenty-seven and still living with your parents,' she began. 'But when this is your home?'

Leo grinned as he carefully brought the car to a stop outside. 'Don't forget, I also get all my meals cooked for me.'

'By Perry, who's an incredible chef.'

'Yep. But I could still cook for myself if I needed to.'

'If the menu consisted solely of Christmas cake, pudding, biscuits and mince pies.'

'What more do you want?'

'Turkey? Pigs in blankets? Stuffing.'

'I can do them, too.'

'Then we're sorted. You've got all the important food groups accounted for.'

Leo smiled. 'Speaking of nosh, by the time we've got all this up to your room, it'll be time for dinner.'

Uncertainty prickled again in her guts. 'Are you sure—'

'Yes! My folks are ecstatic you're staying, especially with Mom in LA shooting a film, Summer in London poncing about for social media, Henry and Libby spending more time at their cottage, Estelle and James at the livery, and Connor either on shift or at his house in the village. Without any grandchildren yet, Dad's panicking about his empty nest. Having you here redresses the balance, and he and Mammy adore you. *Everyone* adores you.'

Ella smiled, but his words were a painful reminder that her own family thought the absolute opposite of her.

A woman in her fifties exited the manor and gave them a wave.

Leo leaned across Ella and opened her door. 'Go on. We all love you and want you here, even Bridget, who's half dragon.'

Ella got out of the car and was pulled in for a hug by the manor's housekeeper, a brisk and forthright woman who kept the staff on their toes, as well as Leo's wayward father.

'Darling Ella, I'm so glad you're coming to stay with us.'

'Hey, why don't you ever call *me* "darling",' Leo complained.

Bridget narrowed her eyes. 'Have you tidied your room yet?'

Leo looked up and to the left, his forehead furrowed, then gave Bridget what Ella knew was his self-titled 'winning' smile. 'Yes, I have.'

Putting her hands on her hips, Bridget's eyes were now slitted. 'When? Last year?'

'Yesterday,' he replied confidently, as Ella bit her tongue to stop a laugh from escaping.

Bridget slapped his shoulder. 'Stuff and nonsense. Kicking your dirty clothes under the bed then throwing blankets over the rest of the piles of rubbish does not, and I repeat *not,* constitute tidying. I've told the girls not to touch your room until I can send them in without the risk of catching a disease.'

'Hey! It might be a bit messy but I'm very clean! I wash and everything!' Leo turned to Ella. 'I smell nice, don't I?'

She swallowed her grin. 'Very nice.'

'There!' Leo said to Bridget. 'And I told you I would clean my own room.'

Bridget folded her arms across her chest. 'Where's the vacuum cleaner kept, then?'

'Under the stairs,' Leo replied definitively.

'Nope.'

'I meant the other stairs.'

'Still no.'

'A cupboard?'

'Which one?'

Leo stared at Ella intently, as if willing her to save him.

'You know where it's kept,' she said to him.

'I do? I mean, yes of course I know, I've just temporarily

forgotten because I'm so excited that my BFFFFFF is coming to stay.'

'So, you're blaming Ella for the fact you have no idea where any of the vacuum cleaners are kept?' Bridget asked acerbically.

'There's more than one?'

Ella winced as Bridget's nostrils flared and she drew in a sharp breath.

'There's a box room halfway down Leo's corridor,' Ella began quickly, 'hidden behind a bookcase, which contains two vacuum cleaners, several mops, toilet rolls, towels, soap, other toiletries and cleaning products, as well as bed linen and extra pillows, blankets and duvets.'

Leo looked puzzled, then comprehension dawned. 'Yes! I remember now! I mean, I already—ow!' he cried as Bridget slapped him a second time.

'Tidy it up by Monday morning, or I'm going in with a bin bag.' She pointed her index finger at him menacingly.

'I'll lock it.'

'And I've got a full set of keys,' she replied before turning back to Ella and giving her another hug. 'Like I said, darling. I'm so glad you're here. Now let's get you inside.'

'I DON'T KNOW WHEN YOU LAST SAW HIS ROOM,' BRIDGET said to Ella as they walked through the manor, Leo following. 'But it's an absolute disgrace. He's messier than his father.'

'I don't think I've been in there since we were about eight,' Ella replied.

One of Bridget's eyebrows raised. 'It was definitely tidier then.'

'Summer's worse than I am,' Leo protested.

'It's a two-horse race,' Bridget replied sternly, before

smiling again at Ella. 'Anyway, I've put you in the room next to his in the vain hope you might exert a positive influence.'

'What?' Leo cried. 'I thought she was going in the Rose Room on the second floor!'

'Who's "she"? The cat's mother?' Bridget asked sharply. 'And *I'm* in charge around here.'

'I mean "Ella",' Leo mumbled, visibly shrinking under Bridget's stony gaze.

She ignored him. 'Now Ella, you remember the duke doesn't approve of locks on any doors, however if you feel more comfortable, I can give you the key to your room. Normally, the inhabited rooms are only locked when we've got a tour on.'

'I'll be fine, thank you.'

'Well, you've got Leo to one side, and Willow then Summer on the other, so you won't be alone in that wing of the house.'

'And I'll protect you if there are any burglars,' Leo said.

Alarm flashed through her like lightning. 'Is that likely?'

Bridget directed a terse sigh at Leo, then turned again to Ella. 'We haven't had a break-in for twenty-five years. The manor is very safe.' She reached a panelled door and opened it. 'This is you, dear.' Inclining her head to the door beside hers, she sniffed. 'Leo's is that one. After you've unpacked, you can see for yourself how much of a state it is.'

Ella looked at Leo. His face had paled. 'Bridge, can you help Ella out? I've got to, erm...' Without waiting for a reply, he dropped the bags he was holding at their feet and dashed into the room next to Ella's.

There was a scraping sound, as if he was pulling a large piece of furniture up against the door.

'Don't you dare mark the floorboards, young man!' Bridget shouted.

'Sorry!' Leo called through, as Ella giggled.

Bridget rolled her eyes, but they were sparkling. 'Don't ever let him know,' she whispered. 'But I love the little scamp as if he were my own.'

'I love him too,' Ella replied. 'There's no-one quite like Leo.'

The two women smiled at each other.

'Come on, let's get you settled,' Bridget said, leading Ella into the room next to Leo's.

HALF AN HOUR LATER, ELLA KNOCKED ON LEO'S DOOR.

'Hang on!' he yelled from inside.

Smothering her grin, she waited.

A minute later, the door was flung open and Leo faced her, out of breath and red-faced, his dirty blond hair sticking up in all directions. 'Hi!'

Ella snorted at the sight of him, her laugh getting bigger and bigger at his affronted expression, until she was bent over and howling.

Leo leant against the doorframe and crossed his arms. 'I'll have you know, this look is considered extremely attractive by many, many ladies.'

She tried to stop her laughter and failed. The stresses of the day had found one outlet through her tears and were now finding another through humour.

'You're... you're very fexy,' she finally managed.

'I'm triple F fexy.'

'Weren't they your GCSE grades?' she asked, before backing off a few paces as he raised an eyebrow. Her tummy turned over at the look he gave her. It was dark and dangerous in a wholly unexpected and surprisingly exciting way.

Then his sunny smile was back. 'To be fair, that's not far off. I'm not as clever as you.'

'You are. You just didn't make the effort.'

He shrugged. 'Maybe. Anyway, are you ready to see my extremely clean and tidy room?'

'I most certainly am.'

Leo backed inside and Ella followed, casting her eyes around the large, high-ceilinged room. It was a mirror of hers, with an en-suite bathroom on the left sharing a wall with her one, and tall windows that overlooked the formal gardens at the back of the manor.

But all the details flew out of her head as Ella stared at the walls, her jaw hanging slack.

'You... I...' She gazed at him in awed confusion. 'Why?'

He gave her a look as if her question was nonsensical. 'Why do you think? Because I love them.'

Ella's feet moved of their own accord to the wall behind Leo's bed and a framed A4 piece of paper she'd forgotten ever existed. Suddenly she was nine again, at Foxbrooke primary, sitting on a small plastic chair at a low formica table and letting her imagination fly out through her fingers.

'That's the first one you gave to me,' Leo said.

Even though it was drawn by a child, it was done with such precision and care. A fairytale castle stood on a hill, a winding path travelling from the top of the hill to the bottom. On the left of the picture was a woman with long black hair and a flowing dress. On her head was a crown, and she was holding hands with a man with short blond hair who was also wearing a crown, and a sword hanging from a belt at his waist.

In case anyone was confused as to who Ella had drawn, there were helpful arrows pointing to the figures with the words 'Ella' and 'Leo'. At the very bottom of the piece of paper she'd written, 'To Leo from Ella X'.

Her hand went to cover her heart. 'I remember giving this

to you,' she whispered. 'Just before my parents said I wasn't allowed to play at the manor anymore.'

'Because my family are such reprobates.'

'The irony,' she replied bitterly.

Leo slung an arm around her and pulled her against him for a hug. 'Don't let them stop your happy-ever-after, Princess Ella.'

She held onto his arm as it lay across her upper chest and gave it a squeeze. 'It's so strange seeing it again.' She turned her head, taking in all the other pictures she'd given Leo over the years. 'Oh, look! The film strip I made! You've still got it!'

Stuck above the dado rail was a strip of sugar paper, six inches tall and two metres long. Ella had drawn a story featuring princesses, princes, lions and dragons. The paper was made to be rolled up, and as you unrolled it, the story unravelled with it.

'I can't believe the Sellotape has lasted this long!'

'It didn't,' Leo said behind her, the warmth from his breath tickling her ear. 'I used bookbinding tape to fix it.'

A lump formed in Ella's throat as she gazed at her work. So many memories were attached to the drawings. They were now waking up, lifting off the paper and swirling around her. She wanted to be happy, but instead felt lost, as if she'd forgotten the most important parts of who she was.

'Oliver never liked them,' she said flatly.

Leo sighed behind her, then took a breath, but said nothing.

'He said...' Ella couldn't finish the sentence. It was too painful. 'Thank you for keeping all of them, even the crap ones.'

'Oi! They're brilliant and I love them almost as much as the artistic genius who created them.'

She huffed. 'Hardly.'

Leo turned her so they were facing each other. 'They *are* brilliant, and you *are* a genius. Just because your drawings are small doesn't mean they're not mighty.'

She nodded, unable to speak without fresh tears flowing.

The sound of a gong echoed along the corridor and Leo's eyes lit up. 'Dinner! Excellent!' He patted his stomach. 'Man cannot live on limoncello and lebkuchen batter alone. Not when roast lamb is on the menu. You hungry?'

Ella didn't know anymore if the pain in her stomach was due to grief, hunger, anxiety, or all of the above, so she nodded again then glanced once more around the room.

'Tidy enough for you?'

'Very.' She frowned. 'Didn't you used to have a four-poster bed?'

'Yeah, but it was meant for sixteenth-century sized people and was annoyingly small, so we moved it into your room.'

'Am I annoyingly small?' she asked with mock outrage.

'No! Not at all! You're, er... perfectly proportioned and century appropriate.'

She narrowed her eyes.

'And not annoying in the slightest. Promise.'

Shaking her head at him, she gazed again at his bed. 'How big *is* that?'

'Seven feet squared. It's an Emperor.'

'Do you *need* a bed that size?' Ella's face suddenly flushed as she imagined Leo in it with a woman. 'Sorry, that's inappropriate. Silly.' Casting her eyes down, she moved towards the door.

'I need a big bed because of my sleep disorder.'

There was a thump behind her and she turned to see Leo sprawled in the middle of his bed, rumpling the bedcovers with his arms and legs as if making a snow angel.

'I also sleep jog.' He turned on his side, attempting to pump his limbs as if sprinting.

By now the pillows were on the floor, the duvet was twisted around his legs, and the sheets were around his lower arm.

Ella couldn't help but belly-laugh at how ridiculous he looked.

'I'm going to trademark "bedercise",' he continued, out of breath. 'Then become an influencer, like Summer. It's amazing what people will spend money on if you're as fexy and fandsome as me.'

'Don't you want dinner?'

'Definitely!' He rolled to the edge of the bed. 'I'm starv—fuuuck!' he cried as he failed to disentangle himself from the bedcovers and fell to the floor with a painfully-loud thud.

Ella went to help him, her cheeks hurting from laughing so much. 'You are such a loon sometimes.'

He grinned at her, his face red and his hair even more dishevelled than earlier. 'But I cheered you up, didn't I?'

'Yes, you did.' Reaching forward, she smoothed his hair back into place. 'Now come on, let's eat.'

❧ 5 ❧

'Do you know who's going to be at dinner?' Ella asked as she and Leo made their way down the main staircase, his ancestors peering at them from their gilt-framed portraits.

'Probably just Dad, Mammy, and Willow. Maybe Connor? You can see why Dad's freaking out. Especially when Henry and Libby, and Estelle and James, have yet to give him any grandchildren.'

Ella smiled. Arthur Foxbrooke may have been a committed naturist who ran infamous sex parties and had two wives, but he loved his family and wanted them around at all times.

The first time Ella had stayed at Foxbrooke Manor, her tummy had been so tied up in knots she'd been unable to eat or speak. Now she was closer to Leo and his siblings than she was to her half-sisters and had got over most of her feelings of social inferiority.

However, when she entered the ornate dining room, the mahogany table lit by candlelight, she froze.

'Gram-Gram!' Leo cried. 'What a delightful surprise!'

Ella's breath stuttered at the sight of Arthur Foxbrooke's mother, the Dowager Duchess of Somerset, sitting on her son's right. Wearing what looked like a vintage Chanel evening dress, and jewellery that screamed 'you could never afford this, peasant', Gram-Gram's spine was straighter than a poker, and her gimlet gaze was harder than diamonds.

Currently, it was fixed on her youngest grandson. 'Don't you know the meaning of "dressing for dinner"?' she asked caustically as Leo bounded towards her like a golden retriever who didn't know the meaning of fear.

'I do!' He gave her a loud kiss on her cheek. 'And that's why I'm not naked. You're looking splendid tonight, Gram-Gram. How's things?'

'I mean, *denim*?' she continued. 'And that ridiculous footwear? Do you think you're *American*?'

Willow, Connor, and Dervla were already on their feet, creating a protective wall of love and affection between Gram-Gram and Ella, as she gazed in panic at her own jeans and Converse trainers.

'Ignore her,' Willow whispered, pulling Ella in for a tight hug. 'She's only on her first sherry.'

Dervla put her arms around the two of them. 'I'm so glad you're here.'

Leo was now speaking in a terrible American accent to his grandmother. 'I sure do, Gramma!'

'Oh, leave him alone, Mater,' Arthur grumbled to his mother. 'Don't scare him away. He's practically the only one left.'

Connor gave Ella's arm a squeeze, his expression full of sympathy and understanding.

Ella swallowed her emotion as she realised Leo must have told them about Oliver.

'What are you all muttering about?' Gram-Gram called over. 'Give the gel room to breathe!'

The cuddle huddle broke apart, and Ella faced Leo's father and grandmother. The first, she was inordinately fond of. The second, not so much.

'Ella!' Arthur roared, coming forward and lifting her from the floor in a bear hug. 'You moving in has made my day! If you want or need anything, anything at all, you must simply ask.' Her feet found the floor again as he released her. 'And you know I can supply—' he gave her a wink, '—*anything*...'

'Dad!' Leo, Willow and Connor chorused.

'What?' he replied indignantly. 'I'm being a good host!'

'Come along, darling.' Dervla took Arthur's arm and led him back to his position at the head of the table.

Leo returned to Ella's side. 'You're next to me.'

Her eyes met Gram-Gram's. Usually there were so many people at dinner she could successfully avoid all interaction with the woman who was at the opposite end of the class spectrum to her.

But now? What should she do? Curtsey?

'Good evening, your grace,' she managed with a small nod.

Gram-Gram's eyes softened from Sauron intensity to Voldemort levels, and she inclined her head. 'Ella.'

Ella took her seat on the other side of Leo, grateful to have him as a buffer between her and Gram-Gram and to be opposite the friendly faces of Dervla, Connor and Willow.

'Is this it?' Arthur asked despondently. 'And on a Saturday night, no less.' He sighed. 'Well, at least Summer's due back tomorrow morning, and if Henry and Libby, and Estelle and James, aren't here, we must cross our fingers that they're procreating.'

'Arthur! Really now,' Gram-Gram said.

'What? Don't you *want* great-grandchildren?'

'Of course, I expect Henry to produce an heir. But one does not discuss the particulars. *Especially* over dinner. And besides.' She sniffed. 'They're not married.'

Arthur sat back in his chair and frowned. 'D'you think that's what's holding up proceedings?' he mused, his gaze unfocused.

Ella sensed everyone around the table holding their breath, awaiting whatever destination his crazy thought-train would visit next.

'I've got it!' He slammed his hand on the table so hard the empty plate in front of him jumped. 'By Jove, I've got it!'

'Got what?' Dervla asked.

'Double bally wedding! It's the Winter Ball in two weeks' time! That can serve as the wedding reception! Kill three birds with one shindig. Then there's no excuse not to get on with baby-making.'

Ella watched Leo exchanging glances with his siblings, then all of them gaze at their mother.

She took a big breath. 'Arthur—'

'Poppycock suggestion,' Gram-Gram interrupted. 'And one neither Henry nor Estelle will want any part of.'

Arthur deflated, then gazed hopefully at his children who were present.

'Don't look at us, Dad,' Connor said, holding up his hands. 'We're all single, and so is Summer.'

Arthur's eyes briefly flicked Ella's way, then he nodded. 'Alright, alright, I'll wait. I suppose one day you'll do what your parents want.'

'And when are *you* going to behave the way *I* would like?' Gram-Gram asked him.

There was a short pause, then Arthur threw back his head and roared with laughter. 'Got me there, Mater! Fair play, fair play!' He wiped the corners of his eyes. 'I suppose I could always get another dog?'

'No!' chorused his children. Arthur's two current dogs, Caligula and Borgia, were more undisciplined than their owner and wreaked havoc wherever they went.

There was a crackle of static and a voice came through a radio on the table next to Arthur's plate. 'Red Leader to the dining room. You ready for launch? Over.'

Arthur pressed the call button. 'Foxbrooke One here. Ready for launch? No, we're ready for dinner! Ha ha ha! Over!'

'Incoming! Over.'

Arthur dropped the walkie-talkie to the tablecloth and swigged a mouthful of wine from a cut-crystal goblet. 'Isn't technology marvellous!' He then stood and went to the door, opening it to let a woman through who was pushing a trolley laden with food. Arthur helped her place the dishes on the table.

'Evening everyone,' she said, then inclined her head at Gram-Gram. 'Your Grace. We've got roast lamb and gravy, potatoes roasted in goose fat and rosemary, steamed cavalo nero and peas with garlic butter, and roasted carrots with redcurrant jelly, balsamic vinegar and smoked paprika.'

'Sounds scrumptious, Perry.' Arthur rubbed his hands together. 'Steve still on for the panto read-through tomorrow?'

'Yep. He can't wait to be the ugliest sister there ever was,' she replied with a grin, then addressed the others around the table. 'You've got raspberry pavlova with the last of the raspberries from the garden for dessert, along with honey and toasted nut ice cream, and a flourless chocolate torte with a healthy splash of rum and whipped cream.'

Leo made a sound of delight, and Ella's tummy rumbled. The food at the manor was heavenly, and a thousand steps up from the cheap meals she'd been eating in an attempt to save money.

'I'll be off now,' Perry said. 'Coffee machine's on the side and I've replenished the chocolates. Anything else, you know where it is. Enjoy your meal, everyone!'

There was a chorus of enthusiastic thanks from around the table as she departed. Then Leo reached for the dishes to serve Gram-Gram first, before passing them to Ella.

'Thank you,' she said, knowing he wouldn't eat until her plate was full.

Everyone settled into a happy silence as they tucked in, Ella suppressing a moan of pleasure at how delicious the food was. Mouthful by mouthful, her stomach unknotted and her nervous system unwound. No matter what was going on outside the manor, here, with Leo and his family, she was safe.

'I've been thinking about a new dish for Christmas Eve this year,' Arthur said to no-one in particular.

Leo's cutlery paused halfway to his mouth. 'Are we going to like it?'

'Of course! Takes about a week to prepare, though.'

Ella ran her mind over all the dishes she'd learned about when studying for the Christmas quiz and came up short.

'Where's this idea from?' Leo asked, clearly following her thought process.

'Eastern Europe. Been meaning to do it for a few years now, but never got around to it.'

Ella's gaze darted to Leo, seeing her amused horror reflected back as the penny dropped.

Leo eyeballed his father. 'No, Dad,' he said firmly.

'But you don't know what I want to do!'

'Does it involve a bath?'

'A bath?' Gram-Gram asked, clearly trusting Leo's ability to predict his father's behaviour.

There was a naughty twinkle in Arthur's eye. 'Maybe...'

'What is it?' Willow asked her brother.

'Christmas carp.'

'Carp?' Gram-Gram enunciated. 'Dreadful eating. You might as well eat mud.'

'But that's what the bath's for!' Arthur said excitedly. 'A week in clean water and the taste is completely different! Found out all about it after we caught those chappies pilfering the ones in the lake a few years ago.'

'Dad!' Willow exclaimed. 'You can't keep a fish in a bathtub!'

'Why not? It's just like a tank, but bigger. And if you won't let me have any more pets, then this will have to do. I'm going to call him Clarence!'

'Which bath are you planning on using?' Dervla asked mildly.

'The two-person jacuzzi in Henry's bathroom. It's bally huge, and I thought the bubbles would help aerate the water.'

Dervla nodded, seeming satisfied. However, her children and mother-in-law were not.

'Have you told Henry and Libby?' Connor asked.

'Why would I need to? They're living at the cottage now.'

'What about Mom?' Willow added.

Arthur pulled a face. 'I'm not quite sure what Vivi will make of the idea.' He turned to his other wife. 'Deedee darling?'

'I'll speak to her. It is organic, after all. And if you fish Clarence out of the lake at the right phase of the moon, he'll be biodynamic as well. I know Vivi's not that keen on fish, so I'll ask her what she thinks when I speak to her later.'

Willow made a sound of frustration, then gazed across Connor at her mother. 'Mammy, please. Just no!'

'I agree with Willow,' Gram-Gram said. 'It's a preposterous idea.'

Arthur raised his knife and fork in the air. 'But it's traditional!'

'So is a burnt sheep's head in Norway and Mopane caterpillars in South Africa, but it doesn't mean we have to eat them here,' Leo said.

'Humph,' Arthur replied. 'You're no fun.' He turned to Ella. 'I've also had some more ideas about the costumes Steve and I should wear for the panto.'

Alarms went off inside Ella. She was in charge of scenery painting and helping Willow with the costumes for the pantomime dame. But this year there were two dames to fit. The decision had been made not to have a wicked stepmother, just two ugly sisters, with Jan Perry's husband, Steve, playing one, and Arthur the other. Arthur had been playing the role of dame for as long as there had been a pantomime at Foxbrooke, and each year his ideas for costumes got more outlandish.

'I did an interweb search for ugly sister costumes and found some topping ideas,' Arthur began.

'But, Dad,' Leo replied, 'those are professional pantos with a much bigger budget and full-time staff. Ella's teaching almost up to Christmas and doesn't have time.'

Arthur's brow knitted with worry as he gazed at her. 'That's true. But I can do most of the work?'

'Why don't you tell me your ideas, and I'll see if we have time to make them happen,' Ella said. 'I might be able to get some of the sixth-formers to help.'

'Could you? That would be splendid!' Arthur dropped his cutlery and leaned forward. 'I was thinking of Clarence at the time, and thought it would be bally amusing if I was dressed as a massive fish for one scene, and Steve was a chip!'

Ella's mind whirled as she wondered how they might make the outfits.

'For our initial entrance, I want us to be dressed in Harajuku street style. Steve in bright pinks and yellows like a unicorn, and me as a goth, whilst "Here Come the Girls" plays.'

'O-kay…'

'Then, for the forest scene where we meet Dandini, I thought I could be a ham sandwich and Steve could be a scone.'

Ella's brain was in overdrive, her circuits moving so fast she feared they would melt.

'I fancy using my regency wig for the palace ball scene,' he continued. 'So maybe those costumes could be Jane Austen meets Madonna. And we can reuse the schoolgirl outfits from a few years ago for the second kitchen scene. For the finale, I want to be a glitter ball and Steve to be a traffic light.'

Dear god. Ella cleared her throat. 'I'm not an electrician—'

'Scott is! You can chat about it with him tomorrow. Steve also had some ideas, but his are plain daft.'

Leo snorted beside her.

'And what *are* his ideas?' Ella asked, hoping for something a little more straightforward.

'Darth Vader and Princess Leia.'

'Darth Vader isn't a woman.'

'He thought we could make her outfit pink. Or he could be a Wookie in a bikini. But like I said, his ideas are silly. Mine are much more on point.'

'I thought we'd decided to recycle costumes from previous years,' Willow said. 'Those ideas sound insanely complicated.'

Arthur looked at Ella hopefully, as if she held his happiness in her hands.

'Would you be happy if I could find them online? Otherwise we'd be constructing from scratch and I'm not sure how long it would take.'

Arthur's face fell.

'But we could always embellish any we bought,' she continued in a hurry. 'And make them unique.'

He perked up again. 'Jolly good! We need to make sure I'm a spectacle! And Steve, of course.'

Gram-Gram sniffed. 'You're always a spectacle.'

'Thank you, Mater! That's a compliment indeed!'

Ella swallowed her grin and continued eating. Hopefully Arthur would be mollified if she could find sufficiently outrageous costumes online and then add some bling.

'Do you know if Libby has found anyone to play Prince Charming yet?' Ella asked Connor. He was the Musical Director for the show, and Libby was directing now that Vivienne was delayed on a film set in LA.

'She sent me a message saying she'd found him and wanted it to be a surprise for us all tomorrow.'

Leo groaned. 'She hasn't persuaded Henry to take the role, has she?'

Connor shook his head. 'He'd never do it. And anyway, Summer's playing Cinders, so that won't work.'

'She could have asked me,' Leo said. 'I'd be a brilliant Prince Charming.'

'But you're Buttons, the comic relief, and Cinderella's best friend. I can't imagine you playing any other part.'

'And you are perfect for that role,' Willow added.

Leo rolled his eyes and turned to Ella. 'Could *you* see me as Prince Charming?'

'Er...' Her mind blanked. Once, many years ago, she'd thought he was her perfect man. But Leo wasn't interested, instead encouraging her to go out with Zach, then falling for Lila as soon as she'd arrived in the sixth form. Ella hadn't thought about Leo as anything more than a friend for twelve years, but as she gazed at his handsome face, lit by the soft glow of the candles, a tiny flame flickered inside her, heating her cheeks with unfamiliar feelings.

'Leave the poor girl alone,' Arthur scolded. 'Not every female in Foxbrooke wants to drop their knickers for you.'

Leo's face burned with embarrassment, his gaze going to his father. 'Dad!'

'What? You're always telling us how successful you are with the ladies!'

Ella sank a little lower in her chair. She'd heard the rumours about Leo's personal attributes and prowess.

'That's not—it's not—' Leo swept a hand through his thick hair. 'Look—'

'Darling,' Dervla interrupted. 'You're perfect, just as God made you. And it doesn't matter how many women enjoy your talents.'

'Mammy!' Leo cried.

'He takes after me in that department!' Arthur said happily. 'Foxbrookes are the best fu—'

'Will you be *quiet*!' Gram-Gram banged her knife on the table. 'I came here for a meal with my family, not a ticket to the zoo.'

Arthur chuckled. 'Fair enough. I promise to behave. At least till the coffee's poured.'

THE REST OF THE MEAL PASSED PEACEFULLY, AND GRAM-Gram departed shortly after eight-thirty, assisted by her companion and live-in nurse, Marie.

Arthur wanted to continue talking to Ella about his costume ideas for the pantomime, but she was struggling to keep her eyes open, hiding her yawns behind her water glass.

'Dad, can this wait until tomorrow?' Leo asked. 'We've had a really long day.'

Arthur glanced at his watch. 'Honestly, the youth of today. When I was your age, I—'

'Already had three kids but was still partying until the small hours and living your best life.' Leo pushed his chair back. 'Yes, we know. But I'm the real star of this panto and looking this good requires sleep, so I'm off to bed.' He turned to Ella with a smile. 'Fancy joining me?'

There was an excruciating pause, then Leo's expression went from relaxed to panicked.

'No! Sorry, I didn't mean *together*. Shit! Sorry Ella! I meant we could go up to bed together. At the same time. But of course in different beds. In different rooms.'

Willow snorted with laughter. 'Smooth, Leo. So smooth.'

Ella covered her embarrassment with a laugh. 'It's how he wins all the ladies' hearts.'

Leo shook his head. 'I'm so sorry.'

'It's fine. Don't worry.'

She went to pick up her plate, but Arthur reached forward and placed his hand on the edge. 'Leave that, my dear. We'll sort it out.' Getting out of his chair, he pulled her in for a hug. 'I'm so glad you're here. Sleep tight now. Everything will be better in the morning.'

Ella said goodnight to everyone, then walked with Leo through the manor and up to her room, pausing with her hand on the door. 'Thank you for today. Thank you for everything.'

Ordinarily, he would have hugged her goodbye, but he didn't move. 'Sleep well.'

'You too.' She nodded at him, then went into her room, closing the door behind her.

. . .

After using the bathroom and getting into her pyjamas, Ella lay awake in the darkness, smelling and feeling how different this room was from the one she'd shared with Oliver for so long. Even though they'd only split up that morning, the fact she'd moved her essential belongings out of their house and was now staying in Foxbrooke manor made it seem so much longer ago. When she thought of Oliver, she still felt numb with shock that her future had vanished with just a handful of words.

Her phone buzzed beside her.

Leo: Sorry about being a muppet earlier. I hope I didn't make you uncomfortable

Ella: Never. I love you just the same x

Leo: Phew. I'm still your BFFFFFF? X

Ella: Forevs x

Leo: Thank god for that. Sleep well, my bestie, and if you have bad dreams, or need company, your protective lion is next door X

Ella: Thank you. For everything xxx

Leo: Anytime X

❧ 6 ❧

Butterflies fluttered in Leo's stomach as he knocked on Ella's bedroom door the following morning. He was always pleased to see her, but nerves didn't normally accompany the excitement.

Frowning, he tried to rationalise the feelings. *We're on the countdown to Christmas. Today's the first rehearsal for the panto. The quiz is nearly here and the Beardy Boys are determined to beat us. Ronnie Chamberlain's coming out of prison.*

However, as he inspected each thought, he had the niggling sensation he was ignoring something big and extremely important. Like staring at hoof prints in the snow and failing to see reindeer on the roof.

The door opened and Ella burst out laughing as she saw what he was wearing. 'We must be psychic!'

He glanced at her sweatshirt and grinned. 'I told you I'm telepathetic.'

'Are we naughty for wearing these to the read-through?'

'Never! We're on the nice list.'

'But Finn and Scott are going to be there.'

'Exactly! We've got to psych them out. Now come on, let's get breakfast.'

He gave Ella the side-eye as they set off down the corridor. She was trying to smother a grin.

'What?' she finally cried.

'Come on, you can admit it. You wore that sweatshirt just as accidentally-on-purpose as I did.'

She let out a guilty snort of laughter, then glanced around as if to make sure they weren't being overheard. 'Maybe...'

Leo slung his arm around her and squeezed. 'There's my partner in crime. Don't forget now, 'tis the season to be winning!'

'Sleighing it at the Christmas quiz?'

'Yes!' Joy filled his heart. 'God, I love you. Best bloody friend in the world.'

Ella grinned, then glanced forward. They'd reached the top of the staircase and it was impractical for Leo to continue side-hugging her.

But he didn't want to let go.

Internally giving himself a shake, he released her. 'I wonder if Summer's back from London yet?' he mused as they stepped down the wide staircase.

'This early?'

'You're right. She normally doesn't even open her eyes until after nine. It's such hard work being an internet sensation.'

Ella smirked. 'Well then, all the more breakfast for us.'

'Yep. Being this epic requires regular refuelling. And right now my stomach is demanding eggs, bacon, black pudding, hash browns, and coffee with cream so thick it can be sliced.'

He took Ella's hand as they reached the ground floor and jogged forward, tugging her along with him.

'What are you doing?' she asked as he pulled her down the corridor.

What *was* he doing? He wasn't sure. He just knew it had to involve holding her hand.

'Making sure we're not late,' he replied. 'And burning off enough calories to justify a Danish pastry as well.'

LATER THAT MORNING, LEO AND ELLA WANDERED THROUGH the manor to the ballroom. A large stage had been erected along one end. This was for the band playing at the annual Winter Ball in two weeks' time, then for the pantomime.

Henry, Leo's oldest brother, was setting out chairs in a circle with Libby, his fiancée. As soon as Libby saw them, she bounded forward. 'You're here!'

'Can we help set up?' Ella asked.

Libby's auburn hair whipped from side to side as she shook her head. 'We're good to go, although we could use this quiet time to chat through the set design and painting if you've got a minute?'

'Of course! I've got my sketchbook with me.'

'Wonderful! This is the first panto I've directed since drama school and we never had anyone as talented as you on board back then.'

Ella blushed, and Libby led her off to the side.

Leo ambled over to Henry. 'Let me guess. She's persuaded *you* to play Prince Charming?'

Henry pulled a face. 'No way. She's got me stepping out of my comfort zone, not leaping out without a parachute.'

Leo smirked. 'Who's she found to play him then?'

'I've no idea. She won't even tell *me*. But it must be someone special as she's about to burst with excitement.'

'So this morning is the big reveal?'

'Yep.' Henry gazed over at Libby and Ella, smiling at his fiancée as if she was responsible for everything that was right with the world. 'I love seeing her this happy. She's in her element.'

'It's lucky that Mom's doing reshoots and doesn't have time to direct.'

'Yeah. Although she told me she's relieved. If you didn't grow up with panto, then it's always a bit weird. It's a particularly British phenomenon and even after all these years, she doesn't really get the appeal.'

'Oh, yes, she does!'

Henry smirked. 'Oh, no, she doesn't!' They grinned at each other, then Henry lowered his voice. 'How's Ella doing?'

Grey clouds scudded across Leo's eternally blue sky. 'As you would expect, but it's better she's staying here rather than still in their house.'

'Hopefully we can be enough of a distraction for her.' Henry frowned. 'I know we didn't like Oliver, but I never imagined he would treat her this way.'

Leo nodded, his hands clenching into fists.

'Thank goodness she's got you.' Henry patted Leo's shoulder. 'You're her best friend and older brother, all rolled into one.'

Henry was speaking the truth, but for some inexplicable reason, Leo tensed at his brother's words.

'I'm the perfect package,' he replied, his voice sounding oddly hollow.

'Yes, you are. If anyone can keep her spirits up, it's you.'

Willow entered the ballroom, her blue hair in two pigtails, followed by Connor. 'Morning everyone! Are we the only ones here so far?'

Libby gave them a wave from where she was sitting on the edge of the stage. 'We've still got ten minutes till start time. Willow, do you want to look at Ella's ideas? They're stunning.'

'Sure!' Willow went over and Connor came to Leo and Henry's side.

'How's Ella?' he asked quietly.

'No tears so far this morning,' Leo replied. 'So I'm taking that as a win.'

Connor's concerned expression softened a little. 'Well, we're all here for her.'

Leo nodded, but his throat tightened with sudden irritation. *He* was Ella's best friend. It was *his* job to be there for her, not anyone else's. He stopped short at the irrational thought. *What is wrong with me today?*

'You okay?' Connor asked.

He forced a smile. 'Yeah! Of course! I—'

The ballroom door opened and two broad and bearded men entered. Finn had been best friends with Henry, Connor and Estelle since they were children, along with Jack, who was now married to Eveline, Foxbrooke's vicar. Scott was a long-time friend of Finn's, whom he'd met through work.

Scott and Finn were also half of the Beardy Boys, the arch rivals of the Noel it Alls.

Breaking away from his brothers and glad to escape his thoughts, Leo strode forward. 'It's the perpetual bridesmaids!' He glanced over his shoulder at Ella. 'Look who it is! Foxbrooke's finest runners-up!'

The two men stared at Leo's sweatshirt.

Scott, the more good-natured of the two, shook his head. 'Tosspot.'

Finn growled.

'What was that, Finley? I'm afraid I'm not conversant in Bear.' Leo turned to Ella as she made her way across the room towards them. 'Do you speak Loser, Ella? I don't, because I always come first.'

'So say all the women in Foxbrooke,' Finn said.

'Oi! At least I'm actually getting—' He broke off as Ella reached his side.

'And it's also the title of your sex tape,' Finn continued.

Scott snorted, then gazed at what Ella was wearing. 'Seriously? You too?'

Her eyes widened innocently. 'What?' She pulled the bottom of her sweatshirt away from her body and gazed at it. 'Oh! This old thing? I can't remember what it says. Leo, can you read it out for me?'

Bringing a hand to his chin and furrowing his brow, Leo fought to keep a delighted smirk off his face. 'It says "The Noel it Alls, Christmas Tour", and then there's a list of dates spanning the last five years. Wow, they *have* been rather successful.'

'Do you know them?' Ella asked Finn and Scott. 'I could get you their autograph if you like?'

Finn crossed his arms and lifted his chest. 'Enjoy it while it lasts. Because *this* year, you're going down.'

If Leo hadn't known Finn all his life and knew underneath the gruff exterior lay a heart of gold, he would have been legging it by now. Finn's expression was terrifying.

'Name all of Santa's reindeer,' Ella asked.

'Dasher, Dancer, Prancer, Vixen, Comet, Cupid, Donner, and Blitzen,' Scott said quickly.

Ella's face lit up. 'Wrong—'

'Plus Rudolph and Olive, if you want to include them,' Finn added.

Ella's face fell.

'What's the name of the reindeer popularised in a nineteen-ninety-five parody song?' Leo asked.

'"Leroy, the Redneck Reindeer",' Finn replied without missing a beat.

Fuck.

'How many of the reindeer are female?' Ella asked.

'All of them. Because male reindeer shed their antlers in the winter,' Scott said triumphantly.

Double fuck.

One corner of Finn's mouth twitched upward. 'Like I said, enjoy it while it lasts.'

'There's no need for us to enjoy it,' Leo blustered. 'Because we're still going to win. We're—'

'Morning everyone!' came a booming voice from the door.

Arthur entered the room with Dervla and Steve Perry, the other ugly sister. As they said hello to everyone, Ella pulled Leo to one side.

'They've upped their game!' she hissed.

'They'll never beat us.'

'But if all four of them are studying properly? And what if they draft in someone else? You're allowed up to five on a team and we've only got the two of us. Should we start looking for reinforcements?'

Leo hesitated. It made sense, but he liked it being only the two of them. 'Who would take it seriously enough?'

She pulled a face. 'And people are scared of being on our team because we're so competitive.'

'That's not a bad thing! Did you know, the Chinese symbol for competitive is the same as the ones for "bloody fucking epic" and "the best in the world"?'

'If only. We're going to have to double down on our studying.'

'Deal.' Leo held up his hands and Ella high-fived him. 'And now you're staying at the manor, we'll have way more time together to practise.'

She nodded. 'We lost six years ago because Oliver messed with my head. This year I'm not going to let him, or *anyone* else, put me off my game.'

Fierce love and pride bloomed in Leo's chest and he pulled Ella in for a hug. 'You're the best.'

She squeezed him tightly back. '*We're* the best.'

'Okay everyone!' Libby cried. 'Let's get started.'

Ella slowly disengaged from Leo's arms, and they went to the circle of chairs and sat next to each other.

Two seats were still empty.

Arthur glanced at his watch. 'Summer should be here by now.'

'It's okay,' Libby said. 'We can give her another five minutes.'

'And where's Prince Charming?' Willow asked.

'Maybe they've eloped!' Arthur squeezed Dervla's hand. 'We might get grandchildren sooner than we thought!'

Finn shifted in his chair and re-crossed his arms. He was overly grumpy when it came to Summer, and Leo always thought he took his role of 'older brother by proxy' far too seriously.

Libby laughed. 'Maybe? I think they know each other already.'

Now everyone followed Finn's lead and leaned forward.

'Who is it?' Willow asked. 'This has been the best-kept secret ever in our family!'

Libby blushed as she smiled. 'He wants it to be a secret until today so he can meet you, or *re*-meet you, in person.'

Leo's brain flicked through all the people he knew. Who on earth was it and why the big drama?

'How did you find him?' he asked.

'He actually found *me*,' Libby replied. 'I'd posted on the social media account for the improv company I own with Claire that I was directing the Foxbrooke panto and didn't have a Prince Charming, and he sent me a DM. It was such a surprise, as he's actually quite famous.'

'What? More famous than me?' Arthur asked indignantly.

Libby smiled. 'You're *infamous*, Arthur. And nobody can take that glorious thunder away from you.'

Arthur appeared satisfied. 'Ha! Good stuff.'

'To be honest, we might as well start,' Libby said. 'Ella, can you read Summer's lines until she gets here?'

'Sure!'

'Fantastic! Okay, so we've got four and a half weeks till opening night,' Libby continued. 'Ella's already been painting the backdrops and Finn's started constructing the flats. As soon as the Winter Ball is over, they can be brought in and rigged up. Willow and Ella have begun work on the costumes, and Connor and Willow have prepared the musical score. You've all had the final script now for a couple of weeks, so hopefully the lines will be familiar, even if you're not yet off the page. We won't bring in background artists for a few weeks, but they've been training at the dance school in Radstock, so they know what they're doing. Ticket sales have been good, but I expect to sell out by the middle of next week once word gets out about Prince Charming—'

'Oh, for the love of *god*, Libby my dear,' Arthur exclaimed, bouncing in his chair. 'Who the devil *is* the chap?'

She grinned at him. 'Patience is a virtue, Arthur.'

'It's a bally *sin* in my book. I'm an instant-gratification kind of fellow.'

'We know, Dad,' Henry said.

'Anyway,' Libby continued. 'Why don't we make a start? Dervla, you ready?'

'Yes, darling. Are you going to set the scene, or shall I just dive right in?'

Libby jiggled in her seat, seeming as excited as Arthur. 'I'll set the scene.' Sitting upright, the script resting on her lap, she opened her eyes wide and leaned forward to gaze at everyone.

'The house lights are down, and faint music plays, promising a fairytale like no other. Slowly, the lights come up, just enough to reveal the front curtain which shows a woodland in winter. An owl hoots—'

'Twit-twoo!' Arthur shouted.

'Then a figure appears, and the spotlight illuminates... Fairy Cakes!'

Leo's gaze went to his mother. She held out a wand he remembered belonging to Summer when she was little and began.

'In a land where hope's the only thing worthwhile, a girl with humble roots and just a smile. Will dance through hardships with kindness and grace, in search of love, in this enchanted place. Will she find it? Will she win? If you're sitting comfortably, let's begin.'

'I think you should say "shitting comfortably",' Arthur said. 'Much funnier.'

Henry let out an audible sigh. 'Dad, there's already more toilet humour in the panto than in the entire Foxbrooke sewerage system.'

'Humph,' his father replied. 'Libby?'

'I think in this instance, Henry's right. And we don't want to detract from you and Steve, do we?'

Leo smothered a grin as he watched his father contemplating a scenario where anyone might take the spotlight away from him.

'Ah! Good point, well made. Alright, carry on!'

'There's a puff of smoke, the spotlight cuts out, and Fairy Cakes disappears,' Libby continued. 'The front curtain lifts to reveal a village marketplace with a post to one side holding signs for Bath, Bristol, and Uranus. Villagers are milling about onstage, along with Buttons, a servant at Hardup Hall and Cinderella's best friend. Cue opening dance number led by

Buttons with the song "I Gotta Feelin" by the Black Eyed Peas, changing the word "night" to "day". Connor, anything you want to add here?'

'No, all good. We can start blocking the song at the next rehearsal.'

'Fab. Okay, then rapturous applause and Buttons begins!'

Leo sat up straighter. 'Hello everybody!'

Everyone else in the circle murmured, 'Hello, Buttons.'

'Oh, my goodness! Golly gumdrops, pear drops, strawberry laces, Percy Pig Phizzy Tails, and "insert latest revolting TikTok-famous sweet here"'—Leo broke off. 'Do we know what it is yet?'

Libby shook her head. 'Trends come and go so fast, we want to be right on the money with that reference. My plan was to ask Summer right before the dress rehearsal. She'll know.'

'Okay.' Leo cleared his throat. 'I didn't know tonight's audience were half-asleep zombies! Any dopier and I'd think you all came from Midsomer Norton! Shall we try that again? HELLO EVERYBODY!'

'Hello, Buttons!' everyone shouted back.

'That's much better!' Leo continued. 'Although—hang about! How did you know my name when we haven't yet been introduced? Are you my number one stan? Well, I *am* pretty popular around here.'

'The village children throw vegetables at Buttons, then run away, followed by the adult villagers,' Libby said, 'leaving the stage empty. Buttons picks the veg up and puts them in a basket.'

'See! People love me so much they give me free food!' Leo said. 'I'm going to turn this into a delicious soup for my favourite person in the whole wide world.'

'Cue background music, "My Heart will Go On", by Celine

Dion,' Libby said. 'Buttons holds the basket as if it were a person and waltzes across the stage.'

'Cinderella! That's who I love,' Leo continued. 'But I think she only sees me as a friend. She lives at Hardup Hall with her two ugly sisters, and she's as perfect as perfect can be. I've been out this morning buying her chocolate buttons in the hope she can love me as much as them.' He sighed. 'Do you think I have a chance with her, boys and girls?'

'Audience plant, currently Ryan or Tommy, will yell "no" at this point,' Libby said. 'Buttons is outraged.'

Leo stuck a hand on his hip. 'Oh, yes, I do!'

'Oh, no you don't!' everyone around the circle chorused.

'Oh, yes, I do!'

'Oh, no you don't!'

'Oh, yes, I do with knobs on, pinch, punch, first of the month and no returns!'

'Buttons walks to the edge of the stage,' Libby said.

'I love Cinderella more than anything. Even more than cheese. When I see her, my head spins and I get a funny feeling in my undercrackers. Will you help me win her heart, mums and dads, grannies and grandads, nanas and grandpas, aunts and uncles, nieces and nephews, and boys and girls?'

'Audience plant yells "yes", and if anyone yells "no", Buttons will make a joke about them definitely coming from Midsomer Norton,' Libby continued. 'Then Cinderella enters from upper stage left.'

'Oh! It's her! Right, wish me luck. It's time for me to tell her how I really feel!'

'Hello, Buttons! Hello, boys and girls!' Ella said.

'Hello, Cinderella!' everyone chorused.

'Isn't it a beautiful day!' Ella continued. 'The sun is shining, the birds are singing, and I'm with my bestest friend. What have you been buying in Foxbrooke today, Buttons?'

Libby's phone rang and she got to her feet. 'Carry on. It's probably Prince Charming.' Dashing to the edge of the room, she took the call.

'Well...' Leo said.

'Have you been buying presents for all the boys and girls in the audience?'

'Er.'

'Oh Buttons, you're so kind! You've bought them chocolate buttons!'

'No, Cinderella, I—'

'Would you like any chocolate buttons, boys and girls?'

'But—'

'Yes!' everyone cried.

'Cinderella throws packets of chocolate buttons into the audience,' Ella said. 'Only stopping when she lifts out a carrot.' She glanced up as a frowning Libby turned back to the group.

'Everything okay?' Henry asked as she retook her seat.

'Um...' Libby's gaze was unfocussed, her skin pale. 'That was Summer. She can't do the panto anymore.'

Leo's heart sank.

'What? Why not?' Henry asked.

'She's, erm, been given an opportunity she can't afford to pass up and is flying out to Mexico this afternoon for a month.'

There was a pause as everyone digested her words. Leo knew just how much work Libby had already put into the pantomime, and how challenging it would be to find a good-enough replacement for Summer at such short notice.

'Oh,' Arthur said. 'Well, at least she'll be back in time for Christmas.' He looked at his middle daughter. 'Willow can take her place.'

'No way!' Willow exclaimed. 'I can play the piano, but I can't sing for toffee. We need someone who can act, sing, dance, *and* looks the part.'

The air seemed to crackle, and Leo's pulse accelerated as everyone's gazes, including his own, settled on the person sitting next to him.

'Yes!' Libby cried. 'Ella's perfect!'

'Me?' she gasped.

'Hear, hear!' Arthur said. 'You're always standing in for people who've missed rehearsals in the past. You play any role thrown your way with perfection!'

'Yes!' Dervla agreed. 'And you've got the voice of an angel.'

'Remember this summer when you and Leo sang the whole Ubergraft concert for us when we were guarding the fence at the festival?' Scott said. 'You were as good as the band.'

Finn nodded his agreement.

'And you're really pretty,' Willow added. 'And practically the same size as Summer, so I won't need to alter any of the costumes I've already made.'

'Oh, thank goodness,' Libby said. 'This solves everything! I can't believe the perfect person has been right under our noses all along, but we just didn't see it!'

'Wait a minute,' Leo started. 'Don't you—'

'Oh Leo,' his father interrupted crossly. '*You* may be immune to Ella's charms, but the rest of us aren't. You don't think she's pretty enough? Good enough?'

'No, that's not—'

'Open your eyes! And I'm sure if we all helped, she'll easily manage the set painting as well as the lead role.'

'Yes, definitely,' Willow said. 'We'll all help.'

Leo crossed his arms and fumed at his family. He didn't doubt Ella could play the part with her eyes shut, but that wasn't why he was raising objections. His father, in particular, tended to make up his mind about something without consulting anyone affected. Leo knew Ella was a people pleaser, and he didn't want her to be bullied into saying 'yes', when she'd much rather be saying 'no'.

'I think what Leo is trying to say,' Henry said calmly, 'is that nobody has actually *asked* Ella if she wants the part.'

Leo raised his hands. 'Exactly.'

'Oh, Ella, I'm so sorry,' Libby said. 'I got carried away and didn't think. Would you like to play Cinderella?'

The look on Libby's face was so full of expectant hope that Leo's heart sank. Saying no to her request was the equivalent of kicking a puppy.

'You'd be really helping us out of a tight spot,' Arthur added.

'Dad!' Leo shouted.

'What?' his father replied, his mouth hanging open in confusion.

Leo wanted to yell at them that Ella already felt obligated enough staying at the manor indefinitely and also free of charge. His father saying that to her was unintentional emotional blackmail.

'Just—don't, okay. This has to be Ella's decision.'

'I know! I was just saying—'

'I'll do it,' Ella interrupted. 'I'll play Cinderella.'

Everyone except for Leo, Connor, and Henry whooped, clapped, or cheered.

'Are you sure?' Henry, Connor and Leo asked at the same time over the din.

Ella nodded, her cheeks pink and her expression determined, as if accepting her fate.

Libby leapt out of her seat and hugged her. 'Thank you! You'll be brilliant!' Her phone rang, and she pulled it out. 'Ella, your Prince Charming has arrived! Let me get him from the main entrance!' She dashed off.

Leo wanted to take Ella to one side and check she was

making the right decision for her, but Willow was already monopolising her attention, talking about the dress that turned instantly from rags into a ball gown. So instead he worried in silence. He was the assistant marketing manager for the Theatre Royal in Bath, and in the run up to Christmas, with their own professional pantomime running for weeks, he couldn't take any more time off to help with the Foxbrooke one. He'd just have to work evenings and every weekend to make sure Ella wasn't swamped.

Suddenly, everyone fell silent.

Leo glanced up.

Libby stood just inside the door, her face bursting with excitement. 'Ladies and gentlemen, let me introduce you to the secret ingredient in the Foxbrooke panto this year... Playing Prince Charming is the handsome, the famous, Mr Zach Price!'

Ella sucked in a shocked breath, and Leo's blood ran cold. He reached for her hand and she gripped it tightly as Libby threw the door open wide and a man entered.

Pushing a pair of designer shades up into his perfectly tousled black hair, he raised a hand. 'Hey, everybody.'

Zach Price. Leo's ex-best friend, Ella's first ever boyfriend, and the man who'd tried to destroy her.

7

Leo leapt to his feet, but Ella pulled him straight back down.

'Bloody hell,' Scott murmured. 'I'm playing his best mate!'

'Isn't that—' Arthur began before Dervla loudly shushed him.

'This is brilliant!' Steve said excitedly.

Zach may have been one of the most famous actors in the UK, but his smile was strained as he gazed at the group. The only people who didn't know what he did nine years ago to Ella, were Libby, Scott, and Steve.

As Libby led Zach across the ballroom towards them, Scott bounded over to shake his hand. 'Hi! I'm Scott and I'm playing Dandini.'

'Zach. Great to meet you. Is the beard staying or going?'

'Not going anywhere. But it makes for more comedy if we give you a fake one for when you're pretending to be me.'

'Love it.'

'You mentioned you knew the Foxbrookes,' Libby said to

Zach as they reached the circle of chairs. 'So you probably already know most of the people here?'

Leo went to move again, but Ella held him in place, her fingers digging painfully into his arm.

'Yeah, I—'

Steve got to his feet, grabbed Zach's hand, and pumped it up and down. 'Steve Perry. One of the ugly sisters. Huge fan!'

Arthur, Dervla, Finn, Henry, Connor, and Willow were all gazing uneasily between Ella, Zach, and Libby, as if waiting for Ella's cue as to how they should behave.

Leo knew Libby would be devastated after his family kicked Zach out of the manor. But she would understand once they told her what he'd done to Ella, and Leo would help her find a new Prince Charming.

Putting a hand over his heart, Zach dipped his head at Steve. 'Thank you. I hope I can do justice to this role.'

'And you were in the same year at school as Leo and Ella!' Libby continued with a huge smile, still riding high on a roller-coaster of excitement and failing to notice that most of the other passengers had fallen off.

Leo's blood now went from ice to boiling point. He didn't give a flying fuck why Zach was here, but it was time for him to go. He pushed out of his seat, but Ella was faster, standing in his path.

'Nice to see you again.' She gave Zach a little wave. 'It's been so long since we were at school together, I can hardly remember our time there. It feels like a lifetime ago.'

Zach's face relaxed. 'It's good to see you.'

Ella dropped her hand, reaching behind her back as if grasping for a lifeline. Leo took it, feeling how cold her fingers were. Why was Zach here?

'Ella's our new Cinderella!' Libby said.

Zach's eyes widened. 'But I—'

'Summer has to work, so Ella's stepped in to save the day,' Libby continued. 'I don't know if Ella ever sang when you were at school, but she's got a beautiful voice. The two of you are going to be perfect together!'

Zach smiled at Ella, his gaze... *hopeful?*

Untangling her fingers from Leo's, Ella sat back down.

Leo remained standing, grinding his teeth as he eyeballed Zach.

'Let me re-introduce you to everyone else!' Libby said.

As she went around the group, Leo took his place next to Ella, his hand resting on the edge of his thigh, palm facing up in invitation.

She didn't take it, her knuckles turning white as she gripped her script.

'Okay, everyone!' Libby said with the enthusiasm of a newly-qualified primary school teacher after a triple espresso. 'Why don't we move onto the next scene in the kitchen, with the arrival of—'

'The star of the show!' Arthur roared. 'Me!' he added, in case anyone was in any doubt.

'Don't you mean *stars?*' Steve asked. 'There are *two* ugly sisters.'

'Quite right. Apologies, Steve.' Arthur cleared his throat. 'The arrival of the stars of the show! Miss Fanny Munchin and her younger sister, Miss Tittie Munchin!' He turned to Libby. 'Are we entering to "Here Come The Girls", or "Dontcha Wish Your Girlfriend Was Hot Like Me"?'

'Well—'

'We could do a medley?' he continued. 'Add in "Bad To The Bone", and "I'm Too Sexy" by Right Said Fred?'

Libby glanced at Connor.

'We could possibly—' he began.

'Splendid!' Arthur interrupted.

'However,' Connor continued, 'we don't want to detract from the other scenes with the ugly sisters. They can't peak too soon.'

'No chance of that,' his father retorted. 'I can go all night. Isn't that right, Deedee?'

Dervla planted a kiss on his cheek. 'Yes, you can, you big stud.'

Henry sighed. 'Dad, that's—'

'And Steve,' Arthur continued, turning to his left. 'You're more than a two-pump chump, aren't you?'

Steve puffed out his chest. 'The force runs strong in me.'

'Dad!' Leo ground out. 'Can we move it along? I can't be here all day.'

'Why not? Have you got a hot date?'

Leo kept his gaze on his father, but in his peripheral vision Ella's head snapped up and Zach leaned forward.

'No, Dad, but I've...' What excuse could he give? He was flailing around in fog, trying to find his bearings. 'Ella and I have to practise for the quiz.'

'Ha!' Scott cried. 'You're running scared. Get ready to be a big fat number two.' He held up a massive hand and Finn high-fived him.

'Are you still competing?' Zach asked Ella.

'Yes,' Leo replied.

'Need another teammate?' Zach continued.

Ella sucked in a breath, the edges of her script crumpling in her grasp.

'No,' Leo said coldly. After what had happened in the past, Zach had the fucking *nerve* to go there?

'You can join our team,' Scott said to Zach. 'We're Foxbrooke's pub-quiz champions eleven months out of the year, and in a few weeks we're going to make it twelve.'

'Cool, thanks,' Zach replied. 'I'd love that.'

'You'll have to borrow a beard, though.'

'Huh?'

'We're the Beardy Boys.'

'Can we get on with it?' Leo snapped. He didn't want to draw attention to Ella, but for her sake, he wanted to get the read-through done and dusted.

'Oh, er, yes, of course.' Libby's forehead puckered in confusion at his tone.

Henry placed a hand on her leg and glared at Leo.

Fuck. 'Sorry, Libby,' Leo muttered.

She gave him her sunniest smile. 'That's alright! Okay, let's go to the kitchen at Hardup Hall, where Cinderella is mopping the floor and Buttons is peeling vegetables. Ella, take it away!'

A lump settled in Leo's throat as Ella cleared hers. She suddenly seemed so small. Leo wanted to take her in his arms and shield her from Zach and the centre-stage role she'd never signed up for. An hour ago Ella had got a bit of her spark back, roasting Scott and Finn, then sharing her ideas for the set and costumes with Willow. Now she was hunkered down in her chair, her legs crossed away from her ex-boyfriend.

'Oh Buttons,' she began. 'Do you ever dream of falling in love?'

'Not at all,' Leo replied.

'You don't? Why ever not?'

'Because I'm already in love.'

'You are? How wonderful! Who are you in love with, Buttons?'

'Buttons turns to the audience,' Libby said.

'What do you think, girls and boys? Should I tell Cinderella how I feel?'

'Hopefully the audience will be shouting "yes",' Libby continued. 'But if anyone shouts "no", then Buttons will make a joke about people from Twerton getting everything backward.'

'Are you sure?' Leo asked. 'You don't *sound* very sure?'

'Audience will now be screaming "yes",' Libby said.

'Okay! I'll do it!' Leo took a deep breath. 'Ella, I love you.'

There was a charged silence as Leo ran the words he'd just spoken over in his head.

'I mean—'

'And I love you too, Buttons,' Ella interrupted. 'As a friend.'

'Cinderella dances around the kitchen with the mop as if it were a person,' Libby said, 'whilst Buttons pulls a sad face to the audience.'

'But I'm dreaming of meeting my one true love,' Ella continued. 'Someone who will sweep me off my feet.'

'Buttons grabs a broom,' Libby said.

'I can do that,' Leo said.

Ella laughed. 'Oh, Buttons, you are funny.'

'So, that's the sweeping box ticked,' Leo continued. 'What else does your one true love have to do?'

'He will be kind.'

'Buttons pats his pockets, finds some more sweets and reluctantly throws them into the audience,' Libby continued.

'That's me,' Leo said. 'And what does he look like?'

'Oh, I don't know. Most likely tall, dark and handsome.'

Like those pricks, Zach and Oliver, Leo thought bitterly.

'Buttons grabs a navy tea towel and puts it on his head, then stands on a chair,' Libby said.

'Look, Ell-*Cinder*ella, your dream man is right here!'

'Buttons, you are the sweetest. Thank you for cheering me up. But you're my *best* friend, not my boyfriend.'

'Music starts,' Libby said. 'And Ella dances with the mop around the kitchen whilst singing, "I Want To Know What Love Is", by Foreigner. Buttons joins in with adapted lyrics, trying to tell Cinders that he is the man for her. After the song, a klaxon sounds.'

'Buttons!' Ella cried.

'Cinderella!' Leo answered.

'They're here!' they both said together.

'Buttons and Cinderella dash around the kitchen, tidying, as the two ugly sisters enter through the audience,' Libby continued.

Arthur got to his feet and struck a pose. 'Dontcha wish your girlfriend was as hot as me?' he roared.

Steve stood, wiggling his hips. 'Dontcha wish your girl-friend was as sexy as me?'

'Fanny picks on a man in the audience,' Libby said.

Arthur sat with a thump on Scott's lap. 'Well hello, sailor! Is this the bus stop? 'Cos I am here to pick you up!'

Scott snorted with laughter.

'What's your name, gorgeous?'

'Scott.'

'And where are you from?'

'Foxbrooke.'

'Ooh, very la-di-dah! I had a tryst with the Duke of Somerset once.'

'Oh, no, you didn't,' Steve retorted.

'Oh, yes, I did!'

'Oh, no, you didn't,' everyone chorused.

'Oh, yes, I did!' Arthur continued. 'We played "hide the sausage" in his back passage!' He gave a heavy sigh. 'And the poor man has never been the same ever since.'

'Poppycock, Fanny!' Steve cried.

'Yes, there was plenty of both,' Arthur said, with an exag-gerated wink.

As Arthur and Steve continued their banter, Leo let it wash over him. He'd been looking forward to the read-through for months, but now he couldn't wait for it to be over. His head was buzzing and his stomach was knotted with frustration. As if Ella hadn't suffered enough recently, now Zach was crashing back into her life and re-awakening memories Leo had tried his best to help her forget.

When Buttons' lines came up, Leo tried to give them some oomph, but his heart wasn't in it.

Ella didn't look up from her script once as she read the part of Cinderella.

'That's fabulous, everyone!' Libby cried as the scene ended. 'Next up, during the scene change, we have Fairy Cakes and then our first time meeting Prince Charming and Dandini in the enchanted forest!'

Leo clenched his jaw as Zach and Scott sat up straighter. It would have been easier to get rid of Zach if he'd been crap, but the moment he opened his mouth, Leo was transported back to being a teenager, acting with him in the school play. Even then, it was obvious Zach had talent as well as looks, and that combination had taken him far away from Foxbrooke and made him a household name.

But along with remembering Zach's acting ability came other memories. Memories Leo had put in a box over a decade ago and deliberately forgotten about. Memories about Ella. They prickled across his skin, making him want to shake out his limbs. That, or punch Zach.

Many years ago, Leo had been so in love with Ella, she'd taken over his thoughts, whether he was awake or asleep. He'd never known a life without her in it, and he'd loved her as much as his own sisters. However, when puberty hit, this love suddenly felt different. *Very* different.

Leo had spent the whole of year ten plucking up the courage to ask Ella out, but when his best friend, Zach, told him he also wanted to date Ella, Leo had stepped back. Since that moment, either he, or Ella, had been in a relationship with someone else, and Leo had never again thought of her the way he did when they were both fifteen.

Would things have been different if he hadn't stepped aside for Zach? What would Ella have said all those years ago if Leo had told her how he felt? Or would the story have still ended the same way, with her turning him down and choosing Zach?

'Fantastic!' Libby cried. 'Now Prince Charming, disguised as his manservant Dandini, happens upon Cinderella gathering firewood in the enchanted forest.'

Fuck. They were there already?

Leo flicked forward through the script, dread filling his veins.

'But soft!' Zach said, sending a chill down the back of Leo's neck. 'What light through yonder forest breaks? It is the east, and this maiden is the sun!'

'Oh, hello,' Ella said, her eyes still glued to the script in her lap. 'Have we met before?'

Zach nodded, his gaze never leaving her. 'In my dreams, I have met you. Are you real? Or will you vanish when I open my eyes?'

'But your eyes are open now.'

'So my wishes have come true. Tell me, who are you?'

'Oh, I'm just a servant girl. What is your name?'

'Prin—Dandini. Have you ever dreamt of falling in love?'

The silence in the ballroom was electric. No-one moved a muscle as they watched Zach. Already off-script, he spoke to Ella as if they were completely alone. Leo's heart thudded faster and faster inside his chest.

'Y-yes,' Ella stuttered, her voice almost a whisper.

'And did your one true love look like me?'

She swallowed. 'Mostly.'

'Mostly? How am I different?'

'I never expected a beard.'

Zach mimed pulling it off. 'And now?'

'Oh! Yes! You are...'

'Your dream man?'

This was a nightmare. Leo was going to be sick.

'Yes. Oh, yes,' Ella said, her voice almost inaudible.

'Cue music,' Libby said. 'Cinderella and Prince Charming sing "Endless Love" by Lionel Ritchie. At the end of the song they kiss—'

'No,' Leo said forcefully.

Everyone's eyes flicked to him except for Ella's, who were still fixed on the script in her lap.

'No?' Libby asked tentatively, a crease appearing between her brows.

'It's a family show,' Leo continued, fully aware he was making no sense.

'Hear, hear,' Arthur said. 'It would be inappropriate.'

Libby's mouth fell open. 'It's just a peck!'

'Can't take any chances with the woke brigade,' Arthur continued. 'Might get us cancelled.'

'Cancelled?' Libby repeated, her eyes wide. 'Why?'

'Um... corrupting the youth and all that?'

Leo held his breath as Libby stared in confusion at the man who was a committed naturist and organised sex parties.

'Arthur,' she began. 'Don't you think your idea to name the ugly sisters Fanny and Tittie Munchin is slightly more problematic than a chaste kiss between Cinderella and Prince Charming?'

Leo glanced around the rest of the group. Those who didn't know the history between Zach and Ella were staring at Arthur as if he'd just grown another head, but Henry, Connor, Willow, Finn and Dervla were gazing at Ella with concern.

'Er...' Arthur flapped his hands in the air as if that would summon a more coherent argument.

'It's about consent,' Leo said. 'Ella shouldn't be forced to kiss anyone.'

Libby's eyes widened in shock. 'Oh my goodness, I'm so sorry Ella, Zach, for not considering this. Really, I had nothing more than a quick peck in mind, but Leo is right. We'll only have a kiss if you're comfortable with it.'

'Fine by me,' Zach said, his hands open and his posture relaxed. 'Ella?'

'Fuck's sake!' Leo exploded. 'Put her on the spot, why don't you?'

Libby froze, glancing in confusion between Leo and Zach.

Henry took her hand and shot another warning look at Leo. 'Why don't we have a short break?'

'Yes. Yes, of course,' Libby replied brightly. 'Great idea! Okay everyone, meet back here in fifteen?'

As soon as Scott and Finn stood, Ella pushed back her chair and fled the ballroom.

Leo leapt to his feet and followed, but Zach was quicker, making it to the door first.

Pushing through into the corridor outside, Leo grabbed Zach's arm before he could chase after Ella. 'What the fuck are you doing here?' he snarled.

Zach shook him off and took a step back, his hands raised in a gesture of surrender. 'Look, I'm sorry. I—'

'Sorry? *Sorry?* For what, exactly?'

Zach sighed, then took a big breath. 'I—'

'Actually, I don't give a rat's arse,' Leo interrupted 'You're going back in there to tell Libby you've changed your mind.'

Zach shook his head. 'I'm not doing that.'

'Oh, yes, you are.'

'Oh, no, I'm not,' Zach replied with a rueful smile.

Leo shoved him. 'Is this a fucking joke to you? Get out of my family's house and get out of Ella's life.'

Zach held up his hands again. 'Can we just talk?'

'No.'

'I want to explain.'

'Not fucking interested. You—' Leo broke off as the door to the ballroom opened and his mother stepped into the corridor, her anxious eyes flicking between him and Zach.

'Darling, is everything alright?' she said to Leo before turning to Zach and opening her arms, drawing him in for a hug. 'It's been far too long, young man. How's your mammy and daddy? Kurt?'

'Mum!' Leo hissed as she gave one of her legendary cuddles to the least deserving man in Foxbrooke after Oliver and Ella's dad.

'Not too bad, Mrs F,' Zach replied. 'Kurt's coming back from Australia for Christmas.'

Dervla drew back to look into Zach's eyes, her hands squeezing his upper arms. 'That'll be nice. Having the whole family back together. Ah, it's so lovely to see you again. And such a surprise having a star like you in our little panto.'

Zach's cheeks coloured, and he glanced at Leo. 'I'm back for a few reasons,' he began haltingly. 'And one of them is to apologise to Ella for what I did back when...'

Leo bristled at the look of contrition on Zach's face. It appeared genuine, but that only went to show what a great actor he'd become.

'You took your fucking time,' he snapped. 'Has it taken you this long to realise what an utter bastard you were to her?'

'Leo!' Dervla cried.

Zach shook his head, his expression haunted. 'Leo's right. I should have reached out years ago, but—' He ran a hand through his thick black hair. 'I don't want to give you any excuses because they're not good enough.'

'So why now? And why crash our panto?' Leo continued, his anger still raging like a wildfire.

Dervla frowned at Leo, then cupped Zach's face as if he were another of her children. 'Ella will understand, I'm sure.'

Zach swallowed, his gaze flicking between the two of them. 'Ronnie Chamberlain is being released early.'

Dervla froze. 'Oh.'

So the Price family *had* been contacted. Leo's jaw clenched even tighter. It wasn't just conjecture and hope on Michelle's part. This news made it real.

'He'll be out in time for Christmas,' Zach continued. 'And the news has brought back everything for all of us. But we need to face it and move on rather than running away or living in anger.'

'And Kurt?' Dervla asked.

'He booked his flight home from Oz before we knew about Ronnie, but he's not going to change his plans. He doesn't want what happened to affect his whole life.' Zach turned to Leo. 'Please, let me speak to Ella.'

Zach may have been genuinely sorry for what he did, but after the shock of Oliver dumping her the day before, the last thing Ella wanted was another ex-boyfriend throwing her for a loop.

Leo shook his head. 'Not today. She's been through enough recently.'

'She has? What's going on in her life? Mum said she's got a boyfriend.'

Zach's words were more petrol being dumped on the fire of Leo's anger. Zach was acting like he had some kind of claim over Ella. As if he had the right to know about her life and be the one to comfort her.

Taking a harsh breath, Leo opened his mouth to eviscerate him, but his mum interrupted.

'Best not to speak to her about the boyfriend,' she said quickly. 'He ended their relationship yesterday, and it came as a bit of a shock.'

Zach may have been an incredible actor, but Leo recognised hope in his expression underneath the concern. Blinding fear whistled in like the wind. Did Zach think he could get back with Ella?

'Just leave her the fuck alone, okay?' he ground out before striding off down the corridor.

NO, NO, NO, NO, NO. THE WORD REPEATED IN LEO'S HEAD LIKE a drum, keeping pace with his feet as if marching him into battle. If Zach's unexpected arrival had stirred up a storm of memories inside him, he could only imagine what Ella was going through.

Zach ruined her life once. He's not going to do it again.

But at the edges of Leo's righteous indignation, a voice he didn't want to hear whispered: *maybe she still has feelings for Zach? Maybe she* would *want to get back together with him.*

Entering the manor's empty kitchen, Leo paused at the doorway.

'It's only me,' he called out. 'Can I come in?'

There was a pause, then a muffled voice replied, 'Yes'.

Leo made his way over to the old fireplace. Built for roasting whole animals as well as feeding everyone in the manor before the advent of modern ovens, it was enormous. Ducking his head a fraction to step under the stone lintel, Leo turned to the right, where a huge bread oven had been built into the side. Through the opening were a pair of Converse trainers and Ella's clasped hands as she hugged her knees.

Leo leaned in. 'I can't believe you can still fit in there.'

'It's because I'm half munchkin,' she replied. 'Look, my head doesn't even touch the ceiling.'

'Right, I'm coming in. Budge up.'

'You won't fit.'

'Yes, I will. I'm at my racing weight, and Estelle dragged me along to one of Isaac's yoga classes last month.'

Ella giggled as he clambered inside. 'One yoga class isn't going to turn you into Stretch Armstrong.'

'I disagree,' Leo grunted as he tried to turn around. 'You know nothing of my pretzel powers. I—ow! Fucking hell!'

He sat on the floor with a thump and rubbed the back of his head, his back hunched as it followed the curve of the brick wall.

'You okay?'

'Never felt better, although I think two adults is the max this oven can take, so it's rubbish for playing sardines.'

'Do you remember when Henry and Connor got stuck up the chimney?'

'Yep. Mom and Mammy had a fit, and Dad suggested passing them some brushes so they could give it a good clean while they were up there.'

The sound of Ella's laugh lifted Leo's soul. Reaching out a hand, he placed it next to hers. This time, she took it and squeezed.

'His family knows about Ronnie coming out,' he said quietly.

'I couldn't believe it when he walked in,' she murmured. 'It was like a nightmare spinning out of control and into the real world.'

'I'm going to speak to Libby. Explain why he needs to go.'

Ella shook her head. 'She's so excited and we don't have

anyone else good enough to play the part. I just need time to process it. I'll be okay. All I need to do is keep my distance.'

An unbidden image of Zach kissing Ella flashed into Leo's mind with a jolt.

'You know, for years I imagined what I would say if I saw him again,' she continued. 'I always thought I would bump into him on the high street, or at school if he ever came back to talk to the kids. I never expected it to be here.'

'You don't have to play Cinders. Asking you in front of everyone was unfair. Willow can do it.'

'It won't work. You know she can't sing very well. And I was at some of the auditions with Libby. The other candidates made Willow look like a pop star.'

'But—'

'Honestly, this is what I need right now. Something so terrifying it will force me to think of something other than Oliver, my dad, or Zach.'

'Surely the Beardy Boys beating us in the Christmas quiz is *more* terrifying?'

'It's on a par. But now I know Zach's on their team, it gives me even more of an incentive to beat them.'

The clenched fist around Leo's heart released its grip slightly. Zach might have wanted to rekindle something with Ella, but it seemed his wish wasn't reciprocated.

'Why is he here? Why does he want to be in the panto?'

Leo swallowed. 'He said he had a few reasons, and one of them was to apologise to you for what he did.'

'Oh.'

'You really don't have to do this. You need to put yourself first for once. Everyone will understand.'

She was silent. They both knew he was speaking the truth, but Leo also knew that once Ella had made a commitment, she wouldn't shy away from it, no matter how difficult or unpleasant.

The silence between them grew heavy and sad.

Shuffling closer, Leo put his arm around her. 'You'll find your Prince Charming one day.'

She huffed. 'Well, I hope he's as kind and dependable as you are.'

Ella's words jabbed uncomfortably in his stomach. *What about 'sexy'?* He blinked at where his thoughts had taken him. *What's got into you? You don't want her to think of you as sexy.*

He cleared his throat. 'I truly am Buttons. The most dependable friend you could ever wish for.'

'You're more than that.' She let her head drop to his shoulder. 'You're funny, and loyal, and sweet.'

'Don't forget devastatingly handsome.'

'Of course.'

'With washboard abs and buns of steel.'

She giggled. 'I'll take your word for it.'

'And a world-leading authority on Christmas.'

'You'd better be. I've never been more determined to win the quiz than this year.'

Leo kissed the top of her head. 'We've got this.'

She squeezed his hand. 'We do. Now I think we'd better get Cinders and Buttons out of the oven. I don't want this panto to turn into Hansel and Gretal.'

'Luckily Michelle's not around,' he replied before thinking. 'Or we'd be cooked by now.'

Ella snorted, then clapped a hand to her mouth. 'Leo!'

He grinned. 'I didn't *say* she was a witch.'

She gave him a look.

'I just *thought* it. Now come on, let's get this read-through over and we can get back to cramming for the Christmas quiz.'

❦ 8 ❦

Pulling the collar of her coat tighter around her neck against the icy wind, Ella pressed the doorbell for the third time in as many minutes.

Has it only been a week since I was last here?

It seemed like a lifetime ago.

The last time she'd stood on this spot, she'd been living with Oliver and looking forward to an afternoon with Leo, then the panto read-through on Sunday.

Now Oliver had dumped her, their house was empty and on the market, she'd agreed to play Cinderella, and her Prince Charming was none other than Zach Price, her first ever boyfriend and the man who'd tried to ruin her life.

Thank god for Leo and his family.

The front door opened and Michelle's heavily made-up eyes narrowed to slits. 'You're late.'

Ella instinctively glanced at her watch. 'I—'

Michelle thrust her phone screen out, showing the time: three minutes past eleven.

A sudden wave of tiredness crashed through Ella, almost

knocking her off her feet, and she reached for the cold brick-work for support. Coming from Foxbrooke Manor to this was like leaving heaven and immediately arriving in hell.

I can't do this anymore.

She took a step back. 'I don't have to be here,' she said, her normal filters blunted by emotional exhaustion.

Michelle's eyes widened to comical proportions. Lurching to grab Ella's arm, she stumbled on the doorsill and pitched forward with a gasp.

Knees buckling as she failed to hold her stepmother's weight, Ella fell backwards, landing with a painful thud on the concrete path as she cushioned Michelle's fall.

'My leg!' Michelle cried. 'My fucking leg!'

Ella froze as the flashback slammed into her. She was trapped again, listening to the terrified screams of her half-sisters, her stepmother's howling, her father's frantic shouts. Her body was paralysed with panic, her vision filled with the memory of broken glass and blood.

'Help me!'

Flung back into the present moment, heart racing, and sweat prickling her skin, Ella lifted Michelle up. 'I'm sorry, I'm sorry, I'm s-sorry,' she stammered.

'Just get me back inside.'

Ella supported her stepmother as they entered the house, casting her eyes around for the nearest stick. There wasn't one in the hall, so they went into the living room. Michelle sat with a heavy thud on the sofa and closed her eyes.

In the silence that followed, Ella's pulse began to slow, and she became aware she'd been hurt by the fall. Her coccyx was throbbing, her right leg and arm ached, and her elbow was burning. Taking off her coat, she saw blood soaking through her sweatshirt. She pulled up the sleeve to see a livid graze.

'You gonna complain about a scratch when I'm like this?' Michelle asked.

Ella hastily tugged the sleeve back down. 'No, of course not. Can I get you anything? Ring the doctor?'

'No. They never give me what I want. Waste of fucking time.' She rested her head back and let out a long sigh, then eyeballed Ella. 'When were you going to tell me about Oliver?'

'Er...' *You never read my messages. I've only just got here, and anyway, why on earth would I tell you?*

'I knew this would happen. Don't know why you keep falling for posh twats. You think you're better than us, but you're not.' Reaching forward with a grunt, Michelle picked up a vape from the table and took a long drag. 'Got anything else to tell me?'

Ella knew enough of her stepmother to know this question was a trap. 'Zach Price is back in Foxbrooke and playing Prince Charming in the Christmas panto.'

Michelle sneered. 'That's not going to save him.'

A panic bomb detonated inside Ella. 'What do you mean?'

There was a nasty gleam in Michelle's eyes. 'You don't know?'

'Know what?'

With her foot, Michelle nudged a magazine towards Ella. 'Talking shit about your dad when his younger brother was up to his neck in it? And now snorting charlie in some fancy club with his new celeb mates? Wanker.'

Ella lifted the magazine. On the cover was a photo of Zach looking wide-eyed and wasted, a smear of white powder under his nose. The headline read 'Soap star sacked after drugs shame!'

Oh, no. Poor Zach. She dropped the magazine, not wanting to read any more.

'You feeling sorry for him?' Michelle asked incredulously.

'After what he did to us? He got what was coming. And if he thinks he can save his rep by poncing around on stage in a so-called "family" show, he's mental.'

'Zach never took drugs when we were together.'

'Well, he's started now.' Michelle cackled. 'I think me and the girls should go to the panto and give him a nasty surprise.'

'Please!' Ella cried. 'Don't do anything!'

Her stepmother shrugged. 'We'll see. But you tell him from us he'd better watch his back. And when your dad gets out, he'd better not still be in Foxbrooke.'

HURRYING AWAY FROM MICHELLE'S HOUSE OVER FOUR HOURS later, Ella tried to shake off the thoughts, memories, and feelings that stuck to her skin like superglue. Oliver had bulldozed the carefully constructed foundations of her life and now her past was colliding with her present; two earthquakes hitting her from either side. Emotionally battered and bruised, the only thing keeping her from completely falling apart was the support she had from Leo and his family.

Leo. He was her rock and her happy place. Someone who loved her just the way she was and had never let her down.

You trusted Oliver. Zach. Look where that got you.

But Leo's not like that!

How do you know? What happens when the Foxbrooke family's charity runs out?

Dread twisted in her stomach at the thought. The only thing she had to offer in return for their kindness was to make herself useful. That was why she'd agreed to play Cinderella. She'd confront every one of her demons and fears if it meant she could repay Leo and his family for everything they were doing for her. If she didn't step up, then she'd just be taking advantage of them.

But now Zach had been thrown into the mix, and she was expected to kiss him. The thought made her feel ill, but compassion followed. Zach may have enjoyed the high of whatever drugs he'd taken, but in the photo he didn't look happy. He didn't seem like the Zach she'd once known and loved. His life was crashing around him, and now Ronnie was being released early.

Rubbing her forehead in an attempt to massage the stress and pain away, Ella crossed the road and turned left, taking the longer route back to the manor to avoid walking past her old house. Leo had helped her clear out all her belongings, and she'd cancelled the next month's rent payment. She was already too far into her overdraft to afford it, and the deposit she'd paid to Oliver's parents was for the same amount. They could keep that instead. It wasn't as if they'd need to pay for repairs or cleaning, as she'd left the place immaculate.

Stop thinking about it! Let it go!

Entering the manor, she jogged up the stairs to her room, tore off her dirty clothes, and got into the shower.

The hot water soothed her aches and pains and cleansed away some of the sickness that arose each time she spent any time at her stepmother's. Glancing at the graze on her elbow, the sight of fresh blood sent another memory from the past to shock her into stillness. Would she ever be able to forget? Or at least feel detached from what had happened?

Come on! Focus on the future. You've waited for this day for a year now. Don't ruin it!

Tomorrow was the official opening of the Bath Christmas Market, but from three until eight p.m. tonight, residents of the county of Bath and North East Somerset were allowed in to enjoy the market before it became overcrowded with people from all over the South West. Ella and Leo's visit was yet another of their Christmas traditions, and Ella couldn't wait.

Throwing on clean jeans and a t-shirt that read 'I'm not an elf, I'm just short', she went into the corridor and knocked on his door.

No answer. She'd texted earlier to say she would be running late, and he'd replied to say for her to find him when she was ready.

Ella knocked again, louder this time.

'Come on in,' Leo shouted from inside, his voice muffled.

Opening the door, she entered his bedroom.

He was nowhere to be seen.

'I'm just finishing up in here,' he called from the bathroom. 'Ella's coming later and we're off to the Christmas market.'

Ella opened her mouth to reply, but suddenly wasn't sure what to say. Who did Leo think was in his bedroom?

Then he wandered out of the bathroom, a white towel around his hips, his head inside another one as he rubbed his wet hair. Water dripped off the hard planes of his chest to the floor.

'I'm thinking of wearing the t-shirt which says "I *am* an elf, I'm just tall",' he said into the towel. 'What do you think? Good call?'

Ella didn't reply, her mouth dry as she stared at his body. Normal cognitive function had been suspended, to be replaced with the kind of urgent and carnal feelings one should never have for one's friends. She knew Leo took care of himself, but she never imagined he was hiding all *that* under his clothes. Before she could stop the movement of her eyes, they tracked down his six-pack, following his happy trail to its final destination: the bulge underneath the towel.

'Willow?'

Ella's gaze shot guiltily back up to Leo's head as he removed the towel from his face and stared back at her.

'Sorry! Sorry!' she began, her face on fire and her hands

raised as if fending off attacking birds. Stepping backwards without knowing where she was going, she collided with the edge of Leo's enormous bed and fell backwards onto it.

'No, er, my fault.' He dashed back into the bathroom, slamming the door behind him.

Scrambling off the bed, Ella ran for the door. 'I'll be in my room!' she called out. 'Just knock when you're ready!'

Without waiting for a reply, she dashed into the corridor. And straight into Willow.

'Oh my god, are you alright?' Willow held onto Ella's shoulders, gazing at her with concern. 'What's happened?'

Ella's heart was beating so hard she almost couldn't speak. 'I knocked, and Leo said to come in, but he thought I was you, and he was...'

Willow rolled her eyes. 'Was he naked? Honestly, he's as bad as Dad.'

'He had a towel on. I didn't see, erm, anything.'

'Thank goodness for that. When we were in our teens, he used to forget to tie his dressing gown up properly. All. The. Time. He only stopped when Estelle started carrying a riding crop with her, threatening to whack "Little Leo" with it.'

Ella gave a hysterical laugh, and Willow frowned. 'Shall I make you a chamomile tea for the shock?'

'I, er—'

The door to Leo's room flung open, and he entered the corridor, buttoning up his jeans. His wet hair was sticking up in all directions and his t-shirt was askew.

'Ella! I'm sorry, I—'

'No, no, it's entirely my fault,' she interrupted.

Willow slapped the back of her hand against his chest. 'You gave poor Ella the fright of her life.'

'Ow! I thought she was you! You said you were coming up to discuss my panto costume!'

'I should have said something when I came in,' Ella said quickly. 'I'm to blame.' She stared at the tall elf on Leo's t-shirt. 'Sorry. I didn't mean to invade your privacy like that.'

He sighed. 'Please don't apologise. There's nothing to be sorry for.'

She shook her head, still too embarrassed to meet his gaze.

'Well, as Ella's back now, we can discuss the costume another time,' Willow said. 'Have an amazing time at the Christmas market!'

'Do you want to come?' Ella asked.

Willow smiled and shook her head. 'Thanks, but no thanks. I'm going first thing in the morning in a couple of weeks, when it's guaranteed to be fairly empty.' She gave Ella a quick hug. 'If I don't catch you later, I'll see you tomorrow at breakfast or at the rehearsal.' Giving them both a wave, she strolled off down the corridor.

Ella held her breath. What could she say to bring normality back to her friendship with Leo?

'Nice t-shirt,' he said.

Letting her breath go with a whoosh, she finally brought her eyes up to meet his. 'You, too.'

'We're twinsies. Shall we wear the hats with the elf ears to complete the look?'

Ella nodded, relieved Leo was acting as if nothing weird had just happened. 'Definitely. Unfortunately, I'll be wearing at least two layers on top of this t-shirt, so no-one will see it.'

His brow furrowed. 'I think next year we'll have to get Christmas coats.'

'Or jumpers three sizes too big, so we can wear at least two of them.'

He raised his hand. 'Plan.'

She high-fived him. 'Are we still getting food there?'

'Definitely. It's going to be bratwurst, roast chestnuts, mince pies, and glühwein all the way.'

'Shall I be the designated driver, then?'

Leo's phone rang in his pocket. 'I don't mind driving if you want to drink.' Pulling it out, he frowned at the screen, then his eyes widened. 'Fuck!'

'What is it? You need to get that?'

'Er...' He ran a hand through his hair as he stared at the phone.

The call cut out, and a few seconds later there was a buzz signalling the missed call.

'Let me guess,' Ella joked. 'You've forgotten you had a hot date scheduled for tonight?'

Leo's cheeks darkened.

Oh god. Creeping, mortifying feelings of inadequacy and shame crawled under her skin. She was a cuckoo in the nest of the Foxbrooke family. The unwanted gooseberry in the fruit salad of Leo's life.

'Leo, I—'

'I'll cancel.'

'Yes, absolutely. We can go to the market another time.'

He glanced at her in shock. 'No, I'm going to cancel my— the date.'

'What? No, you can't!'

'Yes, I can.'

Ella twisted her fingers together until they hurt. 'Leo, no. Please. I won't be able to enjoy myself knowing you've let someone else down.'

'But I don't want to let *you* down. I want to be with you.'

'You see me every day. The market's here for at least the next two weeks. Is she—' Ella took a deep breath. 'Someone you've been dating for a while?'

He shook his head as he frowned at the phone. 'I haven't met her yet.'

'Well then, you have to go!' She forced a smile. 'She might be "the one". Your fairytale happy ending. Your Princess Charming!'

'Ella—'

'Please don't cancel her, Leo. It's not fair.' Ella backed away down the corridor. 'I'm going to find Willow. I need to chat to her anyway about the costumes. I'll see you tomorrow, okay? Have fun!'

Without waiting for a reply, she turned and ran.

He shook his head as he glanced at the phone. I have not her...

Well, then you have to call. She forced a smile. She might be cross, but she's happy enough. Your Dad...

Hi, son! I said. Hang on, I'll get the...

With the corridor empty I went cold. When I tried to sing to her anyway it was the feature. I'll let you remember. How?

Without asking anyone, she found and...

❦   9   ❦

Striding up Park Street in Bristol, Leo checked his reflection in a shop window. Under the woollen coat were his smartest jeans and a tailored shirt, and his Converse trainers had been replaced by a pair of brown brogues. His outward appearance was date-ready, however, his mind was not. It was jumpy and irritable, as if itching powder had been sprinkled in his brain, stopping him from focusing on the evening ahead.

Why did you arrange this date so close to Christmas?

It's still November.

Near enough.

And you didn't know Oliver was going to dump Ella and kick her out of their house.

I should be back there with her.

And stand up—fuck! What's her name again?

Stopping in a doorway, Leo pulled out his phone to check who he was meeting.

Ellie. Okay. Easy to remember. Ellie, Ellie, Ellie.

He kept repeating the name as he approached the entrance

to the bar. A blonde woman was just ahead of him, and he instinctively held the door open for her.

'Leo?'

He stared blankly at her for a second before realising she was his date for the evening.

'Yes! Sorry, brain fart—I mean freeze. Ella? Right?' He held out his hand. 'Leo.'

She took it. 'It's actually Ellie.'

Fuck's sake! 'Sorry. Please feel free to call me Leon, Lenny, or anything else that springs to mind.'

She smiled. 'I think I can manage Leo.'

He held his free hand out and she passed through the door into the bar.

'Ellie, Ellie, Ellie,' he muttered under his breath.

She turned. 'Is it that difficult to remember?'

Huh? Did I say that out loud? 'Um...'

'Or are you a serial dater?'

He attempted a winning smile. 'Not intentionally. Although I've had some exciting flings with Corn Flakes, Rice Krispies and Shredded Wheat.'

Ellie stared blankly at him.

'Cereal dater? As in breakfast cereal?'

Shut up! You're sounding like a spanner!

Ella would have loved that joke.

Yes, but she's not here, is she? Ellie is. Ellie, Ellie, Ellie.

The restaurant manager approached them. 'Good evening. Do you have a reservation?'

Leo cleared his throat. 'Yes, table for two under the name Foxbrooke?'

The man checked his tablet. 'I have you here. Welcome to L'Art de Vivre. Please, follow me.'

Leo extended his arm again for Ellie to go ahead of him, shaking his head at himself. If these were his social skills, it was no wonder since Lila ended their on-off relationship, he hadn't managed to hold a new one down for longer than a few weeks.

The restaurant manager took Ellie's coat and pulled out her seat before Leo could do it. 'Your server will be with you shortly. Have a fantastic evening with us and enjoy your meal.'

Ellie gave him a dazzling smile. 'Thank you.'

Putting his coat over the back of his chair, Leo sat, trying to think of something, *anything* to say. He thought he wanted a girlfriend, but getting one was such hard work and he never seemed to get it right. The women he met were always lovely, but there was no spark, no real connection.

'So,' he began. 'What line of work are you in?'

Oh, way to go with the chat-up lines...

'I'm a secondary school teacher.'

He brightened up. 'Cool! My best friend's a teacher.'

'What subject?'

'She teaches art.'

Ellie paused, her brow furrowing slightly. 'Your best friend's a woman?'

'Yeah, we've been friends since we were in primary. She's awesome.' Leo smiled as he thought of Ella, feeling at ease for the first time since he'd left the manor. 'And she's always been an amazing artist. I've still got the very first drawing she ever gave me. It's a picture of us as a prince and princess in front of a castle. She even drew arrows pointing at us with "Ella" and "Leo" written next to them. It's super cute. I had the picture framed a few years ago, along with loads of other drawings she's given me.'

'*Ella?*'

'Yeah. Ella Chamberlain. Do you know her?'

Ellie shook her head. 'But she sounds like a really special person.'

Leo sighed happily. 'The best. I love her as much as my own sisters.' He frowned. 'Actually, I probably love her more because she's never once annoyed me.' He grinned across the table and lowered his voice as if imparting a secret. 'But don't ever tell them that.'

Ellie was looking at him strangely. 'And things have never been weird between you and her?'

'Weird? In what way?'

'You know. Like you fancied her or something.'

Leo waved his hand dismissively. 'Not really. I had a massive crush on her once, but that was years ago. Things are never weird between us.'

But even as he said the words, his cheeks heated, remembering the shock earlier when he realised it wasn't Willow seeing him half-naked, but Ella. That moment had been *extremely* weird, but he still couldn't pinpoint exactly why.

Picking up her menu, Ellie ran her eyes over it. 'You booked the table under Foxbrooke. Is that your surname?'

Leo tensed. 'Uh-huh.'

'Like the village near Bath?'

'Yep. Have you seen the specials board? The coq au vin sounds excellent.'

Ellie had put her menu back down and was gazing at him quizzically. 'You're not related to the Duke of Somerset, are you?'

Leo stared intensely at the wine list. 'Hmm?'

'The crazy guy who runs orgies at his stately home and has about five wives.'

Leo bit the inside of his cheek to stop a sigh from escaping. Often, he managed to avoid talking about his family until the third date. But sooner or later his potential girlfriends would discover who his parents were. Reactions went from shock and horror to excited curiosity. Sometimes women didn't seem bothered, but by then they'd usually decided Leo wasn't right for them for another reason.

He met Ellie's gaze and attempted to smile reassuringly. 'He only has two wives, and he's got a heart of gold.'

Her eyes lit up. 'So, you know him then?'

'Yeah. He's my dad.'

Ellie's excited expression froze, then crumpled into remorse. 'Oh god, I'm so sorry! I had no idea.'

Leo shrugged, as if it didn't matter, even though it always did.

'Is he *really* your dad?'

He nodded.

'Wow. My parents are accountants.'

A handsome waiter with black hair and flashing dark eyes appeared, giving his full attention to Ellie. 'Mademoiselle, have you seen anything you fancy tonight?'

Ellie blinked as she stared up at him, her cheeks turning pink. 'I, er... What would you recommend?'

He came to her side and bent down, his cheek inches from hers as if he was reading the menu for the first time and his eyesight was failing. 'Let me see what you might like.'

Ellie swallowed and leaned towards him.

Leo resisted the urge to roll his eyes. This was a first. Usually, his dates waited until the end of the night before they made it clear they weren't interested in him. Was it the blond hair that put them off? His family? His crap jokes? Or just the total lack of chemistry between him and whoever he was attempting to date?

As the waiter eye-fucked Ellie and exaggerated his French accent to the point of caricature, Leo thought back to Lila, the only long-term girlfriend he'd ever had. With her platinum-blonde hair, she had similar looks to Ellie. *And an attraction to dark-haired men.* She would always finish with Leo before sleeping with someone else, so he could never accuse her of cheating. But when the thrill of her new fling wore off, or he treated her badly, Lila would return to Leo, knowing he would take her back.

Why did I? At the time, he'd believed he was in love. But now, looking back, was he just in love with the *idea* of being in love? Was he trying to find some normalcy amidst the chaos of a family with one dad and two mums?

'And for you, Monsieur?'

Snapped into the present by the waiter's voice Leo ordered, then forced his posture to relax. Even though Ellie reminded him of Lila and what a fool he was to have stayed with her for so long, he smiled.

'What subject do you teach?' he asked.

'Maths.'

Leo tried not to flinch. He barely scraped through his GCSE in the subject.

Ellie rolled her eyes. 'That's the usual reaction I get.'

'Sorry, I've got a real mental block about maths. My brain shorts out if anyone mentions the word. I remember trying to learn quadratic equations and thinking, "what's the point"?'

'But they're amazing!' she exclaimed. 'They're a fundamental concept in algebra. They develop problem-solving and critical thinking skills, they're widely used in other STEM subjects, and they can model economic and business issues. Like calculating profit maximisation and cost minimisation. The skills you learn from solving quadratic equations can be applied to so many areas in life!'

Leo clenched his jaw, fighting a yawn. 'Maybe it was just how they were taught to me then. I could never get my head around them.'

Ellie frowned. 'That's such a shame.'

It is? He forced himself to nod.

She paused, then seemed to come to a decision about something. 'Okay! I know what we're going to do!' Pulling a pen from her bag, she opened out her paper napkin. 'My mission tonight is to change your mind about maths and teach you a quadratic equation!'

WHEN THEY LEFT THE RESTAURANT A FEW HOURS LATER, LEO still couldn't do a quadratic equation, and Ellie had been slipped a piece of paper by their waiter, presumably with his number on it.

'Thank you for a lovely evening,' Leo began, breaking the awkward silence. 'I've really enjoyed meet—'

He broke off as Ellie touched his arm. 'Look. You're a really sweet guy, but I can't see us being anything more than friends.' Withdrawing her hand, she took a deep breath. 'Honestly, I don't know why you agreed to this date.'

What? 'Er, why not?'

She gave him the kind of sympathetic look you might give a toddler who'd just dropped his ice cream on the floor. 'Leo, I think you need to be looking for a girlfriend closer to home.'

He frowned. 'You mean someone who lives nearer to Bath?'

Ellie rolled her eyes. 'I mean Ella.'

'*Ella?* But she's just a friend.'

'Maybe, but whenever you mentioned her, you lit up like a Christmas tree. You said you loved her more than your sisters, so maybe you need to ask yourself if that's because your love isn't actually platonic?'

He shook his head rapidly. 'Not a chance. She's my best mate. That's all.'

'If you say so.' Leaning forward, she pecked him on the cheek. 'Thank you for the date and good luck in the future.'

Without waiting for a reply, she turned and walked up the street away from him.

Leo watched her go, his head still moving slowly from side to side. Ellie may have been a maths genius, but she was dead wrong about his relationship with Ella. And even if his feelings for her might change in the future, he would never do anything about them. He didn't want to jeopardise their friendship, and she was still grieving the loss of Oliver.

Anyway, you're not her type, he thought to himself as he made his way back down the road towards the car park. Ella went for tall, dark and handsome, not tall, blond, and... the best-looking Foxbrooke? The boy next door? The guy whose primary residence was in the friend zone?

Sudden irritation scratched its nails down his mental blackboard. Why did he keep bothering with these dates when they only ever ended the same way? And besides, he didn't have time for this right now. Ella, the panto, the quiz. Christmas in general. He needed to make *them* his priority. Dating just got in the way.

Pulling out his phone, he deleted his dating app, feeling lighter as the icon disappeared. He could reactivate it in the new year.

THE MANOR WAS QUIET AS LEO ENTERED, SO HE PADDED UP the stairs towards his room, his stomach tensing at the thought of seeing Zach again at the panto rehearsal the next day. An apology to Ella was one thing, but if he followed it up by asking her out, Leo was going to lose his shit, no matter who was around to witness it.

He smiled to himself at the thought of turning the story of Cinderella on its head. Buttons, the lovesick best friend, grabbing Prince Charming's sword and running him through with it. Maybe he could suggest the idea to Libby?

Reaching the corridor with his bedroom, Leo's ears pricked up at a sound. *Moaning? Crying?* Was someone having sex far too loudly? If anyone *was* having sex, then he needed to get into his room as quickly as possible and find a pair of earplugs to block out the noise.

His senses on high alert, Leo stepped forward. *Please let it not be Ella and Zach. She deserves so much more.*

'Stop! No!' Ella cried out from up ahead.

His heart pounding, Leo sprinted forward and pushed the door to her bedroom open.

The room was dark, but the light from the corridor illuminated her alone on the bed, thrashing wildly and tangled up in the sheets.

'Don't do this! Please! No!'

Jesus Christ. Flicking on the main light, he leapt onto the bed and took her hand. 'Ella! It's me, Leo. Wake up.'

She turned towards him, her eyes wide open but unseeing, her breath panicked as if struggling to stop a monster tugging her down to the depths.

'Wake up, love. It's just a dream. It's okay. You're okay.'

Ella suddenly stilled, and Leo knew she was awake.

Then she burst into tears.

'Hey, hey.' He drew her trembling body into his arms. Her pyjamas were damp with sweat, tendrils of hair wet against her forehead. 'I know it felt real, but you're back now. It's just your mind playing tricks on you.'

She nodded as she wept, clinging to the front of his shirt.

Leo rocked her gently until her sobs lessened. 'Was it about the accident?' he asked quietly.

She nodded again. 'Michelle fell onto me earlier and it gave me a flashback. I think the nightmare was my mind trying to process it.'

'Michelle *fell* onto you? How did she manage that?'

Ella raised her head, her eyes puffy and tear-soaked. 'I was at the door and she was mad at me for being three minutes late, even though I'd been waiting longer than that for her to let me in.'

Leo's jaw tightened. *That fucking woman.* He wished she lived on the other side of the world. There, or in hell where she truly belonged.

'I was so tired and pissed off, I told her I didn't need to be there. She panicked and reached for me, but tripped over the doorsill and fell.'

'You could have stepped to the side?'

Ella gave him a look. 'It's better that she landed on me. I can cope with a few bumps and bruises, but she can't.'

A chill ran through him. 'Are you hurt? Do you need a doctor?'

She shook her head. 'I'm fine. My elbow's the worst, but it'll heal in a couple of days.'

'Let me see.'

Lifting the sleeve of her pyjama top up she showed him the graze. 'See, it's fine.'

'It doesn't look fine. That's an owie and a half.'

Ella smiled. 'I haven't heard that word in such a long time.'

'Want me to kiss it better? That's Mammy's cure for owies.'

She let out a small laugh. 'Go on then. Take the pain away, Doctor Foxbrooke.'

Leo contorted his mouth as if preparing for a professional gurning competition.

'What on earth are you doing?'

'Getting the owie removal machine ready for action.'

Ella snorted. 'You look like the world's most unsuccessful ventriloquist.'

'I'm actually auditioning to be the dummy,' he replied, the pain in his heart easing as she giggled. 'Okay! They're primed and good to go!'

Lifting her elbow, he placed a soft kiss over the scrape.

Ella shivered.

'Did that hurt?'

'Um, a tiny bit.'

'Perhaps you need another dose?' Before he could question what he was doing, Leo brushed his lips over her elbow again. A jolt of awareness shot through him and he froze. *What the hell are you doing?*

Moving away, he grinned at Ella's shocked face. 'Cured?'

'Um, yeah.' She blinked, then smiled back. 'Good as new!' Glancing down at her pyjamas, she pulled a face. 'I should probably change out of these.'

Leo got off the bed. 'I'll leave you to it. You okay now?'

She hesitated. 'I'm worried about falling asleep again. Do you mind staying a bit longer?'

'Not at all. I can stay as long as you need.'

'Thank you.' She took a fresh pair of PJs from a drawer, then went into the bathroom to change.

Leo stood by the side of the four-poster bed, suddenly unsure of himself. Had he crossed a line by kissing Ella's elbow? Why did it feel as if he had? And why did it feel so... *different* to normal?

Ella re-entered the room, her long hair brushed and falling around her shoulders in black waves. Leo had the sudden urge to run his fingers through it.

Woah! Get it together, you creep!

Getting onto the bed, Ella gestured to it. 'There's enough

room for you. I know it's not as big as your dictator-sized one next door, but it's big enough.'

He got onto the bed next to her. '*Dictator*-sized?'

'Sorry, Supreme Leader-sized. Is that right?'

He rolled his eyes. 'It's an Emperor.'

'Apologies, your eminence. And thank you for slumming it in this antique four-poster bed.'

'Still too small for sleep jogging,' he grumbled. 'And too high off the ground. I'll fall out and give myself an owie.'

'Well, if you do, I promise I'll kiss it better.'

Without thinking, Leo threw himself out of the bed, landing with an almighty crash on the wooden floor. 'Fuck!'

He looked up to see Ella's laughing face as she peered over the edge of the bed at him. 'No kisses if it was intentional.'

'That hurt way more than I thought it would. I don't know why I did it.'

'Because you're selfless when it comes to cheering me up. Now come and tell me how your hot date went.'

He got back into the bed next to her. 'Bloody marvellous. Best first date yet.'

'Oh. Really?'

'Yep. She spent most of the meal trying to teach me how to do a quadratic equation and left with the waiter's phone number in her pocket.'

'What?'

'She's a maths teacher, and the waiter was *extremely* French.'

Ella clapped a hand to her mouth, but it didn't stop the laughter from bursting out. 'Oh, my god! That sounds horrendous!'

'She also said I was a "really sweet guy", but that we would never be more than friends.'

'I'm sorry. Did you really like her?'

He shrugged. 'Not as a girlfriend. And she also looked a lot like Lila, which was weird.'

Ella didn't reply.

'Anyway, on the way home, I deleted the dating app.'

'Why?'

'I can't be arsed right now and besides, I don't have time.'

'Sorry.'

'Huh? What for?'

'I'm taking up more of your time than usual.'

He took her hand. 'I want to be with you. Spending time hanging out with my BFFFFFFF is the bloody best. There's nowhere else I'd rather be.'

'Are you sure?'

'Yes! Surely you know that by now?' He pulled her in for a hug, and she rested her head on his chest. 'All the women I date eventually decide they just want to be my friend, but I've got more than enough already and the bestest friend in the whole world. No-one can take your crown, Princess Ella.'

She gave him a squeeze. 'I just want you to be happy.'

'I am happy. If it makes you feel any better, I'll reactivate the app in January. But until then, nothing is more important than you.'

'I thought nothing was more important than winning the Christmas quiz?'

'That's you-adjacent. If we weren't on a team together, I wouldn't care as much.'

'Thank you.'

Leaning down, he kissed the top of her head, the floral scent of her shampoo sending his thoughts flying from his mind. *Concentrate!* 'Anytime. Do you want me to turn the main light off? Put the sidelight on instead?'

'Yes, please.' She moved away from him and flicked on the lamp by her side of the bed.

Leo cut the main light, got back onto the bed, and held out his arms. 'Hug?'

Ella nodded and settled herself back against him. 'Thank you. I feel as if I won't have any more nightmares if you're here.'

'Was it a bad one?'

She sighed. 'Yeah. It felt so real.'

'Want to talk about it?'

'You really want to hear the story again?'

'If it helps, then yes. I think every time you tell it, you become more confident in the truth of what happened. Not the bullshit Michelle and her demon spawn spew at you.'

Ella's small body shook with laughter. 'Unfortunately, they'd rather blame me than take a good hard look in the mirror.'

'That option's out. The mirrors would immediately shatter.'

'Leo!' Ella managed in between her giggles.

'It's true. And they've been banned from the Co-op after they soured all the milk.'

'You're very naughty.'

'Yep, and they're not very nice. Mammy loves everyone, and even she struggles to give them the time of day. I'm glad Henry paid for Summer to go to private school, so she wasn't in the same year as Billie-Mai at Foxbrooke Secondary.'

'Me, too.'

A hush settled on the room, the only sounds being the faint creaks from the old house and an owl in the distance.

'My nightmares usually start with the accident itself,' she began hesitantly. 'But this one started before we even left the house. I'm back in the hall trying to talk Dad out of it. But he's just shouting at me and telling me to do what I'm told. And no matter what I say, I can't change his mind. He's getting angrier and angrier until he leaves and slams the door behind him.'

Letting out a steady breath, Leo imagined what Ella must

have gone through that night when she was only fourteen. Ronnie Chamberlain had the bright idea of stealing a car and staging a crash to get a huge insurance payout. The more people involved, the more lucrative. The plan was for him to drive into the family car when Michelle was at the wheel and the three girls were in the back. Ronnie would then wipe his prints from the stolen car and jump into the one with his family in it, then claim that a joyrider had crashed into them.

Only it didn't turn out as he'd planned.

'I only got in the car because I wanted to protect Kyla-Marie and Billie-Mai, and try to talk Michelle out of doing it,' Ella continued, her voice tired.

'I know.'

'But of course she wouldn't listen. I remember how dark and wet it was. The water smeared by the greasy wiper blades and catching the light from the street lamps. It made it really difficult to see the road, but the speedometer kept creeping up. I knew she was going too fast.'

Hugging Ella a little tighter, Leo dropped another kiss on the top of her head.

'In my dream, I'm yelling at Michelle to slow down. To stop. Not to take this risk. But she's furious with me. She turns to yell at me over her shoulder. But then Dad's car hits ours from the right-hand side. Everything is always in slow motion from that point. The two cars travelling sideways. The girls screaming. Michelle's body being thrown about like a rag doll. Then the ear-splitting thud as we crash into a tree on the left. Michelle's not moving, and there's broken glass and blood everywhere. Then Dad's there, but he can't get to us because the tree has staved in the doors on my side, and his car has crushed the ones on the driver's side.'

The fire crew had taken nearly an hour to cut Michelle out of the car and free her daughters, who, miraculously, were relatively unharmed. Ronnie had then grabbed the two younger girls and got a friend to drive them to the hospital to see Michelle, leaving Ella still stuck in the back of the car.

'If I'd been sitting in the front passenger seat, I would have died.'

Leo nodded. 'Thank god you weren't.'

'They're never going to stop blaming me for what happened.'

'You know it's not your fault. None of it is.'

She sighed. 'But Dad being put away *is* my fault.'

'Bullshit. We just sped up the inevitable. Who knows how many more people might have died if we hadn't told the police where his lock-up was? Come on, love. You know I'm right.'

Another sigh. 'Dad coming out early is bringing everything back from that time.'

And Zach returning. 'What can I do to help?'

She gave him a squeeze. 'Just keep being the best friend a girl could ever have.'

The corners of Leo's eyes unexpectedly pricked with tears. He loved Ella so much and wanted to protect her from anything bad in the world, starting with her family.

'Maybe tell me a happy story?' she asked.

Leo smiled. *"Twas the night before Christmas, when all through the house, not a creature was stirring, not even a mouse...'*

'Perfect.'

'The stockings were hung by the chimney with care, in hopes that St. Nicholas soon would be there...'

Leo continued the story that both he and Ella knew by heart, speaking softly in the hope it might lull her to sleep.

'Again,' she murmured when he got to the end.

Halfway through the second rendition, Ella's breathing changed and her body became heavy in his arms. Leo kept talking, making sure she was truly asleep.

'*But I heard him exclaim, ere he drove out of sight—"Happy Christmas to all, and to all a good night!"*,' Leo finished, not wanting to move and wake Ella up.

Holding her in his arms, he listened to the deep, rhythmic sound of her breathing. How lucky he was to have her in his life.

'Love you, Ella,' he whispered, before carefully resting his head back and closing his eyes.

❧   10   ❧

Ella awoke slowly the next morning from the deepest sleep, as if floating down to earth from the fluffiest cloud in heaven. At the edge of her awareness was a niggling sensation. Some unpleasant memory she couldn't quite reach.

The bed smelled different, too. A spicy and comforting scent she knew was good, but had never been in bed with her before. Something heavy was draped over her side and she was holding something warm.

Opening her eyes, she saw a hand nestled between hers. The brief flare of panic in her chest extinguished the moment she remembered who was with her. *Leo*. He'd stolen her nightmares and guarded her sleep.

Carefully turning to her other side, Ella gazed at him. Had she ever seen him asleep before? Still dressed in his smart clothes from the previous night, he looked like a fallen angel with his messy blond hair and tawny stubble. Leo was beautiful in a wholly masculine way.

As if sensing her watching him, he stirred and opened his

eyes, his full lips parting in a lazy grin. 'Morning, Princess. How did you sleep?'

She smiled back, her heart lighter than air. 'Like a log, Prince Leo. And you?'

His grin got bigger. 'Like an even bigger log. Vanquishing dragons is hard work.'

'Is that why I slept so well?'

'One hundred and ten per cent. The floor around your bed is littered with their scaly corpses.'

'And are you going to clean them up?'

There was a mischievous glint in his eyes. 'That's Bridget's job.'

'Leo!' Pushing up to sit, Ella poked him. 'Your mess, your problem.'

He laughed. 'But I don't know where the vacuum cleaner is, remember?'

She prodded him again, and he flinched, his laugh getting higher in pitch.

Her fingertips hovered above his ribs. 'Are you ticklish, Prince Leo?'

'No?'

'Really?' She pounced on him. 'So you won't mind if I do this, then?'

'Nooo!' He rolled onto his back, batting at her hands.

Leo could have overpowered her in an instant, but his attempts to stop her had as much power behind them as a butterfly's wings, and his laughter was so joyous that Ella couldn't help but join in.

Straddling him, she continued her assault, not realising how much of her enjoyment was derived from the hard muscles of his body under her fingertips and the feel of him between her thighs. But then he raised his palms in a gesture of surrender and she finally stopped.

There was a beat as her eyes locked with his and the air around them changed, becoming heavy and charged with energy. The realisation that she'd never been in a position like this with him before hit her like an electric shock, pulsing through her cells and flickering across her skin.

What are you doing? Get off him!

Leaping away, she headed for the bathroom, her heart thudding painfully and her hands tingling. 'I need to take a shower. See you in fifteen mins for breakfast?' She didn't wait for a reply, closing the bathroom door behind her.

Ella blinked as she stared at her crimson cheeks in the mirror, double-checking the person in the reflection was actually her. She looked... alive? Happy? Aroused?

Oh my god, no!

Turning away, she sat on the toilet, her hands on her face as if they could absorb the heat radiating from it.

He's your best friend, not a sex toy! But as the thought popped into her head, her body reacted, blood rushing between her legs and her nipples tightening to aching points.

At the sound of drumming water on the far wall, she glanced up. In the bathroom next to hers, Leo was in the shower.

Stripping off her pyjamas, Ella stepped into her shower, gasping as the cold water hit her sensitised skin. She didn't turn up the heat. There was far too much inside her as it was.

Do NOT think of Leo naked a few inches away!

But her mind inconveniently removed the word 'not' from the instruction, and whether she squeezed her eyes tightly shut or focused on the tiles in front of her, all she saw was him.

Shivering, she quickly washed, not allowing her hands to linger where they wanted, then dressed and left the room.

Leo entered the corridor at the same time as her, wearing a Roger Hargreaves 'Mr Christmas' t-shirt. He laughed as he clocked her 'Little Miss Christmas' one. 'We are definitely telepathetic.'

'You realise you've jinxed it now?'

'Never! We are one mind. Like the Borg, but more festive.'

Ella crossed her arms as if she could hold in her racing heart. 'Really?'

'Yup!' Putting his fingers to his temples, Leo wiggled his eyebrows. 'I am reading your thoughts right now.'

Oh god. She swallowed. 'And what am I thinking?'

'Hang on.' He frowned. 'Download in progress…'

Ella tapped her foot and tried to look bored.

'Leo is the best-looking Foxbrooke,' he began in a high-pitched voice.

'I do NOT sound like that!'

'And probably very hungry after a night fighting dragons,' he continued in a falsetto. 'So we should probably head—'

Grabbing his arm, Ella marched him along the corridor.

'But I haven't finished reading your mind,' he protested, his voice still several octaves higher than normal.

She shot him a look. 'Do you want to sound like that permanently?'

'No, definitely not,' he replied in a voice so deep, the vibrations rumbled from his arm up into hers.

Ella snorted with laughter. 'Glad we're on the same page.'

Pulling his arm from her grip, Leo interlaced his fingers with hers and squeezed. 'Always.'

'You alright?' Leo asked Ella as they left breakfast and strolled through the manor towards the ballroom.

She forced a smile. 'Fine.' She'd been trying to act normal, but the image of Leo lying on the bed between her legs kept popping into her mind and demanding she examine it with a forensic level of detail. 'Why do you ask?' She held her breath as she waited for his answer.

Leo slowed, his brow creasing with concern. 'Zach?'

Her breath whooshed out. 'It'll be fine. I actually feel really sorry for him. It can't be nice having your face plastered on the cover of a magazine and everyone knowing why you've lost your job.'

Leo huffed. 'Pretty ironic, considering his stance on drugs before.'

'He must have been really unhappy for it to have got that bad.'

'Or too full of himself to notice.'

'Leo...'

He stopped walking, his body tight with tension. 'Zach was the one who went to the press after Kurt was stabbed and accused you of selling drugs in school, when he knew it was Kurt who'd been doing it. Zach was the one who threw you under the bus to save his family's rep. He turned almost everyone against you and nearly got you expelled, for god's sake.'

'I know,' she replied quietly.

'It was a witch hunt, and he was the fucker with the pitchfork goading all the sheep on. I'll never forgive him for what he did to you.'

A lump of emotion sat in Ella's throat, so big she could hardly speak. 'I know what he did was bad, but a kid had already died of an overdose. Then Kurt was caught in a county lines feud and left for dead. Zach lashed out at the easiest target—'

'Which makes him a coward as well as an arsehole.'

She shrugged. 'You said he wanted to apologise. Hopefully, we can all move on, even though Da—Ronnie's about to get out of jail.'

'And what if *he* hasn't moved on?'

Ella paused. The prospect of her father coming back to Foxbrooke with retribution on his mind made her want to be sick. 'We have to trust the police and probation service. He can't put a foot wrong or he'll be straight back to jail.'

Leo nodded, a muscle ticking in his jaw.

'It'll be okay,' she said, even though she didn't believe it. 'And we can't let worries about a potential future take our minds off the most important things in life.'

'Like winning the Christmas quiz?'

She grinned. 'Absolutely.'

ENTERING THE BALLROOM WITH LEO, ELLA WAS RELIEVED TO see they were the last to arrive. The rehearsal could start without time for Zach to come and talk to her. She wasn't ready for that yet.

'Morning, Cinders and Buttons!' Arthur boomed from the stage.

Ella raised a hand in return, keeping close to Leo as they made their way over. Libby had a script in one hand, a pen in the other, and was bouncing on the balls of her feet, her face alive with excitement.

'Okay, everyone!' she said. 'Let's have a quick catch up before we get down to it!'

'I've alread—' Arthur began.

'Got down to it at least twice since sunrise?' Libby interrupted.

'How did you know what I was going to say?' Arthur's jaw dropped. 'Was Deedee that loud?'

Leo exchanged exasperated glances with his siblings, and Dervla giggled.

'I have no idea,' Libby replied. 'I just know if there's an innuendo hiding anywhere, you'll be the first to find it.'

'Ha! Too bally right!' He struck a pose. 'And that's why I make the best pantomime dame!'

Steve cleared his throat loudly.

Arthur turned. 'On a par with you, Steve, of course!'

'Grab a chair, everyone,' Libby said, 'and we'll go through the plan for today.'

Leo dragged two chairs over, positioning them on the opposite side of the circle to Zach. Ella sat, sensing Zach's eyes on her.

Be brave! Raising her head, she met his gaze.

Zach gave her a tentative smile and mouthed, '*Hi*'.

Ella forced her lips to curl upwards, even as all the upsetting memories he'd created spilled out of the boxes she'd put them in. Zach had betrayed her trust so completely, yet she could still see the person Leo had encouraged her to fall in love with. When Zach had turned on her, he'd acted from a place of deep anger and pain, and Ella knew how out of character that behaviour had been.

'How many gifts in the twelve days of Christmas?' Scott asked as he sat on the other side of her to Leo.

'Three hundred and sixty-four,' she replied without missing a beat, glad to have a reason to turn her attention away from Zach.

'Where was the candy cane invented?' Scott continued.

'Germany. And why was it shaped that way?' she countered.

'Er...'

Finn leaned across Scott. 'J for Jesus.'

'And why are they red and white striped?' Ella asked.

Silence.

Leo put his index finger and thumb against his forehead, making the letter L.

'There isn't any significance,' Scott blustered.

'Prepare for a smackdown, boys,' Leo said gleefully. 'Go on, Ella. Deliver the killer blow.'

'The white represents purity, and the red symbolises Christ's blood,' Ella said with a smile. 'And another significance of the shape is if you turn the cane upside down, it represents a shepherd's staff.'

Scott frowned at her and swiped his phone open.

'It's quicker just to google "is Ella right",' Leo said. 'Or "will we always come second to the Noel it Alls?" Spoiler alert, the answer for both is a resounding "yes".'

Finn growled and Ella smothered a grin.

'Okay!' Libby said. 'Let's get started.'

Leo raised a hand. 'Can I propose an important motion?'

Her eyebrows raised, but she still smiled. 'Yes, of course. What is it?'

'Thank you. I'm concerned about people's commitment to the spirit of Christmas.'

Henry rolled his eyes. 'Leo, it's still November.'

'Only thirty days to go! The countdown is on!'

'The dress rehearsal is in twenty-two days,' Connor said.

'This is all about dress,' Leo continued.

Libby looked confused, and Henry put a hand on her knee. 'He wants us to wear Christmas jumpers or t-shirts to every rehearsal.'

'Bingo!' Leo replied happily. 'Ella and I have committed fully to this idea, but the rest of you are lagging behind.'

'I'm game!' Steve said. 'I've got some brilliant *Star Wars* ones.'

There were other murmurs of assent around the circle.

'Finn?' Leo asked.

'I don't have one.'

'Yes, you do. I bought you one last year with a picture of the Grinch on it.'

'I had to throw it away.'

'What?!' Leo spluttered. 'Why? He's your brother from another mother!'

Finn shrugged. 'I used it as a work t-shirt and it got trashed.'

Leo shook his head. 'And that's why you don't deserve to win the Christmas quiz. No respect.'

Henry cleared his throat and Leo raised his hands. 'That's all. Carry on, Libby.'

'Okey dokey! Well, the first piece of amazing news is that thanks to our star—'

'Me!' Arthur cried happily.

'The *other* star,' Libby continued, 'Zach. We've completely sold out of tickets and there's a waiting list for any returns!'

Applause rippled around the circle. Leo didn't join in.

'The Winter Ball is in six days, so a week today we can really start calling this space our own.' Libby turned to Finn. 'How are you getting on with construction of the flats?'

'I've done as much as I can before the final assembly in here,' he replied. 'And they're already painted thanks to Ella, Willow and Leo.'

Libby clapped her hands. 'That's fantastic news! Willow, Ella, how are the costumes coming along?'

Ella caught Willow's eye and gave a brief nod, wanting her to speak. Nerves about Zach were biting in her tummy.

'In hand,' Willow replied. 'There have been a few... *creative* differences with one member of the cast, who shall remain nameless—'

'They release doves at bloody weddings!' Arthur grumbled. 'I don't see why I can't let a few pigeons out from underneath one of my dresses!'

Libby blinked at him.

Henry sighed heavily. 'That sounds like a health and safety catastrophe, not to mention inhumane, Dad. And how on earth would we get any in the first place, then get them back out of the ballroom once you'd let them go?'

'Easy! We'll borrow them from that chappie in the village who breeds racing pigeons. They'll be out from under my dress, across the ballroom, and back in their box before the rapturous applause dies down.'

'I'm sorry, Dad, but it's a hard no,' Henry continued.

'But—'

'The costumes will be ready on time,' Willow interrupted.

'And the score's arranged,' Connor added. 'So it's just a case of blocking the routines.'

'Fantastic news!' Libby beamed at him, then glanced around the rest of the group. 'And how are you all getting on with learning your lines?'

'I'm off script,' Zach said, as Dervla, Steve, Scott and Leo nodded.

Ella kept quiet. She knew all the lines, but the thought of being the centre of attention on stage and acting being in love with Zach meant the words often kept flying out of her head when she tried to remember them.

'Ella?' Libby asked.

'Um... I do know them, but then I have a complete mind blank. Sorry.'

'That's completely normal,' Libby said, an encouraging smile on her face. 'It'll get more familiar as we block it out. And I'll always be ready for a prompt on the night if you get stuck.'

'I can help,' Zach said.

Ella felt Leo bristle beside her.

'We can have extra rehearsals together,' Zach continued. 'I can teach you some of the tricks I learnt at drama school.'

'Thanks, but I think I'll be okay,' she said hurriedly before Leo could speak.

Zach glanced at Leo, then gave Ella a friendly smile. 'Well, the offer's always there. I'll give you my number so you can call whenever you need.'

'Thank you, Zach,' Libby said. 'That's really kind. And Ella, you know you can also ring me at any time.'

Ella nodded, feeling everyone's eyes on her as if she was expected to make a decision on who her personal acting tutor would be.

'Okay then,' Libby continued. 'Why don't we start with the forest scene where the ugly sisters meet Dandini who's disguised as Prince Charming?'

'Hurrah!' Arthur leapt to his feet, making for the stage.

Everyone else stood, and Willow came to Leo's side. 'Can I check if your costume fits better now I've altered it?'

'Yeah, sure,' he replied. 'Have you got it with you?'

'On the table over there. It won't take long.'

Leo glanced at Zach, who was in conversation with his mother, then at Ella. 'You alright?'

She nodded. 'Absolutely fine. You go.'

'Alright. I won't be long.'

As Leo turned to follow his sister, he reached to the back of his neck and pulled his t-shirt up and off.

Ella stared, mesmerised, at the corded muscles of his back rippling under the skin. Then she remembered where she was and who she was looking at, and spun around.

Straight into Zach.

'Hi,' he said.

'Hi,' she replied, her cheeks on fire.

He smiled and raised an eyebrow.

Oh god. Does he think I'm blushing because of him? She stared blankly back at him, not knowing what to say.

Rubbing the back of his neck, his gaze fell away. 'I, er... I wanted to talk to you. If that's okay?'

Ella crossed her arms over her stomach, holding her nerves inside, then nodded.

'In private?'

She looked around. They weren't being overheard, but were standing in the middle of the ballroom. Without waiting, she strode to the far corner of the room and turned, her heart beating uncomfortably fast as she imagined what Zach might be about to say.

Facing her, he put his hands in the pockets of his jeans and stared at the wooden floor, taking breaths, but exhaling without speaking.

Then he shook his head and let out a terse sigh. 'I've been working on this speech for years, but now I can't remember how to start it.'

Ella remained silent. If this was meant to be an apology, she wasn't going to help him out. Her heart hurt with old memories, as if a scar were being stretched.

Raising his eyes, Zach held her gaze. 'I'm sorry, Ella. For everything I did to you.' His expression was desolate. 'When Kurt got stabbed, I blamed myself. He was my little brother, and it was my job to protect him. But instead I was...'

'Sleeping with the enemy?' Ella's voice was dry and brittle.

Zach swallowed. 'I didn't want to believe Kurt was working for your dad. I wanted to keep everything black and white. Divide the good guys from the bad ones. I was too much of a coward to go after Ronnie, so I lashed out at you.'

Ella rocked back on her heels as his words hit her.

'I thought you had to have known everything your dad was up to. The bad batch of drugs. Kurt's involvement. And I didn't want him to get into trouble with the police, so I tried to throw everyone's focus to…'

'Your girlfriend,' Ella whispered, hugging herself tighter.

Zach's eyes were liquid. 'I'm so fucking sorry. I'll never forgive myself for how I treated you.' A tear spilled down his cheek and he swiped it away. 'And it's been eating me up ever since. I thought I could outrun my shame, but it's followed me like a shadow.'

Ella clenched her teeth together to keep her own emotion from escaping.

'I don't know if you know,' Zach continued. 'But I've been sacked from *Swallowdale*. For taking drugs.' He sighed. 'I'm fully aware of the irony. I'd never touched them until last year, but I got caught up in playing a part. Not the one on the soap. The character of Zach Price, the guy the media thought I was. But that was never me. I'm not some bad boy who likes to party. That was who Kurt wanted to be. I was just the geeky kid who loved being on stage. You know that.'

Ella shrugged.

'The drugs helped me escape from my demons, but then the comedowns were like being dragged into hell. Deeper and deeper every time. I haven't touched anything since I got sacked and I never will again.'

'Is that why you're here? To try and rehabilitate your public image?'

There was a tiny hesitation, then Zach nodded. 'It's one of the reasons, I'm not going to deny it. But it's only part of the picture. I wanted to see you. To apologise. To rebuild the bridges I burned. And I want to be closer to Foxbrooke. To my folks. Maybe get a job nearer home.'

Ella didn't know what to say. For years she'd dreamed of an apology, believing it would mend all the broken parts of her. But now she just felt exhausted and empty.

'I don't know if Leo told you, but Kurt's coming back from Australia for Christmas.'

She nodded.

'And then we were told Ronnie's being released early.'

A knife of ice plunged deep into her belly. 'Michelle told me. And she thinks Dad wants to settle some old scores.'

Zach's expression darkened. 'Would he come after Kurt? Our folks? *Me?*'

'I don't know. He'd be mad if he did.' She paused. They both knew 'sane' wasn't a word often associated with her father.

'Can I speak to the police?' Zach asked. 'Tell them what you've just told me?'

'Of course.' She gave a helpless shrug. 'But to be honest, he could be talking about any number of people he's fallen out with over the years.'

'Maybe he's talking about whoever told the police where his lock-up was?'

Ella was silent as fear choked her. Could her dad have found out it was her and Leo who shopped him? And if he did, what would he do?

Zach reached out as if wanting to touch her, then ran his hands through his hair instead. 'I'd really like to talk more. Make amends. My folks say there's an incredible restaurant on the high street that opened a couple of years ago. Can I take you there for a meal? It's closed tonight and Monday. So maybe this coming Tuesday?'

Ella's mind reeled. Did he think this was a date? 'It's the last few weeks of term so I'm a bit snowed under at the moment.'

He smiled. 'Of course. Are you going to the Winter Ball on Saturday?'

She nodded.

'Great! Maybe we can chat more then? Have a dance for old time's sake?'

'Er...'

Glancing over Zach's shoulder, Ella saw Leo striding across the room towards them. He may have been dressed as Buttons, with a garishly bright blue and yellow costume, but his expression was thunderous.

Zach followed her gaze and took a step backwards, his palms raised as Leo reached their side. 'I was apologising to Ella. Well, I've started at least.'

Leo nodded, his focus on Ella's face as if checking she was alright.

'It's okay,' she said.

'And I was asking if she was going to the Winter Ball next weekend.'

Leo's eyes narrowed as they flicked to Zach's. 'Yes. She's going with me—my family.'

Zach's smile was relaxed and affable. 'Great! I'm really looking forward to it.'

Ella nodded, then turned to Leo. 'I think we should get back?'

Without waiting for either of them, she made her way across the ballroom, her mind churning with everything Zach had said. She'd never expected to see him back in Foxbrooke, let alone acting the part of Prince Charming on-stage and off. And now he would be at the ball as well? Wanting to dance? She'd been looking forward to spending the evening with Leo, but after this morning, would it be better if she kept her distance from him? Her feelings were confused, her brain utterly scrambled. Right now, she didn't know which way was up and which way was down. All she knew was that she couldn't jeopardise her friendship with Leo because of a crazy rebound crush.

❦ II ❦

Buzz. Buzz. Buzz.

Ella woke from a dream about a swarm of bees pulling Santa's sleigh and groggily reached for her phone.

> Leo: Are you awake yet?

> Leo: Are you awake yet?

> Leo: Are you awake yet?

> Leo: I know your phone's set to vibrate and is right by your bed because we discussed this last night

> Leo: In case the bed was so comfy you didn't want to wake up

Ella glanced at the time. *Already eight o'clock*. Despite the stresses of Zach, her dad and the panto, she'd never slept better. The only night she'd had a deeper sleep was the one when Leo had shared her bed over a week ago.

Leo: Come on, Princess Ella. Wakey-wakey, rise and shine!

Leo: Do you really want me to get Dad's hunting horn?

Leo: Or a set of bagpipes? I'm positive he's got some stashed somewhere

Leo: Okay. I'm going to take a shower and sing really loudly and see if that does the trick

Leo: Did it work?

Leo: Seriously? Are you STILL asleep???

Leo: Come

Leo: on

Leo: Ella!

Leo: Wake

Leo: Up!!!

Ella: You made me dream that bees were pulling Santa's sleigh

Leo: She stirs!

Leo: Can I come in now?

Ella: Give me five

Leo: Seconds?

Ella rolled out of bed and drew the curtains. Even though the winter sun had just risen, it was hidden behind thick grey clouds and the sky was dark.

Ella: I need to make myself presentable

Leo: You're a princess. You're always presentable

Ella: Hardly

Leo: You're the most beautiful woman I know

Her heart skipped a beat. *He's your friend! Don't make things weird with him!*

Messing up her hair, she took the most unflattering selfie she could and sent it to him.

He sent back a gif of Bugs Bunny with hearts popping out of his eyes.

Ella replied with one of Stanley Hudson from the US version of *The Office* yelling, 'Have you lost your mind?'

Another gif pinged in of Dwight Schrute saying, 'Let's put it this way... No.'

Laughing, she went into the bathroom, had a quick wash, cleaned her teeth, dragged a brush through her hair, then dressed in her jeans and a t-shirt which read, 'Keep calm. Santa is coming'.

Ella: I'm ready

She heard Leo's phone beeping in the corridor outside, then he flung open the door and entered the bedroom with his arms outstretched, showing off his t-shirt that read, 'I can't keep calm. Santa is coming'.

They gazed at what the other was wearing, then cracked up.

Leo lifted a hand for Ella to high-five him. 'Legend.'

She grinned and slapped his palm with hers, warmth filling her chest like gooey marshmallows. *God, I love him so much.* The thought made her whip around, hiding her flaming cheeks. *As a friend!* Lifting a wrapped package from the bed with trembling fingers, she turned to face him.

He was disappearing back into the corridor. 'Two secs!' he yelled over his shoulder, then re-appeared a moment later with a rectangular-shaped package, wrapped with golden string and adorned with a bow.

He held it out. 'Happy first of December.'

'Leo...' She took it, raising an eyebrow, then handed him the gift she'd made in return. 'This looks and feels like it contravenes the guidelines.'

He sat on the edge of her bed. 'I'm thinking outside the box. And anyway, mine are always a bit rubbish compared to yours.'

She sat beside him. 'No, they're not! It's the—'

'Thought that counts? I know, I know. But I'm about as creative as a caterpillar.'

'Caterpillars turn into butterflies. That's pretty magical.'

Leo gazed at her and opened his mouth.

Ella held her breath. There was something new in his expression.

Then the look disappeared. 'You go first.'

'Okay,' she exhaled, undoing the ribbon.

Leo put the gift she'd given him to one side, his hands splayed on his thighs as if forcing them to stay still.

With a nail, Ella picked at the edge of a piece of tape, then peeled it off.

Leo huffed. 'Just rip it!'

She raised her eyebrows. 'If I do that, I can't recycle the paper.'

He rolled his eyes.

'And it's more exciting to build up the anticipation.' She picked at another line of tape. 'The slower I go, the more plea-surable the experience is.'

'I'm more of a rip-it-off-and-job-done-in-less-than-ten-seconds kind of guy.'

She smirked. 'So I've heard.'

Leo's eyes bugged out, then the corner of his mouth twitched. 'Ella Chamberlain. Are you making a joke about my, er...' He trailed off, his cheeks darkening.

Ella raised an eyebrow, trying to act cool, even as her heart thumped against her ribcage. *Are you flirting? Jesus! Stop it immediately!*

He indicated the bed where they were sitting. 'You know...'

'Your approach to changing your sheets and making your bed?'

Letting out a breath, he gave her a cocky grin. 'That's Bridget's job.'

'Leo!'

'I kid! I kid!' He leapt out of tickling range. 'I make my own bed. Even though it's a pain in the arse because it's so big.'

'And whose fault is that, then?'

'Dad's?'

Ella shook her head and went back to opening her gift. 'This is definitely not regulation-sized.'

'Nothing about me is regulation-sized,' Leo replied proudly.

She snorted with laughter, even as her mind conjured up pictures she knew full well she shouldn't be imagining. Quickly pulling the sides of the wrapping paper away, she saw what he'd done.

'Oh my god, Leo! This is amazing!'

Inside a cardboard frame were numbered boxes for each day up to Christmas Eve, and he'd decorated every one with enough glitter and gold stars to stock a preschool stationary cupboard for a week.

Opening the box for the first of December, Ella pulled out a spiced plum liqueur miniature and two Baci chocolates.

She smiled at him, her heart full. 'I love these!'

'I know. Now go on, open them.'

Undoing the cap, she put the bottle to her nose. 'It smells like Christmas!'

'Try it.'

The liquid ran like fire into her belly. 'That's so good!' She held the bottle and a chocolate out to Leo, but he didn't take them. 'Come on. Sharing is caring. And anyway, if you didn't want one, you wouldn't have given me two.'

'Oh, go on then.' He grinned and took them. 'You've twisted my arm.' Sipping from the bottle, he hummed with appreciation, then held his chocolate up. 'Let's see what message we have today.'

Unwrapping the foil, they each took out the slip of transparent paper, which held a quote about love.

Leo chuckled, then read his one out. '*A true friend knows all there is to know about you, yet still likes you.*'

'Perfect! Now mine.' Her hand pressed against her chest as she read the quote. 'Oh, this is beautiful!'

'What does it say?'

Her throat tightened, but she managed to speak. '*With your kisses have I painted my starry sky.*'

There was a beat as Leo gazed sympathetically at her, then opened his arms. 'Hug?'

Nodding, she leaned towards him, resting her head on his shoulder, her nose pressed against the warm skin of his neck.

'The official court hugger is here,' he said, holding her close.

The sound of his voice was a deep rumble vibrating into her. Ella felt safe in his arms, but it wasn't a wholly comfortable sensation. Leo smelled amazing, but she had the overwhelming desire to kiss his neck where his pulse touched her lips in time to the beat of his heart.

'Thank you,' she whispered, the movement of speech pressing her mouth against his skin.

His pulse sped up.

Oh, no. You've made it weird! Abort!

Pulling away, she focused on the chocolate, popping it in her mouth. 'Hugs and chocolate!' she said with forced cheerfulness. 'All a girl ever needs.'

Biting through the crisp shell, Ella resisted the urge to moan as the perfect amount of chocolate, sugar, cream and praline coated her tongue.

'Well, you've got forty-six left,' Leo replied.

She risked a glance up. 'Hugs?'

He pulled a face as he ate his chocolate, then swallowed. 'The supply of them is infinite. I meant the chocolates. You've got two a day.'

'And you'd be happy for me to eat both of them?'

There was the briefest of pauses. 'Absolutely.'

'Sharing is caring?'

He grinned. 'And supports one of the many meanings of Christmas.'

'Along with peace and goodwill to all men—'

'And women.'

'And batteries not included?'

'One hundred per cent!' Leo paused, then shuddered. 'Did I ever tell you about the Christmas where our folks didn't have enough batteries for all the toys they'd bought us?'

'No. What happened?'

'Mom and Mammy took the batteries out of *their* toys and gave them to us...'

Ella shrieked. 'Oh, my god! No way!'

Leo shook his head as if he couldn't quite believe the story himself. 'Yes way. You know what they're like. Enormous libidos.'

'But even bigger hearts.'

He smiled. 'Very true. I wouldn't change them for the world.' He lifted the present she'd given him. 'Can I unwrap mine now?'

'Yep!' Ella loved watching Leo opening gifts she'd made. He was like the proudest parent, always loving whatever she'd produced, even if she wasn't entirely happy with the quality.

He tore the paper, then held up the advent calendar she'd made, his eyes alight. 'Holy shit, Ella! This is incredible!'

She'd drawn Foxbrooke Manor, with numbers on the windows and a twenty-four on the front door.

Leo ran his finger over the illustrations, as if Ella had just presented him with his first child who'd been born clutching a winning lottery ticket. Finding the window with a number one, he carefully opened it, then burst out laughing. 'Me! As Santa!'

'I couldn't have drawn anyone else for the first window.'

'You could have drawn you?'

'But I don't live here.'

He gazed at her askance. 'Firstly, yes, you do live here. And selfishly, I never want you to leave. And second, you're my BFFFFFFF, so you have to be behind at least one of the windows.' His eyes narrowed. 'Have you drawn Dad's bloody dogs?'

'Maybe.'

'And did you draw Perry and Bridget?'

'Er...'

'*They* don't live here.'

'But they're part of the manor.'

'As are *you*, you noggin-headed ninny pants.'

She snorted.

'Honestly, if I asked Bridget who she'd rather have here, me or you, you know full well she'd choose you over me every time.'

'Only because I'm tidier and know where the vacuum cleaners are.'

Leo harrumphed. 'Hogwash, balderdash, and poppycock.'

Ella laughed. 'You sound exactly like your dad.'

His nose scrunched up. 'Bugger. Next step down that slippery slope and I'll be wandering semi-naked down Foxbrooke high street yelling, "Hullo!" to everyone.'

'Could be worse.'

Leo didn't reply, and Ella knew he was also thinking about *her* father.

Picking up the miniature bottle of plum liqueur, Leo passed it to her. 'Finish this off and let's go to breakfast. It'll be okay, I promise.'

Taking it, she drained the contents. 'How did you know what I was thinking?'

'I told you, I'm extremely telepathetic. Especially when it comes to you.' He placed his fingertips on her temples and affected a look of extreme concentration. 'Right now you're thinking about Christmas tree shopping this afternoon, followed by the Winter Ball.' Dropping his hands, he raised an eyebrow. 'Correctamundo?'

She smiled. 'Your powers are extraordinary.'

'I know, right?'

'But the tree's going in *your* room.'

'Nope. Yours.'

'But your room has more floor space. I've still got boxes of my stuff cluttering this one up.'

'We'll move them.'

'Where and when? I also need to buy a dress for tonight. It's been so busy with school and the panto, I haven't had time.'

'Just borrow something from Willow. Or raid Summer's wardrobe.'

Ella shook her head. Each time Leo or one of his family did something kind for her, she felt the weight of it, as if she were accruing a debt she'd never be able to pay back.

Getting off the bed, Leo grabbed her hand and squeezed. 'Can we continue this discussion over breakfast? I can argue better with a full stomach.'

She nodded. 'Sorry.'

'You do know each time you say that word, an elf dies in Santa land?'

She gave him a look. 'So what *should* I be saying?'

He grinned. '"Yes, Leo. I love it when you're always right".' Tugging her off the bed, he moved towards the door. 'Now come along, Princess. You've got to get your strength up so you can face the wicked witch and be back in time to choose a Christmas tree.'

AT FIVE TO ELEVEN, ELLA KNOCKED ON HER STEPMOTHER'S front door, her heart more buoyant than it had been in a long time. It didn't matter what Michelle threw at her, literally or figuratively. That afternoon she was selecting a tree with Leo for his room, buying a nice dress with the money she had from not paying Oliver's parents rent for December, then attending the Winter Ball at the manor. The thought gave her goosebumps, butterflies, and tingles where they shouldn't be.

What is wrong with you?

Being with Leo always made her feel better. But now, whenever she thought of him, her skin prickled, her heart raced, and her stomach swooped and dived like a swallow in a summer sky. She was torn between wanting the sensations gone and craving them more than her next breath.

And now, waiting to be let into her stepmother's house, she was full of nervous energy, bouncing on the balls of her feet like an athlete preparing to sprint. This would be the fastest house clean she'd ever done.

If Michelle ever comes to the door, that is…

Eventually there was the sound of a key turning, then the door opened.

'Thank Christ you're here,' her stepmother said in a hoarse whisper.

Ella rushed forward. 'Oh, my god. Are you okay?'

One hand on the door, the other braced on the wall, Michelle started coughing, her puffy face getting redder with every hack, until Ella was terrified she would stop breathing. Eventually Michelle drew a ragged breath, then spat a ball of greeny-yellow sputum on the concrete path next to Ella's trainers.

'Of course I'm not fucking okay,' she wheezed, reaching for Ella's arm. 'I need you.'

Supporting her stepmother's weight, Ella helped her into the house. In the living room, Michelle collapsed onto the sofa, her breath laboured and sweat breaking out across her skin. Glancing around, Ella saw with dismay the piles of used tissues, dirty takeaway containers, and empty cans and bottles. The space was at least twice as messy and filthy as normal.

She crouched by the sofa, noting Michelle's stained pyjamas. 'What can I do first to help?'

'Need Lemsip Max,' she rasped. 'Tissues, Lucozade, more vapes.'

'Any food?'

'Dairy Milk, Haribo, Krispy Kreme. Stuff that's easy to eat.'

'Chicken broth?'

Michelle shot her a withering look. 'I need food. Not hippy shit.'

'Okay. Have Kyla-Marie and Bille-Mai been helping you at all?'

Her stepmother's eyes filled with tears as she shook her head. 'I don't want them catching this.'

Ella swallowed her anger. 'Has the doctor seen you?'

'He says it's just a cold.'

'Do you have a fever?'

'No.'

'I'll be as quick as I can at the shops. Can I borrow your keys so I can let myself back in without you having to get up?'

'Just leave it on the latch.' Hauling herself upright, Michelle began coughing again, phlegm rattling in her chest.

Ella glanced around wildly for a tissue, but there were no clean ones left. Grabbing an empty box from the floor, she held it for her stepmother to spit into, trying not to gag as green flecks hit her hand.

Leaving the box with Michelle, she stood. 'If there's anything else you need. Just text, okay?'

Her stepmother nodded and closed her eyes.

Ella: Michelle's ill. Just dashing to the shops to get supplies for her. Not sure how long I'll be but I'll keep you updated

Leo: No worries. I'll stand by. And if you need anything, just ask X

Ella: Will do. And sorry xxx

Leo: Don't apologise! You just killed an elf in Santa land!

Ella: Ha ha

By the time Ella returned to her stepmother's home, it was midday. Once Michelle was settled, she began cleaning the house, her eye on the time as the minutes seemed to pass as quickly as seconds. How on earth was she going to have time to select a Christmas tree *and* go into Bath to buy a frock before all the shops shut?

At three p.m., she sat on the top step of the stairs, wiped her sweating brow with her sleeve, and checked her phone.

> Leo: How's it going? I wish I could help, but I know my presence would only make things worse

> Ella: I'm not even halfway through cleaning the house because she keeps calling me down for things. Honestly, I think she's really lonely as well as feeling rotten

> Leo: Where are Mani and Pedi?

Ella snorted with laughter.

A hoarse whisper came from downstairs. 'What are you doing up there?'

'Just checking my messages,' she called back. 'I'm about to move onto your room. I promise I won't touch the lights.'

There was no reply.

Ella stood and made her way into Michelle's bedroom. It was an absolute tip, with used tissues and empty take-away boxes on the bed.

> Ella: Michelle doesn't want them to visit in case they catch what she's got

> Leo: But your immune system's coated with Teflon?

Ella: I promise to keep my distance from you
when I get back

Leo: What about my hugs? I need my five
a day

Ella: Isn't that meant to be about vegetables?

Leo: How much friendship and emotional
support can I get from broccoli? Hugs are
better

Ella: I've got to put my phone away and get
the rubber gloves back on. It's far worse here
than normal. I'm really s***y but there's no
way I'll be done in time for Christmas tree
shopping

Leo: We can go another time X

Ella: But when? Rehearsals will take up
tomorrow, then we're both back at work. I
don't want to wait until next weekend. Would
you be able to go without me? xxx

Ella waited, watching the dots appearing and then disappearing as Leo wrote his message. She was desperately torn, but didn't want to leave Michelle's until the place was clean and her stepmother had everything she needed.

Leo: Of course. I'll send you photos so you
can decide which one you like the best X

Ella: Thank you xxxxx

Leo: Any time XXX

❧ 12 ❧

True to his word, half an hour later, Leo sent through a series of photos of Christmas trees leaning against a fence in the yard of a local farm.

Sitting on the floor of Michelle's bedroom, a pang of loneliness speared Ella's heart. Even though she didn't miss Oliver, she missed the sense of belonging she had with him. She saw their relationship and home as proof she'd made different life choices to her parents. But now the house and boyfriend were gone, and she was back to square one.

No, you're not! You've got a great job, and you've got Leo and his family.

She rubbed her forehead, trying to remove all the negative thoughts swirling around like rubbish caught in the wind.

Oliver didn't even like *Christmas. And can you imagine having his folks as in-laws for the rest of your life?*

Her ex had never seen the point of getting a Christmas tree. Too much fuss and bother for such a short amount of time, then pine needles stuck in the carpet for the next twelve months. So Leo always helped her choose a tree for their house and decorated it with her.

Leo: You still there?

Ella: Yeah, sorry

Leo: AN ELF JUST DIED!!!

Ella: I apologise

Leo: AND ANOTHER!

Ella: I didn't say the S word!

Leo: It was the same sentiment. Elves are sensitive and fragile creatures

Leo: Just like me

Leo: Come on then, which tree do you like the best?

Ella: Any of them. I trust you

Leo: And that's why you're my BFFFFFFF

Ella: How are you getting it back to yours?

Leo: Roof of Estelle's Defender. What time do you think you'll be back to decorate it? And don't you still have to get to town to buy a dress?

Ella: I've run out of time to do both. The tree
will have to wait until tomorrow night at the
earliest, but I've also got to prep for school
next week. Dammit!

Leo: I know this is unorthodox, and quite
frankly against protocol, but if you tell me
which box has the decorations in, I could do
the tree whilst you head to Bath?

Leo: And if you think I've done a crappy job,
we can find some time next week to redo it?

Ella bit the inside of her cheek to stop a sob escaping. The
last two weeks of the school term were always the most hectic,
and the one before the Christmas break was especially so with
scene painting and costume sewing for the panto, as well as
revising for the Christmas quiz.

Leo: Princess?

Ella: Honestly, that would be amazing. I'm
feeling a bit overwhelmed at the moment xxx

Leo: No worries. Your prince is here to save
the day!

Ella: Just let me know how much the tree is
and I'll send you the money

Leo: Which box are the decorations in?

Ella: The one with XMAS DECS on the side.
But I don't think the lights will be enough for a
tree taller than seven foot

Ella: And don't forget to tell me how much
it is!

Leo: Got to go. A man just tried to take one of my carefully curated trees X

Ella: See you later xxx

At four p.m., Ella dashed down the stairs of her stepmother's house. If she ran back to the manor to collect her car, she could be in Bath by five. Most of the shops stayed open until six, so she had just enough time to make a panic-purchase.

You could just wear the same dress you normally do?

It's green. The theme for the Winter Ball is black and white. I don't want to stick out.

Poking her head into the living room, she gazed at Michelle on the sofa. 'All done. Can I get you anything else before I leave?'

Michelle opened her mouth to speak, but began coughing instead, her face turning puce. Rushing forward, Ella passed her a fresh box of tissues, immediately smelling alcohol as her stepmother hacked. Glancing around, she saw two opened cans of pre-made gin and tonic on the side table.

'Don't leave me,' Michelle whispered as she drew ragged breaths, her eyes bloodshot and liquid.

'I have to—'

Michelle's hand shot out to grab Ella's. 'I don't want to be alone.'

Her heart sank as she gazed at her stepmother. She looked tired and vulnerable, her lower jaw wobbling and tears tracking down her cheeks. There would be no time to get a dress now.

Just cut your losses for this year.

'We can get pizza. Watch a bit of telly?' Michelle whispered. 'Please?'

Ella tried to keep her voice steady. 'Of course.'

'You're a good girl,' her stepmother rasped. 'You look after me.'

'I just need to message—tell people I won't be back until later.' She took out her phone.

'You can stay the night. Use Kyla-Marie's room.'

Clenching her teeth together to stop a scream escaping, Ella gave a tight nod, then sent Leo a message.

> Ella: I'm so sorry but I can't make the ball. Michelle wants me to stay the night. She's not well and has also started drinking. I need to make sure she's okay and the tablets she's on don't react badly with the booze. Please apologise to your folks and Willow for me as well xxx

> Ella: Going to turn my phone off. She'll only get annoyed if I look at it

> Ella: I'm so sorry but I can't leave her xxx

Turning off her phone, she forced a smile. 'Can I make you a cup of tea?'

ELLA CHEWED THE STODGY BREAD AND PLASTIC CHEESE OF the pizza Michelle had ordered, whilst a mind-numbing dating show blared on the television. In another reality, she was drinking champagne with Leo and his family in a stunningly decorated room of the manor as they waited for the gong to announce that dinner was served.

She hadn't turned her phone back on, not wanting to be reminded of what she was missing.

Just get through tonight. There'll be another ball next year.

At the sound of knocking on the front door, Ella raised her

head, then glanced at Michelle, who was now asleep on the sofa, snoring loudly.

Getting up, she went to answer it, her mouth gaping at the sight of the person standing outside.

'Dervla! What are you doing here?'

Leo's mum brushed past her into the house. 'Shift change,' she said with a smile, then went to the living room door and gazed at Michelle. 'How much has she had to drink?'

Ella came to her side. 'At least two gin and tonics. And she wanted me to collect the pizza rather than have it delivered, so she probably drank more when I was out.'

'Right you are, then. Willow's in the car outside to take you home.'

'You can't give up your evening for this!'

Dervla cupped her cheek. 'Yes, I can. I know Michelle from years ago. We were mums together at the local playgroup when Summer was a baby. She won't give me any trouble. You've done enough for her today. You need a night off.'

'But—'

Dervla herded her towards the front door. 'Let me do this for you, darling. Is this your coat?'

Ella nodded. 'But—'

'No buts about it.' Opening the front door, Dervla gently pushed her outside. 'You shall go to the ball!'

Before Ella could argue any more, the door was shut behind her.

On the road, a car was parked with the engine running. Willow pushed the passenger door open. 'Your carriage awaits!' she cried. 'Get in!'

Ella did as instructed, her brain struggling to process the change of plan.

Willow eased the car away from the kerb. 'I know you

didn't have time to pick up a frock, but I rang Summer and she told me to take anything from her wardrobe.'

'Is she sure?'

'Yes! Half the stuff in there is unworn as she keeps getting sent things but has no time to even look at them.'

'Whose idea was this?'

'Me and Mammy's. We were helping Leo with the Christmas tree when your message came in.'

'Is he okay?'

Willow paused before replying. 'He'll be fine.'

Ella rubbed her chest. The guilt made it hurt. 'Does he know I'm coming back?'

Willow shook her head. 'Me and Mammy didn't tell him our plan in case you didn't go for it. He'll be chuffed to bits when you turn up.'

Butterflies took off inside Ella's tummy. They seemed to have taken up permanent residence there, reminding her of their presence whenever she thought of Leo or saw him. Suddenly, she was aware of how filthy she was after an entire day at Michelle's, and how much she wanted to look her best for him.

It doesn't matter! He won't notice or care!

'When we get back, grab a quick shower, then meet me in Summer's room,' Willow continued. 'I'll blow dry and fix your hair, and we can choose a dress. We'll probably miss the main course, but I'll get a couple of plates sent up, then we can go downstairs for pudding.'

'Thank you,' Ella said, her voice unsteady.

Willow reached over and squeezed her knee. 'Anytime. The ball's not the same without you.'

. . .

THE ENTRANCE HALL OF THE MANOR WAS PACKED WITH people dressed to the nines, handing coats to attending staff. Unclipping a low rope from the bottom of the main stairs so they could pass, Willow led Ella up to the corridor where their rooms were.

'I'll be as quick as I can,' Ella said to her. 'Ten mins, tops.'

'Great. Don't bother with make-up. I can do it for you once we've got you into the dress and done your hair.'

'Thank you. For everything.'

'No probs. And don't be too cross with Leo.'

'Cross? For what?'

Willow grinned and made for her own room. 'I'm going to get ready myself. See you in a bit.' She gave Ella a wink, then disappeared.

What could he have done? Entering her bedroom, Ella stopped just inside the door, her hand flying unconsciously to cover her heart.

Oh, Leo...

The main lights were off, but the room was illuminated with the soft glow of thousands of fairy lights adorning an enormous Christmas tree. The boxes holding the majority of her belongings had been wrapped to look like huge presents then placed at the base of the tree, and the branches were heavy with decorations; hers, and ones she'd never seen before.

Padding across the floor in awe, Ella took them in. A tiny dove with real feathers, a felted mouse, glitter ball baubles, a model of Elvis dressed in a Santa hat, a trio of robins with red sequinned breasts that sparkled in the light. She tracked them up to the ceiling. Leo must have used a stepladder to decorate the tree, as it was at least ten feet tall.

'Leo,' she murmured aloud as her vision blurred with unshed tears. 'What did I do to deserve you?'

Swiping her fingers across her eyes, she took a deep breath.

She wasn't going to thank him when she looked a mess and smelled like her stepmother's house. Ripping off her clothes, she dashed for the bathroom. Hopefully, a hot shower, Summer's clothes, and Willow's magic would make her feel as beautiful as the tree.

'OH MY GOD, ELLA!' SUMMER SCREAMED THROUGH THE phone as Willow held it up. 'You look amazing! Divine! Stunning! The belle of the ball!'

Ella grinned shyly at her. 'Thank you so much. This dress is incredible.'

'It's yours. Keep it. I could never do it justice.' Summer turned away from her screen. 'Mario! Come and look at my friend!'

A deeply tanned and indecently gorgeous man dressed only in board shorts strolled towards Summer's beach lounger and leaned over her shoulder.

'She's going to a ball at my folks' place,' Summer said to him. 'Isn't she beautiful?'

Mario stroked his stubbled chin. 'Sí.' He lowered his head a fraction, eyeing Ella through thick lashes. 'Do you have a boyfriend, beautiful?'

Her face flushing, Ella shook her head.

'Would you like one?' Mario continued.

Summer screeched with laughter and batted him away. 'You outrageous flirt! She's on the other side of the Atlantic.'

Mario shrugged. 'For someone that delicious, I would travel to the ends of the earth.'

'My, oh my,' Willow murmured, turning the screen around to see what Mario looked like.

'And who are you?' he asked her.

'My sister,' Summer said to him. 'And she only goes for

squeaky-clean good guys, so you've got no chance.' Standing, she strolled away from Mario towards the azure water. 'Honestly, it's a nightmare here. The men are too charming for their own good and all look like supermodels.'

'How you must suffer,' Willow replied drolly.

Summer snorted. 'I'm actually really looking forward to getting home. It's paradise here, but it feels weird to be on a beach in December.'

'Do you know when you'll be back?'

'Hopefully by the Christmas quiz.' She glanced past Willow to Ella. 'Don't crush the Beardy Boys too spectacularly this year. I don't think Finn can take it.'

'They've really upped their game,' Ella replied with a grimace. 'It'll be a close-run thing, but please don't tell them I said that.'

Summer mimed zipping her lips shut. 'Your secret's safe with me. Now bugger off and have the best time tonight. And thank you for stepping in to play Cinders on my behalf. You're the best.'

'No worries.'

As Willow said her goodbyes to Summer, Ella turned to gaze at herself in the full-length mirror again, blinking at her reflection to make sure it was really her.

The bodice of the dress was a white silk corset, decorated with jewels, and moulded around her breasts to give her support and a cleavage she wasn't used to showing off in public. The straps were superfluous, hanging off her shoulders around her upper arms with white feathers carefully stitched onto silk bands. The skirt of the dress reached the floor and was made from white taffeta, decorated with more jewels and feathers and given body by a net underskirt. It was a designer dress for a swan princess, and Ella had never worn anything as beautiful before.

Willow had curled her hair, so it now fell in long ringlets around her bare shoulders, a section pinned back with a jewelled clip, and she had artfully applied make-up so subtle that it hardly appeared there, whilst also making Ella feel like a model.

Willow held out a sparkling necklace. 'One finishing touch coming up.'

'Oh, my god! Please tell me they're not real diamonds.'

She grinned. 'Family heirloom.'

Ella took a step back. 'I can't wear that!'

'Oh, yes, you can. It doesn't go with the dress I've got on, and someone's got to show it off. Now turn around.'

Reluctantly, Ella faced away from Willow and allowed her to fix the necklace around her neck. The butterflies in her stomach were now fluttering so fast she wasn't sure if they wanted her to run away and hide, or make a grand entrance. Even though hundreds of people were downstairs, the only one who occupied her mind was Leo. Would he notice the dress? Would he like it? Would he like *her* in it?

Shaking her head to try and dislodge the thoughts, she took a deep breath then turned to Willow, who was typing a message into her phone. 'I'm ready if you are?'

'Uh-huh, two secs.' Willow slipped her phone into a hidden pocket of her black dress, linked her arm with Ella's, and led her towards the door. 'Time to shine, my friend.'

'Does Leo know I'm here?' she asked as Willow propelled her along the corridor.

'I told him I had a surprise for him and to meet me at the bottom of the stairs.'

'Oh.' The butterflies were now thrumming their wings against the inside of her skin. 'And I'm the surprise?'

Willow gave her a look. 'Of course you are! He was in such an almighty grump earlier when he thought you wouldn't be here. He said he couldn't be bothered to go to the ball at all.'

'Really?'

'Yep. Mom made him promise he would show up.'

'She's back from LA?'

'Arrived home earlier than planned this lunchtime.'

Ella's stomach twisted. Dervla was missing a reunion with her wife to babysit Michelle for her.

'Don't worry.' Willow gave Ella's arm a squeeze. 'Mom, Mammy and Dad spent the whole afternoon in their bedroom. They've got the sex bit out of the way for at least twenty-four hours.' She grinned. 'Now allow yourself to have fun. Okay?'

Ella nodded. She had the sudden feeling she was about to jump out of a plane for the first time with no idea where she would end up or even if she was wearing a parachute.

Willow ground to a halt. 'Stay here a sec.' Dashing forward, she peeked over the ornate banister. 'Don't move!' she yelled, then came back to Ella's side. 'Right then, off you trot.'

Ella's heartbeat was now filling her throat. She gazed wide-eyed at Willow, her mouth open but too dry to form words.

'Shoo! It's not a grand-enough surprise if I'm with you.' Willow flicked her fingers as if urging a reticent child forward. 'Go on! It's not often I get to surprise one of my top three brothers. I'll follow on in a bit with the shovel to scrape his jaw off the floor.'

Ella wanted to roll her eyes, but all she could think about was Leo waiting at the bottom of the stairs, not knowing she was about to walk down them. Before she could chicken out and grab Willow's arm, she turned and forced her feet forward, keeping her gaze ahead on the far wall and Leo's ancestors staring at her from their portraits.

But when she rounded the corner, her eyes fell to the living, breathing man standing at the foot of the stairs, and the rest of the world faded away. Dressed in black tie, his eyes blazed so brightly she had to blink. Leo was the sun at the centre of her solar system, pulling her inexorably towards him by the force of his gravity. She reached a hand to the polished wood of the banister to steady and anchor herself as her breath came quicker and quicker, her lungs pushing against the confines of the corset.

Ella was floating, her body drawn to Leo as if reuniting with a missing part of itself. And she was also falling, tumbling into a terrifying realisation so profound that she knew the truth of it from the depth of her bones to the edges of her soul.

She was completely, hopelessly, and endlessly in love with her best friend.

Leo couldn't breathe. Couldn't move. Couldn't think. All he could do was feel.

As Ella descended the stairs towards him like an angel from heaven, he barely registered what she was wearing. All he saw was her. It was as if he'd been wearing dark glasses for years and now they'd been ripped off to reveal her shining so brilliantly it was blinding.

The love he'd had for her when they were teens hadn't gone away just because he'd hidden it under a rock, then forgotten where the rock was. It had been growing, maturing, building in magnitude until this precise moment. And now it devastated him.

How did I not see?

The frustration he'd felt earlier when Ella had been stuck with Michelle. The fury he felt towards Oliver and Zach. The butterflies in his stomach when Ella was around, then the pain in his chest when she wasn't. Every thought and every feeling had the same root cause: love.

But this love was no longer that of a friend. Now her kindness, her humour, her creativity and her beauty added up to something even bigger, even deeper, and the sum total of everything he'd ever wanted.

Ella had stolen his heart in the beginning, and now Leo knew she would own it forever.

She stopped on the first step so their faces were level, her voice a little breathless as she said, 'Hi'.

Leo's brain fired, misfired, then every circuit shorted out into an overwhelmed silence.

Say something!

Ella swallowed. 'You look very... handsome.'

Come on! 'You, too,' he finally managed.

Ella blinked. 'Oh.'

Shit! 'In a girly way. I mean, for a girl—a woman. Like a woman. You're a handsome woman.'

Her eyes widened, suddenly glassy, as if she'd presented him with her prettiest picture and he'd immediately blown his nose on it.

Jesus Christ! Ella had just had her heart and life trampled on by Oliver, and now Leo was describing her as 'handsome' when she'd never been more beautiful. *Fix this, you utter twat!*

'Sorry, I'm just shocked you're here and I've developed Foot-in-Mouth disease.' He reached a hand out to take hers, then immediately second-guessed himself and shoved it in his trouser pocket instead. 'You look really—' He broke off, panicking that if he used the word 'beautiful', she'd know how he really felt and it would make her deeply uncomfortable. 'Nice,' he finished confidently, then inwardly cringed.

'Hey Leo!' Willow bounced down the stairs. 'Isn't Ella the most gorgeous woman you've ever seen?'

Tearing his gaze from Ella's face, his cheeks scorching with embarrassment, Leo faced his sister. 'Yes, of course.'

'We got the dress from Summer's wardrobe. I think it's a

couture sample from Aunt Simone. Doesn't she look amazing in it?'

Leo kept his eyes on Willow as he nodded, hoping that silence was the best way to salvage the situation.

His sister pulled a face. 'I'm not the one wearing it, you numpty.'

Steeling himself, as if about to face an army of Cupids with their bows drawn and him in their sights, Leo forced himself to look properly at Ella.

Then immediately wished he hadn't.

Fuck, fuck, fuck, fuck, fuck!

The corset framed her top half, accentuating her waist and presenting the creamy softness of her breasts like a pudding he wanted to dive headfirst into. Her long black hair fell in curls, as glossy and lustrous as a raven's wing. Leo wanted to feel the locks against his face as he kissed and sucked down her neck, swirling his tongue in the hollow at the base of her collarbones.

Molten heat burned from his cheeks into his chest, moving like lava, lower and lower, to pool in his abdomen and thicken his cock.

Stop! Think of something else! Anything else!

But he couldn't. Desire for Ella was hitting him like a thousand-tonne truck full of fireworks driving into an active volcano during a meteor shower. He needed to run. Hide. But the only place he could think of was under the skirts of Ella's dress, burying his tongue in her—

'See?' Willow said to Ella with a smug grin. 'Told you I'd need a shovel.'

'Willow!' Ella hissed, her face flushing with embarrassment.

He glanced up, the sight of his sister providing a much-needed bucket of cold water. 'Huh?'

Willow's eyes were sparkling. 'To scrape your jaw off the floor after you saw Ella.'

Leo was floundering, the ground no longer solid and the air too thick to breathe. Not knowing what to do, he rubbed the back of his neck, surreptitiously pulling the collar of his shirt away from his sweating skin, then frowned at his sister.

'Don't make Ella uncomfortable,' he said gruffly. 'I'm just surprised she's here, that's all. And of course she looks incredible. She always does. She doesn't need one of Aunt Simone's dresses or glass slippers to make me see that. She could wear her Converse for all I care. She's beautiful, whatever she's got on.'

Or off… Fire flared in his groin at the thought of removing Ella's dress. *Does it have buttons? Ribbons? A zip? Stop thinking about it!*

Willow was laughing. 'Go on, Ella, show him.'

What the—

Leo's eyes bulged as Ella lifted the hem of her dress to reveal—her Converse trainers.

Oh, thank fuck. He forced what he hoped was a carefree grin. 'Your dancing shoes?'

She nodded. 'I'm ready to hit the "I don't need a man" room.'

'The *what?*'

'Don't you remember what Finn renamed the Party Room last year?' Willow said to him. 'Because of all the Beyoncé, Aretha, Taylor, and Meghan Trainor?'

'He called it that?' Leo asked. 'But we spent most of the night there.'

'Because you don't need a man, either,' Willow replied.

Leo's breath caught in his throat. *Hear that? Ella doesn't want or need a man right now, and when she does, it isn't going to be you.*

He took two steps back and inclined his head in the direction of the music that was drifting into the entrance hall. 'Shall we?'

Willow linked her arm with Ella's. 'What do you want to do first? Dancing, drinking, or dessert?'

'Sorry,' Leo said automatically. 'I didn't think. Have you eaten anything?'

'Willow got a couple of plates sent up earlier, but we haven't had any pudding yet,' Ella replied.

Leo's mouth watered as he gazed at her. *Get yourself together!* He swallowed. 'Well then, we'd better hotfoot it back to the dining room before Finn finishes his and moves on to all of ours.' Forcing another smile, he led the way, his hands thrust deep in his pockets to stop him from reaching for Ella. Tonight was going to be a torturous exercise in self control.

'Leo?' Ella asked hesitantly, as they made their way back up the stairs at the end of the night. 'Is everything okay?'

'Hmm?' His hands were clenched into fists inside his pockets. He'd spent the evening trying to act normally around Ella, but had second-guessed every word he said, every look he gave her, and any physical contact between them. Even Finn had noticed how robotic he'd been, asking if it was because he knew the Noel it Alls were going to get thrashed by the Beardy Boys at the Christmas quiz.

'I'm so sorry about earlier,' she continued.

'Huh?'

'Staying with Michelle.'

'It was fine. I understood. No worries at all.'

Leo kept his gaze ahead, but sensed Ella's eyes on him, and heard her breathing in, then stopping, as if she wasn't sure what to say next. His heart thudded painfully inside his chest. He didn't know what to say, either. The only thing he knew with absolute certainty was that he had to keep his feelings for her to himself. She'd been dumped by her long-term boyfriend, was probably still in love with him, and had never seen Leo as anything more than a friend. Added to the mix was Zach coming back on the scene and her dad about to be released from prison. The last thing she needed was Leo declaring his love out of the blue in some desperate hope it might be reciprocated.

They walked in silence down the corridor towards their rooms, the small space between them seeming to get bigger and bigger with every step.

Ella paused by her door. 'You were very naughty about the tree,' she said quietly.

Leo dragged his eyes to meet hers, her uncertainty and beauty making his heart ache. Now the floodgates to his feelings had been opened he was drowning in them.

He smiled and shrugged in response. The tree was nothing. He'd walk to Lapland and bring one back from Santa's yard if it would make her happy. Collect snow from the North Pole to make her a snowman. Knit her a stocking from reindeer yarn.

'So, see you tomorrow morning at mine for chocolates and booze?'

'Huh?'

'Advent calendars?'

'Oh yeah.' He took a step back. Suddenly, the thought of sitting on Ella's bed reading out quotes about kisses and love seemed more dangerous than eating an uncooked Christmas dinner.

A tiny notch appeared between her brows, her eyes clouding with confusion and uncertainty. 'Have I done something wrong?'

Fuck! 'No! Nothing!'

'Then what's the matter? You've been so different this evening. You know you can tell me anything?'

I can't tell you I'm in love with you. Taking a deep breath, Leo pondered what lie he could come out with.

'Is it about Zach? Were you worried he was going to be there tonight and upset me?'

Leo blinked. He'd completely forgotten Zach was meant to be there.

'I meant to tell you he went to London on Friday for a meeting and won't be back until tomorrow for the rehearsal.'

Leo squeezed his fists tighter inside his pockets. How often was Zach messaging her? Were they going to get back together?

'Libby told me,' Ella said hastily. 'She thinks it's about a new job.'

Leo's breath rushed out before he could stop it.

Ella gave him a rueful smile, as if she'd guessed what had been bothering him all evening. 'I'm okay with Zach now. His apology was sincere and I've always understood why he did what he did, even though it was wrong.' She reached forward and put her arms around him. 'I'm alright. I promise.'

Unclenching his fingers, Leo pulled his hands from his pockets and hugged Ella back, his posture stiff as he willed his cock not to follow suit. He suppressed a groan as he held her. She fitted so perfectly in his embrace. The feel of her body against his, the scent of her. It was achingly familiar but also seared him like a brand down to his bones. How could he live with this pain in his chest? How could he go back to treating her just as a friend, now that his eyes and heart were truly open?

Lowering his head, he rested his cheek against her hair, breathing in deeply. Ella's ear was resting on his chest. Could she feel his heart beating? His skin was tingling, heat prickling in waves like wind rippling across the surface of the sea, signalling the first whispers of an oncoming storm.

He pulled away, his gaze averted. 'Night-night, Princess,' he managed huskily, then went into his own room and closed the door behind him.

Leo: Morning Princess. Go down to breakfast without me. I couldn't sleep so I'm off for a run. I'll catch up with you at rehearsal X

WITH HIS HAND ON THE DOOR TO THE BALLROOM, LEO closed his eyes and took a deep breath. *Come on. Act normal.*

His muscles were still screaming in protest at the two-hour run he'd subjected them to, and his head was splitting from lack of sleep. He tried to remember the last time he'd actually slept well.

Over a week ago. When you spent the night in Ella's bed.

He shook his head. How had he been so blind for so long about his feelings for her? Was his moral compass so well fixed he'd only allowed himself to acknowledge he loved Ella when they both were single?

Go me, he thought dolefully. He wished he wasn't in love with her. He'd made everything weird between them and her unhappy. What a useless best friend he was right now.

'Is the door locked, honey?'

He glanced up to see his mom sashaying down the corridor towards him. Wearing a red silk dress, Vivienne looked like she'd just stepped off a catwalk.

'Morning, Mom. No, I'm just trying to collect my thoughts.'

Vivienne frowned and raised her hand to his forehead. 'You got a fever?'

'I went for a run just now.'

'Oh dear. That's my least favourite form of cardio.'

The smile came easily to Leo's face. His Mom was naturally slim and eschewed any form of exercise that took place outside of the bedroom she shared with his dad and mammy.

'Is it good to be home?'

'Yes, and it's nice to know I can relax with Libby directing the pantomime this year.'

'You don't mind?'

Vivienne leaned closer. 'I'll try not to interfere.'

Leo snorted. 'So, why are you coming to the rehearsal, then?'

She gave a casual shrug. 'To offer any assistance if needed.' He raised an eyebrow, and she smirked. 'Anyway, why are you skulking outside?'

'Um.' What to say? He'd never been any good at lying, and he hadn't worked out what excuse he could give for his radical change in behaviour.

Vivienne waited patiently.

'I realised last night I'm in love with Ella,' he said in a rush. 'But I can't say anything because she's my friend and still hurting from Oliver dumping her. And now Zach's here and I think he wants to get back with her, and if she wants that, then I have to support her, but—' He broke off and rubbed the middle of his chest. 'I love her so much and it hurts.' He hung his head.

'Honey.' Vivienne's voice was gentle as she took his hand. 'We never understood why you stepped back at school and encouraged Zach to pursue her.'

Leo's head snapped up in surprise. 'You knew I loved Ella back then?'

She nodded, her gaze filled with compassion.

'Who else knew?'

'I think only Deedee. We didn't discuss it with your father because…'

Leo huffed. 'Because he wouldn't have been able to keep his mouth shut.'

Vivienne's head inclined regally, acknowledging the truth of his words. 'But you've got a second chance now.'

He shook his head. 'She'll never see me as anything other than a friend.'

'You don't know that.'

'Mom. Zach and Oliver are all "tall, dark and handsome". I'm not her type.'

'Have you asked her?'

'There's no way I can do that. Can you imagine how awful it would be to turn me down, then still live here and have to see me every day?'

'I understand your concern, but don't hold off forever telling her how you feel. Love is more than what someone looks like. The two of you are so well-suited. You have been since you were little kids. It's like you're two sides of the same coin.'

Leo let out a heavy sigh. There was no way he was going to risk his friendship with Ella by blurting out how he felt. She'd been through enough already.

Vivienne took his arm and led him into the ballroom. 'Come on, honey. You can do this.'

✿ 14 ✿

The ballroom was already full of people, but Leo searched for Ella. She was wearing a t-shirt that said 'Yippee Ki Yay!' and chatting to Willow. Despite how miserable he'd been feeling, his heart lifted as she noticed him, pointed at his 'Nakatomi Plaza Christmas Party 1988' t-shirt and gave him two thumbs up.

'See?' Vivienne murmured. 'Two sides of the same coin.'

She left his side, wandering over to Libby, who appeared to be in a heated discussion with his father.

Leo hung back, unsure of where to go and what to do. The door opened behind him and he turned to see Zach entering, out of breath, a rucksack over his shoulder.

He came to Leo's side. 'Glad I'm not late. How was the ball last night?'

'Good. How was London?'

His face brightened. 'Really great. I can't say much until the contract's signed, but it looks like I've got a new gig.'

'In London?'

'Yeah.' Zach shucked his rucksack to the floor and ran his hands through his hair, his gaze on Ella.

Leo's gut tightened. The sooner Zach was out of Foxbrooke, the better.

'Mate,' Zach began. 'Can I have a quick word?'

Leo's pulse quickened. 'Uh-huh.'

Zach's expression was bashful, looking at Leo through impossibly long, dark lashes.

And this is how blokes like him always get the girl.

'I wanted to ask… if you could put in a good word for me. With Ella.'

Leo didn't reply, ice running in his veins.

'Like you did before,' Zach continued. 'When we were at school. You know, be my wingman.'

Leo froze, the fury inside him crystallising in his fists.

Zach took a step back, his palms raised and his eyes wide. 'Okay mate, no harm no foul, eh?'

'Don't,' Leo gritted out. 'Just don't.'

'Look, I've apologised to Ella. We're good now. I want to make it up to her. Try again, you know?'

'No.'

Zach frowned. 'Don't you think that's up to her?'

'Hi Zach! Hi Leo!' Libby called over. 'You ready to get started?'

'Sure thing!' Zach said, heading towards her. 'Love the t-shirt!'

Libby was wearing one with the words, 'There's no business like snow business'. Leo splayed his fingers, trying to get the blood moving back into them and away from his pounding heart. His worst fears about Zach were true. One long-overdue apology and he thought he could just waltz back into Ella's life and pick up where they'd been before he tried to ruin her life.

'We're going to start with the forest scene with Cinders

and Prince Charming,' Libby called out. 'I've agreed for Arthur to trial *one* of his ideas to see if it works.'

Leo's gaze fell to his father. He was wearing a t-shirt that said, 'What happens under the mistletoe, stays under the mistletoe!' and carrying a black metal box attached via an extension lead to the mains.

'Foam machine!' he cried. 'Used it at one of the sex parties! Fantastic fun and gave the place a spring clean at the same time! I've adjusted the setting, so it looks like snow. Going to make the panto extra festive!'

'It's just a trial, Arthur,' Libby said. 'If it makes the stage slippery, then we can't use it.'

'I honestly don't know why you won't let me try my other ideas,' he replied grumpily.

'Dad.' Henry crossed his arms. 'There is no way in hell we're letting Caligula or Borgia on stage.'

'But they're hunting dogs! Why d'you think Prince Charming's in the bally wood in the first place?'

'They're *not* hunting dogs, Dad,' Henry replied testily. 'They're a bloody menace.'

'Well then, let me put Zach on a horse. What an entrance that would make. Properly regal.'

Henry and Libby turned as one to eyeball Dervla and Vivienne, who were sitting hand in hand enjoying the show.

'Mom?' Henry gritted out. 'Mammy? We've only got two and a half weeks till opening night.'

Dervla's eyes were sparkling and Vivienne was struggling to hold back a smile. 'Arthur, honey,' she began. 'Try the snow machine first.'

His shoulders deflated a little, then he nodded. 'Okay, okay.' He clambered onto the stage and stood to one side. 'Righty-ho, I'm ready to snow! Ha ha!'

Libby gave Ella and Zach a bright smile. 'Are you happy to try this? No worries if you'd rather not.'

'Sure thing!' Zach leapt onto the stage with the grace of a panther. He extended a hand to help Ella climb up, and Leo gritted his teeth.

'Connor?' Libby asked. 'You ready?'

He was sitting to the side behind an electric piano and gave her a thumbs up.

'Okay, why don't we go from just before the song?' Libby continued. 'Ella, can we go from the bit about Zach being your dream man?'

Leo levelled a death stare at the back of Zach's head.

'Can I start the snow?' Arthur asked.

'Go for it,' Libby replied.

There was a whirring sound, then tiny flecks of foam shot out of the end of the machine into the air.

'And cue Ella!' Libby cried.

'Yes!' Ella said to Zach. 'You are...'

'Your dream man?'

'Yes. Oh yes!'

Was she acting, or was it for real?

'And cue music,' Libby continued.

Connor played the opening bars of 'Endless Love' by Lionel Ritchie, and Zach and Ella held hands and began to sing to each other as fake snow fell gently around them.

'This is bally brilliant!' Arthur yelled from the side of the stage, waving the nozzle of the foam machine in the air.

Zach suddenly pulled Ella into an embrace and began waltzing her around the stage. She looked shocked, but didn't stop singing.

Libby clapped her hands. 'Fabulous! Love it!'

'I'm going to turn it up a notch,' Arthur called out. 'See what it can do!'

'I think it's perfect as it is,' Libby replied loudly. 'We don't need any more.'

He ignored her and the machine stepped up a gear, throwing larger flecks of foam into the air.

Zach and Ella were now whirling in circles, singing about endless love in a flurry of fake snow.

'Dad!' Henry shouted. 'Turn it off!'

But as the music swelled and Zach and Ella crescendoed, Arthur didn't appear to hear his eldest son.

Panic flashed through Leo as Ella slipped.

Zach held her up, but his own foot began to slide.

Leo ran forward, watching in horror as Zach and Ella spun together towards the edge of the stage.

At the last second, Zach let go of her, pivoting and pushing her back to safety, then fell backwards off the stage to the floor with a sickening crack and a cry of pain.

The music stopped and everyone rushed to his side.

Leo leapt onto the stage to Ella. She sat on the floor in a sea of foam, rubbing her elbow.

'You okay? You hurt?'

'I don't think so. Just my arm a bit.'

Zach screamed, and Ella's face went white.

'I'm calling an ambulance,' Henry shouted.

Leo helped Ella to her feet, and they went to see what had happened.

Zach was on the floor, his face twisted in agony and his right leg bent at an unnatural angle.

'Oh my god,' Ella whispered, her knees buckling.

Leo held her up, fear cutting into his chest. Was she remembering the accident? The injury to Michelle's leg?

'L-Leo,' she stammered, her teeth chattering.

Hoisting her into his arms, Leo rushed to the rear of the

stage, down the steps at the back, and whisked her out of the ballroom through a side door.

Ella clung to him, her clothes damp from the foam, as Leo strode through the manor. Fear and anger fuelled his feet as he jogged up the stairs, going straight to her room and sitting with her on the edge of the bed.

'Th-thank you,' she whispered.

'Can I run you a hot bath?'

She shook her head. 'Just hold me.'

So he did, rocking her in his arms whilst planning exactly how he was going to murder his father.

'It's not his fault,' Ella murmured.

'Huh?' Was she thinking about Zach?

'Your dad. He gets overly excited about things. That's all.'

'Well—'

'And it's not Zach's fault, either.'

'Are you reading my mind?'

She poked his arm. 'We're telepathetic, remember?'

The corners of his mouth twitched. 'I didn't know your skills were as highly attuned as mine.'

'Yes, they are,' she replied, her voice sounding stronger. 'Right now, you're thinking "how far can I push it before she starts tickling me?"'

The snort of amusement came out before he could stop it. 'That's *one* of the things I'm thinking about.'

Twisting her head so she could gaze up at him, Ella gave him an open-mouthed look of astonishment. 'You can think about more than one thing at once?'

He raised an eyebrow, trying to appear cool, even as his love for her was overrunning his heart and making his eyes sting. 'I'll have you know, I can be thinking about lunch whilst eating breakfast.'

'Wow,' she deadpanned. 'That's next-level skills right there.'

Leo smiled with relief, knowing she was recovering from whatever hellish memories Zach's fall had triggered.

Carefully easing off his lap, Ella sat beside him. 'Yes, I *was* thinking about Michelle when I saw his leg. And no, I don't think it's my fault he fell, even though a part of me wants to blame myself. It was an accident.'

'Caused primarily by my muppet of a father.'

She gave him another poke. 'I can't have a monopoly on complicated fathers, you know.' Before he could reply, she passed him a Baci chocolate from her bedside table. 'Your reward for hard labour.'

'Hard labour?'

'Voluntarily going for a run first thing this morning, then training for the World Wife-Carrying Championships in Finland by hauling me all the way up here from the ballroom.'

Leo's heart skipped a beat. 'Are we married then?'

She blushed. 'I think you're allowed to carry anyone's wife in the competition.'

'But I want to carry my own,' he replied belligerently. 'And as I've been training with you, does that make us married now under Finnish law?'

The colour in her cheeks deepened. 'I don't remember a proposal, let alone a wedding.'

Leo unwrapped the chocolate, popped it in his mouth, then carefully folded the foil wrapper into a thin strip.

'What did the motto say?' Ella asked, her voice getting higher.

Leo lifted it and pretended to read. 'You're my favourite person in the universe. I love you more than Christmas. Please, will you marry me?' Without meeting her gaze, he dropped the scrap of paper to the floor and held out the strip of silver foil. 'Left hand, please.'

Ella's laugh was breathless, but she held out her hand for

him to wrap the foil around her fourth finger and twist it into place. 'Is this a proposal *and* a marriage ceremony?'

'Yes, according to an obscure Finnish law I just made up.'

'But I haven't agreed to any of it.'

Leo's heart plummeted into his stomach. What the hell was he doing? Dragging his eyes to meet Ella's, he pulled a face. 'Sorry about that. Pretty please?'

She gave a nervous laugh. 'Er... okay. Since you asked so nicely, my answer's yes.'

His pulse was racing so fast it was chasing the breath from his body, but he attempted a carefree smile. 'Excellent. Honeymoon in Lapland? See the northern lights? Sleigh rides? Meet Santa?'

'All the above with whipped cream and marshmallows?'

Leo's brain temporarily suspended normal function to remind him exactly how creamy and edible Ella's breasts had looked in her dress the previous night.

Then his phone buzzed, and he pulled it out, glad of the distraction.

'It's Connor,' he said. 'Asking if we can come back to the ballroom.'

THEY MADE THEIR WAY BACK DOWNSTAIRS IN SILENCE, although Leo was sure Ella was thinking the same as he was: what on earth would happen now Zach had most likely broken his leg?

In the ballroom, the mood was sombre. Arthur was seated with his head bowed like a child who'd been sent to the naughty step, and Libby's eyes were red from crying.

Willow rushed forward and gave Ella a hug. 'You alright?'

She nodded. 'I'm fine now. Sorry, I just had a bit of a freak out.'

'Don't be sorry, it's totally understandable.'

'How's Zach doing?'

Willow pulled a face. 'The ambulance left a few minutes ago. Mammy followed them to the hospital to keep Zach company until his folks can get there.'

Leo glanced over to where Connor, who was a nurse, was sitting, his expression grim. 'What did Connor say about Zach's leg?' he asked Willow in a low voice.

'He'll be in plaster for weeks,' she whispered back. 'He said it's a really bad break.'

'Fuck.'

Willow nodded. 'Come on, let's sit down and try to work out what to do.'

As they sat with the rest of the group, Libby gave them a small smile. 'Thank you for coming back. Ella, are you hurt at all?'

She shook her head. 'I'm fine. It was more of a shock than anything else.'

'My dear, please accept my sincere apology,' Arthur said to her, his eyes damp with unshed tears.

'Of course,' she replied. 'It did look very pretty at the beginning.'

Arthur perked up. 'My thoughts exactly! Maybe, if I just keep it on a low—'

'No,' chorused Henry and Connor loudly.

'Okay, okay,' he mumbled.

'Right then,' Libby said, her tone artificially perky. 'I never want to assume the worst, but I trust Connor's professional judgement, and therefore we need to accept that Zach will not be able to perform in the pantomime.' She took a deep breath. 'Which opens in two and a half weeks.'

'Who else could play Prince Charming at such short notice?' Steve asked.

Libby puffed out her cheeks, then sighed. 'No idea. It would have to be someone who knew the words, songs, and dance moves, or at least could learn them in record time.' Her head swivelled slowly to face Henry.

Henry swallowed, his expression rigid with terror, then turned to gaze at Finn. 'How about Finn?'

'What?' Finn replied, his jaw hanging loose. 'Sorry, but no way. I'm about as charming as dry rot. Henry should do it.'

'Connor?' Henry continued desperately. 'He can sing. Willow can do his job of the music.'

Willow's head was a blur as she shook it. 'I can't. I'm nowhere near good enough.'

Leo felt Ella, tight with tension beside him. She'd never signed up to play Cinderella in the first place, and now she had no idea who her next leading man was going to be. And the others were right. Finn and Henry would be awful, and Connor was in charge of the music.

'Okay,' Libby said. 'Why don't I put a call out on social media? Explain the situation and see if we can find someone —*anyone* to step in.'

'No,' Leo said. He hadn't thought of an alternative, but he knew he couldn't stand by and see Ella go through more stress and be expected to kiss a random stranger.

Libby turned to him. 'Do you have another idea?'

'Yes.' His mouth moved five steps ahead of his brain. 'I'll do it.'

'You?'

'Yes. I know all the words already.'

'But you're Buttons,' Libby continued.

'You can be Buttons,' he replied, feeling more confident with every word. 'The part is often played by a woman, so the audience will buy it. You're a brilliant actor and know the lines as well as I do. The costume is loose-fitting so you'll just need the trousers and sleeves taking up a bit. You were going to be in the wings for every performance anyway, so you might as well be on stage.'

Silence.

Then Libby's face broke into a sunny smile. 'That's a fantastic idea!'

Henry looked like he'd just escaped the firing squad. 'One hundred per cent.'

Finn appeared similarly relieved. 'Definitely. Thanks, Leo.'

'Bally marvellous!' Arthur said. 'The show's back on the road!'

Leo glanced around the circle. The black mood had lifted and everyone looked excited again. He turned to Ella. 'Are you alright with this?' he murmured.

'Yes, of course. Why wouldn't I be?'

Leo didn't know how to reply. Suddenly, all he could think of were the kisses written into the script. He needed to talk to Ella about them. He didn't want to be like Zach and assume she'd want to kiss him, no matter how chaste they were meant to be.

Yes. He'd talk to her after the rehearsal. Make it clear she didn't have to do it.

'Alrighty then!' Libby got to her feet. 'Let's dive straight in with Cinders and Prince Charming at the ball. Ella, Leo, you both ready to fall in love?'

❧ 15 ❧

'**Y**ep, all good!' Avoiding looking at Leo, Ella jumped to her feet, her wits scattering like sugar grains falling from a tipped bowl.

Do I want to fall in love with him? She let out a little huff as she made for the stage. *That ship has already sailed.*

Shaking her head, she clambered onto the stage.

'Sorry,' Leo said behind her.

'What for?' She turned to face him, her heart leaping at his proximity.

'Me volunteering for the role.'

'I told you, I'm fine with it.'

'Then why were you just shaking your head?'

Because I'm in love with you more than I was in love with Zach and Oliver put together. Because I'm going to have to kiss you, and I want to do that more than win the Christmas quiz. Because I don't want to lose our friendship. Because I'm seriously worried you can read my mind. Heat flooded her cheeks as the answers ran around her head like excited children wanting to be let out to play.

Leo ran a hand into his hair and sighed, as if her silence was confirmation of his thoughts. 'Look,' he began.

'Honestly, it's fine.' The tip of her thumb fiddled with the foil ring on her finger. 'I was just...' But as she gazed at him, her brain lost the ability to come up with a convincing lie. All she could think about was what would happen if she actually married him. Shared a bed with him. The hard heat of his body above her, *in* her.

He huffed. 'You're a rubbish liar.'

'Okay!' Libby said. 'Now the stage is dry, let's take it from Cinderella's entrance.'

'Hang on!' Arthur cried. 'Wait for us! Come on, Steve, shake a leg!'

'Ella,' Leo murmured urgently as the two ugly sisters clambered onto the stage. 'You don't have to kiss me.'

'But—'

'It doesn't matter what's in the script. You don't have to do it.'

But I want to! she internally wailed.

Connor played incidental music, and Leo moved away.

Frustration tightening her insides, Ella went to the back of the stage.

'Her Royal Highness, Princess Incognito!' Connor cried.

'Ooh, look what the cat just dragged in, Fanny!' Steve said as Ella walked forward.

Arthur reared back as he gazed at Ella. 'Who does she think she is? Waltzing into my party like that?'

'It's a ball, Fanny.'

'Waltzing into my ball—'

'You've only got one, Fanny?'

Arthur struck a pose and winked at the audience. 'Quality, not quantity, darling. Anyway! We need to keep her away from the prince!'

'Too right. Dressed like that, she could get any Tom, Dick, or Harry.'

Well, she's welcome to Tom and Harry, just as long as she stays clear of my Di—'

'Fanny! We're too late!'

Ella met Leo in the centre of the stage, her heart fluttering as she gazed at him.

He stared blankly at her, spots of colour appearing on his cheekbones.

The silence extended.

'The girl from the forest!' Arthur stage-whispered to him.

Leo started. 'Ell—the girl from the forest.'

'Dandini. You've lost your beard.'

'Er, yes. I only wear it on Tuesdays and Thursdays,' he replied quickly, as if worried he might forget more of his lines. 'I can't believe you're here.'

'I can't either.'

He held out his arm. 'Pinch me. I need to make sure I'm not dreaming.'

'I can't do that.'

'Kiss me then—I mean, er, you don't have to—'

Raising her head, Ella leaned forward to kiss him, but he immediately reared back. Losing her balance, she fell forward. Leo stumbled as he took her weight, and they both fell to the stage in a heap.

'Good grief!' Arthur grumbled. 'What's the matter with you, Leo?'

'Sorry,' he muttered, his gaze fixed on the floor as he helped Ella to her feet.

'Shall we try that again?' Libby said. 'Let's go back to "pinch me". And Leo, just relax. You're doing fine.'

Ella nervously played with the circle of foil on her finger, as if it would magically make Leo's feelings for her match hers for him.

Leo looked utterly miserable. He rubbed his frown lines then extended his arm robotically towards her. 'Pinch me. I need to make sure I'm not dreaming.'

'I can't do that.'

He stood stock still. 'Kiss me then.'

She paused, the tip of her thumb picking at the fake ring he'd given her. Was it coming loose?

Leo's head started to move towards hers as the ring slipped off her finger and fell to the ground. Reaching instinctively for it, she head-butted Leo's chest as he came in for a kiss. He leapt back as if shot, and Ella fell to the stage on her hands and knees.

'Sorry, I'm so sorry,' she mumbled.

'No, I'm sorry,' he replied, his words terse and clipped.

'What on earth was that?' Arthur cried. 'Call yourself a Foxbrooke, Leo? We're lovers, not lump hammers! The apple fell so far from the bally tree with you, m'boy, it landed in Paulton Tesco.'

'Arthur,' Libby said firmly. 'It's been a very stressful morning. Give them a break.' She smiled at them. 'Let's move onto the clock striking midnight.'

TWO HOURS LATER, THE RELIEF AND JOY EVERYONE HAD expressed at Leo taking the role of Prince Charming had been replaced by a low-level worry that hung in the air like a bad smell.

People weren't smiling anymore. They looked as anxious as Ella felt as Leo stumbled over his lines. His performance was slightly better if she wasn't on stage, but the moment the two of them were together, they had the ease of a summit between the leaders of North and South Korea.

Ella wanted to weep. Where had her laughing and joking best friend gone? Leo appeared frazzled to the point of exhaustion, tiptoeing around her as if they'd just met and he didn't know how to act.

Now he was standing near the door with Libby, his body language signalling utter dejection. Libby glanced at Ella and beckoned her over.

She approached with leaden feet.

'Sorry for being so bloody useless,' Leo said to her as she came to their side.

'You're not!' Libby said warmly. 'This is completely new and you haven't had a chance to prepare mentally for it. It doesn't help with all of us watching.'

He shrugged.

'I think the two of you need to spend some time together in private.'

Ella's heart pounded as Leo glanced at Libby in shock.

'Working on some trust exercises and practising your parts,' she continued. 'I've got a whole list of ideas on the improv company website.' She pulled out her phone, tapped on the screen, then handed it to Ella. 'Have a look at these and decide which ones take your fancy. Don't worry about the rest of the rehearsal. I'm not concerned about your lines. I just need you both to feel comfortable with each other.'

'Of course we do,' Leo immediately replied. 'Ella's my best friend.'

'I know, but you're now in a situation none of us planned for. When you've chosen a couple of exercises, take the rest of the afternoon off to give them a go. Director's orders. Okay?'

Ella nodded and Libby gave her arm a squeeze, then walked away.

In the silence that followed, Ella scrolled through the list, her eyes unfocused, then held the phone out to Leo. 'You choose. I'm sure they're all fine.'

He didn't take it. 'I only want to do what *you're* comfortable with.'

She bit the inside of her cheek to stop a sigh from escaping. *Be a good friend!* Channelling the eternally optimistic Libby, she forced a smile and checked the list again. 'Okay, we can do the guided walk, the mirror exercise and the trust fall. You happy with that?'

'If you are, then yes.'

'Okay. Two secs.' She strode across the ballroom with Libby's phone. When she returned, Leo held the door open for her and they passed into the corridor.

'So,' he began. 'Guided walk. What's that?'

'We really should use a blindfold.' She glanced around as if one might magically appear.

Leo closed his eyes. 'I promise I won't peek. What are you going to do?'

'I've got to lead you with verbal instructions only.'

'Okay, I'm ready.'

'Um. Turn ninety degrees anti-clockwise.'

'Maths?' he spluttered. 'Already? If only I'd paid more attention on my last date.'

A pang of jealousy struck her heart. *Get over yourself!*

'Ella?'

Holding onto his shoulders, she twisted him around to face the right direction.

'I thought you weren't meant to touch me?'

She let go as if she'd been burnt.

'Don't get me wrong,' he continued. 'I'm not objecting. I'd much rather you just took my hand.'

'Are you sure?'

'Of course. I don't need a silly game to tell me how much I trust you.'

Excitement jumping in her tummy, Ella reached for his hand, a shock of electricity running up her arm at the contact.

He shivered, then squeezed. 'That's better. Now, guide me.'

Tugging lightly, she started along the corridor, Leo by her side. Being this close, he seemed taller, broader, taking up the space around them and so much of her heart that it pressed against her lungs, making her breathless.

She led him through the ground floor of the manor until they reached the bottom of the main staircase.

Leo opened his eyes and blinked. 'Right. My turn.'

Ella closed her eyes, her senses now wholly focused on the feeling of her hand in Leo's and the pounding of her pulse.

At a slight pull from him, she lifted her foot, but misjudged the height of the step and stumbled.

Leo hauled her upright and into the side of his body.

'Sorry!' she gasped.

'No, no. My fault. I forgot to give you the measurements in millimetres.'

She pulled a face at him, even though her eyes were still closed.

'And as I'm so crap at maths,' he continued, the smile evident in his voice, 'we'll have to try a different approach.'

Before she could guess what that might be, her feet were off the floor and she was back in his arms.

Her eyes flew open. 'Leo!'

'Don't you trust me?'

'Of course I do, but this is the second time you've done this in one day and I'm heavy!'

'No, you're not. And now I'm Prince Charming, I have to be even more buff and manly.'

'Washboard abs and buns of steel?'

She felt his stomach tense against her side, and a dart of pleasure struck her lower abdomen.

'I'll have a ten-pack by the time we enter the World Wife-Carrying Championships. Now close your eyes and trust me.'

Ella did, allowing herself to drown in the sensations of being carried by Leo as he continued up the stairs. His body was powerfully strong, and the heat from it radiated out through his clothes and into her.

All too soon, she was in her bedroom and her feet were carefully lowered to the floor.

Opening her eyes again, she saw Leo moving away to turn on the Christmas tree lights, filling the room with a soft and magical glow.

'Right, what's next?' he asked.

'A mirror exercise.'

He nodded decisively, then strode towards her bathroom.

'What are you doing?' she asked as she followed.

Leo stood in front of the sink, gazing earnestly at his reflection. '*Mirror, mirror, on the wall, who's the fairest of them all?*' He made his voice high-pitched. '*Ella is!*'

She snorted with laughter. 'That's not what we're meant to do.'

'Now your turn.' Tugging her into the bathroom, he positioned her in front of the mirror, then stood behind her with his hands on her shoulders. 'Off you go.'

Grinning at his reflection, she began. '*Mirror, mirror, on the wall, who's the fairest of them all?*'

'Ella is!' Leo squeaked behind her. 'Didn't you hear me the first time?'

She rolled her eyes but couldn't help another laugh escaping. Finally, the weirdness between them was gone.

'What's next?' he asked.

'Trust falls. We have to fall backwards and hope the other person catches us.'

He pulled a face. 'I'll crush you.'

'Maybe we could put pillows on the floor?'

'It's too much of a risk. I don't want you getting hurt.'

'Could we do it on the bed? In a kneeling position, maybe?' The moment the words were out of her mouth, she regretted every single one of them. Without glancing at his reaction, she pulled away, going back into the bedroom.

He followed her. 'Okay, let's give it a go.' Kicking off his trainers, he stood on the four-poster bed, his head almost touching the canopy. 'You fall first.'

Ella slowly unlaced her Converse. 'This is silly.'

'Yeah, but we're good at being silly, and it means we can go back to Libby and say we did exactly what she wanted us to.'

'*Mirror, mirror on the wall*? Since when was *that* a trust exercise?'

'We improvised. That alone earns us a gold star. Now come up here and fall over.'

Shaking her head, she climbed onto the bed and faced away from him. 'You ready?'

'Yep!'

She let herself drop backwards, immediately feeling Leo's strong arms around her.

'What's my rating on Trust-Fall-Pilot?' he asked, his mouth right by her ear.

'Definitely a five out of five,' she replied, knowing she had to move, but wanting to stay right where she was.

He eased her up to stand. 'Right, your turn. But I'll crouch and you can kneel behind me.'

They swapped positions on the bed, and Ella dropped to her knees, her arms spread wide.

Leo crouched in front of her, wobbling as he struggled to

keep his balance on the soft mattress. 'You read—fuck!' he cried, toppling backwards.

Unprepared for him to fall without warning, Ella fell back to the bed with his weight on top of her.

'Shit!' He leapt off and crouched above her. 'You okay?'

She couldn't keep her giggles inside. 'This is ridiculous!'

Leo's concern melted into a heart-stopping smile. 'Hashtag nailed it.' He lay on his side next to her, his head propped up on his hand. Magic seemed to dance in the air between them, but then his smile dimmed. 'Ella,' he began softly.

'Yes,' she replied, her heart beating faster.

'You don't have to kiss me in the panto.'

A wave of disappointment crashed through her. 'It's fine! I don't mind. It's just a peck.'

He frowned. 'But I never want you to do anything you don't want to.'

An insane flash of bravery moved her vocal chords before she could stop them. 'Maybe we could practise first? So we know what to expect?'

His eyes widened slightly and his gaze dropped to her lips for a fraction of a second. 'Um, yeah. Good plan.' He swallowed. 'If you're sure?'

'I think it's for the best,' she replied, trying to keep her voice level.

'Definitely.' Leo's voice seemed to have dropped several octaves.

'So... I give you permission to kiss me.'

'Now?'

She nodded, no longer able to form words. Her body was burning with anticipation, desire blazing through every part of her, stealing the oxygen from her lungs. Leo looked unsure, his cheeks heightening with colour, but Ella no longer cared or questioned if this was real for him or not. All she cared about was that he did it before she combusted on the spot.

Then, just as she was terrified he wouldn't, he lowered his head and brushed his lips across hers.

The pleasure was so sudden, so acute, that she gasped. Never before had a kiss felt so powerful, the flicker of a butterfly's wings from the other side of the galaxy knocking her world off its axis.

Leo withdrew, his pupils so huge that only a tiny ring of brilliant blue remained.

'Again,' she whispered, freezing as she realised she'd vocalised her thoughts.

He didn't reply, only brought his lips back to hers with a soft warm pressure that sent sharp prickles of light shooting through her like stars. This time he didn't pull away, dropping kisses along her jaw and down her neck that made her head spin.

He's kissing me. He's kissing me.

Ella's breath came quicker, trying to keep pace with her frantic pulse and the chaos of her thoughts and feelings. Grabbing his back, she clutched the ridges of muscle, feeling them ripple with the laboured movement of his breath. Was he as affected as she was? The thought disappeared, lost in a whirlwind of sensation as Leo kissed his way back to her mouth, taking her lower lip between his and gently tugging.

The moan began deep in her chest, vibrating through her before she could stop it. He slanted his head, capturing her mouth, his tongue meeting hers as if wanting to taste the sound of her desire and feel her pleasure as his own.

It was too much and not enough, a sensory riot bursting through every cell. Recalibrating every setting, every truth, showing her a new reality beyond anything she'd ever experienced before.

His tongue slicked against hers with licks of molten fire, and his fingers ran through her hair, clasping her head to pull her closer. Every inch of her skin was alight, her blood boiling, her mind white hot in its focus. *More. More. More...*

Shifting beneath him, she spread her legs, urging him to press his weight where she wanted it most. He did, circling his hips, rolling the solid length of his arousal across the epicentre of her need, over and over again.

Pleasure shot from her mouth to her clit, burning bolts of lightning that made her quiver with their intensity. Clenching her core, she chased a feeling that curled deep inside. There was no room in her mind to question what was happening, where this was leading, or who she was with. She'd ceded all control to Leo as he led her towards the edge of the horizon and into the heart of the sun.

Time lost all meaning. There were just his hands holding her tightly to him, his lips and tongue making her burn, and the throbbing, yearning pleasure in her pussy that pulsed with each roll of his hips. Her heart was tripping over itself, pounding so fast she didn't know if she would survive. Wrapping her legs around the back of his, her arms clamping around the broad expanse of his back, she held on tighter as he pushed her higher.

He moved faster, grinding his pelvis against hers, groaning into her mouth. The sound ignited the touch paper of her climax and she started shaking. Tiny whispers came to her. *This isn't possible. This can't be happening.* But they were instantly burnt to ash by the inescapable force of her oncoming release as it built and built to the point of no return.

It didn't matter that they were fully clothed. Leo was already in her body, mind, and soul. Carrying her, guiding her, leading her. Chasing the bright light of the charge as it crackled inexorably on towards a mountain of gunpowder.

Tearing her mouth from his, Ella panted into his neck, her muscles taut, her hips rising to meet his.

Then the charge reached the centre of her, detonating an orgasm so powerful it ripped a scream from her throat. Holding on for dear life, sensation scorched through her, a blast of light that shuddered through with the power of a supernova.

The shockwaves kept coming, amplified by the energy pouring off Leo. He kept pushing the pleasure on until he gave a harsh cry and collapsed on top of her, his face buried in the crook of her neck, his breath heavy and ragged.

Ella floated, her eyes open but unseeing. Every part of her was humming at a new frequency, buzzing in technicolour. There was no past. No future. Only the perfect present.

But then, like the first drops of rain on her parade, thoughts fell from the sky to wash away her happiness.

What just happened? Oh my god, I threw myself at him. I used my best friend like a giant sex toy. I made everything weird. So weird. I'm going to have to leave. Move out. But where?

'Breathe,' Leo mumbled into her neck.

Ella did, realising her panicked thoughts had stopped her breath. 'I'm so sorry,' she gasped, her chest filled with stabbing anxiety.

He raised his head, his eyes drowsy. 'What for?'

Her cheeks flamed. 'Using you.'

Something flickered in his expression. Was it hurt?

'In what way?'

'Like a sex toy,' she mumbled.

There was a pause as his forehead creased. 'You think I didn't want what just happened? That I didn't enjoy it?'

Now Ella felt the flush of embarrassment all the way to the tips of her toes. She nodded.

Leo rolled fully off her and took her hand.

'What—' Her sentence cut off when he placed her fingers over the very wet crotch of his jeans. 'Oh.'

'*That's* how much I enjoyed it.'

What now? Never in her wildest dreams did Ella ever imagine being in this situation with Leo. Sure, she'd been in love with him before, but their relationship had always been that of friends. Ever since they'd been little kids. What on earth was going to happen now?

Leo's gaze was searching. 'Are you alright?'

I don't want to lose you. I can't lose you. Fear crawled like spiders under her skin. *He felt sorry for me. His date didn't pan out, so he's horny. He didn't know how to say no to me.*

'Ella?'

Indecision kept every word locked inside, so she nodded.

'You don't seem okay.'

Don't ruin everything! 'I'm f-fine.'

Abruptly, Leo sat up, his legs bent, resting his head in his hands. 'Fuck!' he growled. 'I'm sorry, Ella. I'm so fucking sorry.'

She pushed herself to sit, her hand reaching for his arm, then withdrawing. 'Don't apologise. Honestly, there's nothing to be sorry for!'

He didn't meet her gaze, just huffed and slowly shook his head.

Tears filled her throat. She'd never before felt so wretched. 'Leo, I'm the one who should be sorry. I've ruined everything. I —' She broke off as he raised his head, his hair sticking up in all directions, his expression anguished.

'You haven't ruined anything.' His voice sounded tired. 'You're my best friend. Nothing you could ever say or do will change that.'

Swallowing her tears, she tried to smile.

His face became bleaker as he took hers in. Seeming to make a decision, he got off the bed.

Icy terror gripped her. 'Where are you going?'

'Just for another run. I'm going to leave you in peace for a few hours, maybe go to Connor's for dinner later.'

'Oh... okay. So, er, I'll see you tomorrow?'

His smile didn't reach his eyes. 'Sure.' He paused, as if deciding what to say next. Then he turned and left.

As the door closed behind him, Ella stared at it in shock and disbelief. She'd just been rocketed to heaven, but was now dropping into a dark pit with no clear way out. All she knew was that she had to make things right with Leo. If that meant giving him space to process what had happened, then so be it. But she couldn't allow one silly mistake of hers to destroy a lifetime of friendship.

❧ 16 ❧

Waking up in the darkness of the early morning, every part of Ella's body hurt. Her eyes were sore from too much crying, her head was splitting through lack of sleep, and her bones ached. There were still two more weeks of school left before the Christmas holidays, but she didn't feel like getting out of bed to face any of it.

How could she fix things with Leo? Her tummy flipped at the thought of seeing him again. However, the excitement was tempered by nerves. How could it not be weird after yesterday?

Getting out of bed, she went to the bathroom and stared at herself in the mirror, not quite believing that she was looking at the person who'd had the best orgasm of her life thanks to her one hundred per cent platonic best friend.

She needed to talk to someone about it. But who? Not Leo. Nor his family. And definitely not her absent mother, her uncaring stepmother, or her uninterested half-sisters.

Ella's mind jumped to Lila, then quickly backtracked. Lila was still her best female friend, but she now lived in California, so conversations were sporadic and they usually just communicated through voice notes every few months.

And anyway, she's the love of Leo's life, Ella thought bitterly as she brushed her teeth. Sure, they'd broken up years ago, but Leo hadn't had a girlfriend since. *Well, none that you know of.* And it didn't matter how many times Lila had dumped him in the past, he'd still come running the moment she wanted him back.

Back in her bedroom, Ella dressed and turned on her phone, hoping for a message from Leo. Messages pinged in. However, the first one she saw was from Kyla-Marie.

> Kyla-Marie: I can't believe you left Mum with that slapper

> Kyla-Marie: Ure such a selfish bitch

Sitting on the edge of the bed with a thump, Ella hung her head. Yesterday, Dervla had told her Michelle had been much improved after a night of sleep, and hadn't kicked off to discover Dervla looking after her instead of Ella.

Unbidden, fresh tears dropped onto her clenched hands. *Why does it always have to be so bloody hard with them?* Swiping her fingers across her cheeks, she took a big breath and opened the messages from Leo.

> Leo: Night-night, Princess, and sweet dreams. I'm staying at Connor's, so I won't see you at breakfast. Chat at lunchtime? X

> Leo: Morning, my BFFFFFFF! Hope you slept well. And remember… If you ever use a word that starts with S and ends with ORRY, then AN ELF DIES IN SANTA LAND!!!!!

> Leo: #ElvesAreForLifeNotJustForChristmas

Smiling for the first time since Leo had left the previous day, Ella typed out a message.

Ella: That goes for you too, you know

His reply came through almost immediately.

Leo: She wakes! How did you sleep?

Ella: It was suboptimal

Leo: Dammit! I forgot to remove the pea from under your mattress

Ella: Ha ha

Leo: If it makes you feel any better, my sleep was rubbish, too. Connor's spare bed was designed with elves in mind, not people

Ella: #ElvesArePeopleToo

Leo: Yeah. Bloody small ones

Ella: Lol

Leo: Have you had breakfast?

Ella: Not yet. Still trying to wake up properly

Leo: Okay, I'll leave you to it then. Your start time is earlier than mine and I don't want you to be late

Ella: Chat at lunchtime? I'm free at one for half an hour

Leo: Does Santa live at the North Pole?

Ella: When he's not in Lapland

> Leo: True. Can't make a mistake like that in twelve days' time

Ella: I hope we win

> Leo: We will. We Noel it All, remember?

Ella: If you say so

> Leo: I do. Now go to work and sleigh it X

Ella: You too x

LEAVING THE SCHOOL GROUNDS JUST AFTER ONE, ELLA turned her phone on and headed for the park. She couldn't have a conversation with Leo in the staff room, and she needed fresh air after a centrally-heated classroom filled with too many sweaty teenagers. The run up to Christmas was always manic, but this year there was so much more to deal with than normal. Crossing a line with Leo was the last straw, and Ella was emotionally as well as physically exhausted.

As her phone connected, it buzzed with notifications for missed calls. Her heart sank as she stared at the screen. *Oliver's parents.* No prizes for guessing why they were calling. Her rent payment for December should have gone out of her account on Saturday. Entering the park, Ella perched on a wooden bench, the frosted wood cold and hard even through the thick layer of her coat.

Her thumb hovered over their number, irritation needling her. Why had they called so many times this morning? She was at work. Their son was also a teacher, so they knew the score.

But you're an art *teacher. It's just colouring in and coffee breaks.* Ella shook her head, remembering Oliver's dad's words. Not ever having to see Oliver's parents again was one reason she was glad her relationship with him was over. Another was that Oliver never treated her half as well as Leo did.

Nor ever gave you an orgasm that made you see stars.

Don't think about that! Leo's your friend!

A brief pang of guilt hit her. Guilt for asking Leo to kiss her, and guilt for moving on so quickly from Oliver.

But you hadn't had sex with Oliver for months! You knew in your heart of hearts things weren't right. And you're not moving on from Oliver, you're moving back to Leo.

Even if we can never be together.

Before the internal argument could continue, she called Oliver's parents.

'Fitzcannon,' an officious voice barked when the call connected.

Ella repressed an eye roll. Why couldn't he just say his first name? Or, 'Hello'?

'Hi, Fabian, it's Ella here. I'm just returning your calls.'

'Miss Chamberlain. Finally, you deign to pick up your phone.'

'I've been teaching all morning and only just switched it on.'

He snorted as if he didn't believe her. 'I've been calling because there seems to be an administrative error on your end.'

Here we go. 'In what way?'

'Your rent payment is yet to arrive.'

Ella took a deep breath. She would not be bullied. Leo had been right for her to cancel the payment, as she didn't trust them to return her deposit.

'I moved out over two weeks ago, ensuring the property was left immaculate for the estate agent. I—'

'That has no relevance to your rental obligation. We expect the money by the end of the day.'

'No.'

'Excuse me?'

Ella squeezed her free hand into a fist, trying to find the confidence she didn't feel. 'No. You can keep my deposit, which is for the same amount. Then we're quits.'

'We are most certainly *not*, young lady! That money is earmarked for vital repairs.'

'What repairs? I left the place in better condition than when Oliver and I moved in!'

'The... the back fence needs replacing.'

'Which has nothing to do with the fabric of the house *or* me.'

'We knew you'd pull a stunt like this.'

Angry tears stung her eyes. 'I've been paying through the nose to live with your son and you never charged *him* rent. If we'd had a contract, which we *didn't*, I would have had at least three months to vacate the property, not one.'

'Scum. That's what you are,' Fabian spat down the phone. 'Just like your parents. Thank god Oliver finally saw sense. You know—'

Ella cut the call, then blocked their number, her fingers shaking.

Her phone rang again. *Leo. Thank god.*

'Hi.' Her voice was already wavering.

'Ella? What's wrong? What's happened?'

She took a shuddering breath, trying not to cry. 'Oliver's dad just rang, wanting to know why the rent money for December hadn't come through.'

'Thank fuck you stopped the payment.'

'He was furious.'

'Course he was. Wanker. I'm so sorry, Ella, but you did the right thing. They would never have given you your deposit back.'

'You're right. He said they were going to use it for "vital repairs".'

'Repairing what? It's a bloody show home.'

'I said as much. He said the back fence needed replacing.'

'Arsehole.'

'He said I was scum,' she whispered.

'He said *what?*' Leo shouted.

'I've blocked his number.'

'Jesus, Ella. I'm so fucking sorry!'

'Leo, you've already killed two elves with this conversation.'

He gave a strangled laugh. 'True. Although I think they'll pop back into existence the moment I've murdered Fabian Fitzcannon. Get rid of one nasty piece of work and two nice things have to happen. It's how karma works at Christmas.'

Ella let out a long slow breath, her stress levels easing. 'Thank you. For everything.'

'I don't feel I've done much. Please, can I slay the Fitz-cannons?'

'Slay as in kill, or sleigh as in the thing Santa pulls?'

'Both. I'm going to borrow Santa's sleigh and joyride— sorry, "joy to the world ride" into their house, slaying them in the process.'

She snorted. 'Thank you for telling me to cancel the payment. And thank you for making me feel better.'

'You know what would make you feel even better?'

Her heart and stomach lurched. *Having sex with you?* 'Er, what?'

'The *Muppet Christmas Carol!* Tonight should be movie night.'

She exhaled in a rush. 'Good plan. But it can't be a late one as I've got school tomorrow.'

'You back around six?'

'Should be.'

'Well, I'm finishing here at three, so I'll come home and prepare picnic food we can eat whilst we watch the movie. I'll have you in bed by nine, I promise.'

I'll have you in bed by nine. Ella closed her eyes as arousal rushed around her body.

'You'll get at least eight hours of beauty sleep by my calculations,' Leo continued, seemingly unaware of the double meaning of his words. 'Which is seven and a half hours more than you need. Deal?'

She nodded.

'Ella?'

'Yeah, sorry. That's fine.'

'An elf just died! Now I really have to remove the Fitzcannons from the world, or there won't be enough elves left to wrap all the kiddie's presents properly.'

Ella giggled. 'You can't kill them.'

'Think of the children!'

'Lunatic.'

'But you still love me.'

'Of course I do,' she replied, hiding her truest feelings in plain sight.

'Excellent. I'll spare their pitiful lives in a charming show of princely benevolence and see you later.'

Finishing the call, Ella sat on the bench watching a dog walker and feeling the winter stillness all around her. She'd hopefully seen the last of the Fitzcannons and things were back on track with Leo. Last night was just a blip in their friendship and one they'd already worked through and moved on from.

So why did she feel an emptiness inside rather than relief?

Come on! It's fine. It's better this way. Giving herself a shake, she stood. She had work to focus on, then the Muppets to look forward to. That film was not only one of her favourites, but also had a zero per cent chance of inducing sexy thoughts about Leo.

At half-past six, showered and nervous, Ella knocked twice on Leo's door.

'Who's there?' he called out.

'Mary!'

'Mary who?'

'Mary Christmas!'

The door opened to reveal a laughing Leo, who then clocked her t-shirt. 'No way!'

She was wearing one that said, 'All I want for Christmas is you pigs in blankets'. He pointed at his, which had the words, 'All I want for Christmas is you to win the Christmas quiz' on it, then raised his hand for her to high-five him.

She slapped his hand with hers. 'This is getting uncanny.' Looking past him into the room, she blinked at what he'd done.

His room was immaculately tidy, with strings of fairy lights criss-crossing the high ceiling and framing the windows. At the foot of the bed was a huge television mounted on a wheeled stand, and across the counterpane was a red picnic blanket covered in food on plates decorated with paintings of holly and ivy. His pillows were hidden under a mountain of cushions that Ella recognised as having come from one of the drawing rooms downstairs.

'Oh, my god, Leo. This is amazing!'

He shrugged, looking relieved and also proud of himself. 'Hungry?'

'Absolutely. I haven't eaten since breakfast.'

'What? Why not?'

She pulled a face. 'After the delightful call with Oliver's dad,

I couldn't stomach anything. And the afternoon was so full-on, I forgot about lunch.'

'Well then, milady, a feast awaits! Please, take a seat.'

Taking off her trainers, Ella climbed onto the bed and sat cross-legged, gazing at the food, her mouth watering.

'We've got clementine and chilli halloumi skewers, maple and mustard pigs in blankets, hasselback potatoes wrapped in bacon, blue cheese and sage filo bites, smoked salmon, cream cheese and dill blinis,' Leo began. 'Then for pudding, we're having dates stuffed with dark chocolate—'

'My favourite.'

'I know. Then Christmas popcorn and Christmas rocky road as per your special secret recipes that only the two of us know, but also now Perry, as she helped me with everything.'

'I was wondering how on earth you managed to do this in a couple of hours.'

'Well, I am your BFFFFFFFF.'

'Have you just added another f?'

'Yep! For fast.' He grinned at her expression. 'And a jug of cranberry and orange juice with soda water.'

'No mulled wine?'

Leo hesitated briefly. 'No alcohol on a school night.'

'In a house where at least two different wines are served with dinner every evening?'

'Er—'

'And I've got a miniature behind every window of my advent calendar?'

'Um...'

A sudden thought hit Ella like a slap to the face. *Oh god. Does he think if I have anything to drink, I'll leap on him again?*

'It's the countdown to the quiz. Our brains need to be functioning optimally.'

Not constantly imagining having sex with you, then?

'And the miniatures are tiny. You'll have metabolised any alcohol before you get to school.'

'I don't think my headteacher would be pleased to know I'm on the booze every morning.'

He smirked. 'I bet he's got a bottle of whisky stashed in his desk drawer.'

Ella laughed to cover up her worries about why Leo didn't want them to drink. 'Probably.'

'Tuck in then, you've got a calorie deficit to make up for.'

Her stomach grumbling, she filled her plate and started eating. The food, of course, was delicious, made even more enjoyable because of the person she was sharing it with. Leo chatted about what was happening at the Theatre Royal in Bath where he worked, and the preparations for their pantomime, which was starting next week and would be running for a month. The two of them had plans to see it the night before the Christmas quiz, and Ella couldn't wait.

'Want to eat pudding whilst we watch the movie?' he asked when they'd demolished the savoury dishes. 'After all, one of them *is* popcorn.'

'Absolutely. And thank you, that was amazing.' She started collecting the plates, but Leo batted her hands away. 'You make yourself comfortable. I'm just going to run these downstairs.'

'You sure I can't help?'

'Positive.' He pulled a tray out from under the bed, piled the plates and dishes onto it, then carried them to the closed door. 'Ah.'

Leaping off the bed, Ella opened it for him, failing to avoid ogling the way his arm muscles filled the short sleeves of his t-shirt. She followed him into the corridor and he gave her a quizzical look.

'I just need to get something,' she said, then moved away from him and entered her room.

The advent calendar he'd made her was propped up on her bedside table, the ring he'd created from the Baci foil wrapper lying next to it. She hadn't had the heart to open the calendar that morning without him, especially with things so awkward and unresolved between them. But now their relationship was back to normal. On the surface, at least.

Inside, she yearned for him. When she'd been a teen, she'd had many dreams about kissing Leo, but the reality had blown her mind and set her body on fire. Now she knew exactly what it felt like and she craved more. Her finger touched the tinfoil ring. Would that ever be their reality?

She shook her head. *Marriage? Get a grip. He's a friend. Don't hound him for more and end up pushing him away forever.*

Leaving her thoughts in her room, Ella re-entered Leo's, arranging the pillows at the end of the bed and putting the dates, rocky road, and popcorn in the middle as a food wall to help her hand from straying to a Leo-shaped dessert that definitely *wasn't* on the menu.

When he arrived back, his gaze fell to the advent calendar. 'You didn't open it this morning?'

'It didn't feel right without you there.'

'But it's yours!'

'And you put two chocolates behind each window.'

He grinned, then went to his side of the bed and showed her the calendar she'd made for him. 'I didn't open mine either.'

She smiled. 'Guess who's behind the second window?'

His mouth twisted as he frowned in concentration, then he seemed to give up the attempt. 'No idea. Give me a clue?'

'I thought you could mind read?'

'Yeah, but you weren't actively thinking about who it was. If you do, *and* give me a clue, then I'm bound to get it.'

'Okay.'

Putting the calendar on the bed, Leo crawled forward, reaching towards her.

'What are you doing?' she asked, her pulse suddenly rocketing.

His hands withdrew immediately, his expression crestfallen. 'Shit, sorry. I, er... I thought if I touched your head I might get a visual download.'

Taking his hands, she placed his fingers on her temples, then closed her eyes.

With the loss of her sight, her other senses ramped up. Leo didn't speak, but she heard the hitch of his breath, felt the touch of his fingertips. Her skin buzzed with awareness of him, electricity raising every hair on her body and making her shiver. She inhaled deeper, trying to breathe him in.

Then his hands withdrew. 'I... I don't know,' he said, his voice hesitant.

She opened her eyes. 'I don't know either. I can't remember who I drew.'

He laughed, his expression once again cocky and carefree. 'Well, that explains everything! Why didn't you say? I thought my powers had deserted me.'

She grinned. 'I like to keep you on your toes.'

He lifted the window to reveal a picture of his father, dressed as Santa. 'Love it! Now open yours whilst I get the movie started.'

'Ooh! Bailey's! Yummy!' Ella exclaimed as she opened the window, pulling out the tiny bottle and the two Baci.

'Today is a double chocolate day,' Leo replied, jumping back onto the bed with the remote.

'Quadruple if you count the chocolate-filled dates and rocky road.'

'Yep. We're going to be off our heads in about ten minutes.'

He started the movie and settled back into the mountain

of pillows next to Ella. She passed him a chocolate and he opened it, discarding the wrapper with the motto about love to the bed next to him.

See! If he wanted anything more than friendship, he would have read it out!

Opening her one, she put the motto in her pocket to read later, and focused on the film.

An hour and twenty-five minutes later, after having sung all the songs and said their favourite lines out loud, Leo glanced at his watch.

'It's only just gone eight. Another movie?'

Ella nodded. She was exhausted, but wanted to prolong the evening until she couldn't keep her eyes open any longer. Whenever she was with Leo, life wasn't just better, it was perfect.

He cued up *The Family Man*, and she rested her head back. The film was one of her favourite Christmas movies, but now she saw it in a whole new light. What would her life have looked like if she'd got together with Leo instead of Zach when they were at school?

But he didn't like you then. He encouraged you to date Zach.

She blinked, as if it would reset her thoughts, which were caught in a loop. Her eyelids were heavy, and it was getting difficult to keep them open. Maybe she could let them close and just listen to the film? She knew it so well she didn't need the images. She could let it play out in her mind.

Pleasure moved through Ella's veins like late-summer honey; thick and sweet. Leo was gazing down at her, his golden hair a halo of light, his bright blue eyes blazing.

'Ella,' he murmured, the sound rippling across her skin like butterfly kisses.

Her fingers ran down his naked torso. 'Leo.'

Leaning down, he dipped his tongue into the hollow at the base of her throat, then kissed his way up to her lips, whispering her name again.

Arching up to him, she held his head, pulling him closer. Desire burned in her chest, flaring as her tongue met his. She was writhing underneath him, desperate to have him inside her.

'Ella.' Her name on his lips amplified every sensation.

She was panting now, clawing at his trousers to get them off. 'Leo!'

'Ella.'

Her climax was close but still too far away to catch, the frustration too much to bear. 'Leo, I need you. Please.'

'Ella!'

Her eyes shot open as she tumbled from her dream, her heart pounding and her mind scattered.

Leo was gazing down at her.

Fully clothed.

Pushing up to sit, her limbs uncooperative, Ella tried to reconcile where she'd just been with the reality of where she was now. The room was darker, the only illumination coming from the fairy lights. The TV was off and the bed was cleared of food.

How long have I been asleep? And did I say anything? She fell back to the bed, staring at the ceiling crisscrossed with tiny lights.

'Did I...?' She didn't know how to finish the sentence.

Leo didn't answer, so she turned her head to face him. He was looking away, his arms clasped around his knees, his cheeks red.

Oh god. 'What's the time?' she finally managed.

He cleared his throat. 'Just after ten. You fell asleep about twenty minutes into the movie, so I turned it off and tidied everything up.'

Ella's body hummed with remembered pleasure, a dull ache between her thighs that her fingers wanted to relieve. Her arms and legs were heavy, her mind still not up to speed. She wanted to be back in her dream with Leo's lips on hers, his hips pressing her into the mattress, his—

'What did I say?' She needed to know how much she'd embarrassed herself.

He swallowed. 'Nothing.'

Ella knew he was lying. She knew he was helping her save face. Giving her an out. But she was drunk with sleep and sex hormones, and her body overruled her mind.

'I was dreaming about you.'

'A nightmare then?' His gaze was still ahead and his voice was strained and mocking.

'No. It was the best dream I've ever had.'

A muscle twitched in his jaw and he finally brought his gaze to meet hers, his eyes flicking down and back up her body as if he was powerless to stop them.

The movement fanned the flames of her desire, quickening her pulse. *Did* he want her? Or at least enough to satisfy a physical need? Right now, she was too horny to care if his feelings matched her own. She needed him more than she could bear.

Leo swallowed again, his lips parting as if to speak, but no words came.

'You really don't have to,' she said haltingly. 'If you don't want—'

'I'd do anything for you.' His voice was hoarse. 'Anything.'

She inched her hand slowly over the mattress until it rested by his bent leg. 'Will you—' She broke off when his hand reached for hers.

The moment their fingers touched, the erotic charge that had been building inside her released with a snap of energy, making her gasp.

'Ella.' His voice held a warning and a plea.

'Please, Leo.'

His fingers tightened around hers. 'What do you want?'

'You,' she whispered. 'I want you.'

❧ 17 ❧

Blood roared in Leo's ears, urging him to take everything Ella seemed to be offering, then take some more. His cock was painfully hard in his jeans, his muscles primed and his heart about to explode. If watching Ella sleep was an emotionally charged experience, then kissing her, touching her, loving her body with his, might end him.

But it would be worth it.

If she needed a physical release to help her get over Oliver, then Leo would be the man to give it to her. No-one else. There was no other person on earth who loved her more than he did. No-one he trusted more to worship her body and guard her heart like he could. And when she was done with him in the bedroom? He'd go back to being just a friend. Even if it killed him.

She tugged on his hand and he lay beside her, his free hand stroking down the side of her face to cup her jaw. Ella was so fucking beautiful it hurt. Like an angel had kicked him in the nuts, then throat-punched him till he couldn't breathe.

Take it slow. 'Are you sure?'

She nodded and let go of his hand. Then reached down and palmed his cock.

'Fu—aaahh!' he cried incoherently, jerking away from her as the pleasure struck him like lightning. Squeezing his eyes tightly closed, he willed his climax to recede, then took a ragged breath and dared himself to look at her again.

Her lips were parted, her face flushed with uncertainty as well as desire. 'Are *you* sure?' she asked hesitantly.

The question was so patently ridiculous he raised an eyebrow.

Her breathless laugh knocked down the final barrier of his restraint. Covering her body with his, he bracketed her head with his forearms and lowered his lips to hers. He was already raging with desire, but when her tongue stroked his, fire scorched a path to his cock, eviscerating everything in its wake. He was molten with heat, every part of him burning for her.

Spreading her legs, Ella wrapped them around the back of his, holding him tighter to him as their kiss intensified. There was nothing languid or gentle about it. Her fingers clutched his head as if holding on for dear life, her breath rapid and frantic.

Leo had never known passion like this. Love and lust crashing together like the meeting of two oceans. He was lost in pleasure, battered and turned inside out by it. But even as stars filled his head, warning of an oncoming blackout, he still wanted more.

Tearing his mouth from Ella's, he kissed her jaw, then sucked and nipped down her neck as she writhed and panted in his arms. He wanted to worship every inch of her. Then do it again and again, until his love had seeped down to her bones.

Moving her hands from his head, she tugged the bottom of his t-shirt up. He sprang to his knees, ripped it over his head and threw it to the floor.

Ella stared at his chest, then licked her lips and swallowed. Leo had never felt prouder. More potent. More determined to give Ella anything and everything she wanted. He flexed, tightening every muscle, and was rewarded by the widening of her eyes, her pupils now so dilated they were dark lakes he wanted to dive into.

'Washboard abs,' she whispered.

Leo couldn't think of anything to say in response. His breath was laboured as he watched her run her fingers across his skin, trailing fire in their wake.

'You're so beautiful,' she continued.

He shook his head. 'You are. You're the most beautiful woman I've ever known.'

A beat passed, and her fingers stilled. Had he said the wrong thing? Moved too fast?

But then, before he could work out what to do next, she tore off her t-shirt, undid her bra and tossed it to the bed.

Leo's mind stuttered to a stop.

He'd spent so many years fantasising about seeing Ella's breasts that now it was actually happening, his brain couldn't compute the reality or distinguish it from a fevered dream. Blood rushed from his head, making him dizzy with lust. His fingertips tingled and his cock throbbed.

Another look of uncertainty flickered in her expression, and he cursed himself. *Get it together and be the man she deserves!*

Reaching down, he drew circles around her breasts, each pass moving a little closer to the hard buds at the centre.

'I need you to know,' he began, his voice low and gravelly, 'how much I've wanted this. And if I appear hesitant, then it's just because I can't believe I'm touching you like this.'

The flesh of her breasts tightened with goosebumps as her breathing quickened.

'But if you want me to stop at any moment, just say. Promise?'

She nodded, her eyes glistening in the low light, then placed her hands over his, guiding them to the centre.

As he grazed the pads of his thumbs over her nipples, she let out a little whimper. He rolled them between his fingers and thumbs, power and pleasure surging inside him with each soft cry she made. He was single-minded in his determination to learn exactly how to please her. How to drive her so wild with desire that it was *his* name on her lips when she came.

Her hips were subtly rocking, her hands ghosting over his arms, his sides, anything she could reach as if she was restlessly trying to alleviate an itch that kept growing in intensity.

Relieving his own desperate craving, Leo lowered his head and sucked a nipple into his mouth, his tongue roughing over the tip.

Ella reacted as if shot, crying out and grabbing his head to hold it in place.

He licked faster, wishing he had more hands, another mouth. He wanted to gorge on Ella, taste every part of her at once, bring her the same ecstasy that was currently rushing through him in waves.

'Oh, god. Leo!'

In his mind, the sound of Ella crying his name was accompanied by trumpeters and a choir of angels. Nothing would ever feel as satisfying as this moment.

But then she undid her jeans and pushed them, along with her underwear, down to her knees, and Leo realised he'd reached the top of a mountain of happiness only to discover there was another, bigger one right in front of him.

Moving to his side, he cradled Ella in the crook of his left arm, angling her lips to his as his left hand found her breast and his right skimmed down the skin of her stomach to cup her pussy. Beneath his palm were soft curls, warmth, and the most secret, private part of her that he wanted to love with every part of him.

He drank in her whimpers and cries as his tongue tangled with hers. He didn't move his right hand, just held still as she pushed up into his touch. Then she put her hand over his and pushed his middle finger down into her wet heat.

Oh god, oh god, oh fuck! Leo fought for control as Ella squeezed around his finger. *Think of her! Make it good for* her!

Corralling his feelings and emotions, he forced himself to remain detached, running his middle finger up the cleft of her pussy to circle her clit with the slickness of her arousal. The bud was hard and swollen, so he moved gently, learning how to please her.

Wrenching her mouth from his, Ella gasped, drawing in lungfuls of air as he rolled her nipple with one hand and stroked her clit with the other. He sensed her muscles tightening with every ragged inhale, quivering as if she were teetering on a knife's edge.

He drank in her expression, watching every flicker, every tiny response to what he was doing. Pleasuring Ella was like receiving the ultimate gift. One he would keep in his heart for the rest of his life.

Her eyes met his, her gaze frantic and wild, her cheeks bright with colour. 'Leo! I'm—'

He kept up the movement of his fingers, the pace steady and relentless as she began to fall apart.

Ella. Ella. My Ella.

'I'm going. I'm going to—' her words cut off as her breath stopped, her body stiffening.

Yes. He continued to stroke her as she shuddered on the bed, gasping for air, the tremors continuing to radiate out in waves.

Then, eventually, when she became as limp as a rag doll, he held her to him, nuzzling her neck, his heart so full of love it threatened to spill from his eyes.

She turned her head, her mouth seeking his, and he kissed her with everything he was and everything he had. Her hand reached for his trousers, but he pulled away. She owed him nothing. Her pleasure was his pleasure, and he was desperate to prove himself to her. If he could show her how good it could be with him, then maybe, just maybe, she might consider him for the long haul, not just for now.

Shifting down the bed, he tugged her jeans and pants off.

She raised her head, her cheeks pink. 'What are you—?'

Kneeling, he took one of her feet into his hands, pressing his thumbs into the instep.

Ella flopped back on the pillow. 'Oh my god,' she murmured. 'That feels so good.'

Leo mentally pinched himself as he gazed at her naked form lying on his bed. How had he got so lucky? He continued kneading and massaging, then moved to the other foot, revelling in every little moan and sigh she made.

When her limbs were heavy and languid, he pressed kisses to the ends of her toes, then kissed his way slowly up her legs, waiting for her to part them as he went. Her hands were flexing by her sides, her breath coming deeper.

Taking his time, he sucked and nipped up her inner thigh, drawing the soft flesh into his mouth. She was twitching now, her desire ramping up again, until her legs finally spread in open invitation.

Leo took it, licking up the length of her slit and circling her clit with his tongue.

She jerked at the contact, but her hands flew to his head to keep him in place.

He smiled and did it again.

'Oh, my god! Holy shit,' she moaned. 'That feels... just—ah!'

He wrote 'I love you, Ella,' on her clit over and over, each letter he drew making her breathe a little faster until she was panting.

Then he stopped, resting his head on her inner thigh, drawing her scent into his nostrils and savouring the taste of her on his tongue.

'Leo,' she whimpered.

Inching a finger inside her, he slowly rubbed it against the front wall of her channel, feeling her clench around him. He added another finger, then drew letters over her clit again, this time writing, 'All I want for Christmas is you'.

She was tightening with each breath, chasing another climax. Leo poured out his love for her through his tongue, his fingers, his soul. Painting the centre of her pleasure with the words, 'All I want for forever is you'.

As he reached the final letter, Ella stiffened beneath him. He thrummed the tip of his tongue against her clit and she let out a strangled scream, her inner muscles clenching rhythmically around his fingers as her orgasm kept coming. He held her tightly as she thrashed on the bed, shuddering, shaking, her breath returning in disjointed gasps.

She pulled ineffectively on his hair, and he trailed kisses up her torso until he reached her lips. Her kiss tasted of pleasure, gratitude, and love.

The words he'd used to bring her to orgasm still lingered on his tongue. Could he say them out loud? Tell her how he felt?

No. This is enough for now. Take what you can and be patient.

Her head drew back. 'That was the most incredible thing I've ever experienced,' she said shyly.

Happiness bubbled up inside him. 'Am I now the fexiest man you've ever met?'

She nodded. 'And the most fandsome, fantastic, and funny. I'm the most fortunate festive friend in the whole flipping world.'

Friend. The word stabbed Leo's stomach. He wanted so much more than just that. But he covered his fear with a smile. 'I think we need a new Christmas tradition.'

She raised an eyebrow.

'Starting on December the first, you should have as many orgasms per day as the calendar states. Yesterday, to the best of my knowledge, you had one. And today, at least with me, you've had two. What do you think of my cunning plan?'

She blushed. 'So, on Christmas Day, I'm having twenty-five?'

'Yep. I'm up for it if you are?'

'And what happens *after* Christmas?'

You decide to give me a chance, long-term? He grinned. 'We start all over again, preparing for next year.'

'But what about you?'

'Me?'

'Yes, you. Would you like to, er...' The fire in her cheeks burned hotter as she inclined her head towards his crotch, his arousal still painfully obvious. 'Um. Have sex with me?' she finished in a mumble.

Leo leaned forward to whisper in her ear. 'More than you can imagine.'

He felt her smile against his cheek. 'I don't have any condoms, but I presume you might?'

'They might not be in date.'

Ella leaned back to gaze at him sceptically.

He shrugged, suddenly awkward. 'It's been a while.'

She blinked.

'Not as many women as you might think find me fexy.'

'Well, their loss is my gain. And, if you want, we don't have to use a condom.'

Now it was his turn to stare in confusion at her.

'After Oli, I didn't know if he might have been unfaithful, so I got myself tested. Everything came back negative, and I've got an IUD fitted, so I won't get pregnant.'

Leo felt a pang of disappointment at the last part of her sentence, as if now they'd been intimate, part of him had already decided they were at the 'marriage and kids' stage of their relationship.

Then the realisation of what she was offering nearly made him ejaculate in his jeans for the second day running. Ella was suggesting they have sex without a barrier between them. The thought of being bare inside her, coming deep in her pussy made his head spin.

'But only if you want to,' she continued in a rush. 'I don't want to put you under any pressure.'

He took a deep breath, trying to calm his rioting heart. 'I've never had sex without a condom before and I got tested after my last relationship. There's nothing I want more than what you're offering.'

Her smile was full of relief. 'More than winning the Christmas quiz?'

'More than that, *and* a white Christmas put together. More than anything.'

'You might be disappointed.'

'Never. There's more chance of me meeting Santa on the roof of the manor than that.'

She reached tentatively for the top button of his jeans. 'So...?'

He covered his hand with hers. 'You've got to be up in a few hours.'

'I don't mind.'

'*I* mind.' Leo knew how exhausted Ella was, and he also knew once he got naked, he wouldn't be able to leave her alone. Then there was his fear that she'd wake up the next morning with some kind of regret. The first time they had sex, he wanted to be sure she'd be into it as much as he would be.

Her expression faltered, and she sat up. 'Should I go then?'

'What? No!' Hauling her back to the bed, he cradled her in his arms. 'You can if you want, but I'd really love it if you would stay the night here. I always sleep better when you're with me.'

'I've only ever slept next to you once before.'

'Best night's sleep of my life.'

She giggled. 'I think you're just worried you'll get lost in this stupidly enormous bed.'

'Well, if I do, I'll sleep jog until I find you.'

LEO LEFT ONE STRING OF FAIRY LIGHTS LIT, SO WHEN HE finally came to bed next to Ella, he could still make out her face in the semi-darkness.

Taking her hands, he brought them to his mouth for a kiss. 'Night-night, Princess Ella.'

She leaned forward and kissed him on the lips. 'Night-night, Prince Leo,' she replied softly, then closed her eyes with a happy sigh.

Leo kept his open, watching Ella's face relax and listening to the changes in her breathing as she drifted off to sleep. Only when he knew for certain that she was dreaming did he voice what his heart wanted him to yell from the rooftops.

'I love you, Ella,' he murmured, before closing his eyes, her hands still wrapped in his, and let himself follow her into sleep.

❧ 18 ❧

The first part of Ella to wake up the next morning was her sense of smell. There was a spicy, woodsy, warm and comforting scent in the air. It enveloped her in feelings of happiness and safety. Like drinking mulled cider in front of a crackling fire in a luxurious cabin in the middle of a winter woodland.

Leo.

He was spooning her, one arm holding her close like she was his favourite childhood teddy bear.

Snuggling back into the cradle of his body, Ella let the memories from the previous night wash through her, waking her up more effectively than a double espresso. Leo kissing her. Leo kissing her *everywhere*. His body. His words. The orgasms that shattered her into a million points of light. The promise of even more to come.

As if sensing the quickening of her heartbeat, he stirred behind her. 'Morning, Princess,' he said, his voice gravelly and deep, rumbling into her back and sending vibrations of pleasure straight between her thighs.

'Good morning, fair prince.' She stretched, accidentally-on-purpose pushing her bottom back against his already hard cock.

He responded by kissing her neck and bringing his hand to her breast. 'Good? It's spectacular,' he replied in between kisses. 'Best morning of my life.'

Ella smiled, then gasped as he rubbed her nipple through her pyjama top. This was the best feeling in the world. Nothing could beat it.

Then Leo stilled. 'What's the time?'

The question was a bucket of iced water over the head. Panicking, Ella sat up and glanced at the bedside clock.

Five past eight. She should have been at school twenty minutes ago.

Leo sprang from the bed. 'Get washed and dressed and I'll see you outside the front door in ten.'

Ella stumbled to follow him. 'Where are you going?'

'Grabbing you some breakfast, then getting my car so I can drop you off.' He snatched his t-shirt and trainers from the floor, then ran from the room.

Seven minutes later, Ella dashed out of the manor and leapt in Leo's car. 'Thank you so much,' she said breathlessly as he drove off in a shower of gravel.

'Anytime.' He flashed her a grin. 'The bag at your feet contains an all-you-can-eat breakfast roll, a pain au chocolat, a thermos of coffee, a bottle of the manor's spring water, and a portion of leftover shepherd's pie for lunch.'

'That's amazing.'

'Oh, and an apple because you're a teacher and I'm your pet.'

She giggled. 'What kind of pet?'

'A lion, of course.'

'How could I forget?' Ella glanced at her watch as Leo sped along Foxbrooke high street. 'Aren't you going to be late for work as well?'

'It's fine. They're cool. I can make up the time at the end of the day.'

A couple of minutes later, Leo swung his car through the school gates and screeched to a halt.

Ella turned to say goodbye, suddenly hyper-aware that this was a moment when a girlfriend might kiss a boyfriend.

'Don't overthink it,' Leo murmured, then cradled her jaw to bring her mouth to his. He brushed his lips over hers, making them tingle. 'See you later?'

She nodded, getting out of the car on unsteady legs.

Leo gave her a salute, then drove off, leaving Ella feeling as if he'd taken half of her with him.

Libby: Morning! How did the trust exercises go? Do you feel more comfortable with Leo now? X

Ella: Great, thank you. I think things will be better now x

Libby: Wonderful! Are you up for another quick rehearsal tonight? Willow's finished your transformation dress and I want to make sure it works alright, so I thought we could run through the scene before the ball with you and Dervla?

Ella: Yes! Of course. Straight after dinner?

Libby: Perfect! Thank you! X

Ella: No worries. See you later! x

. . .

Ella: I hope you got to work okay? Xxx

Leo: All good. I'm going to work a bit later tonight, so I'll see you this evening? xxx

Ella: I'm going to try out the rags-to-riches dress, so I should be in the ballroom. Do you want me to save you some dinner? Xxx

Leo: Don't worry. I'm going to grab something in town before I leave xxx

Ella: Okay. Thank you for this morning xxx

Leo: Thank you for last night… X

MOVING FROM TASK TO TASK DURING THE DAY, ELLA'S cheeks heated every time she thought of Leo, to the point where a colleague asked if she had a fever, and a cheeky sixth former asked who she had a crush on. By the time she entered the ballroom after dinner, she was jumpier than a cricket on a hot tin roof, convinced that everyone could see her thoughts as she replayed what had happened with Leo the previous night.

'There's our star!' Libby said excitedly as she came forward to give her a hug.

Ella glanced around to check Arthur wasn't in the room to object.

Libby grinned. 'The other star is on his way.' She lowered her voice. 'Apparently he's got a surprise for me.'

'You'll love it!' Dervla called from the stage. 'He's been working on it for months now.'

Ella shared a look with Libby. What did Arthur have up his sleeve this time?

'And is there any reason why you can't tell me what it is?' Libby asked Dervla.

'He likes to make a grand entrance,' she replied. 'And surprises. But I promise you, this one is completely safe.'

Libby took a big breath and squared her shoulders. 'In which case, I am cautiously excited.' She turned back to Ella. 'Right, let's get you into this dress and see if it works.'

On a table in front of the stage was a pale blue gown adorned with sparkling crystals. Libby rummaged under the voluminous skirts. 'I just need to get into the middle—' She broke off at the sound of barking. 'Oh no.'

The ballroom door opened, and Ella breathed a sigh of relief when Steve entered, a large, shaggy dog by his side. Chewy was a Briard; a French herding and hunting dog who Steve and Jan had bought because of his resemblance to Chewbacca. Despite his size, he was well trained, unlike Arthur's demon hounds, Caligula and Borgia, who were not only big, but bonkers and extremely badly behaved. They only ever paid attention to Estelle Foxbrooke's boyfriend, James, however unfortunately he lived with Estelle at her livery on the other side of the estate park.

'Hi everyone!' Steve said. 'I was about to pick up Jan and thought I'd pop by and see if anyone's heard how Zach is getting on?'

A pang of guilt hit Ella's stomach. Since last night, she hadn't thought about him once.

Chewy came to her side and pushed his head against her leg. Tangling her fingers into his long coat, she scratched behind his ears.

'He's not great,' Dervla replied. 'But it was a clean break and he should be out of plaster in a few weeks.'

'We've got him a get-well card for everyone to sign,' Libby added. 'And Willow's putting together a food hamper which I'm going to take to the hospital tomorrow.'

Steve frowned. 'Poor lad. Do you think people will want their money back once they find out he's not in the panto anymore?'

'Hopefully not, but we've put out a press release, and Zach still wants to come and support us. I'm going to create the role of a narrator and give him some of Dervla's lines.'

'Good idea.' Steve nodded his head at the dress. 'Is that the magic one?'

Libby smiled. 'Yes! Want to see how it works? Ella was just about to test it.'

'Absolutely!'

Putting her hands back under the skirts, Libby lifted the dress and helped it over Ella's head. 'Now pick up the first layer of the skirt and pull it to the top of your head like a scarf,' she instructed.

The underside of the blue fabric was brown, and another skirt lay underneath, a copy of her patchwork Cinderella dress. It meant it now looked like she was wearing her tattered dress with a shawl over her head and shoulders. All she needed to do to transform herself was drop the skirt back into place to reveal the ballgown.

'That's so clever,' Steve said. 'Are we still having some fireworks go off? Arthur said—'

'No,' Libby interrupted firmly. 'We're not having *any* fireworks. We'll have a bit of dry ice just before Dervla waves her wand, then Finn will flash the lights as Ella twirls. That should be effective enough without creating any fire hazards.'

'Shall I give it a go on stage now?' Ella asked.

'Yes, that would be great. Why don't you go from the scene where you come back in from the garden with the pumpkin?'

Ella nodded and went to the back of the stage and up the stairs, Chewy following. The flats were constructed from canvas stretched over wooden frames, and Finn had started securing them to stands with casters so they could be easily moved around. Pulling open the centre of one of them that had been painted to look like a door, Ella entered the set for the kitchen at Hardup Hall, Chewy by her side.

'You've made a new friend!' Dervla said. 'And look at your dress. It's gorgeous!'

Ella gave her a twirl. 'It's turned out so well!'

'Hang on!' boomed a voice from the ballroom door. 'I've got Priscilla!'

Arthur was entering the room, his backside first, and pulling behind him—

'Oh, my god!' Libby cried. 'Is that real?'

An enormous pumpkin sat in a wheelbarrow.

'Certainly is!' he replied proudly. 'I've been growing her for months! Priscilla edged out Percy, Phoebe and Pedro in the size competition.'

'But how on earth is Ella going to carry it?' Libby asked. 'It must weigh a ton!'

'Aha! I knew you'd ask that! I've already carved out the centre, so it's not that heavy. Look!' Reaching into the wheelbarrow, he lifted it with a grunt. 'See! Easy!'

Next to Ella, Chewy's ears pricked up, and he growled.

'Chewy! Shush!' Steve called out.

'Okay,' Libby said. 'Ella, are you happy to give it a go?'

'Sure!'

Arthur wheeled the barrow to the front of the stage, and Ella stepped forward to meet him.

Chewy barked loudly.

'What is it?' Ella asked him as Steve yelled at him to shush again. Then she looked at the pumpkin and her stomach dropped.

Arthur caught her eye. 'Don't show Libby yet,' he whispered. 'I want to—'

'Don't show me *what?*' Libby asked, striding forward. 'Arthur, what—oh my god, you have *got* to be joking!'

He'd hollowed out the pumpkin from a hole in the side, then put a cage door across the opening. Inside were four white mice.

'Well, you won't let me use the dogs *or* a horse,' he said belligerently. 'I really don't see what the problem is.'

Libby put a hand to her forehead. 'For one thing, it's cruel—'

'No, it's not. They're perfectly happy. And they've got a much bigger cage when they're not in Priscilla.'

'It's scary for them—'

'How do you know? Oh, come on, Libby. Please? Just let me try this one little idea.'

Libby let out a heavy sigh. 'Only if Ella is happy to give it a go.'

Ella nodded, even though she wanted to run in the opposite direction. The only thing she hated more than mice were spiders and snakes.

'Hurrah and Huzzah!' Arthur exclaimed. 'Now see if you can hold it, Ella.'

Bending at the knees, she took a deep breath, then lifted it from him. It was heavy, but the weight was just about manageable. The bigger issue was how unwieldy it was, and how much interest Chewy was currently showing in it.

'Okay,' Libby said brightly, as if holding onto her sanity by a thread. 'Ella, see if it's possible to come safely through the door whilst holding it. There will be a table later which you can put it straight onto.'

Coming forward, Dervla took the pumpkin from Ella, so she could pull up the top layer of her skirts and put them over her head, turning her gown into a ragged dress and shawl. Carefully taking the pumpkin back from Dervla, she pushed the door open with her bottom and stepped through, Chewy still growling at her heels.

Behind the flat, she heard the ballroom door open and Leo's voice greeting everyone. Her tummy flipped with nervous excitement and she hooked her toe around the edge of the canvas door to open it.

'Hey Ella!' he called out as she came back onstage, then stared at what she was holding. 'Bloody hell, is that thing real?'

'Meet Priscilla!' Arthur cried. 'Newest addition to the family. And—'

'Hang about. You've got *real* mice in there?' Leo exclaimed as he strode forward. 'But Ella *hates* mice!'

The fabric of her dress was smooth, and the unwieldy pumpkin was beginning to slip.

Don't drop it! You can't hurt the mice!

'Chewy, shush!' Steve shouted as his dog growled again.

Suddenly the ballroom doors were flung open with a crash, and Satan's hellhounds bounded into the room, spittle flying from their bared teeth as they barked.

'Caligula! Borgia! No!' Leo and Arthur roared, as Libby stood in their path, her arms spread wide, a small ray of sunshine trying to fend off two category-five cyclones.

Ella watched in slow-motion horror as the dogs dodged Libby and leapt onto the stage, heading straight for her and a barking Chewy.

Stumbling backwards through the door in the flat, still holding the pumpkin, there was a thud as something hit the canvas, then claws ripped a hole through the material.

She heard more yells and screams from the other side, two

more almighty crashes, then the entire flat tipped towards her. Falling to the floor, Ella crouched over the pumpkin, her arms over her head, and braced for impact.

It didn't come. Only the feeling of something light bouncing off her back.

Still huddled in a ball, her eyes tightly closed, her heart trying to exit through her ribs, all Ella could hear were people shouting and screaming, the frantic barking of dogs, and Leo's voice.

'Dad! Mammy! Steve!' he roared. 'Get them out of here!'

Ella turned her head and opened her eyes. The flat was lying in pieces around her, but miraculously, it had fallen so the light canvas door was over where she was huddled. It had hit her, then bounced open again.

The muscles in Leo's arms were straining as he held Caligula and Borgia's collars. Wrestling them off the stage, his father took one dog, his mammy the other, and they headed out of the ballroom. Steve dragged Chewy through another door.

Libby rushed to Ella's side. 'Are you alright?'

'C-can you take the m-mice?' she stammered.

'Of course.' Taking the pumpkin from her, Libby rushed out of the third door to the ballroom as Leo came forward.

His expression was tortured, his hands running over her. 'Are you hurt? Talk to me.'

Ella shook with adrenaline and relief. 'I-I'm okay. I'm okay.'

Leo let out a noise that was half laugh and half sob, then clasped her to him. 'Jesus, Ella. I was so worried. I'm so sorry. I'll have him put down.'

She pulled away. 'You can't! It's not the dog's fault!'

He skewered her with a look. 'I was talking about my father.'

'Oh.'

There was a brief pause as they stared at each other. In the stillness, primal fear turned into primal need. Cheating death had made every cell in her body want to affirm life. And there was only one way she could think of to do this.

They reached for each other at the same time, Leo's lips crashing into hers with an urgency that matched her own, his tongue drinking her in like a parched man finding an oasis. Pleasure flooded her veins as she clung to him, pulling him closer as if she could merge her body with his, tugging the hem of his shirt from his trousers so she could feel his skin. Her desire for him was desperate. Painful. As if she could only feel safe and whole again with him buried inside her.

Pushing him away, she tore the Cinderella dress off, then reached for the top of his trousers.

'Ella.' Leo was panting, his hands bunched into fists on his thighs.

'Yes?'

His gaze was incendiary. 'Upstairs. Now.'

She nodded, and he helped her to her feet and off the stage. Holding hands, they ran from the ballroom, through the ground floor, then up the stairs.

Leo led her into her bedroom, then pulled off his trainers and removed a sock, hanging it on the outside door handle.

'What's that for?' she asked breathlessly.

'Everyone in this house knows not to disturb anyone with a sock on the handle. But to make doubly sure.' He dragged a chest of drawers against the door, then faced her. 'Where were we?'

'Taking all our clothes off.'

He swayed a little, his eyes blank, then slapped his cheek. 'Yep. Just checking I haven't died and gone to heaven.'

Undoing the top three buttons of her shirt, Ella pulled it off, then took off her bra.

Leo's jaw hung slack as he stared at her breasts.

Tugging off her shoes and socks, Ella shimmied out of her jeans.

He still didn't move.

'Leo!'

'This is actually happening,' he said, his voice faint.

'Well, it *would* be happening,' she replied as she stepped out of her pants. 'If you got with the programme.' Filled with a sexual confidence she never knew she had, she sauntered over to him, bringing her lips a hair's breadth away from his. 'Do you need assistance?'

Suddenly, her feet left the ground as Leo lifted her into his arms. Locking her legs behind his back, Ella kissed him with her heart and soul. Jokes, ideas, thoughts about how this might play out sank to the bottom of her mind, lost under the swelling ocean of her arousal and the frenzied need to have him fill her.

Her back hit the softness of the bed, her front covered by the hardness of his body. His lips were hot and firm, his tongue stroking hers with liquid fire that inundated her, tingling her fingers, sensitising her breasts, pooling in her core, and making her toes curl. One of his hands ran through her hair, the other rubbed her aching nipple until she cried out. His kiss deepened, became more demanding, as if feeding off her pleasure. Shifting to one side, his hand covered her pussy, his middle finger easing inside.

Ella tore her mouth from his as her hips bucked to meet his touch. 'Oh god, yes!'

Another finger joined the first, thrusting as his thumb circled her clit with agonising precision. She couldn't keep track of the sensations or the speed of her orgasm as it came hurtling towards her. It was too much too soon. She wasn't prepared. She couldn't survive.

'Leo! Leo!' She wanted him to slow down, even as her pelvis rocked to meet his thrusts.

Then his head dipped to her breast, and he sucked her nipple hard into his mouth.

The climax hit with the power of a freight train, slamming the breath from her body and shuddering through her like an electric shock. Her vision was lost to blinding light that fizzed and popped behind her eyes, then ricocheted through every cell.

Leo's fingers kept pumping, his thumb circling, his tongue roughing her nipple, until her breath returned with a tortured cry, the pleasure continuing to turn her inside out.

But even as her head swam with stars and her limbs refused to work properly, Ella felt the emptiness within, the urgent need that had yet to be satiated. Lurching to sit, she wrenched at the buttons on Leo's trousers to undo them as he dragged his shirt off. Then he shucked off the rest of his clothes and covered her naked body with his.

This was it. The moment she'd fantasised about for so long. The wish she never believed could come true. She was skin-to-skin with Leo, his body about to join with hers, their intimacy changing from that of best friends to lovers.

Angling her hips, she felt the hardness of his cock against her entrance and pushed up onto him an inch, gasping at the sweet stretch.

His head lifted, his expression dark and desperate. 'You okay?' he asked, his voice strained.

She nodded, utterly overwhelmed with the enormity of her love for him.

'I,' he began. 'Ella, I—'

Was he going to stop? Did he doubt how much she wanted this? She held him tighter. *I love you. I love you.* 'I—' She swallowed. 'Please don't stop.'

As his eyes held hers, everything else disappeared. Nothing else existed or mattered except the two of them together and the slow slide of his cock as it eased inside her. She held his gaze as she breathed through the tightness, feeling her inner muscles relax and stretch to accommodate his size.

She couldn't speak, her throat too constricted with emotion. He pressed further in, the tendons in his neck taut, then let out a short, ragged cry as he filled her completely.

I love you, I love you, I love you.

Leo was as deep in her body as he was in her soul. Possessing her, shaping her, binding her to him. No matter what might happen in the future, Ella knew in this lifetime she would never, *could* never stop loving every part of him with every part of her.

Their bodies began to move together as if obeying a will that went beyond conscious thought. A sensuous, sinuous undulating of their hips that sent pleasure radiating from Ella's core to the edges of her skin and beyond.

She locked her gaze with Leo's. Nothing had ever felt so raw. So real. So all-encompassing as this before. There was no comparison. He was her everything.

Ella breathed with him, her hips following the roll of his, moving with the swells of sensation as the storm built. His cock nudged deeper and a bolt of pleasure struck her pussy, pushing out a cry. He did it again. Then again. Driving the waves higher and splitting open the sky with lightning.

She was gasping to stay afloat, to keep her eyes open. The energy was pouring off him. Crackling from his skin into hers, whipping the tendrils of her climax together, whirling it tighter and tighter until it squeezed a last breath from her lungs.

The last thing she saw before her orgasm broke was his face. The tender anguish. The exaltation. The joy.

Then the release crashed through her with more power

than she could contain. It barrelled through with unrelenting force, breaking her apart from the inside out. The sensations were full and deep, sparkling and sharp. They had the depth of the ocean, the energy of the sun, and the strength of the earth to move mountains. Wave upon wave of intense feeling, pushing on and on.

Leo's hips snapped faster and her own pleasure swelled again as she felt him reaching the point of no return. She clutched him to her as his breathing disintegrated, his cock pounding deep inside her. Then he cried her name, his voice hoarse, his body jerking with his own release.

She held him as he shook above her, this strong and powerful man seemingly as wrecked as she was by what had just happened. As his breathing quietened, Leo nuzzled her neck, pressing kisses to her skin and whispering her name.

Swallowing the tears of emotion that filled her throat, Ella locked her arms tightly around him, never wanting to let go. Her world had been altered irrevocably, but questions immediately rose from the well of her self-doubt to prick the bubble of her happiness. How long would Leo be happy with this new state of affairs? And if he changed his mind, how could she live going back to being just friends?

❧ 19 ❧

Striding through Foxbrooke the next Saturday on the way to her stepmother's house, Ella had a spring in her step. The sleety rain didn't bother her, she wasn't affected by lack of sleep over the past week, and the frantic rush to get everything done at school before the holidays wasn't stressing her at all.

All because of Leo.

Who knew it was possible to feel *this* happy? Her heart was buoyant, floating on a sea of contentment. She'd never smiled so much. Laughed so much. And as for the orgasms? They were made from rainbows and shooting stars, and delivered multiple times a day by a blond-haired god with devilish sex skills.

She knew it couldn't last. Life had shown her that. Just when you thought you had everything set in place, the tablecloth would be pulled away, scattering and breaking everything. Sooner or later, reality would come knocking for Leo. Reminding him there were better options than a broken best friend with a family of entitled scroungers and bargain-basement gangsters.

But for now, Ella forced these doubts to the bottom of her mind. She would ride the Leo wave through Christmas, holding on for dear life until it broke, making sure she bottled every drop of happiness to be savoured when everything changed.

WHEN MICHELLE FINALLY OPENED HER FRONT DOOR, ELLA had a smile ready. 'How are you feeling?'

'Like you give a shit,' her stepmother scowled. 'Abandoning me last weekend and letting that pikey into my house.'

Don't rise. Just don't. 'I'm sorry, but I had other commitments I couldn't cancel. Dervla said you had a nice chat.'

Huffing, Michelle limped back into the house, and Ella followed her into the living room.

'I need you to put something up,' Michelle said, collapsing into an armchair with a sigh and pointing at a package on the floor with her foot.

'What is it?'

'It's for your dad. Open it.'

Ella did, discovering a polyester banner, bigger than a beach towel, decorated with the words, 'Welcome home! We missed you so much!' and pictures of balloons. Her heart beat faster. 'Do you have a date for his release?'

'Yeah. Next Friday. So you'll need to be back here in the morning to clean instead of Saturday.'

'I can't. I'm at work.'

'Then throw a sickie! Fuck's sake, Ella, put your family first for once.'

Angry tears rose in the back of her throat. 'What do you think I'm doing right now?' she asked, her voice tight with frustration. 'It's the last day of term next Friday. With prize-giving and parties for each class. I can't miss it.'

Michelle threw her hands in the air. 'Well, you can't come in the afternoon as he'll be back by then and wants a bit of quiet time with his family.'

Which clearly doesn't include me. Ella bit the inside of her cheek. Her mother had never wanted her, and her father and stepmother even less. Why on earth was she here? Why did she keep slaving for no appreciation or kindness when Michelle's daughters could have stepped up at any time?

'Look.' Michelle's tone softened, as if realising she'd gone too far. 'You're welcome to join us next Saturday night for pizza. You'd like that, wouldn't you?'

'I can't,' Ella replied dully. 'It's the Christmas quiz.'

'So?'

'We've been preparing for months. It's—'

'And? Your dad's been locked up for fucking years!'

'Can I come in the afternoon instead?'

'No. We're going out.'

Ella briefly closed her eyes, all the euphoria from the last few days draining away faster than water through a sieve.

'Well?'

Calmness settled on Ella like falling snow. It didn't matter if Leo and his family asked her to leave the manor the moment she returned there later, she would never seek refuge here. It was better to be totally alone in the world than treated like this.

She opened her eyes. 'Why am I here, Michelle?'

Her stepmother's mouth opened, her lower lip wobbling as if unsure what words to form. 'What are you on about?' she eventually replied.

'Every week I clean and tidy your house, parcel up your packages and take them to the post office, do other odd jobs and spend what little money I have buying you things you could easily afford to pay for yourself. And in return, you treat me like scum. So, I'm asking again. Why am I here?'

Michelle's face was scarlet with rage as she pushed to stand. 'You owe me,' she snarled, spittle flying from her mouth. 'I wouldn't be like this if it wasn't for you!'

'That's not true.' Ella's voice was calm despite the storm that raged inside. 'You and Dad decided to stage the car crash, not me. You were the one behind the wheel and driving too fast. I was a child, begging you not to do it. The accident was *your* fault, not mine.'

'You ungrateful little bitch,' Michelle replied, her voice low and ominous. 'After everything I've done for you. Taking you in after your slag of a mum left. No wonder she fucked off if this is how you behave.'

'Dad's going to be back soon, and you have two adult daughters to help you. You don't need me.'

Michelle's stick whipped through the air. Deflecting the blow with her forearms before it hit her head, Ella staggered backwards, adrenaline rushing through her blood, screaming at her to flee.

'You think you're better than us,' Michelle spat. 'Like all the Foxbrookes. But you're not. You're not one of them and will never be. You weren't good enough for Oliver, and you'll never be good enough for them. You're pathetic. Running after that posh twat, Leo, hoping one day he'll shag you out of pity?'

Ice cold fear stabbed Ella's heart.

Michelle's eyes gleamed at her response, a scornful smile on her lips. 'So, he has? After fucking his way through the whole of Foxbrooke, he's finally reached the bottom of the barrel.'

Ella was shaking so hard she could hardly speak. 'I—I'm going to go now.'

'It won't last, even if he's stupid enough to think it might.'

She laughed, the noise cutting like a knife into Ella's skin. 'Can you imagine the wedding? Foxy on one side with his whore wives and bastard kids, and us on the other?'

Ella couldn't. It was like staring into hell.

'But it'll never come to that,' Michelle sneered. 'He'll see sense, just like Oliver and Zach did. Face it, Ella. No-one wants you.'

Ella's feet moved of their own accord, stumbling towards the front door as Michelle followed, screaming obscenities. Making it outside before another blow could fall, she ran down the path, onto the street and away, her stepmother's voice still ringing in her ears.

Only when she was almost back to the manor did her pace slow, tears tumbling from her as fast as her gasping breaths. She couldn't believe she'd finally walked away from Michelle. But there was no relief, only emptiness and the fear of what was to come.

Her phone pinged in her pocket and she pulled it out.

> Kyla-Marie: You selfish little bitch! How could you leave Mum like that?

> Kyla-Marie: Just you wait till Dad hears what you've done

Ella blocked her number, then continued towards the manor with leaden feet. Was her stepmother right about Leo? Would he tire of her as Oliver and Zach had done?

Shut up! Stop it! You know Leo. He's a lion with a heart of gold. Even if he didn't want to sleep with you anymore, he'd still be your friend.

Entering the large open space in front of the manor gates and Saint Saviour's church, Ella turned right towards the park. She couldn't face seeing anyone until she'd composed herself.

Her phone buzzed again. Was it Billie-Mai messaging to tell Ella how evil she was? Sighing, she took it from her pocket and gazed at the screen.

> Leo: How does Good King Wenceslas like his pizza?

Wiping her eyes, the corners of her mouth twitched.

> Ella: I don't know. How does Good King Wenceslas like his pizza?

> Leo: Deep pan, crisp and even...

She laughed out loud, a spark of happiness lighting the darkness in her chest and chasing the demons away.

> Ella: Lol. I know we were meant to be making Christmas wreaths later on, but are you free now? I can be in the arboretum in about ten minutes, but I don't have secateurs or a bag x

She watched the dots appearing, then disappearing. Finally, his message came through.

> Leo: Meet you at the Himalayan Cedar in a bit? XXX

> Ella: Yes xxx

RUBBING THE SLENDER, SCALE-LIKE LEAVES BETWEEN HER fingers and thumb, Ella brought them to her nose and breathed in deeply. The scent was grounding, anchoring her to the here and now. Surrounded by trees far older than herself in the quiet calmness of the estate arboretum, she felt connected and rooted. Both to who she was on the inside, and also to an utterly different world to the one she'd just left behind at her stepmother's.

Michelle had been wrong about a lot of things, but one image Ella couldn't erase from her mind was the inside of Saint Saviour's church if Leo and her ever got as far as marriage. The idea of his family on one side of the church and hers on the other made her stomach roll. It would be like trying to mix crude oil with spring water. The thought of her dad and stepmother swanning around the manor. Seeing what they could pinch without being caught made her want to vomit. And if her biological mother showed up, which flavour-of-the-month boyfriend would she have on her arm? Ella shook her head to try and dislodge the pictures in her mind, but they were stuck like burnt food to the bottom of a pan.

In the distance, striding along a sandy path through the trees, she spotted Leo, a bag over his shoulder. Lifting an arm, she gave him a wave.

He froze, then bolted left behind a tree.

A giggle bubbled out of her. They hadn't played their game of 'inept spies' for years.

The top half of Leo's face appeared around the side of the trunk, then he crept across the grass like a long-legged spider attempting to be stealthy, until he'd hidden behind another tree, closer to her.

The Himalayan cedar had long, languorous branches that reached to the ground. Pushing her way through them to the trunk, Ella climbed up a couple of branches to hide. Through the thick green foliage, she caught glimpses of Leo as he got closer, running from tree to tree.

Reaching the cedar, Leo pushed through the branches as if hacking his way through a dense jungle, then stood with his back to the trunk. 'What is a Christmas tree's least favourite month?' he stage-whispered.

'Sep-*timber*,' she cried, then jumped off her perch and stood in front of him, her heart pitter-pattering in her chest.

Leo's cheeks were ruddy from the exertion, but his gaze was steady and questioning as he took her hand. 'What happened?'

'Dad's coming out next Friday. Michelle wanted me to clean that morning and wouldn't accept that I couldn't because it was the last day of term.'

Ella could tell Leo was trying to remain impassive, but a muscle still twitched in his jaw.

'She said I could see him next Saturday night, but I said it was the Christmas quiz. I then asked why I kept helping her every week when she's so horrible to me, and Kyla-Marie or Billie-Mai could have done it.'

Leo's hand tightened around hers.

'I told her I wasn't going to do it anymore. And she...'

'Didn't take it very well?'

Ella shook her head.

'How do you feel now?' he asked quietly.

'Empty and sad. I thought I'd feel relieved, but I don't. And I'm worried how Dad will react when he finds out.'

'We'll cross that bridge when we come to it.' Leo drew her in for a hug. 'I'm so proud of you.'

Ella sank into the warmth of his embrace, wanting to disappear inside him and live there forever. Far away from her family; safe and untouchable.

'There's been a lot of chapters ending in your life over the last few weeks,' Leo continued. 'And it's been bloody awful for you.'

She nodded. And what was Leo now? A new chapter, or a short and steamy story with an ending only a few pages away?

Her heart was tired. She didn't have the strength to ask him what he thought of their relationship. That question could wait until the pantomime and Christmas were over. The new year would be a new start, whether Leo still wanted to be in her bed or not.

'It's going to be okay,' he murmured into her hair. 'I promise. And there are plenty of fun things to focus on. Reigning triumphant at the Christmas quiz for one.'

'I hope so.'

'We're unstoppable. The Beardy Boys don't stand a chance. And the night before, we'll be at *Aladdin*.'

She smiled against his chest. The Theatre Royal's pantomime was always brilliant and one of her and Leo's Christmas traditions. Because he worked at the theatre, he got two free tickets, and they were always in the best position, right in the middle of the stalls.

'I can't wait,' she said. 'It'll help take my mind off my dad.'

'Exactly. And next week's going to be so busy at work, you won't have time to think.'

ENTERING THE THEATRE ROYAL A WEEK LATER WITH HER hand in Leo's, excitement shivered up Ella's arm. In his place of work, he was acting like they were a couple. How right he'd been about time flying. With the countdown to the end of term, as well as preparing for the Christmas quiz, rehearsals for Cinderella and finishing the set painting, by the time she got to the end of each day, she'd barely been able to keep her eyes open. But then the moment Leo's lips touched hers, it had fired up reserves of energy she never knew she had. Nothing felt better than being in his arms, and the orgasms he gave her wiped every thought or worry from her brain.

'Hey Leo!' one of the ushers said with a smile as he scanned their tickets.

'Hi Mike,' he replied. 'You've met Ella before, haven't you?'

He nodded. 'Lovely to see you again. Enjoy the show!'

She murmured her thanks as they moved down the corridor towards the stalls.

Leo paused at the entrance to the bar. 'Why don't you grab our seats and I'll get us some drinks?'

Ella felt a twinge of inadequacy in her stomach. All she'd done was take from Leo and it didn't sit right with her. 'I'll get them.'

'My treat.' He moved forward to kiss her cheek. 'And anyway, I get a Leo discount.'

Before she could argue, he pressed the tickets into her hand and jogged down the steps into the bar.

Moving towards the stalls, another usher was waiting to guide people to their seats. He frowned slightly at Ella, then his face opened into a smile. 'Ella, right? I'm Jules. Here to see the panto with Leo?'

'Yes. Have you seen it yet?'

He shook his head. 'Not properly. I'll probably go in Jan when the tickets are cheaper.'

'But what about your free ones?'

'Free ones?'

'You know. Everyone who works here gets two free tickets for each new show.'

'No, they d—' He broke off, his expression revealing why he was suited for a job off-stage and not on it. 'I gave them away.' Sweat beaded on his brow at the obvious lie. 'To my granny.'

Ella's blood ran cold. How many hundreds, if not thousands of pounds had Leo spent on tickets for them both over the years?

'Hi Jules! How's it going?' Leo said behind her.

'Er...' Jules replied, before turning forty-five degrees to grab a ticket from an older gentleman. 'Sir, let me show you to your seat.'

Leo pulled a face as he watched him go. 'What was all that about?' He gave a shrug, then handed Ella a glass. 'Prosecco for the lady.'

'Thank you,' she replied automatically, then paused. 'Leo...'

'Hmm?'

'Are these tickets really free?'

His eyes darted from side to side, then finally settled on her. 'No. But I get a discount.'

'Why didn't you tell me? You must have spent a fortune!'

'I haven't. And I didn't want to tell you because I didn't want you to say no.'

'I could have paid something towards them!'

He sighed. 'I know you would have wanted to, but I also knew how little money you had to play with at the end of every month. You're so sweet and kind and generous, Ella. But I'm around you enough to know how short money is.'

She crossed her arms over her chest, defensive and ashamed, as if he could see into every sad facet of her life. 'What do you mean?'

He raised an eyebrow as if asking if she really wanted to go there.

She stared at him unblinking, even as hot, shameful tears welled behind her eyes. She'd grown up with nothing, and despite how hard she'd worked and all her best intentions, thanks to a low-paying job and the extortionate rent she'd been paying to Oliver's parents, not to mention the money she'd spent on Michelle, she was flat broke and had been for years. The fact made her feel like a total failure.

'What do you think makes me happier?' Leo asked. 'Receiving a present from you that you've made, or bought?

Money is a useful tool, but that's it. It doesn't measure you as a person.'

Ella was silent. It didn't matter that he was right, she was still mortified.

'Going to the theatre with you makes me so bloody happy it's almost painful,' he continued. 'There's no-one I'd rather be here with than you. I'm sorry I didn't tell you the truth. I just didn't want you to feel guilty. I wanted you to enjoy the experience as much as I did.'

'Anything else you want to tell me?' she asked with a tentative smile, trying to lighten the mood.

He hesitated, his cheeks colouring.

'Leo?'

'I'm saving it for Christmas.'

'We're at the panto. It doesn't get much more Christmassy than this.'

He grinned. 'Want to bet?'

She rolled her eyes.

'I'll tell you after the panto.'

'This one?'

'No, our one. Now come on, let's find our seats. It's about to start.'

As the curtain rose, Ella set her worries aside and threw herself into enjoying the show. By the time the interval came around, her throat was sore from laughing and yelling.

'I need the loo,' she said. 'The prosecco went straight through me.'

'I'll get the ice creams,' Leo replied.

Digging in her pocket, she handed him her bank card. '*I'll* get the ice creams,' she said firmly.

He took it and gave her a quick salute. 'One salted caramel ice cream coming up. Meet you back here?'

'Yep.'

Exiting through a door, Ella joined the queue for the toilets. When she'd finished, she wandered back along the low-ceilinged corridor towards the stalls, weaving around people stretching their legs and eating mini tubs of ice cream. Side-stepping a large man fanning his face with a programme, her feet and heart stopped dead at the sight of the person in front of her.

Oliver.

He was as familiar to her as her own reflection, but at the same time felt like a total stranger. Wearing a shirt she'd bought for him a couple of years ago, his hair was cut shorter than usual, and part of Ella's brain thought she should compliment him for the new style. But the rest of her was preoccupied with the stunning brunette in Oliver's arms. Long-limbed and grace-ful, she was wearing a green satin sheath dress, her hair cascading down her back in barrel curls. She was whispering something into Oliver's ear and he was smiling. One of his hands drifted down the small of her back to cup her bottom.

A hot flush whooshed through Ella's body, making her light-headed and nauseous. She had to get away, but her feet weren't moving.

As if sensing her presence, the woman lifted her head and frowned.

Oliver turned, his face blanching as he clocked Ella.

Time seemed to slow, giving her mind the opportunity to peruse every excruciating detail of the scene. The woman was extremely beautiful, a natural confidence radiating from her.

She looks a bit like me. But better.

The woman's eyes flicked down and up Ella's body, then she

gave a small, satisfied smile, as if coming to the same conclusion. Her left hand, which had been behind Oliver's neck, moved down to rest in the centre of his chest as if stating ownership. Ella's gaze slid to the woman's ring finger, adorned with a massive diamond.

She couldn't breathe. Stumbling sideways, she held onto the wall for support, gulping in air.

'Er...' Oliver began. 'Lucinda, this is Ella.'

The woman's eyes widened at the news, her mouth forming a perfect 'o' shape as she stared at her.

'Ella, this is my...'

'Fiancée,' Lucinda supplied.

The corridor was getting smaller. Tilting. The edges of Ella's vision darkened.

Then a strong arm was around her, holding her upright.

'Oliver.' Leo's voice was cold and clipped. 'What an unpleasant surprise.'

Ella sagged against him, her lower jaw quivering with the rush of air in and out as she breathed.

'Er, hi, Leo,' Oliver replied.

Lucinda extended her hand, a confident smile on her face. 'You must be the best friend. Lucinda Harrington, Oliver's fiancée.'

Leo didn't take it. 'Since when?' he asked, his voice deadly quiet.

Lucinda returned her hand to Oliver's chest, transferring her dazzling smile to him. 'October. He proposed at the top of a black run in Val d'Isère.' She gave a little laugh. 'Gave me quite the incentive to make it down the slope in one piece.'

Leo turned his attention to Oliver. 'You piece of shit,' he snarled.

'Hey, hey.' Oliver raised his hands in a pacifying gesture. 'Look, I didn't know how to tell her—'

'*Her?*' Leo interrupted. 'Her name is *Ella.*'

'Okay, okay.' Oliver glanced at Ella. 'Can I have a quick word?'

She shrank back into Leo's arms, shaking her head, her heart racing out of control.

'Anything you want to say to Ella, you say here and now,' Leo said. 'Make it quick, then you can both fuck off out of this theatre and never come back.'

'You can't—' Lucinda began.

'Yes, I can. I work here.'

Oliver turned to his fiancée. 'Luce, sweetie, this won't take long. I'll see you back in our seats. Okay?'

'Of course, darling.' She kissed him on the lips, then walked away.

Ella clutched her stomach as bile rose up into her throat. This couldn't get any worse.

Leo tucked her tightly into his side to keep her from falling and eyeballed Oliver. 'Well?'

He ran his hands through his hair. 'Look, Ella. I'm sorry, alright? I didn't know how to tell you, and time kept slipping away, and you kept asking when I was coming home, and—'

'Are you done?' Leo snapped.

Oliver's cheeks reddened. 'You need to pay my parents the money you owe them.'

'What?' she gasped.

'The rent for December. They're giving you another chance to pay before they start legal—'

Leo's fist flew through the air, connecting with Oliver's jaw and knocking him to the ground.

❦ 20 ❦

I gnoring Oliver sprawled on the floor, Leo turned to Ella. 'Are you okay?'

Her face was ashen. 'I'm so s-sorry,' she stammered.

The question cut through the adrenaline pulsing through his body. 'For what?'

'For Oliver. Did you hurt your h-hand?'

Leo wanted to laugh, but then Ella glanced in panic behind him and he braced for impact. Suddenly he was spun around and Oliver's fist was heading his way. Instinctively ducking to the side, the punch only grazed his jaw. However, as Oliver pitched forward, his fist ended its journey by smashing into Ella's shoulder, sending her crashing to the ground.

Despite the blood lust demanding he pummel Oliver to a pulp, Leo dropped to his knees in panic. 'Jesus, Ella! Are you alright?'

She nodded unsteadily, her gaze flicking to the commotion behind him. Leo turned to see Jules and Mike holding Oliver back, expressions of shocked horror on their faces.

'We'll call the police,' Jules said. 'Are you alright, Ella?'

'We saw him punch you,' Mike added.

'Let go!' Oliver shouted. 'Leo hit me first!'

The ushers gazed at Ella as if for confirmation.

'No,' she replied, her voice strong as she got to her feet with Leo. 'He didn't touch him. This man is my ex-boyfriend. Despite cheating on me for months, he's angry that I've moved on with Leo.'

'Yeah right,' Oliver spat. 'In his dreams.'

Putting her arms around Leo, Ella reached up and kissed his cheek. 'Leo is my boyfriend now.'

Oliver shook his head. 'As if.'

Another usher came running down the corridor towards them. 'What's going on? Oh, hey, Leo.'

'Tim, this man assaulted Ella,' Jules said. 'Can you ring the police?'

'This is bullshit!' Oliver yelled.

'Wait!' Ella cried. 'I won't press charges if Oliver promises he and his parents will leave me alone.'

Holding tightly to Ella, Leo stared daggers at Oliver, willing him to do the right thing, whilst also wishing he could punch him again, only harder this time.

Oliver gave Ella a terse nod.

Lucinda entered the corridor. 'What's going on?'

'Is she with you?' Jules asked Oliver, still holding onto his jacket.

'I'm his fiancée,' Lucinda replied icily.

'Let go of me,' Oliver snarled, struggling in their grip.

'Mike and I are going to escort you off the premises,' Jules said to him. 'Then we're going to make a written statement about the incident to support Ella if she changes her mind about pressing charges.'

'What?' Lucinda screeched.

'You're welcome to enjoy the second half of the show,' Jules said to her. 'Or leave with him.' With that, he and Mike frog-marched Oliver down the corridor towards the entrance.

Shooting a look of hatred towards Leo and Ella, Lucinda turned to Tim. 'I need to get our coats.' She disappeared back into the theatre, Tim following.

Leo gazed at Ella's pale face, his heart breaking at the sight of her eyes glistening with unshed tears. 'What do you want to do?'

'Go back to the manor, please,' she replied shakily.

'Okay. Let's get you home.'

ELLA WAS SILENT DURING THE DRIVE BACK TO FOXBROOKE, and Leo didn't know what to say. He'd always thought of himself as easygoing, but the hatred he felt towards Oliver felt like acid burning his insides. And god only knew what was going through Ella's mind right now. She'd loved Oliver for years. Those feelings couldn't be easily turned off, no matter how much of a shit he'd been to her.

Leo's hands gripped the steering wheel tighter as he thought of Lucinda. She couldn't hold a candle to Ella, but he also knew his best friend well enough to know she would have thought Lucinda was somehow better than she was. He repressed a sigh. It didn't matter what Lucinda looked like, her very existence would have made Ella feel inferior and question herself.

I love you. I love you. I love you, Ella. The words ran around his head, but he wouldn't let them out. Not until he knew they wouldn't make her run a mile. The last thing Ella needed was him declaring his love and expecting her to reciprocate when she was processing her break up with Oliver, her decision to walk away from Michelle, and the prospect of her dad getting out of jail.

Don't be selfish. Think about what Ella needs right now.

He would wait until the panto was finished before telling her how he felt. Or maybe until Christmas was over, or even the whole year was done and dusted. Could a part of her still be in love with Oliver? At least now she knew for certain there was no chance of them getting back together. *Christ.* Oliver had got engaged to someone else before even finishing his relationship with Ella. *What an arsehole.*

'How's your hand? Is it sore?' she asked quietly as he drove up the long drive towards the manor.

He flexed his fingers. 'Feels fine. How are you doing?'

She rubbed her shoulder. 'A bit stiff. I think I should get into an Epsom salt bath.'

He pulled the car to a stop. 'Good idea. You start it running and I'll get you a drink. Hot toddy? Hot chocolate?'

'Hot toddy sounds perfect, thank you.' She got out of the car and started for the front door, walking stiffly.

Leo rushed to her side. 'You *sure* you're okay?'

Her smile was more of a grimace. 'I'm fine. I promise.'

He wanted to take her hand but was too unsure of what she wanted or needed, so went ahead, opening the door for her.

'I'm so sorry, Leo,' she said as she entered the house.

'No, *I'm* sorry.' He ran his fingers into his hair, scoring the nails across his scalp to help alleviate his frustration. All he wanted was to take her into his arms and pour out his love. But this wasn't the time. 'Go on. I'll be up in a bit.'

She nodded and turned for the stairs.

Fifteen minutes later, Leo knocked on Ella's bathroom door. 'I made you a pot of it,' he called through. 'With Dad's honey and cider brandy. Shall I leave it outside?'

'Can you bring it in?'

He swallowed. Yes, of course he could. But that would necessitate seeing a naked Ella and trying not to react.

'Leo?'

Deep breath. This isn't hard. Although my cock's almost there, dammit!

Opening the door, he focused on the tray as he carried it in, placing it on a wide shelf behind the sink, then pouring the hot toddy into a porcelain cup.

'It's a Sèvres teacup so the toddy will cool down quickly,' he said as he passed it to her, his gaze fixed on the tiles around the bath. 'But the pot is heavy china so will keep the rest at temperature.'

'You should have given me one of the chipped mugs with "World's Best Dad" on the side,' she replied. 'Aren't these priceless antiques?'

He shrugged, now counting how many tiles were in each row whilst his peripheral vision strained to see her. 'I dunno. Probably not, or they would have been confiscated by Gram-Gram to prevent Estelle from selling them.'

'What?'

Eighteen, nineteen, twenty. 'Before Henry finally came home, Estelle had to keep flogging anything that wasn't nailed down to pay for the abject failure of Dad's "interesting" business ideas. She thinks we didn't notice, but we did.'

'Wow. Well, this cup looks the real deal.'

Twenty-one, twenty-two. 'Hmm.'

'Leo?'

'Yup?'

'Are you okay?'

Swivelling back to the teapot, he adjusted its position by a millimetre. 'Yep. Knuckles don't hurt at all, which is pretty disappointing, really. That's the first time I've ever hit anyone and I feel like I should at least have some bruising.'

'I wasn't thinking about that, although I'm glad you're not hurt. You just seem...'

'Hmm?' How he could adjust his thickening cock without her noticing?

'Nothing. It's nothing.'

Hearing the unhappiness in her voice, Leo turned, forcing his eyes to meet Ella's. 'What is it, Princess?'

The beginnings of a frown pinched her forehead, and she was chewing her lower lip anxiously. 'You don't have to be with me.'

What did she mean by that? Right now or in general? Leo dithered, not knowing how to respond.

Her gaze dropped from his as if resigned, then stopped abruptly when it reached the level of his crotch. 'Er... Leo?'

Excited to have finally been noticed, his cock jumped to full attention. 'Yes?' he replied, staring fixedly at the tiles.

'Is that a yule log in your trousers, or are you pleased to see me?'

He let out a frustrated huff. 'Every part of me is *always* pleased to see you. I'm just trying not to molest you after... after tonight's unexpectedly stressful occurrences.' *God.* He sounded exactly like his oldest brother, Henry.

'She's his headmaster's daughter,' Ella said softly. 'Lucinda. I recognised her surname.'

'So he's a suck-up, as well as a cheating bastard?'

'Seems that way. No wonder he got promoted to head of the history department.'

'Well, he's lost the biggest prize of all.'

She gave him a half shrug and a sad smile.

'What can I do to make you feel better?'

Her cheeks coloured. 'If you don't mind,' she began tentatively.

'Yes?'

'Would you please take me to bed and help me forget?'

'Yes,' he replied instinctively, grabbing a fluffy white towel and holding it up for her. It didn't matter if Ella was on the rebound from Oliver and just needed comfort. She'd asked him to help her, and as the dedicated best friend that he was, it was up to him to assist.

How selfless we are! his cock crowed, and he resisted the urge to roll his eyes.

Ella pulled out the bath plug and stood, water dripping from her body. Leo stared, following the rivulets as they dropped from the pink tips of her nipples to run down her stomach into the wet curls between her legs.

Taking the towel from him, she rubbed it over her breasts, hiding them from view. He made a noise of distress, a pitiful whimper that tugged a smile from her lips.

'I need to get dry,' she murmured.

He shook his head, plucking the towel from her hands and throwing it to the floor.

'Le—oh!' she cried as his mouth descended.

She tasted sweet and fresh, like rain on spring flowers. Her skin was warm and wet, puckering with goosebumps as he licked her. He chased every droplet, drinking her in as he drew smaller and smaller circles on her breast until he captured her nipple and sucked. Ella gasped, her fingers running into his hair, sending prickles across his scalp that made him shiver.

Standing in the bath, she was now the perfect height for him to lavish his love on her breasts. Cupping their heavy weight in his hands, the pad of his thumb rubbed one hardened bud, his tongue the other, until her breath was uneven and her hips began to rock.

He raised his head. 'How many presents in total were given in the song "The Twelve Days of Christmas"?'

Ella blinked, her eyes drowsy with desire. 'Huh?'

His fingers and thumbs rolled her nipples, watching her inhale sharply and the colour in her cheeks heighten. 'I'm checking to see if I've made you forget yet,' he murmured. 'How many presents in total were given in the song "The Twelve Days of Christmas"?'

She let out a shaky laugh. 'Three-hundred and sixty-four.'

'Oh dear. I'm obviously not trying hard enough.' He brought his mouth back to her breast, redoubling his efforts, and was rewarded with a low moan.

Keeping his hands where they were, he lowered slowly to his knees, his tongue tracing a path down her abdomen, swirling into her navel, then sinking into the cleft between her thighs.

'Oh!' Her body twitched as he found the nub of her pleasure.

Dropping his hands, he nudged her legs further apart, opened her pussy wider, then licked up her length. She gasped again, but he didn't give her a chance to catch her breath, flicking the tip of his tongue over her clit, then gently sucking it into his mouth.

She clutched handfuls of his hair as he alternated between licks and sucks, feeling her trembling, her muscles tensing. His cock was straining painfully to be free, but he ignored it, driving her on until he felt her nearing the peak of her climax.

He raised his head. 'What year was the first Christmas card sent?'

'W-what?'

His heart leapt at the sight of her dazed expression.

'Touch your breasts.'

The tangent made her look even more confused.

'Touch your breasts,' he repeated.

She did, her eyelids fluttering as she tweaked her nipples, her lower lip trembling.

'What year was the first Christmas card sent?'

'Um—eighteen forty—ah!'

His tongue dived back to her pussy, cutting off her answer as he let himself drown in the taste of her, the sweetness of her bathwater mingling with the heady, musky slickness of her arousal. Her breath was getting shorter, each inhale a gasp.

I love you. I love you. I love you Ella. He wrote the words his heart was crying onto her clit until she stiffened with a cut-off scream, her body shaking.

I love you. I love you. I love you Ella.

Her orgasm kept coming, wave after wave as he poured out his love. Then she fell forward, her hands dropping to his head.

He stood, lifting her over his shoulder, then walked her out of the bathroom and laid her carefully on the bed.

'Eighteen forty-three,' she murmured. 'First Christmas card.'

Grinning, he arranged her limbs, so she was spread-eagled and open for him. He lowered his head and blew a cool stream of air over her pussy. 'When was tinsel invented?'

She shivered, but still managed to reply. 'Sixteen ten.'

He eased two fingers inside her, curling the tips as if beckoning her forward. 'Year the Queen's speech was first televised?'

'Um... I can't think when you—oh!'

Lowering his head, he vibrated his tongue over her clit, rubbing inside her tight channel at the same time.

'Oh, my god! I can't—Leo!'

He didn't pause to ask the question again, thrumming his tongue against her as she shook beneath him, her hands flying to his head to grip handfuls of his hair.

He felt the strength of her orgasm as it hit, ripping through her body like an earthquake. Her inner muscles clamped around his fingers and he rubbed harder against her g-spot.

She convulsed, a guttural cry tearing from her throat as hot liquid gushed over his tongue.

Yes.

He kept stroking, licking, easing her down from the high until she softened and went still.

'Leo?'

'Yes, Princess?' he replied, kissing her inner thigh.

'Did I...?'

He smiled. 'Yes, you did.'

'I've never done that before.'

Good. Raising to his knees, he gazed at her lying beneath him. Flushed, tousled, and so beautiful it hurt.

A satiated smile spread across her lips. 'I can't remember the last question you asked.'

'Shall I ask you some easier questions?'

'Go on then. See how much cognitive function is left.'

'Who's the fexiest Foxbrooke?'

'You are.' She reached for the button of his trousers and flicked it open.

His breath hitched. 'Most fandsome?'

'You, again.' She tugged the zipper down and reached inside his boxers to free his cock.

His muscles tensed at her touch. 'Most well-endowed?'

She stopped and raised an eyebrow. 'How on earth would I know that?'

'Sorry, my brain's not working properly anymore.'

Her hand slowly pumped his length, sending sharp darts of pleasure across his skin.

'But just so you know,' he continued, lights flashing in his vision. 'The answer's me.'

'Hmm...' Her eyes held his as her mouth sank onto his cock.

'Ahh—oh fuck, oh fuck, oh god, oh—'

She released him with a pop. 'When does the Russian Orthodox Church celebrate Christmas?'

'I don't care.'

Ella giggled. 'But it's the quiz tomorrow night.'

'I still don't care.'

She swirled the tip of her tongue around the head of his cock. 'You need to try a little harder, Leo.'

He let out a strangled cry as she licked his slit. 'Any harder and I'll explode.'

Her eyes still locked on his, she sucked him deep, humming her approval.

Lust shot through him like an electric shock, fizzing through his blood and drawing up his balls. Jerking away from her, his hands tightening into fists on his thighs, he sucked air in and out through his clenched jaw.

Her fingers reached for the buttons on his shirt, fumbling to undo them.

She wasn't being quick enough.

Grabbing either side of his shirt, he wrenched them apart, buttons pinging to the floor.

Ella giggled, but when he shucked the remains of his shirt to the bed and pinned her with a stare, her lips parted with a gasp and her pupils dilated into deep pools of longing.

Leo fisted his cock, drawing his hand slowly up and down the rock-hard length as if it might settle his raging desire. 'One last question,' he gritted out.

She nodded, breathlessly.

'Who do you want?'

'You,' she replied immediately, then dropped back to the bed, her legs spread and her fingers parting the lips of her sex wide for him. 'You, Leo.'

His head spun, but his gaze didn't leave hers. Settling

between her thighs, he notched the fat head of his cock at her entrance, then pushed inside with one steady thrust.

The sight of her face, the ghosting of her breath across his skin as she gasped, nearly sent him over the edge. He'd never felt this desire with anyone else before. This depth of need. Ella was the oxygen keeping him alive. The life-force keeping his heart beating.

Fighting to stay detached, he braced himself, withdrawing an inch, then plunging inside her again.

'Yes,' she murmured.

He did it again. And again. Circling his hips as he thrust, massaging her clit over and over.

Her pelvis rocked up to meet his, a flush appearing in the middle of her chest, her nipples rock hard.

'Leo, Leo, Leo,' she whispered with each breath.

Every hair on his body lifted, tingling with pleasure as pride and power rushed across his skin. Every time she exhaled his name, he knew Oliver was being erased from her mind. And now it was Leo's job to replace him in her heart.

Following her cues, he snapped his hips faster, every muscle inside him screaming for release.

Her breasts were mottled with colour that rose into her neck. 'Leo, I...'

'Touch yourself,' he ground out, his control cracking. 'Now.'

Her fingers fluttered to her nipples, and she tugged.

Every atom inside him split as Ella shuddered beneath him, her head thrown back, her back arching off the bed.

Surrendering with a roar, Leo dived into a boiling sea of pleasure, his cock pounding inside her, his balls emptying with sharp spasms of sensation that shot through his body and stole his breath. He drank in the sight of Ella till his vision went blank. Every sense now centred on the exquisite torture of her pussy clamping around his shaft, the release and relief beyond all comprehension.

Gathering her into his arms, he collapsed, his face buried in the crook of her neck, his heart beating hard and wild.

He felt her hands on his back. Stroking, soothing as he shuddered above her. He wanted to tell her how he felt. To yell it from the rooftops. But he clamped his lips shut. *Give her space. Wait till after Christmas.*

And until that time, he would make sure she was so satisfied, the name 'Oliver' never again crossed her mind.

21

'**A**re you sure we haven't gone a bit too far this year?' Ella asked Leo as they stood outside the Horse and Hounds pub on Foxbrooke high street the next night.

He grinned. 'Go big or go home?'

'But what if we don't win?'

'Then we accept our defeat graciously.'

'Really? We do?'

'By screaming we were robbed and immediately demanding a rematch.'

A smile appeared. 'Sounds like a plan.'

'Yep. Knew you'd be on board. Now we just need to psych them out. You ready?'

Ella ran on the spot, punching the air like a boxer preparing to fight. 'Yep. Bring it.'

'That's the Christmas spirit. Right, let me message Willow.'

A minute later, his sister appeared, snorting with laughter at what they were wearing. 'Oh, my god! Do you know if you can even fit through the door?'

Leo exchanged a panicked look with Ella.

'Hang on.' Willow unlatched the second door of the pub. 'Now give me thirty seconds to get the music going.'

She dashed back inside and Leo took Ella's hand. 'We're the Noel it Alls. We've got this. Okay?'

She nodded. 'Destroy all opposition. In a festive way, of course.'

The sound of 'Eye of the Tiger' by Survivor started playing and someone cheered.

'Here we go!' Leo yelled, then extended his arm. 'Ladies first.'

Ella jogged up the steps to the doors, which were being held open by Willow and Connor, and Leo followed her into the pub to a chorus of whoops and whistles.

This year, Ella had constructed giant boxes to fit around them, which they'd covered in wrapping paper, bows and ribbons. They were walking presents nearly a metre wide, and not ideally suited to a pub that was hundreds of years old and filled with people on a Saturday night.

But Leo didn't care. And seemingly, neither did Ella. No matter what she'd been through over the past few weeks, here she was, strutting through the pub like a prize-fighter crossed with a supermodel. Leo followed her lead, posing and singing along to the lyrics as they made their way through the main body of the pub to the back, where the quiz was taking place.

People in groups sat around small tables, dressed in Christmas hats and jumpers. Each group cheered and clapped as Leo and Ella arrived. All except for the Beardy Boys, who were rolling their eyes and shaking their heads.

Scott was wearing a t-shirt with a picture of a sexy Santa on it and the words 'Women love a man with a beard'. Ryan's t-shirt read 'It's the most wonderful time for a beer', Tommy's had the words 'Dashin', Dancin', and Prancin' till I get Blitzen' on it, and Finn's t-shirt was plain black with the words 'This is my Christmas t-shirt' in white block capitals.

Leo went straight to Finn's side, twerking in his face until Finn pushed the giant box away, sending Leo stumbling forwards.

Ella caught him, then pointed at Finn. 'Naughty step! I mean, you're on the naughty list! You're getting coal in your stocking this year.'

'He needs it to warm up his grinchy-cold heart,' Leo added, noting with glee that Scott, Ryan and Tommy were trying not to laugh.

The quizmaster, Derek, was dressed in an eye-wateringly garish jumper with lights embedded in the design that flashed every time he moved. He raised his hands. 'Alright, alright. You haven't won yet.'

'Then why did I slip you twenty quid yesterday?' Leo asked indignantly.

Derek grinned. 'Finn gave me forty.'

'What?' Leo turned to Ella. 'Is there anything left in the bribe kitty?'

She pulled a face. 'Your sexual favours?'

Leo sighed loudly. 'Okay...' He made a move to climb out of his present box.

Derek held up both his hands. 'No, thank you. Not now. Not ever.'

'I wasn't offering them to you,' Leo replied, glancing towards the bar where Derek's wife was pulling pints. 'Janet! Fancy a ride on the Foxbrooke express in return for us winning the quiz tonight?'

Janet didn't look their way but extended a middle finger in Leo's direction, then made the gesture for 'wanker'.

'Rude!' Leo cried, as everyone cracked up.

'Sit down, you muppet,' Derek said. 'Now, are we all here?'

Leo took a seat opposite Ella, and they grinned at each other. Each year, they made sure they were the last to arrive so as to make the biggest entrance.

'We're waiting for one more,' Finn said. 'He's just coming.'

The news triggered a memory Leo had successfully forgotten about. *Zach*. Of course, he had to make an even grander entrance than they'd just done. The light dimmed a little in Ella's eyes. What was she thinking?

Elyse, Ryan's girlfriend, was coming through the pub, clearing a path for Zach in his wheelchair, a pair of crutches across his lap. He was being pushed by—

'Oh my god,' Ella whispered. 'It's Kurt.'

The last time either of them had seen him, Zach's younger brother had been a scrawny kid who thought he was a gangster just because he was selling drugs for Ella's dad. After recovering from being stabbed and nearly dying, he'd left Foxbrooke behind to travel, eventually settling in Australia. Now he looked like a surf god. He'd grown a few inches, filled out with muscle, and his shoulder-length blond hair was sun-bleached and tousled.

Leo glanced between Kurt's face and Ella's, seeing her anxiety, then the moment Kurt clocked her. He stood, his body primed to protect her if Kurt decided to kick off.

'Love the costumes!' Zach said, his attention all on Ella. 'What do you think of my t-shirt?' Flexing his arm muscles as if posing in a body-building competition, he pulled the bottom hem down so she could read the text, 'Aren't we forgetting the true meaning of Christmas? You know, the birth of Santa'.

Ella smiled. 'Love it. And I see you're going full method for your team.'

Zach wiggled his eyebrows and gave her a smouldering look as he passed a hand over his growing beard. 'Do you like it?'

'Hi Kurt,' Leo said before Ella could reply. 'How are you doing?'

'Good.' His gaze flicked warily to Ella. 'How are *you* doing?'

'Oh, you know, same old, same old,' she replied breezily. 'Trying to keep my head down and avoid drama.'

The corners of his mouth twitched as he gazed at the enormous glittery box around her.

Ella looked at it as if seeing it for the first time. 'Oh, this old thing? First thing I grabbed from the wardrobe.'

'And Zach tells me you're playing Cinderella in the panto.'

She frowned. 'Yes. I was in the wrong place at the wrong time and don't know how to say n—n—n—' She broke off. 'See? It gets me in all sorts of trouble.'

Kurt laughed freely, his perfect white teeth contrasting with his deeply tanned skin. 'Can I buy you a drink?' His gaze showed an interest that went beyond catching up as friends.

Leo stiffened, opening his mouth to speak, but Zach was quicker.

'Back off, little brother. I'm the one who owes Ella a drink.' He smiled at her. 'What do you fancy?'

Me! She fancies me now, you dipshit! But even as the thoughts shouted in Leo's mind, he glanced anxiously at Ella to see her response.

Her cheeks were burning. 'Er...'

'Come along, Mr Soap Superstar and Mr Bondi Beach,' Derek said into the microphone. 'Pick your team and let's get on with it.'

'I'll find you in the break,' Zach said to Ella, then swivelled his chair to the right to join the Beardy Boys.

Kurt stayed next to Leo and Ella. 'Is it just the two of you on your team?' he asked. 'Fancy a third?'

No! Fuck off! Biting his tongue, Leo turned to Ella. She was the one who had the most history with the Price family. The decision had to be hers.

'Yeah, sure,' she replied. 'Take a seat.'

Kurt went to grab a chair and Ella whispered, 'Sorry' to Leo under her breath.

He took her hand and squeezed. 'It's fine. It's not going to make a difference. We're still going to win.'

'Okay then, ladies and gents, are we finally ready to get this sleigh in the air?' Derek asked.

Everyone cheered.

'Now, you know the rules,' he continued. 'Mobiles on aeroplane mode or turned off. If for any reason you need to be contactable, your phone can sit in this box next to me. Write your answers on the piece of paper in front of you, and I will mark them during the break. Once I ring my bell, signalling the start of the quiz, you may not leave your seat. No "going to the toilet", or "nipping out for a cheeky fag". If any member of the audience attempts to communicate in any way with you, be it through the medium of sign language, bodily function, or interpretive dance, your team will be disqualified. Do I make myself clear?'

'Yes, Derek!' the entire pub yelled.

'Marvellous. In the unlikely event of a tie, each team will nominate one member to compete in a two-minute rapid-fire round. My word is law and only one person in this pub is ever allowed to challenge my decisions. Remember who that is?'

'Your wife!' everyone chorused.

'Correct! One point to all of you. Now, you've got precisely ninety seconds to make sure your glasses are full, your bladders are empty, and your phones are off. Starting... now!'

As if of one mind, Leo and Ella cracked their knuckles and rolled their shoulders.

'You look like you're taking this very seriously,' Kurt said.

'Nothing is more important than the Christmas quiz,' they both replied at the same time.

His eyes widened. 'Wow. I'm a little nervous now.'

'Glory or death,' Leo replied.

'Festively speaking,' Ella added.

Kurt grinned. 'Well, I'll try not to let you down.'

'Do you know much about Christmas?' Ella asked.

He shrugged. 'The usual?'

'That won't be enough,' Leo replied. 'But don't worry. Ella and I have been in training for the last three-hundred and sixty-three days, so we're going to nail it.'

'Yeah right,' Scott called over. 'You haven't got a chance against us.'

'Wanna bet?' Leo retorted. 'You're going to eat those words with a side order of twice-boiled sprouts.'

Ella pointed two fingers at her eyes, then Scott's. 'Yippee-ki-yay, motherfuckers.'

'Settle down, settle down,' Derek said. 'Honestly. You lot are enough to give me an ulcer.' He lifted a bell and rang it. 'Right! We're off!'

Leo leaned forward, his heart beating faster as Ella lifted the pen, her hand curved around the piece of paper so no-one could see what she was writing.

'Question number one. In the song "The Twelve Days of Christmas", how many—'

'Next!' Leo yelled, as Ella scribbled the answer.

Derek gave them a long-suffering look. 'New rule. If anyone from the Noel it Alls speaks another word, they will be immediately disqualified.'

'Ha!' Finn called over. 'Suck it, losers.'

'And the same rule applies to the Beardy Boys,' Derek continued.

Leo opened his mouth to crow, but Ella gave him a sharp dig in his ribs and he shut up.

'Question number two. What do children in Sweden leave out for Father Christmas?'

Leo looked over Ella's shoulder, nodding as she wrote the word 'coffee'.

'Question number three. 'In the film *Home Alone 2*, who does Kevin meet in the hotel lobby?'

Ella wrote the words 'Donald Trump', then gazed questioningly at Leo. He nodded.

As the questions kept coming, Leo relaxed slightly. They had this in the bag. However, when he glanced over at the Beardy Boys, his stomach knotted. They appeared equally unfazed by Derek's questions. And even worse than the worry of losing the Christmas quiz was the thought he might lose Ella to Zach. The handsome bastard seemed to be spending more time glancing her way than concentrating on his teammates, and his younger brother, sitting on the other side of her, seemed similarly smitten.

The caveman side of Leo wanted to yell at them all to fuck off, kiss Ella till her knees turned to jelly, then carry her out of the pub back to his bed. But he knew he couldn't. Was he the stop-gap? The rebound fling? The only way to forget Oliver? And would she fall back in love with Zach now he'd apologised? Or fall for his surf-dude younger brother?

'What are the six white boomers?' Derek asked, derailing Leo's train of thought. 'A Norwegian folk group famous for singing traditional Scandinavian Christmas songs, Kangaroos who pull Santa's sleigh in Australia, or a group of six elderly men in Florida who celebrate Christmas every day?'

Leo glanced at Ella, seeing his panic reflected back at him. He had no idea what the answer was.

Kurt leaned forward. 'It's the kangaroos', he whispered.

'Are you sure?' Ella whispered back. 'Kangaroos aren't white.'

'And it's traditionally nine reindeer,' Leo added. 'Why kangaroos? And why six?'

Kurt shrugged. 'I dunno. There's just this silly song about six white kangaroos pulling his sleigh when he visits Australia.'

'What do you want to do?' Ella asked Leo.

He pulled a face. 'Your call.'

She nodded, then wrote 'kangaroos'.

Despite her being right to trust Kurt, Leo had a sour taste in his mouth. How bad would it be if they won thanks to him? Visions of Kurt giving Ella a congratulatory kiss made his hands form into fists. This was meant to be the highlight of the year, but all he could think about was Ella choosing to be with someone other than him.

'In which country do people leave beer for Santa?' Clive asked.

'Australia,' Kurt whispered.

'It can't be,' Leo replied testily.

'Why not?'

'There can't be two questions in a row about Australia.'

'Why not?'

'Because... I don't know. There just can't.'

'I don't know the answer,' Ella fretted. 'What should I put? Australia sounds like a good guess.'

Leo nodded, irritation growing like a prickly cactus in his stomach as Ella wrote the word 'Australia'.

'Which country invented the culinary experience known as a White Christmas?' Derek asked.

'For fuck's sake,' Leo muttered.

'We don't know any of these questions,' Ella hissed. 'Could it be America? They invented the song.'

'Is it a drink? Like a White Russian?'

Kurt leaned forward. 'The answer's Australia.'

Leo resisted the urge to roll his eyes. 'Seriously?'

'A White Christmas is a snack made with Rice Krispies, desiccated coconut, and dried fruit.'

'How do you know that?'

'Because I've lived in Oz for the last eight years?'

The cactus in Leo's belly was now doing the cancan. Right now he'd take losing the quiz with Ella over winning it thanks to her latest admirer.

'Leo! What should I write?' Ella asked. 'Australia or America?'

'America,' he replied.

Kurt sat back in his chair, shaking his head.

'What year was the first Christmas card sent?' Derek asked.

Ella immediately scribbled the answer.

The tension in Leo's stomach eased as they correctly answered the remaining questions, and ten minutes later they were done.

Derek collected their answer sheets and sat at his table to mark them. 'Five-minute break, then I'll announce the winners,' he called out.

Zach wheeled over to their table. 'That was fun. Who knew there'd be so many questions about Australia?'

Leo ground his teeth.

'Ella, fancy that drink now?' he continued.

'Um...' She glanced at Leo. 'Do you want anything?'

Zach and Kurt to fuck off to Australia? He shook his head. 'I'm good. Do you think there's enough room at the bar for the two of you?'

Ella patted the enormous box around her. 'People will get out of the way. Zach's famous and I've got presence.'

Despite how annoyed he was, Leo snorted with laughter.

Zach and Kurt gave him an odd look.

'You know, presence as in, "I have a great presence",' Ella explained to them, 'and present with a t because I'm a walking gift.'

'Oh,' Zach said. 'I get it now. And you *are* a gift, Ella. Who wouldn't want to find *you* under their tree?'

Oh shut up, you arse!

Ella laughed nervously.

'I'll come with you to the bar as well,' Kurt said, seemingly keen to get back into the Ella-sphere. 'I can carry the drinks.'

'Okay,' she said in a determined way, as if about to tackle an unpleasant task. 'Let's go and prematurely celebrate our inevitable win.' She glanced through the crowds towards the bar, then froze, her face draining of all colour.

Leo followed her gaze, his heart juddering to a halt.

Ronnie Chamberlain had entered the pub.

22

Leo reached for Ella, his hand clasping tightly around hers as she moved closer to him.

Ronnie looked older, smaller, greyer. His face was lined and his expression grim as he surveyed the pub.

Moving in front of Ella, Leo blocked her from his view.

'What's going on?' Zach asked from his wheelchair.

'Ronnie,' Kurt replied, then stalked to where Derek was hunched over the quiz answer sheets and leaned down to talk to him.

Derek was on his feet in an instant, striding through the crowds to Ronnie's side.

'There's a restraining order against him,' Kurt said quietly. 'Well, several, actually. For me, Zach and our folks.'

Leo wanted to turn and take Ella into his arms, but he needed to know Ronnie was out of the building first. Derek was leading him towards the doors, Ronnie's gaze still sweeping over the crowds. Searching. Then his eyes locked on Leo's, before passing to fix on someone over his shoulder.

Leo turned. Ella had moved out from behind him and was

gazing at her father, her eyes liquid. Then she closed them and tears spilled down her cheeks. Leo glanced quickly back to the front of the pub.

Ronnie had gone.

'Ella, love, come here.' Zach took her other hand and pulled her towards him.

'Do you need a hug?' Kurt moved to embrace her but was foiled by the enormous box around her body.

Tugged in three different directions, Ella lost her balance and stumbled, falling onto Zach.

'Fuck!' Leo dashed to lift her up. She was white-faced and trembling, trying not to cry and failing completely.

Willow came to her side, pushing Leo and Kurt away. 'Shall we get you to the ladies?'

Ella nodded, and Willow led her away.

When the two women disappeared from view, Leo glared at the floor, not trusting himself to even look at Zach and Kurt without exploding. *Remember what they went through? This is difficult for them too.*

'Leo,' Zach began.

'What?' he snapped.

'You need to give her space. This must be hard for her.'

'You think?' Leo's voice dripped with sarcasm. 'Shame you didn't realise that nine years ago. What makes you suddenly the Ella expert?'

Zach sighed. 'Look, I know you're her friend—'

'*Best* friend.'

'But she needs space to be able to move on from her ex.'

'And that's what the two of you are doing right now, is it?'

Kurt took a step back, his palms raised. 'I'm going to get a drink. Want anything?'

'No!' Leo and Zach replied at the same time.

As his brother made a sharp exit, Zach ran a hand through

his hair. 'I know you were there for Ella when I spectacularly fucked up, but I know her in ways you don't.'

Really? I bet I've given her more orgasms in the last couple of weeks than you managed in your entire relationship.

Zach seemed to take Leo's silence as confirmation he was right.

'Look, mate,' Zach continued. 'I know.'

'Know what?'

'You had a crush on Ella when we were at school.'

'I didn't have a "crush" on her,' Leo spat, his voice low. 'I was in love with her.'

One of Zach's shoulders lifted in a half shrug. 'Whatever you thought it was, you were a good friend to me back then. Stepping aside and being my wingman.'

Clamping his jaw shut to stop a torrent of words flying out, Leo stayed silent. He couldn't tell Zach he was in love with Ella again now before finding the right time to tell *her*.

'You think you could do it again?' Zach asked. 'Put in a good word for me. I really want to get back together with her.'

Over my dead body. Taking a slow breath in and out in an attempt to settle the rage snarling in his belly, Leo made his voice calm. 'I'll do exactly what's needed to make Ella happy. Not what I think or hope will make her happy, but what she explicitly *tells* me will.'

Zach's face relaxed with relief. 'Thanks, mate. I appreciate it.'

Connor sauntered over, a drink in his hand. 'Is everything okay over here? People are taking bets as to who's going to win the fight you seem about to have. A celeb in a wheelchair with a broken leg, or a man dressed as a Christmas present.'

Zach laughed. 'We're all good.'

'Thank god for that,' Connor replied. 'To lose one Prince

Charming may be regarded as a misfortune. To lose both looks like carelessness.'

A bell rang and Leo turned to see Derek holding the answer sheets from each team. 'Are we ready, ladies and gents, for the big reveal?'

Zach wheeled himself back to the Beardy Boys' table and Leo looked in the direction of the toilets, his heart squeezing as he saw Ella coming back towards the table.

'You okay?' he asked as she sat. 'We don't have to stay if you don't want to.'

She gave him a watery smile, then squared her shoulders. 'I'm not missing our moment of triumph. You ready?'

He patted the outside of the box. 'Locked, loaded, and ready to go.'

Kurt came back to the table and Leo suppressed a sigh.

'You ready to celebrate the greatest achievement of your life so far?' Ella asked him, her confident tone telling him that the subject of her father turning up was not to be broached.

'Sure am,' Kurt replied. 'Beating my brother at anything is cause for celebration. Is there a prize?'

'Bragging rights and a feeling of smug and self-satisfied superiority.'

'And normally a box of chocolates Derek got from the garage because they were on offer,' Leo added.

'I can see why the stakes are so high. Do you eat them in front of everyone and refuse to share?'

Leo grinned. 'Of course. Although I usually throw the ones I don't like at Finn.'

Kurt glanced over at Finn's hulking form and slowly shook his head. 'You're a braver man than me.'

'Poking the bear is Leo's favourite game,' Ella said. 'Finn's only got one weak spot, and the Christmas quiz is it.'

'Right, you 'orrible lot,' Derek said into the microphone.

'Before I reveal who's won, I'm going to go through the answers.'

Leo and Ella shifted their chairs so they could glance between Derek's table and Finn's without turning their heads.

Each of the Beardy Boys, apart from Zach, adjusted their seats so they could see Derek and the Noel it Alls.

Leo caught Finn's eye and winked at him.

Finn scowled back.

'Losers,' Ella coughed into her hand.

Scott scratched his beard with his middle finger.

'Question one,' Derek said firmly. 'There are three-hundred and sixty-four presents in total given in the song "The Twelve Days of Christmas". Question two. In Sweden, children leave out coffee for Santa to help keep him awake. Question three...'

As Derek continued, Leo kept his eyes glued on the Beardy Boys, looking for any crack in their countenance. However, they either had poker faces worthy of a high-stakes game in Vegas, or they, like the Noel it Alls, had so far got every question correct.

'The six white boomers are kangaroos who pull Santa's sleigh when he visits Australia.'

Finn high-fived Zach.

Fuck.

'Keeping with the antipodean theme,' Derek continued, 'Australia is where people leave out beer for him.'

Finn high-fived Zach again.

Double fuck.

'And the country that invented the snack made from puffed rice, dried fruit, and coconut, is also Australia.'

Finn and Scott high-fived Zach and Leo's stomach plummeted.

'I'm sorry,' he muttered to Ella.

'It's okay,' she whispered. 'They can't have got every question right.'

But as the rest of the answers were read out, Finn's expression got happier and happier, turning him from a growling man-bear into someone old ladies no longer crossed the road to avoid.

'Okay! Here's the moment you've all been waiting for!' Derek cried. 'In third place, with seventy-eight points, is—' he rolled his eyes '—Actually, in First Place Because They are The Best at Everything.'

'What?' Leo, Ella and the Beardy Boys yelled.

Leo's oldest sister, Estelle, stood up at a table along with her boyfriend, James. 'Thanks, Derek. We'll take the chocolates now and be off.'

Derek shook his head. 'Nice try. Next time I'm vetting team names.'

The sigh of relief from Leo, Ella, and the Beardy Boys was audible.

Estelle snorted with laughter and high-fived James. 'That was so worth it.'

'In second place,' Derek said firmly, 'with eighty-one points is...'

Leo and Ella leaned forward.

'...Do They Know it's Quizzmas!'

Huh?

'Which means,' Derek continued, 'we have a tie for first place! Both the Noel it Alls and the Beardy Boys only got one answer wrong!'

Leo hung his head. If only he'd listened to Kurt, they would have won outright.

'So, for the first time in the history of this illustrious tournament, we're playing a two-minute rapid-fire round. Each team must nominate one person. They will stand on either side of me and I'll alternate asking them questions. Each player gets two seconds to answer. If they haven't done so within that time, then I'll move on and they forfeit the question. I'll have a stopwatch, and the lovely Janet will keep score. Okay then, can I have your team representative up here, please?'

Kurt sat back. 'Don't even think of looking at me.'

Ella nodded and gazed at Leo, her forehead creased with worry. 'Can you do it?'

'You sure you don't want to? You know more than I do.'

'My head's in bits. This is a mind game more than anything else. You can stay focused better than I can right now. Please.'

He took her hand and squeezed. 'Of course.'

Leo stood, his arms spread wide as he sauntered to Derek's side. 'The champion has arrived!'

'Don't speak too soon,' Finn growled, looming on the other side of Derek like he'd been woken up prematurely from hibernation by a class of preschoolers playing the recorder.

'Okay, gentlemen, shake hands.'

Leo reached forward as if he was about to take Finn's hand, then whipped his away at the last minute, putting his thumb on the end of his nose, wiggling his fingers, and sticking out his tongue.

Everyone laughed.

Finn's eyes narrowed. 'You're going down, Foxbrooke.'

Leo blew him a kiss.

Shaking his head slowly, as if lamenting having to lower himself to competing against Leo, Finn turned to look out across the packed pub, his arms folded across his massive chest.

'Janet, you ready, love?' Derek asked his wife, who was sitting at the table by his side.

'Yep. Good to go.'

Taking a coin from his pocket, he turned to Finn. 'Heads or tails.'

'Heads.'

Derek flicked the coin in the air, then followed it with his eyes to the floor. 'Heads it is. Finn will be asked the first question.'

Leo huffed, and Finn gave him a predatory smile.

Taking a sheet of paper from his back pocket and a stop-watch, Derek took a step backwards. 'Eyes forward, gentle-men,' he said. 'And silence everyone for this momentous event.'

Leo gazed at Ella. She nodded and gave him two thumbs up.

'In three, two, one... Finn, the song "Jingle Bells" was origi-nally intended for what other holiday?'

'Thanksgiving,' Finn replied without hesitation.

'Leo. Which British monarch delivered the first Christmas message?'

'George the fifth in nineteen thirty-two.'

'Finn. Who invented the Christmas wreath?'

'Johann Hinrich Wichern.'

'Leo. What plant is known as the "Christmas flower"?'

'Poinsettia.'

The questions and answers kept coming, neither man missing a beat. Leo knew that focus was everything, so he kept his eyes on Ella, not allowing anything to distract him.

'Finn. Which Christmas song finally got to number one, twenty-six years after its release?'

Finn hesitated and Leo heard a female voice say, 'Excuse me, coming through.'

Looking past Ella, he saw his youngest sister, Summer, pushing through the crowds to stand at the front.

When did she get back from Mexico?

Tanned and beautiful, she was wearing a shiny red

minidress and red platform heels, with a pair of pink, sparkly reindeer's antlers nestled in her white-blonde curls. She waved at Finn and Leo.

'Leo,' Derek continued. 'Which Christmas song—'

'I didn't get a chance to answer,' Finn interrupted. 'It's "All I want for Christmas is You".'

'Too slow,' Derek replied. 'Leo's question again. Which Christmas song plays at the end of the nineteen eighty-eight film, *Die Hard?*'

Leo glanced at a flustered Finn.'"Let it Snow! Let it Snow! Let it Snow!"'

'Finn. What colour are mistletoe berries?'

'Red,' he replied, staring at Summer.

'No!' Scott cried.

'Fuck! I mean white!'

'Too late! Leo. Which US state was the first to declare Christmas Day an official holiday?'

'Oklahoma.'

A bell rang. 'Time's up! And the winner, by a margin of fifteen points to thirteen, is Leo Foxbrooke, on behalf of the Noel it Alls!'

Ella leapt onto her chair and raised her arms in the air. 'We! Are! Christmas!' she roared, before tearing off the gift box around her to reveal a t-shirt with the words 'This gal just won the Christmas quiz' and an arrow pointing up at her face. Leo followed suit, his t-shirt reading 'This guy just won the Christmas quiz'.

They pulled confetti cannons from bags around their waist and let them off as Willow played 'We are the Champions' by Queen through her phone.

Shaking his head as he laughed, Derek handed Leo a box of Celebrations chocolates. 'Congratulations. Can I pay you not to enter next year?'

'Never!' Leo replied, passing the box to Ella.

She ripped the top off and started throwing the sweets into the cheering crowd.

Leo glanced over at the Beardy Boys, who were shaking their heads and rolling their eyes. Finn stared daggers at Leo and mouthed the words, '*Next year*', then drew a finger across his throat.

Dancing over to them, Leo turned his back to the crowd, revealing the word 'Losers' printed on the back of his t-shirt and an arrow pointing towards the Beardy Boys.

Summer came over and gave him a hug. 'You're such a meany!'

'When did you get back?'

'An hour ago. You missed me?'

'Yep. There's no-one messier than me to take the flak from Bridget.'

'Rude! I'm a minimalist now.'

'Since when?'

'Since I got paid to say I was.' She gave him a wink and flounced over to Finn's table. 'Hey guys! Ignore Leo. You know he's a one-trick pony. You're unbeaten the rest of the year.' She gave Finn a hug, and he froze, then patted her awkwardly on the back.

Ella appeared at Leo's side and threw her arms around him. 'We did it!'

He held her tightly back. *This* was why he wanted to win the quiz. To put a genuinely happy smile back on her face. 'How are you doing, champ?' he murmured in her ear.

'I've been better,' she replied. 'To be honest, I just want to go to bed. But...'

'You don't want to let down your adoring public in your moment of triumph?'

'There is that, but I'm more worried about Dad.'

'Waiting outside?'

She nodded.

'I'll take a quick look now.' Reluctantly releasing her, he made his way through the pub and out the door.

The high street was cold, dark, and empty. There was no sign of Ronnie. Hearing the door open behind him, he turned to see Ella.

'I can't face saying goodbye to everyone,' she said. 'I'm too tired.'

He held out a hand. 'Coast is clear. Let's get you home.'

She entwined her fingers with his and squeezed. 'Thanks.'

Despite the euphoria she'd exhibited five minutes ago, it was clear it had been an act. Ella now appeared as small and deflated as a burst balloon.

Leading her across the road and down the narrow street that led to the church and the manor, Leo mulled over Zach's words. He would give Ella space and wait for the right moment to tell her how he felt, but he wouldn't wait forever. He'd lost one chance to be with her. There was no way he was missing another.

❧ 23 ❧

Sitting in the corner of a room just off the ballroom and wearing her rag dress Cinderella costume, Ella stared at her phone. It had been four days since the Christmas quiz and she'd heard nothing from Michelle, her father, or any other member of her family.

Is it for the best?

She shivered, remembering the moment her dad had appeared in the pub. He'd looked so different: older, smaller, battle-scarred. The moment his eyes had met hers, it was as if she'd been gut-punched.

But despite the panic, her heart had also cried out to him. No matter what he'd done, inside her was still a little girl who loved her dad. How must it have felt, being chucked out of his local pub the moment he set foot in the door? Being ostracised by a community? Even though she was terrified about seeing him, she still wanted to check he was okay.

Dropping the phone in her bag, Ella leant down to tie the ribbons of her brown ballet shoes with trembling fingers. Tonight was the first night of the pantomime. She'd have been nervous enough doing her usual jobs behind the scenes, but this year she was centre stage.

The room was full of people getting changed, but Leo had found a screen so she could have some privacy in the far corner. There was a small table with a mirror on it, a chair, and a rail for her costumes making up the fourth wall of the space.

'Knock knock,' came Zach's voice from the other side of the screen.

Forcing a smile, Ella stood and pushed the clothes rail to one side. Zach was in his wheelchair, a huge bouquet of flowers on his lap.

He held them out. 'For the leading lady on opening night.'

'Oh my god, they're stunning. You really shouldn't have.' Taking them from him, she placed them on her dressing table.

'They're in a pocket of water, so they don't need a vase.'

'Thank you. They're absolutely beautiful.'

'Just like you.'

Ella blushed, not knowing how to respond. Zach had been friendly and respectful, but she had the growing sense that under the mild flirtation, there was a wish for more. She didn't want to make things awkward by telling him outright that she wasn't interested. What if he then turned around and told her she'd been imagining things? The thought was too mortifying for words.

And in front of his family, the panto cast, or in the pub during the quiz, Leo hadn't behaved any differently towards her than he'd always done. Was their physical relationship something he wanted kept secret? Or did he see it fizzling out after Christmas? Ella was too scared of the answer to ask the question. If she knew for sure Leo wanted to finish what they'd tentatively started, she'd never be able to perform on stage without falling apart.

Just get through the week. After the last show, talk to him. Tell him how you truly feel.

'How are you doing?' Zach asked. 'Nervous?'

She nodded.

'I would say "break a leg", but now I actually have, I wouldn't wish it on anyone.'

'Does it hurt?'

'Not anymore, it's more annoying than anything else.' He paused, as if deliberating whether or not to say something, then took a deep breath. 'Ella, I—' He broke off, glancing right.

Leo appeared by his side, a poinsettia plant in his hand, his gaze flicking to the flowers covering half of the small table. 'I wanted to wish you luck and give you this,' he said to Ella, passing her the plant.

'Thank you.' She placed it on the table next to Zach's enormous bunch of flowers.

'And also...' He took something from a paper bag and handed it to her.

She gazed at a chocolate leg wrapped in cellophane.

'I've got them for everyone.' He gave one to Zach. 'I hope you don't think it's in poor taste after what's happened to you.'

Zach grinned. 'I love it. Thanks, mate, you're a good friend.'

Leo gave him a stiff smile in return, his cheeks darkening under the stage make-up.

The silence became uncomfortable.

'The best,' Ella blurted.

The two men's eyes snapped to hers questioningly.

Now it was *her* cheeks that heated. 'Friend. The best friend.'

Zach smiled. 'Absolutely.' He turned to look at Leo, his gaze... challenging?

'I also wanted to thank you for the card you gave me,' Leo said to her. 'It's incredible.'

Ella's blush intensified. She'd drawn a good luck card for Leo in the style of a superhero comic strip, but with him dressed as Prince Charming. In the panels he was vanquishing dragons, and each time he punched one, there was a sound effect reading 'Poweth!', or 'Whameth!'

'Oh, yeah, thanks for the card you made for me,' Zach added. 'I'm going to keep it.'

'Good idea,' Leo said drolly. 'Might be worth something in the future.'

'Exactly!' Zach replied, Leo's sarcastic tone seeming lost on him. 'If Ella becomes a famous artist, I could make a mint!'

'Ten minutes, everyone!' Libby cried from behind the screen. 'Let's huddle up!'

Leo stepped away so Zach could wheel his chair out of Ella's space and into the rest of the room. Ella followed him, her heart thumping in her throat as she saw the entire cast and crew gathering in the middle of the room. This was really happening, and there was no way she could exit stage left and never return.

'Hey.' Leo entwined his fingers with hers. 'You've got this. You're incredible.'

She pulled a face, wanting to vomit with nerves.

'It's true. We're all just lumps of rock orbiting around you. You're the star.'

'I hope you're talking about me!' Arthur interrupted. 'Oh, and Steve, of course.'

Ella blinked, still trying to get her head around the Tokyo street-style-inspired outfits the ugly sisters were wearing for their first scene. Steve looked like a middle-aged man who'd been dressed by Barbie during an acid trip, and Arthur looked like the result of an experiment to breed Hello Kitty with Dracula.

'No, Dad,' Leo said patiently. 'Ella's the star.'

'Humph, well, I suppose the clue's in the name of the show. And she is bally brilliant.' Arthur turned to Ella and smiled. 'I can't believe you've been hiding backstage for all these years, my dear.'

She tried to smile back. 'I kind of wish I was still there.'

'But why? Talent like yours needs to be seen! And we've all got your back. If you go blank, just say the magic word and I'll leap onstage to distract the audience.'

'The magic word?'

'Yes! It's like a safe word during our sex parties. Everyone has to have one. Mine's sprouts because I hate the things. Satan's testicles, that's what they are. Mater used to make me eat them as a child, and I swore the moment I came of age I'd never eat another one.'

'Not even on Christmas day?'

'Pah! Not on your nelly. Tradition my arse. You know, you can use it if you like?'

'Er—'

'Not my arse. Ha! That's exclusively for Vivi and Deedee. Sprouts. You can use the word if you get stuck for a line.'

'Arthur,' Libby said. 'That won't be necessary. Vivienne's going to be our prompter, and I know Ella's going to be fine.' She beamed at her. 'The lights are so bright, you won't see most of the audience, and anyway, they're the friendliest crowd in the world.' Libby gazed around the rest of the group. 'My business partner, Claire, is out there tonight, as well as Estelle and James, to get the audience into the swing of things. They're three of the loudest people I know, and they'll always have your back. Just remember to enjoy yourself, and if anything doesn't go exactly as we've planned, then it will be even funnier! Now, hold hands, everyone.'

Zach moved closer to Ella and grabbed her free hand. She was hyper-aware that on one side of her was the man she was in love with, and on the other was the man she once believed herself in love with.

'Okay!' Libby cried. 'Let's go with "Abracadabra"! In three, two, one...'

'Abracadabra!' everyone yelled, raising their joined hands in the air.

Ella's heart raced. *Come on!* If she could manage to walk away from her stepmother, she could do this.

HOWEVER, STANDING IN THE WINGS FIFTEEN MINUTES LATER, she wasn't so sure. Libby was on stage as Buttons and with each line she uttered, the seconds ticked down to the moment when Ella had to step out of the darkness and into the spotlight. It felt like she was standing on a plank over shark-infested waters, and the wooden board was shortening before her eyes.

She felt Leo's warmth behind her, then his arms around the front of her chest. Leaning back against him, her breath relaxed.

'I'm so proud of you,' he whispered in her ear.

'I love Cinderella more than anything,' Libby said from a few feet away. 'Even more than cheese. When I see her, my head spins and I get a funny feeling in my undercrackers. Will you help me win her heart, mums and dads, grannies and grandads, nanas and grandpas, aunts and uncles, nieces and nephews, and boys and girls?'

'Yes!' the audience yelled.

Leo placed a soft kiss against Ella's neck. 'Go knock 'em dead, Princess.'

He stepped away and she ran onto the stage. 'Hello, Buttons! Hello, boys and girls!' she cried.

'Hello, Cinderella!' everyone chorused.

A thrill raced across her skin. 'Isn't it a beautiful day?' she continued. 'The sun is shining, the birds are singing, and I'm with my bestest friend. What have you been buying in Foxbrooke today, Buttons?'

As the scene continued, Ella felt as if she were two people in one body. There was the person who sang, danced, and interacted with the audience as if they were born to shine, and there was also the shy and terrified person peeking through their fingers at everything as it unfolded.

By the time the interval began, she was running on adrenaline, boosted by the praise and encouragement backstage. During the second act, she felt invincible.

However, as soon as the curtains were whisked across the stage for the final time and the house lights went up, her legs gave way and she fell to the floor with a thump.

Libby and Leo, who'd been standing either side of her for the curtain call, dropped to their knees beside her.

'Ella!' Leo's voice was edged with panic. 'Are you okay?'

She couldn't reply, her body numb, her breath heaving and her vision unfocused.

Libby took her hand. 'After flying so high and so fast, she's run out of fuel,' she said to Leo, 'so she's coming back to earth with a bit of a bump.' She squeezed Ella's hand. 'Can you breathe with me?'

Ella tried to nod, but her entire body was shaking.

'What's going on?' Arthur asked.

'Are you alright, darling?' Dervla added.

There were too many people. Too many sensations. She couldn't cope.

'Ella will be as right as rain in a moment, but needs space to breathe and a bit of quiet,' Libby said. 'Can you all go back to the dressing room, please?'

Leo made a move to stand, but Ella grabbed his arm.

'You can stay,' Libby said to him, then shifted, so she was directly in front of her. 'I know it feels like you can't, but I need you to close your mouth and breathe through your nose. In for two and out for four. Can you try and do that with me?'

Ella gave a shaky nod. Her skin was tingling and stinging, as if she'd been rolled up in an electric fence. Panic screamed inside her, seizing her muscles.

'You're doing great.' Libby's voice was calm and soothing. 'In for two, and out for four. Slow each breath. Feel the sensations leaving your body with every exhale. That's it. Well done. In for two, and out for four. With every breath, you're more relaxed. You're doing great.'

As Libby's voice continued, the stress inside Ella began to ease, the pain slowly leaching out. Then, with a shuddering sob, she crumpled against Leo, utterly spent.

As his arms cradled her, she rested her head against his chest, listening to the rapid thump of his heart.

'What the fuck was that?' he asked Libby.

'Ella got through tonight thanks to extremely high levels of stress hormones,' she replied. 'Now her body knows she's safe, she's crashing. She needs to rest as much as possible.'

'Summer's back,' Leo said. 'Can't she take over?'

Ella shook her head. 'I'll be fine,' she croaked.

'This doesn't look fine to me.'

'You can't kiss your sister,' she continued, trying to make her voice strong.

'What?'

'You're Prince Charming now,' Libby said. 'Do you really want Summer to play Cinderella?'

Leo took a breath as if to speak, but didn't.

'Ella,' Libby said gently. 'It's totally up to you. We can ask Summer to play Buttons, and I can step into your role if you like?'

An image of Henry Foxbrooke watching his fiancée kissing his younger brother popped into Ella's mind and she snorted.

'Ella?' Leo asked.

'Sorry,' she said as she giggled. 'I was just imagining Henry's face if you kissed Libby.'

Libby's face contorted as she tried not to laugh. 'I'm sure he would understand.'

Leo huffed. 'He'd have apoplexy.'

'I'll be fine to keep going,' Ella said, feeling anything but.

'Well, if you change your mind, just let me know,' Libby replied. 'And make sure you take it easy over the next few days. You'll need more strength than you think to get through the rest of the performances, although hopefully it should get easier.'

She nodded.

'Now, I suggest you go straight to bed. You don't need to change down here. I can tell everyone you're okay.'

'Thank you.'

Leo helped her to her feet and held onto her as her legs tingled with pins and needles. They went to the back of the stage and down the stairs, then headed out of the ballroom. Ella's feet moved slowly, every part of her dog-tired and wanting to collapse. Finally reaching her bedroom, Leo paused outside, and a bolt of dread shot straight to her stomach.

'I think it's for the best that I sleep in my own room until the panto's over,' he said, not meeting her eyes.

So this is it. The beginning of the end. Her throat was too full of tears to let any words out.

'You need to rest,' Leo continued, staring at the floor. 'Not have me molest you all night.'

She couldn't say anything. Couldn't move. She was too numb as all of her worst nightmares seemed to be coming true.

'But...' His gaze finally met hers. 'I want to talk to you when this is all over. About us. If that's okay?'

She finally managed a shaky nod.

'But let's wait until Saturday. When the final performance is done. Libby's right. You need to rest.'

I need you!

Leo stepped stiffly back. 'I hope you feel better in the morning.'

Ella nodded again and stepped inside her room, shutting the door behind her.

How did she ever think it would have worked between them? Friendship, yes, but tying her life to his? Her *family* to his? She stumbled into the bathroom, staring at her face as she removed the thick layer of make-up, turning her from a princess back into a commoner.

'Be grateful,' she whispered to her reflection. 'You had a good run of it. Not every tale has a happy ending.'

Finishing in the bathroom, Ella took off her ball gown and got into the four-poster bed. The pantomime ended in three days. Seventy-two hours to prepare herself for the inevitable: Leo saying he wanted to be just friends.

❧ 24 ❧

'**H**as anyone seen Leo?' Libby asked as she strode into the dressing room.

Ella glanced up from her job of retouching Arthur's garish make-up and shook her head.

'Not since the end of the matinee,' Scott replied.

Everyone's eyes swung to Ella.

'I saw him maybe an hour and a half ago?' she said. 'He said he had to run out and do a quick errand.'

Libby looked at her watch and frowned. 'The show starts in less than ten minutes.' She gave Ella a sunny smile. 'I'm sure he's not far away. I'll ring him again.'

An uneasy silence settled on the dressing room as Libby dashed out.

Ella turned back to Arthur. 'Would you be able to finish this yourself? I want to see if I can get hold of Leo.'

'Yes, yes, of course, my dear. Off you trot!'

Grabbing her phone, Ella exited the room, looking for a quiet corner of the manor. She hadn't changed since the afternoon performance and didn't want the public to see her in costume. Despite having made it through every show that week without having another breakdown, she was running on empty and still had one more performance to get through. Then she had to face a conversation with Leo. If he hadn't run away, of course.

'Ella!'

She turned to see Willow sprinting down the corridor, her expression panicked.

'What is it?'

'Leo,' she gasped. 'I had to find you.'

Ella grabbed Willow's arm to steady herself as the floor seemed to tilt under her feet. 'What's happened?'

'I was out the front just now chatting with an old school friend. I told her Leo was playing Zach's role after he broke his leg. And she said she saw him about an hour ago—'

'Where?'

'Getting into a car with your dad.'

'Oh god!' Memories spun out of control in Ella's mind, careering into catastrophic futures. Leo injured, hurt—

'Ella! I'm sure he's going to be okay.'

But she couldn't believe it. She had to find him. Save him. This was all her fault. If she hadn't been friends with him in the first place, he'd never have known Ronnie Chamberlain. He wouldn't have gone to the police about him. He wouldn't be in a car with him now going god knows where.

'Has he rung you? Messaged you?' Willow asked.

Ella pulled out her phone.

Leo: I'm with your dad. Won't be long X

She showed Willow the screen.

'There we go!' Willow said, the relief evident in her voice. 'It's all okay.'

But how? Ronnie hated the Foxbrookes. Had sworn revenge against whoever had turned him in. Why had Leo got in a car with him?

'I've got to go.' Ella ran up the corridor.

'Where?' Willow cried as she dashed to catch her up.

'To look for him.'

'But curtain's up in less than ten minutes!'

'Stall them. They can't start without Leo, anyway.' Leaving Willow behind, Ella sprinted through a set of doors into the public side of the manor. It was filled with smartly dressed people on their way to the ballroom.

'Excuse me, excuse me,' she muttered, ignoring the bemused stares of people wondering why the star of the show was in such a hurry to run in the opposite direction to the stage.

'It's not midnight yet!' someone cried, and people laughed.

Fighting back tears, Ella made it to the front hall.

'Ella!'

She stopped dead, staring as if at a ghost.

'Surprise!' Lila grabbed her in a hug, lifting her off the ground. 'I can't believe it's been so long!' She pulled back, her hands clasping around Ella's upper arms. 'O. M. G. Just look at you! The star of the freaking show!'

'Lila!' Ella gasped. 'What are you doing here?'

'I've come to see *you*, of course, dummy!' She leaned forward and lowered her voice. 'And my Prince Charming.'

'W-what?'

Lila was beyond beautiful with her blonde hair immaculately straight, her cheeks sun-kissed by the Californian weather, and her blue eyes sparkling like the sea.

'I've come back for Christmas, and...' She winked at Ella. 'I just might stay.'

'But, your job!'

Lila gave an artless shrug. 'It was getting boring. Just like the men. New is only exciting for so long, but then you kinda miss what you once had.' She glanced around the hall, an expectant smile on her face. 'So, tell me. How is he?'

Ella's heart plummeted to the pit of her stomach. 'Leo?' she whispered.

'Yeah, of course! Who else? I hear he's still single.'

'Lila?'

Lila's head snapped to Zach, her eyes widening. 'Holy shit-balls! You got bust up bad!'

He smiled. 'You should see the other guy.'

Lila glanced between him and Ella. 'So, you two are all cool now?'

Zach took Ella's hand. 'Yeah, all good.'

'Uh-huh.' Lila raised an eyebrow as she looked at their hands.

Ella pulled hers free. 'Lila, sorry, I've got to dash. I've got to find—' She broke off as Leo entered the front door, out of breath. *Oh, thank god. Thank god.*

His eyes found hers, and he gave her a tentative smile.

'Baby!' Lila squealed, launching herself across the space and throwing her arms around him.

Leo froze, his arms stiff by his sides as Lila hugged him.

'How's *this* for a surprise?' she said, pulling back and giving him a once over.

Ella clutched her stomach as it rolled with nausea. Leo's face was white, his mouth hanging open as he blinked at his ex-girlfriend.

Lila took his arm and pulled him back over to Ella and Zach. 'We've got the whole gang back together!'

'Just like old times.' Zach grinned up at Ella. 'The next thing you know, Ells, we'll be on a double date again at Maccy D's with Barbie and Ken.'

Leo caught Ella's eye, but she glanced away, her heart breaking. Leo and Lila were a blindingly beautiful couple, with their golden hair and bright blue eyes. Their 'Barbie and Ken' moniker may have started as a joke, but it couldn't have been more apt. They were perfect together.

'Ella,' Leo said, 'can I have a quick word?'

She took a step back. 'I've got to go.'

'Me too,' Zach said. 'I'm on stage in a couple of minutes. We'll leave you two to catch up.' He turned to Ella. 'Can you open any doors for me on the way back?'

'Yeah, sure.' She rushed to open the first one at the back of the entrance hall and Zach wheeled himself through.

'You've got about twenty-five minutes before you're on stage!' Zach called over his shoulder to Leo. 'So don't let your romantic reconciliation take any longer than that!'

Ella ran ahead of Zach after he'd pushed through each door. The last thing she wanted was talk to him about what had just happened.

'We found Leo!' Zach announced triumphantly as he entered the dressing room.

'Is he okay?' Willow asked.

'Better than ever,' Zach replied. 'He's with Lila!'

'*Lila?*' Willow and Dervla chorused, glancing Ella's way.

'Yeah. She's come back to Foxbrooke.'

'Where is he now?' Libby asked. 'The panto was meant to start a couple of minutes ago.'

'Ells and I left them in the entrance hall to catch up,' Zach continued with a smile. 'I told him not to take too long.'

'Oh, okay.' Libby clapped her hands. 'Right then, Zach, let's get you on stage. Willow, can you run and let Connor know we're back on track?'

'Sure!'

As everyone bustled about, Ella left the room to stand in

the wings on the opposite side of the stage to Zach. She was overjoyed that Leo was alright, but in a pit of misery at seeing him next to Lila. In her dreams, Leo and her would be together, but that tentative picture of a future with him had just been torn up by the arrival of his ex.

Of course Lila would assume he'd jump back into her arms if she asked, just like he'd always done. Lila was the love of his life, and the fact he'd never had a relationship with anyone else since she left for the States proved that.

The house lights went down, and Zach began. 'In a land where hope's the only thing worthwhile, a girl with humble roots and just a smile, will dance through hardships with kindness and grace, in search of love, in this enchanted place. Will she find it? Will she win? If you're sitting comfortably, let's begin!'

Ella squeezed her eyes tightly shut. *Do not cry!*

Watching from the wings, she tried to feel the same joy as the audience as they clapped along to the opening number.

Just fake it for the next two hours. Don't let anyone down. You can do it.

As the song finished, Libby, as Buttons, interacted with the audience, whipping them into an excited frenzy. She was a born performer, and her confidence only seemed to highlight how unconfident Ella felt.

'Cinderella! That's who I love,' Libby proclaimed. 'But I think she only sees me as a friend. She lives at Hardup Hall with her two ugly sisters, and she's as perfect as perfect can be!'

Ella mouthed Libby's words in an attempt to centre herself as her hands twisted in the fabric of her dress and her heartbeat marked the seconds until her entrance.

'Do you think I have a chance with her, boys and girls?' Libby asked.

The children in the audience gave her an enthusiastic 'Yes,' while the adults roared 'No!'

Libby stuck a hand on her hip. 'Oh, yes, I do!'

'Oh, no, you don't!' the audience countered.

This was it. Just a few short moments and Ella would be on stage.

'Oh, yes, I do!' Libby cried.

'Oh, no, you don't!'

Seeing movement out of the corner of her eye, Ella turned.

Leo.

He rushed to her side, out of breath, his costume unbuttoned and his hair sticking up in all directions. 'I need to talk to you,' he whispered urgently.

'Oh, yes, I *do* have a chance with Cinderella,' Libby told the audience. 'With knobs on. Pinch, punch, first of the month and no returns!'

'Now?' Ella whispered back to him, every part of her tightening with pain. She wanted to scream. Cry. Rage against a world where happiness was being snatched from her grasp, over and over again.

Leo's gaze flicked to the stage.

'I love Cinderella more than anything!' Libby was saying. 'Even more than cheese.'

'I've got to go on!' Ella said to him, her voice trembling. 'Please. Don't do this now.'

Leo cursed under his breath and reached out to take her hand. 'I'm sorry.'

'Will you help me win her heart, mums and dads, grannies and grandads, nanas and grandpas, aunts and uncles, nieces and nephews, and boys and girls?' Libby cried.

'Can we talk at the interval?' Leo asked.

'I think Cinderella is just about to appear!' Libby said, eyeballing Ella.

She tugged her hand from Leo's, fixed a bright smile in place, and ran onto the stage. 'Hello, Buttons! Hello, boys and girls!'

'Hello, Cinderella!' the audience chorused.

'Isn't it a beautiful day!' Ella continued, even as her heart shattered into pieces. 'The sun is shining, the birds are singing, and I'm with my bestest friend!'

ELLA GOT THROUGH THE FIRST TWO SCENES, THEN STOOD IN the wings, watching Leo and Scott as Prince Charming and Dandini.

How would her life look without Leo in it? After seeing him and Lila together, she knew it would be too painful to remain friends with him anymore if he got back with her. The depth of her love for Leo was too deep, too all-encompassing. Having to see him with Lila would pour salt on an open wound that could never truly heal if she was around him.

Just get through Christmas, then think about where else you could live.

Maybe she could look for a job somewhere other than Foxbrooke? Perhaps abroad? Somewhere far, far away from Leo, her dad, her stepmother, Oliver, Zach, and anyone else who knew her and her history. She could have a fresh start. Make new friends. Forge a new life where she wasn't defined by her past.

But underneath the desperate optimism, she was miserable. No matter where she ran, her heart would still be in Foxbrooke with Leo.

The lighting changed and Connor played incidental music.

Taking a deep breath, Ella strolled onto the stage. 'I hope I can gather enough firewood to please my sisters,' she said.

'Sometimes I think that no matter what I do, it'll never be good enough.'

She turned her back on the audience as the words bit like sharp teeth. *Get it together! You can do this!*

'But soft!' Leo said behind her. 'What light through yonder forest breaks? It is the east, and this maiden is the sun.'

Ella dug her fingernails into her palms to stop her tears and turned to Leo. 'H-have we met before?'

Leo's gaze was focused on her in a way that made her breath stutter. 'In my dreams I have met you,' he said softly. 'Are you real? Or will you vanish when I open my eyes?'

Ella swallowed to dislodge the lump of emotion in her throat. 'But your eyes are open now.'

'So my wishes have come true. Tell me, who are you?'

'Oh, I'm just a servant girl. What's your name?'

'Prin—Dandini. Have you ever dreamt of falling in love?'

'Y-yes,' Ella stammered.

'And did your one true love look like me?'

Always. She swallowed. 'Mostly.'

'Mostly? How am I different?'

'I never expected a beard.'

Leo pulled the false beard off and threw it away. 'And now?'

'Oh! Yes! You are...'

'Your dream man?'

Ella couldn't reply without crying, so she nodded instead.

Connor played the opening bars of 'Endless Love', and Leo extended his hand to her.

She took it, feeling warmth, electricity, and the heart-deep knowledge that he was everything she would ever want and need. The love she had for him choked her. She opened her mouth to begin the song, but couldn't make a sound.

Leo sang her lines for her. Singing that she was his first

love, his only love, the one person he wanted to share his whole life with.

Everything else disappeared. There was no audience. No cast and crew watching from the wings. Only her and Leo, held in the magic of a song that promised her everything she wanted and knew she couldn't have.

The stage lights glistened around him like a halo, setting off the gold in his hair and the aquamarine depths of his eyes. Through her tears, he was shining.

As the song came to an end, Leo leaned down towards her, and Ella reached up for his kiss like a flower chasing the sun.

Closing her eyes, she tried to commit the moment to her memory. The soft press of his lips on hers, the sharp and sweet pain in her heart, and the coolness of her tears as they tracked down her cheeks.

If this is the last time, then be grateful for what you've had.

'Coo-ee!' Arthur called loudly from the wings. 'Where are you, Princey-poos! Your little Fanny wants to play!'

'And your Tittie does too!' Steve added.

Ella broke away from Leo. 'I have to go,' she managed, then ran off stage.

CASSANDRA

❧ 25 ❧

Hiding behind the flat, Ella wiped her eyes. She was due back on stage in the next few seconds for a scene with Dervla as the fairy godmother, then a series of scenes in the kitchen of Hardup Hall leading up to her transformation into a princess and leaving for the ball. After that, it was the interval and she could talk to Leo. But did she want to? If he was going to tell her something awful about her father, then say he wanted them to just be friends, she'd rather he waited until the end of the panto so there was no need for her to hold it together any longer.

Drawing on all her reserves of energy, she grabbed a bunch of sticks and went back on stage where Dervla was hunched over, a brown shawl over her head.

'Hello, my dear,' Dervla called out in a wavering voice. 'I wonder if you could help me?'

'Yes, of course!' Ella replied. 'How can I be of assistance?'

As the scene continued, Ella tried to keep her focus on what she was meant to be doing, but her awareness was constantly drawn to the sight of Leo standing in the wings, his gaze fixed on her.

What had happened with her dad before the show? How had Leo got away? And what was he feeling about Lila's return?

The knot of tension in her tummy got tighter and tighter as the pantomime progressed, each word and each scene taking them closer to the halfway point.

Now they were in the kitchen of Hardup Hall again.

Dervla held her magic wand aloft. 'Cinderella! You shall go to the ball!'

'But how?' Ella replied. 'I don't have a ticket, any way of getting to the palace, and my only dress is rags!'

'Minor details, my dear. Do you have Amazon Prime?'

'Er... no. Is that a problem?'

Dervla shook her head. 'We can use my account.' She waved the wand in the air. 'I've got Optimus Prime. Delivery by drone within sixty seconds of your order being placed. Your VIP ticket should be with you in five, four, three, two—'

An envelope whizzed through the air. Ella caught it and read the front. 'Princess Incognito?'

'Well, you can't be announced as yourself with your ugly sisters there, can you?'

'But won't they recognise me?'

'Not with my magic. It's more powerful than a social media beauty filter. Now all I need is a pumpkin, two frogs, and four white mice. Got any lying around?'

'I'll see what I can find in the garden,' she replied, then dashed through the kitchen door where Willow was waiting with her transformation dress. Ella shimmied out of her costume and Willow helped her into the ballgown then lifted the top skirt up and over her head as a shawl to disguise it.

'Where's the fake pumpkin and the cages with the stuffed

animals?' Ella asked, glancing at the empty table behind the scenes.

'We don't know,' Willow muttered. 'Libby and Leo have gone to try and find them. They were there ten minutes ago.'

Ella listened to Dervla's dialogue on the other side of the flat. 'She's going to finish in a few seconds.'

'I know. Can you stall for time?'

Ella nodded, then poked her head through the door onto the stage. 'The mice are missing and the frogs have hopped off,' she said to Dervla. 'Just trying to chase them down.'

'And the pumpkin? It's not like that's got legs.'

'It's, erm... rolled away?'

'Ah,' Dervla replied, then shot a panicked look at Connor sitting behind an electric piano by the side of the stage.

He started playing the opening of 'Holding Out For a Hero', by Bonnie Tyler.

Dervla turned to face the audience, her arms wide and her left foot tapping along with the synthesised drum beat. '*Where have all the pumpkins gone, and where are all the mice?*' she sang with the power of a Viking warrior and the emotion of an Italian footballer. '*Where are all the little frogs... for my magic device?*'

Ella ducked backstage to find Leo, Libby and Willow arguing with Arthur, who was carrying a real pumpkin in his arms.

'Hullo, Ella!' Arthur hefted the pumpkin onto the table. 'Priscilla got lost, so I've brought you Pedro instead.'

'Dad, you promised no surprises!' Leo hissed.

'But it's the last night of the show!' Arthur retorted, then turned to Ella. 'Pedro's a bit lighter than Priscilla, so easy-peasy to carry.'

Dervla was still giving it some welly from the other side of the painted backdrop. '*Isn't there a winter squash that's saved from*

Halloween? Cinders needs a coach tonight, and a taxi's too mainstream...'

Ella checked there was nothing inside the pumpkin, then lifted it into her arms. 'And the stuffed animals?'

Libby rounded on Arthur. 'This is your final warning. Tell us where you've hidden them.'

Arthur's eyes widened at her ferocious tone and his lower jaw wobbled. 'Er...'

'Got them, Fanny!' Steve rushed up the stairs at the back of the stage with a cage in each hand.

'Top job, Tittie!' Arthur replied.

'Thank go—what the fuck!' Leo yelled.

'Dad!' Willow cried. 'Just no!'

Ella stared at what Steve was carrying, her stomach turning over. The mice and frogs in the cages were one hundred per cent alive.

'Don't get your knickers in a twist,' Arthur replied belligerently. 'Fiona and Freddie are going back to the pond after the show.'

'*I need a pumpkin!*' Dervla roared from on stage at ear-splitting volume as Leo, Willow, and Libby continued arguing with Arthur. '*I'm holding out for a pumpkin 'til the end of this scene... He's gotta be big, and he's gotta be plump, and he's gotta be orange, not green...*'

Before she could second-guess herself, Ella pushed open the door with her backside and entered the kitchen set with the pumpkin, plonking it on the small table.

The music stopped and the audience burst into applause. Dervla bowed, then turned to Ella. 'What a beauty, my dear. And the rest?'

'Two secs.' She nipped backstage and grabbed the cages from Steve with shaking hands. When she re-entered the kitchen, there was a collective gasp from

Dervla and the audience as they saw what she was carrying.

Ella put the cages on the table and stepped away.

'Oh, my,' Dervla murmured. 'I see you've gone to a lot of—' she turned to stare at the back wall of the set, '—*trouble*,' she said pointedly.

There was a low chuckle from Arthur backstage.

Dervla gave herself a little shake, then turned her smile back on. 'Now, my dear. Are you ready?'

'I think so. Will it hurt?'

'Not at all. You might feel a little tingly, but that's just the fairy dust.'

There was a whoosh as the smoke machine blew a stream of dry ice across the stage and the lights dimmed, leaving Ella in a spotlight. As Connor played music, she began to twirl.

'With a wave of my wand,' Dervla cried, 'this tattered old dress... will change into a gown, fit for a princess!'

Ella spun faster as Finn flashed the lights on and off. Suddenly, there was an almighty bang, and she flinched as a shower of confetti came over the back of the set behind her.

'Dad! For fuck's sake!' she heard Leo growl.

'Ta-da!' Dervla rushed forward to brush the skirts of Ella's dress down, revealing the ball gown as the audience clapped.

'Thank you!' Ella managed, as her heart hammered inside her chest. 'This is so beautiful!'

'Fit to win the heart of a prince!'

'But I don't want a prince.'

'Say *what* now?'

'I've fallen in love with Dandini.'

'Dan-*who*-ni?'

'A handsome man I met in the enchanted forest.'

Dervla gave a loud harrumph. 'Well, that's not who I saw you marrying in my crystal ball. Did he have a beard?'

'A fake one.'

'Ah! It's all becoming clear.'

'It is?'

'Yep, all will be revealed in the palace ballroom. Now, have you got any shoes?'

Ella lifted up the hem of her dress to show her bare feet.

'Oh, that won't do. It's not a hoe down.' Dervla rummaged in a large bag hanging from her shoulder and pulled out a pair of glass shoes. 'Try these.'

Ella put them on and gave a twirl. 'Thank you!'

'Now, just before I get your transportation sorted, I need you to accept the Terms and Conditions.'

'Of what?'

'My pro bono enchantment services.'

'Oh. Okay, I accept.'

'You don't know what they are yet!' Dervla took a scroll from her bag, dropping the bottom end, so the paper unrolled all the way to the floor. 'Do you want the full version, or the highlights?'

Ella glanced at the kitchen clock. 'The highlights, please.'

'Rightie ho.' Dervla cleared her throat. 'First, I must make you aware that all magic is monitored for quality and training purposes. My name is Fairy Cakes. May I call you Cinderella?'

'You may.'

'Jolly good. Now here are the Terms and Conditions for Enchantment Services, short version. Point one: Agreement to Terms. By accepting the services provided by the Fairy Godmother, hereinafter referred to as the "Service Provider," you, the recipient, hereinafter referred to as the "Client," agree to abide by the following terms and conditions.

'Point two: Nature and Duration of Services. The Service Provider will transform your attire into an evening gown and your transportation into a pumpkin carriage with accompanying footmen and horses. The aforementioned transformations are strictly temporary and will cease precisely at midnight on the day of the service.'

'Midnight?'

'Yes. The magic's only viable for today. And anyway, by then you'll probably have blisters. Those shoes don't exactly look comfortable. Right. Point three: Limitation of Liability. The Service Provider is not liable for any inconvenience or consequences arising from the reversion process. Point four—'

'This is the short version?' Ella interrupted.

'Point *four*,' Dervla continued firmly. 'Acceptance of Risk. The Client acknowledges understanding and acceptance of all inherent risks associated with temporary magical transformations.

'Point five: Governing Law. These terms and conditions shall be governed by and construed in accordance with the laws of the Enchanted Kingdom. By accepting the enchantment and proceeding to the ball, the Client acknowledges having understood, and agreed to these Terms and Conditions. Do you accept this enchantment?'

'Yes.'

'Jolly good! Now let's step outside so I can complete the process and get you on your way!'

Dervla took the two cages, and Ella lifted the pumpkin. They went to the side of the stage as the lights started flickering and a front cloth was lowered in front of the kitchen set. An image was projected onto it of a pumpkin, mice and frogs being transformed into a carriage, horses and footmen, then Ella got into position behind it, seated on a stool with casters.

As she was illuminated, it appeared as if she was inside the projection of the carriage. The image moved across the stage and Willow pulled the stool along with it as Ella waved goodbye to the audience. When the carriage reached the edge of the stage, the front curtains were drawn and the house lights went on for the interval.

As soon as she was hidden from view, Ella slumped with exhaustion.

Leo appeared by her side and took her hand. 'You okay?'

She nodded, unable to meet his eyes.

'I'm sorry about my incorrigible father. Mammy's currently tearing him a new one.'

'It's okay.'

Leo took a deep breath. 'I know it might seem a bit much to deal with right now, but would you come outside for a bit?'

'Why?' she murmured.

'Your dad's there. He wants to talk to you.'

$\mathscr{H}$ 2 6 $\mathscr{H}$

Ella stared at Leo, her heart jumping into her throat. 'Why? What happened earlier with him? Are you alright?'

Leo's smile was warm. 'Everything's okay.'

'But how? You saw Ronnie in the pub. Michelle said he wants revenge on—'

'He knows I told the police where his lock-up was.'

'Oh, my god! Who told him?'

'I did.'

'What?' she cried in panic.

Leo squeezed her hand. 'I told you. Everything's fine. He wanted to see you, but Michelle wouldn't give him your number and he can't come in here because of Zach and the restraining order. I said he could wait in the garden and I'd bring you out in the interval. But only if you wanted to see him.'

'I do. But I don't understand how you're still alive.'

Leo chuckled. 'You'll see.' He handed over her Converse. 'These will be better than what you're currently wearing.'

Taking off the glass slippers, Ella put her trainers on, then followed Leo through to the back of the manor and out a side door. His fingers interlaced with hers, but she pulled her hand away and crossed her arms over her stomach. If he and Lila got back together, then she needed to get used to her and Leo's relationship going back to that of platonic friends.

Outside, the gardens were shrouded in the darkness of a December night, the trees still and quiet. Ella couldn't see anyone.

'He's by the fountain.' Leo shucked off his Prince Charming jacket and placed it over her shoulders.

'T-thank you.' She didn't know if her shivers were from the cold, fear, or both. Had her father really changed? Was any of this real?

Following Leo along a gravel path, Ella passed through a gap in one of the yew hedges and saw a hunched figure seated on the edge of a fountain.

Dad.

Ronnie got to his feet, took a step forward, then stopped.

Ella's mouth was dry, her pulse pounding. Forcing her feet to move, she went forward, Leo by her side. Up close, her father was smaller than she remembered. Thinner. The moonlight accentuated the deep lines in his forehead and the creases in his cheeks.

'Hi, love,' he said hesitantly.

'Hi Dad,' she replied, her voice a whisper. 'How are you doing?'

'Glad to see you.'

'I'll wait by the hedge and give you some space,' Leo murmured, then stepped away.

In the silence that followed, Ella tried to think of what to say. She had so many questions, but was unsure of where to start.

'He's a good lad,' Ronnie said gruffly.

'Leo? But you...' *always hated him*. 'I mean—'

Her father's eyes flicked behind her to where Leo was waiting in the distance and he gave a half smile. 'I was wrong.'

Ella stared at him in shock.

'It's taken me years to even think those words, let alone say them,' he continued. 'But there's freedom in them. Peace. There's no more fighting if you apologise.'

'I told Leo where your lock-up was,' she said in a rush. 'It was me.'

Ronnie smiled. 'Figured as much, even though he swore blind he was acting on his own. You can't bullshit a bullshitter.'

Unbidden, tears sprang from Ella's eyes. 'I'm so sorry,' she whispered.

'Don't cry, love!' He frantically patted his pockets, then pulled out a handkerchief and pressed it into her hand. 'It's clean. I promise.'

Ella wiped her eyes.

'I'm glad you shopped me to the cops,' Ronnie continued. 'It was the right thing to do.'

'What's changed?'

His hand came to a thin gold chain around his neck, rubbing the metal between his fingers and thumb. 'When I went in, all I could think about was getting out and getting even. All this anger was inside me, with no way out. The thoughts were like poison. But I couldn't see that the person being hurt the most by them was me.'

He let out a heavy sigh. 'I started getting chest pains, and they didn't let up. It got so bad I couldn't breathe right. One morning I woke up and just knew I was going to cark it. On the way to the doc, I ran into this bloke. He was always there if you wanted to talk, but I'd always told him to fu—go away. But that morning I knew I had nothing to lose. So... I went with him.'

'Was he a counsellor?'

Ronnie shook his head. 'A chaplain. He listened as I let it all out. Then he told me I was loved, and he prayed for me.'

Ella bit the inside of her cheek as her eyes stung with more tears.

'No-one's ever loved me like that. Like it didn't matter what I'd done or who I was. I didn't have to do anything or be anyone. I cried like a baby and couldn't stop. But it was okay. *I* was going to be okay. And when I left the room, the pain in my heart was less. I felt lighter.'

A ringtone sounded in the stillness of the garden and Ella turned to see Leo with his phone out.

'You okay if I get this?' he asked.

'Yes, I'm fine,' she replied. 'You can go back inside if you need to?'

He gave her a nod and turned away, taking the call.

Ella faced her father again. 'Why didn't you tell me all about this?'

'You had Oliver. I thought you were better off without me in the picture.'

'Did Michelle know?'

'No. I wanted to wait till I was out.'

'What did she say?'

He gave her a rueful smile. 'It wasn't what she was expecting.'

'It hasn't been easy for her.'

'Or you.' Ronnie gazed at her intently. 'Bille-Mai told me what you've done for Michelle. It was what you did for us before I went in. I've—' He broke off, tugging the chain from under his jumper and rubbing the gold cross hanging from it.

'I've been a shit dad, Ella. I know a few words won't fix anything I've done, but I wanted to tell you I'm sorry.'

Any reply stuck in Ella's throat. After all the thoughts about what would happen after her father was released, the fact he might have changed had never crossed her mind.

'The accident wasn't your fault,' he continued. 'It—' He broke off, pinching the bridge of his nose. 'Out of all the things I did... that...' Taking a deep breath, he faced her, his expression tortured. 'I'd give up my life if I could take that night back. You were trying to stop me. You were doing the right thing. But I didn't listen. I never did.'

Ella closed the gap between them and extended her hand.

Ronnie took it, his eyes liquid. 'I'm sorry, love. I'm sorry for everything.'

Ella allowed herself to be drawn into a hug. Getting this version of her dad back was more than she could have hoped for. But would her stepmother ever allow them to have a relationship?

'And don't you worry about Michelle,' he said, seeming to read her mind. 'She's my wife and I love her, but things are going to change. She can't treat you like she's done. None of us can anymore.'

'She hates me,' Ella mumbled.

'Nah, she doesn't.' He hugged her a little tighter. 'She's just jealous and running scared.'

Ella lifted her head. 'Huh?'

The corners of his eyes crinkled as he smiled at her. 'Prison gives you time to think. You're everything Michelle's not, and she feels threatened by you.'

'What?'

'She has to be in control to feel safe, so that's why she acts the way she does.' He paused, his smile turning sheepish. 'I've been learning about myself and studying why people behave the way they do. I've even discovered I have an "inner child".' He grinned at her expression. 'If your eyebrows go up any higher, they're going to fly off your head.'

Ella drew back, embarrassed. 'Sorry, I—'

'Don't say that. An elf just died in Santa land.' As her mouth dropped open, he smirked. 'Leo told me to say that if you tried to apologise for anything.'

She blinked at him in disbelief. 'Is this real?'

He nodded. 'I've got my life back and the chance to do things differently.'

'What are you going to do?'

'Start by making amends if I can. Beg forgiveness from all the people I've hurt. And it's the right time of year for it.'

'Christmas?'

'Yeah. It feels like the big man's on my side.' He let out a long breath. 'I know I've got a lot to make up for. But I want to be the kind of dad you read about in kiddie books. The kind of dad I would have wanted. One you deserve.'

Ella couldn't speak, the lump of emotion in her throat too big to even swallow.

'I'm so proud of you, love. For everything you've made of your life. And the way you've looked after Michelle. You're a saint.' He pulled her in for another tight hug. 'I'll do my best to make you as proud of me as I am of you.'

The floodgates opened, and Ella sobbed into her father's chest.

'Don't cry, sweet pea, you'll ruin your make-up. Don't you have to be on stage in a few minutes?'

Drawing back, she nodded, wiping her eyes and seeing the black streaks of mascara. 'D-do I look like a panda?' she asked shakily.

Ronnie smiled. 'A very pretty one. But you'd better get back inside and fix it.'

'Okay.'

They walked together towards the manor, but her father hung back as they saw Zach in his wheelchair, just outside the back door. 'You go in, love. Leo's got my number, so you can get in touch whenever you want. I don't want to push you. It's on your terms.'

Ella threw her arms around him. 'I love you, Dad.'

He froze. 'I love you too,' he replied gruffly, before drawing back. 'Now go on... Go!'

She jogged towards Zach. Just before she reached him, she glanced back over her shoulder.

Her father had gone.

'Hey, Ells. You okay?' Zach asked. 'Who were you with?'

'My dad.'

'Shit. Did he hurt you? What—'

'No! I'm fine. Honestly. He's changed.'

Zach made a scoffing noise.

'He has,' Ella repeated firmly. 'You'll see.'

There was an awkward silence, then Zach sighed. 'Okay.'

Ella held the door open so he could wheel back through. 'I've got to get back and sort my make-up out.'

Zach didn't move. 'Ells...'

'Please don't call me that.'

'Er, why not?'

Because that's what you called me when you were my boyfriend? Because I don't like it? 'I prefer Ella.'

He nodded. 'I'm sorry. I—' He took a deep breath. 'Look, I'm just going to come out with it. I want us to get back together.'

The words hung in the air.

Zach must have taken her silence as tacit approval as he continued. 'We were so good together. The best. And I know I fucked up, but being back in Foxbrooke with you has shown me just how much you meant—*mean* to me. Whatever you want, Ella, I want to give it to you.'

I want Leo. She sighed. 'I'm sorry, Zach. But I can't go back. I—'

'Are you still in love with Oliver?'

'No.' It might take a long time to fully recover from the depth of his betrayal, but Ella knew any feelings of love for her ex had been completely extinguished. Both by his behaviour, and how irreversibly in love with Leo she was.

'Then would you give me another chance? Give *us* another chance?'

She shook her head. Even if she couldn't have Leo, there was no way she could fall back in love with Zach. That story was finished. 'I'm sorry.'

He nodded, his expression crestfallen. 'Lila coming back really brought it home to me how good it was when you and I were together and she was with Leo. Life just seemed simpler back then. Happier.'

'But it wasn't, really.'

'Yeah, I know. It just felt like it was.' He gave her a sad smile. 'I want you to be happy. And if that's not with me, I'll get over it.' He wheeled in through the back door. 'Take as long as you need to fix your make-up. I'll stall the audience with mildly amusing anecdotes about my time on *Swallowdale*...'

FIFTEEN MINUTES LATER, ELLA STOOD BACKSTAGE AS Connor played the music announcing the start of the second half. She hadn't had a chance to speak to Leo since coming back inside and getting Willow to fix her make-up.

'How did it go?' Leo asked as he came to her side. 'Good?'

'Better than good. I can't believe it, but at the same time I know it's true.'

His smile lit up his face. 'It's a Christmas miracle.'

She nodded.

'And...' The sunshine left his face, and he looked unsure. 'I'm hoping for one more miracle at the end of the night.'

Oh. He must mean Lila. Ella swallowed. 'You don't need a miracle,' she said haltingly.

His eyes widened. 'I don't?'

'No. It's a sure thing.'

He took her hand. 'Really?'

She nodded. 'I, I know she wants you back.'

'Huh?'

Don't make me say her name!

'What—who are you talking about?' His expression was utterly baffled.

'Lila.'

'*Lila?*'

'Yes, Lila,' she huffed. 'Your one true love. The love of your life. The star at the top of your tree. The person you want to meet under the mistletoe. The pig in your blanket—sorry, that sounded awful. Anyway, you know what I mean,' she finished crossly.

Leo stared at her, his mouth hanging open.

'Into position everyone,' Libby cried as the music swelled. 'Ella, don't forget we need you behind the flat for your grand entrance.'

Ella stepped away from Leo, but he didn't let go of her hand, still staring dumbstruck at her.

'Leo!' Libby hissed. 'Positions!'

He blinked, his cheeks darkening, then stumbled towards Scott, his eyes still on Ella.

She ducked out of view as the curtains were drawn and the second half began.

Why had Leo looked so surprised when she'd said Lila's name? And if he wasn't thinking about her when he was contemplating another Christmas miracle, then what *was* he thinking about? The panto finishing without Arthur causing another incident?

All too soon she was announced, and she pasted on a smile and proceeded to the front of the stage.

As Arthur and Steve bantered with each other, Ella gazed up at Leo. He was looking at her as he had when they'd first rehearsed this scene, his cheeks full of colour and his posture taut.

He opened his mouth, but nothing came out.

The silence began to stretch.

'Who does she think she is?' Arthur said pointedly. 'Some girl from the enchanted forest he met in the first half of the show?'

Leo started. 'You're the girl I met in the enchanted forest,' he said quickly.

'Dandini,' Ella replied. 'You've lost your beard.'

'What? Oh, er, yes. I, er—'

'Only wear it on Tuesdays and Thursdays!' Arthur cried, then turned to the audience. 'Honestly, this is what hundreds of years of aristocratic inbreeding does for you. The pumpkin's got more brains than the prince and considerably more charm.'

Leo flushed as the audience roared with laughter. Then he took Ella's hands. 'I can't believe you're here.'

She swallowed. 'I can't either.'

His gaze was all-absorbing. 'Pinch me. I need to make sure I'm not dreaming.'

'I—I can't do that.'

'Kiss me then.'

The sudden silence was overwhelming, as if everyone on stage and in the audience were holding their breath. Ella brought her lips to Leo's, her eyelids fluttering closed as tingles ran across her skin.

He let go of her hands and cupped her face, deepening the kiss, and she gripped his shoulders for support as her head filled with stars. Leo kissed her as if she were the most desirable and precious thing in the world. His touch reverent yet restrained, as if it was taking all of his strength not to consume her in greedy bites. Powerless to resist the swells of desire, Ella opened to him, the sweep of his tongue against hers making her gasp with pleasure.

She was vaguely aware of whoops, whistles, and catcalls from the audience, but she couldn't stop kissing him.

Suddenly Leo was wrenched away from her by Arthur, who was currently over seven feet tall courtesy of lime-green platform heels and a vertiginous wig. 'Princey-poos, this is a *family* show,' he cried, 'not *Love Island*.' He adjusted his enormous fake breasts, which were shaped like traffic cones with flashing red lights at the tips. 'You need to show a bit of decorum and class like me and my Tittie.'

'Too right, Fanny.' Steve wiggled his hips. 'We put the arse into class!'

'Now don't you think you'd like to have a nice waltz rather than attempt the horizontal tango?' Arthur continued. 'And maybe tell this delightful girl your real identity?'

'Shit—sorry—erm...' Leo was looking increasingly flustered. He ran a hand through his hair. 'I'm—'

'He's Prince Charming,' Arthur interrupted, turning to Ella. 'And that's Dandini over there.' He faced Leo again. 'Now, hold her hand out to the side. Other hand on her waist...' He arranged the two of them into a waltz hold, then yelled, 'Connor! Music!' over his shoulder, before turning to the audience and rolling his eyes. 'Can't get the cast these days!'

Connor started playing, and Ella circled the stage in Leo's arms. He was still looking discombobulated, mouthing, '*Sorry*', when his back was to the audience.

'It's okay,' she whispered back, her heart rioting with confusion and expectant hope. His kiss didn't feel like an act, but she couldn't talk to him now until the end of the show as there was no moment when either one of them wasn't on stage.

As the chimes of the clock counted down to midnight, Ella dashed into the wings, passing Willow who was wearing a duplicate of her rag dress, a shawl over her head to hide her face to give the audience the illusion that Cinderella's transformation was immediate.

Backstage, Ella changed out of the ballgown, then crept back to watch Leo perform. He seemed to have got his groove back, speaking his lines with confidence. But then he caught her eye from her position in the wings and trailed off without finishing his sentence.

Ella ducked back out of sight, her heart pitter-pattering in her chest. She couldn't wait for the panto to be over. The uncertainty was making her light-headed and nauseous. What if she'd been wrong? What if Leo wanted her and not Lila? Or was he now confused and couldn't decide between them?

Gripping her head as if she could squeeze the thoughts away, Ella let out a strangled cry.

Just a few more scenes and then it's over. Either way, you'll have your answer.

❧ 27 ❧

Hiding just off-stage, Ella listened to Leo and Scott as they entered the kitchen of Hardup Hall with the glass slipper.

'His Royal Highness, Prince Charming!' Scott announced. 'And you, er, *ladies* are?'

'Her soon-to-be-royal-highness, Miss Fanny Munchin!' Arthur cried.

There was the sound of a scuffle, then Steve spoke. 'No, *I'm* the woman you're looking for! Tittie Munchin at your service, your princeliness!'

'Are you sure this is the last house?' Leo asked Scott.

'Unfortunately, yes. If we can't find Princess Incognito here, then she really has vanished into thin air.'

'Coo-ee!' Arthur cried. 'Your Fanny is waiting!'

Scott cleared his throat. 'By royal decree, whoever's foot fits this slipper shall marry the prince. Are you ladies willing and eager?'

'She's willing, and I'm eager,' Arthur replied. 'Now come on, let's get this show on the road. I've got a wedding to get to.'

'Yes, mine,' Steve said. 'You're going to be the bridesmaid.'

As the two ugly sisters started fighting, Ella moved to stand on the opposite side of the stage to where Leo was facing, so she could enjoy the action without him seeing her.

Arthur had already broken one chair, and was now fighting to fit the slipper onto one of his feet.

'It doesn't fit,' Scott said.

'That's because I'm wearing stockings,' Arthur grumbled. 'Try to control yourselves, gentlemen, whilst I remove them.'

Connor played the opening bars of 'Let's Get it On' by Marvin Gaye, as Arthur tugged the toe of one of his striped stockings whilst leering suggestively at the audience.

'Family show, Fanny!' Steve cried.

As Arthur continued pulling off the stocking, it appeared it was made for someone with an eighty-foot-long leg. Libby took the end and passed it into the audience as Connor changed what he was playing to the theme music from the Benny Hill show, and Arthur tugged the stocking down his leg faster and faster.

By the time the striped stocking had travelled to the last row of seats and back, the audience was in stitches, letting out a cheer when the end finally appeared.

'At last!' Arthur cried. 'And look! It fits!'

Scott lifted Arthur's foot to show the glass slipper hanging off his toe. 'Oh, no, it doesn't!'

'Oh, yes, it does!' Arthur retorted.

'Oh, no, it doesn't!' everyone else chorused.

Steve dragged Arthur out of the chair. 'My turn. Come on, Dandini, let's get it on.'

Connor played the opening bars of 'Let's Get it On' by Marvin Gaye again.

'Not yet!' Steve yelled at him. 'Wait till we're married.'

Steve turned to Leo. 'And you must be gentle with me, my princey-pie. For I am chaste.'

'Yeah, all over Foxbrooke on a Saturday night,' Arthur replied.

Scott knelt down and put the slipper on Steve's foot. 'Oh, no!'

'Oh, yes,' Steve said gleefully.

'What is it?' Leo asked.

Scott swallowed. 'It fits...'

'Ha!' Steve cried. 'Told you! Suck it, Fanny! I'm going to be Princess Charming.'

'What?' Arthur roared.

Steve stood. 'Right. Where's the vicar? Where's my dress? This wedding is on, on, on!' he cried, walking away from the chair and leaving a false leg behind with the glass slipper attached.

'And now it's off, off, off!' Arthur crowed.

Scott picked up the false leg and removed the slipper. 'You two don't have a leg to stand on. Now tell us. Are there any other eligible young women in the house?'

'Um...' Libby began.

'Yes, Buttons?' Scott asked.

Arthur and Steve stared pointedly at Libby and dragged their fingers across their throats.

Libby twisted her hands in the sides of her trousers as she gazed at the audience. 'If I tell the prince about Cinderella, then I'll never have a chance with her! What should I do, girls and boys?'

'Tell him!' the kids in the audience screamed.

'What was that? You want me to *smell* him?'

'No! Tell him!'

'Oh, alright,' Libby's shoulders sagged. 'I love Cinderella so much that I won't stand in the way of her happiness.' She faced

Leo and Scott. 'Your highness, there is another fair maiden in this house. Her name is Cinderella, but I don't know where she is!'

'Do either of *you* know where she is?' Scott asked Arthur and Steve.

Arthur pouted. 'Don't know nuffink!'

'Me too,' Steve added. 'I definitely don't know we locked her in the cellar.'

Leo dashed to the cellar door, but it didn't budge. 'It's locked!'

'Who's got the key?' Scott asked.

Arthur held the key up, then put it down the front of his dress. 'You want it? You're going to have to come and get it!'

Leo and Scott looked at each other in horror.

'After you,' Leo said to Scott.

'No, I insist,' Scott replied. 'After you.'

As they argued, Ella tiptoed behind the back flat to stand behind the cellar door.

There was a puff of dry ice and the lights flashed as Dervla appeared on stage.

'Who are you?' Arthur asked. 'Come to fix the electric, have you? It's on the fritz.'

'I'm not a sparkie, I'm Mistress Cakes, Fairy godmother to Cinderella,' Dervla replied. 'And with my magic you don't need a key, to save Cinders from the cellar!'

The lights flashed again and Dervla opened the door and led Ella onto the stage.

'Princess Incognito!' Leo raced forward to take her hands.

'Prince Charming!'

'The slipper!' Scott said. 'We must check if it fits!' He looked around. 'Where is it?'

'You mean *this* slipper?' Arthur held it aloft.

'Yes! Give it to me!' Scott jumped, trying to reach it.

Arthur flung it offstage, and there was the sound effect of a glass smashing. 'Without a glass slipper, you can't prove she's anyone other than a common-as-muck kitchen maid,' he sneered.

'It doesn't matter.' Leo gazed at Ella. 'This is the woman I want to marry.'

Ella's pulse rocketed. Those weren't the lines he was meant to say.

There was an awkward pause, then Libby jumped in. 'But Cinderella, didn't you show me a matching glass slipper when you got back from the ball last night?'

'Er... yes, I did,' Ella replied, her gaze still fixed on Leo.

'Maybe you should get it?' Libby continued.

'We don't need it,' Leo said. 'All I need is Ella.'

Oh, my god.

'Okey-dokey,' Libby said. 'I'll fetch it.' She dashed behind a flat and immediately returned. 'Found it!'

Leo didn't appear to notice, gazing at Ella as if they were the only people left in the world. 'I love you,' he said. 'I know it might be too soon to say the words, but I need you to know.'

'Shall we see if it fits?' Scott asked.

'Excellent idea,' Libby replied.

'You're my best friend. My soulmate. The other half of me,' Leo continued. 'There's no me without you.'

Ella felt Libby lift her foot and Scott place the slipper on it. 'A perfect fit!' he cried.

Libby pulled the shoe off and tossed it behind her. 'Hurrah!'

'Every part of me loves every part of you,' Leo said. 'All I want is for you to be happy. And if that's not with me, then I'll accept it. I just—'

'I love you too,' Ella interrupted. 'I don't want anyone else but you.'

His eyes widened. 'You...?'

'I love you more than anything,' she replied, giddy excitement bubbling up inside her. 'Even more than Christmas.'

A brief, shocked silence ensued, then Leo's arms were around her, his lips on hers. Ella let herself drown in his kiss, pleasure flooding through her with wave upon wave of emotion. He loved her. He wanted her. After all these years, he was finally hers.

She was suddenly aware that her feet were no longer on the ground. Lifting her head from Leo's, they stared at each other in bewilderment as Arthur, Steve, and Scott carried them into the wings, then ran back onstage.

'Oh Fanny! We've lost our chance with the prince!' Steve cried.

'Well, I spy Dandini,' Arthur replied. 'Come here, gorgeous! I know you prefer Fanny to Tittie!'

As they chased Scott around the stage, Ella gazed at Leo, his smile mirroring her own.

'I love you more than anything,' he said.

'More than winning the Christmas quiz?'

'I'd happily lose every year if it meant I could have you.'

'Are you sure?'

He nodded. 'I was in love with you when we were at school.'

'What?'

'But I stepped aside for Zach.'

'Why?'

Leo shrugged. 'I thought I was doing the right thing. He told me you liked him.'

'I was in love with you, too. I only noticed Zach when you encouraged me to date him.'

He pulled a face. 'I was such a numpty.'

'No, you weren't. You were being a good friend. The best friend. And we've got our happy ending now.'

'Come along, lovebirds,' Dervla chided as she came off stage. 'Time to get ready for the grand finale!'

Libby was leading the audience in a song, giving everyone else time to change into their final outfits.

Ella and Leo dashed to the dressing room, putting on their new costumes, then going to help Arthur and Steve. Arthur was dressed as a glitter ball, and Steve was a working traffic light.

'I'm glad you two have finally sorted things out,' Arthur said to Leo and Ella as they fastened the tapes of his costume and clipped a cycling helmet covered in mirrored squares onto his head. 'Very romantic. I would have shed a tear if I hadn't been trying to save the panto.'

'Well, you *are* the star of the show,' Ella replied with a grin.

'Exactly! That's what I've been saying all along! Next year I think we should do "Widow Twankey, with special guest: Aladdin". You can be Princess Jasmine, Ella. If you're not up the duff, that is.'

'Dad!' Leo growled.

'What? If Libby and Estelle won't give me grandchildren, then you two will have to step up.'

Ella giggled. 'It's pretty early days in our relationship, Arthur. We've only been officially together for about five minutes.'

'What rot. Discounting the sexy times, you've been closer than most couples for the past twenty-odd years!'

Henry appeared by their side. 'Dad, leave them alone and get on stage, or you'll end up at the back.'

'What?' Arthur cried in horror, then turned to Steve, who was rummaging around in a bag. 'Tittie! Stop fannying about! Let's go!'

Steve shuffled forward with the bag in his hand. 'I need you to turn me on.'

'Isn't that your wife's job?'

'The lights!'

'Oh! Yes! Right you are.'

Arthur flicked the switch in the middle of Steve's back and the traffic lights started flashing as if they were trying to cause a car crash.

Arthur chuckled. 'Ha! Bally brilliant! Okey-dokey, let's wrap this thing up. Come on everybody!'

Ella took Leo's hand and they hurried into the wings as the people playing the villagers and courtiers ran forward to take their bow. Next, Scott wheeled Zach onto the stage. They were followed by Dervla and Libby. Arthur and Steve were due next, but the two of them were huddled together behind a flat like naughty schoolboys about to play a prank.

'Dad!' Leo hissed. 'Steve!'

Arthur turned around and Leo groaned. If their costumes weren't ridiculous enough, the two of them had gaffer-taped party poppers to the front of their outfits.

The ugly sisters strutted onto the stage to the biggest cheer of the night, letting off the party poppers as people shrieked with laughter.

Now it was Ella and Leo's turn to shine. As they ran forward together, the audience went wild. Holding Leo's hand, Ella was overflowing with joy and happiness. She'd done it. She'd conquered her fears, stepped out of the shadows and played the role of Cinderella to a capacity audience. Her dad was home and changed for the better. And on top of all that, she'd won Leo's heart.

Dervla raised her wand and everyone fell quiet. 'So now our tale is at an end, we really have to go.'

'Thank you all so much for coming,' Scott continued. 'And we hope you loved the show.'

'We didn't catch a prince tonight, but our search is far from through,' Steve said.

'So run for it when the curtain falls,' Arthur added, 'or we just might come for you!'

Leo squeezed Ella's hand, then addressed the audience. 'True love has conquered all, and Cinderella is now my wife.'

'Our hearts are filled with joy,' she continued, feeling every word as truth, 'as we start our brand new life!'

'And now we'd like to ask you all,' Libby said, 'for one more festive cheer...'

'As we wish you Merry Christmas,' everyone chorused, 'and a very Happy New Year!'

As the audience applauded and cheered, Connor played the opening riff of 'Everybody Needs Somebody to Love' by the Blues Brothers. On stage, everyone danced a simple box set, their feet in time to the beat, as Libby stepped forward.

'Ladies and gentlemen, boys and girls,' she began. 'We're so glad to see so many of you fabulous people here tonight, and we would especially like to welcome all the representatives of Somerset's farming community who have chosen to join us here in the Foxbrooke Manor ballroom at this time!'

There were whoops from the back.

'We do sincerely hope that you all enjoyed our show,' she continued. 'And please remember, folks, that no matter what you do... who you are... whatever it takes for you to live, thrive, and survive, there's still one thing that makes us all the same...' She pointed at the audience. 'You!' She pointed at herself. 'Me!' Then she raised both her hands to encourage everyone to join in with the last word. 'Everybody!'

The whole cast burst into the opening line of the song as the audience joined in and clapped along. *'Everybody... needs somebody... to love...'*

Ella sang at the top of her voice, every tiny hair on her

body lifting with exhilaration. She finally understood the lure of the spotlight. The thrill of feeling the fear and doing it anyway. The rush that came from seeing all the happy faces in the audience. Feeling their enjoyment multiplying inside until it seemed you would burst with it.

A flash of golden hair snagged Ella's attention. A few rows back, Lila was bopping along to the music, a huge grin on her face. Looking directly at Ella, she made a heart shape with her hands, then pointed her index fingers at her and screamed, 'Love you!'

'You too!' Ella yelled back, relief flooding through her at the knowledge that she hadn't lost Lila as a friend because she was now with her ex.

Glancing to her right where Zach was seated, she caught his eye. He gave her a wry shrug and a resigned smile, then mouthed, '*It's okay*,' and gave her a thumbs-up.

She smiled back at him and nodded, reassured that everything was going to be alright. Zach raised his eyebrows and inclined his head at the audience, and Ella faced them again, singing the last lines of the song at the top of her voice. 'I need you! You! You!'

She pointed at the audience, then at Leo as he pointed back at her. 'I need you! You! You!'

As the music came to a roaring end, Tommy and Ryan from the Beardy Boys let off confetti cannons from either side of the stage into the audience. The noise was deafening as people stamped their feet, hollered and wolf-whistled.

Ella glanced up to see the ornate chandelier shaking.

'It'll be fine!' Leo yelled. 'Henry's in charge of health and safety, so we're as safe as houses!'

Holding Leo's hand on one side and Libby's on the other, Ella bowed as the audience went crazy. Finn dropped the front curtain, then raised it again as the stamping of feet increased.

They did four more curtain calls, then the house lights went on.

'Come along, Tittie!' Arthur cried. 'Time to meet our adoring public!' He pushed through the curtains and called out, 'Coo-ee! Who wants a selfie with the most fabulous Fanny in Foxbrooke?'

Steve dashed to follow him. 'And the prettiest Tittie!'

Everyone broke out into laughter as the two of them disappeared.

'Well done everyone!' Libby cried. 'You were incredible! Feel free to mingle with the audience, and we'll have a celebratory party once the ugly sisters have finished with their fans!'

There was a movement at the side of the stage and Vivienne dashed forward, her eyes alight. 'Outstanding!' She embraced everyone she could reach. 'Magnificent!' Usually so poised, her enthusiasm was infectious as she threw out superlatives and hugs with unrestrained excitement.

When she reached Ella, she threw her arms around her. 'Dazzling! You were *born* for the stage!'

Ella squeezed her back. 'I get it now. I almost feel like one of you.'

Vivienne pulled away, her hands on Ella's upper arms and her expression soft. 'Honey, you've *always* been one of us.'

Ella's eyes pricked with tears. No matter how the media portrayed Leo's family, they'd always been there for her. Loved her. Accepted her no matter who her family was.

'Come here,' Vivienne said, drawing Ella back into her arms.

Ella felt Leo hugging her from behind and the vibrations in his chest as he murmured, 'Thank you', to his mom.

'Cuddles?' came Dervla's voice. 'I want in!'

They disengaged with a laugh, and Dervla lifted Ella into the air. 'You know we're never letting you go now?'

She sniffed her tears away, smiling. 'There's nowhere else I'd rather be.'

Dervla exchanged a look with Vivienne, then turned back to Ella. 'You sure you and your handsome prince don't want some private time? Just the two of you?'

Ella felt heat bloom in her cheeks. 'Er—'

'Just remember to put a sock on the door handle,' Dervla continued. 'Then we'll know to leave you alone.'

'Thank you, Mammy.' Leo steered Ella to the side of the stage behind a flat and held her close.

Wrapping her arms around his back, Ella rested her head on his chest and listened to the steady beat of his heart. She had the deep sense that she was finally home. Leo was her safe place. Her harbour. The destination that every road in her life had led to. She was protected by him. Loved by him. And this love flowed through her like a warm golden light, filling every cell with happiness and contentment.

'I love you,' he whispered, kissing the top of her head.

'I love you too,' she murmured, the words sending a thrill of excitement through her.

'Do you want to stay for the party? Or…'

Ella's heart skipped a beat. Right now, all she wanted was to be alone with Leo.

'What do you want to do?' she asked.

He drew back and raised an eyebrow, his gaze incendiary. 'I've just found out the woman I love loves me back. So much as I would enjoy partying with these reprobates, I'd much rather be alone with you. I need to make sure there's no doubt left in your mind as to how much I love you.'

She reached up and pressed a soft kiss to his lips. 'Let's go.'

28

'**O**ur room, or ours?' Leo asked as they stood in the corridor outside their bedrooms.

Ella's heart leapt. This was real. Her and Leo. A few weeks ago, she'd been single and homeless. Now she was with the man of her dreams and living in a fantasy home where she didn't even have to cook or wash up if she didn't want to.

'Because now I've won the princess's heart, I never want us to be apart again,' Leo continued. 'The room on the left has the Christmas tree, but the room on the right has a century-appropriate bed.' He frowned. 'I suppose we could just knock through?'

She attempted a stern expression. 'Leo...'

'Yes, Princess Ella?'

A flicker of uncertainty shivered through her heart. How could such happiness be real?

She swallowed. 'Are you sure about me? About us? Last month—'

Holding her hands, he waited patiently. Somehow knowing she needed to voice her deepest fears.

'You went on a date,' she finished.

'A date where I talked non-stop about you, and at the end of the night, Ellie, who I kept calling *Ella* by the way, told me I should be looking to make *you* my girlfriend, not her.'

'Oh.'

'And don't you think *I* might be worried you're not yet over He-Who-Shall-Not-Be-Named?'

She shook her head rapidly. 'Oliver seems like some weird dream that happened in another life. But I don't think about him at all anymore. Only you.'

Leo's shoulders relaxed a fraction. 'When we were teenagers, I didn't think it was possible to love anyone as much as I did you. But then...'

Lila.

'I fell in love with you all over again,' he continued. 'Only this time it was even more all-consuming.' He gazed at her with understanding. 'It was a surprise, seeing Lila again tonight. But it just reminded me of a part of my life where I was going through the motions. Acting in the way I thought was expected of me. Lila was—*is*...' He sighed. 'Lila. But the person who stole my heart in the beginning, and who has it now, is you, Ella.' He gave her a heart-stopping smile. 'It's you. It's always been you.'

Ella didn't realise she was crying until Leo swept the tears from her cheeks with his thumbs.

'All I think about is you,' he continued. 'All I want to do is make you happy. So if you need me to back off and give you space, you have to tell me.'

She shook her head again. 'I never need space from you. You're my best everything. I just can't believe I could be this lucky. I've never loved anyone the way I love you.'

Leo wrapped his arms around her, pressing her body

against his as if their love could merge them into one person, murmuring his love for her over and over like a prayer.

Ella felt every beat of her heart, love pulsing through her blood. But as she felt the hard length of Leo's arousal pressing into her belly, that love became hotter, needier. Pulling him into her room, she closed the door behind them and locked it.

Confusion moved across Leo's lust-drenched features. 'You got a key? How?'

'Bridget,' she replied with a grin. 'I'm clearly her favourite.'

'I should be mortally offended. But she's got impeccable taste.'

He lowered his head, his lips coaxing hers apart as pleasure coursed through her like a spring tide. She opened to him, her tongue meeting his with licks of fire that made her gasp. His kisses were decadent and debauched, taking everything she had to give, then soul-searingly sweet.

She clung to his broad shoulders, her body thrumming with need, her pulse racing. It had been days since they'd been intimate, and now her need for him was painful in its intensity.

Resisting the magnetic pull of his mouth, Ella broke free, grabbing at the back of her dress to undo it. Leo spun her around, tugged the zip down, and pulled the capped sleeves from her shoulders. The dress pooled at her feet and she stepped out of it, then took off her bra. Leo dropped to his knees to take off her ballet pumps, then tore off her pants.

She stood naked above him, trembling with desire, her skin prickling with electricity. He stared up at her, his eyes blazing with intent, his cheeks coloured with passion. Then, still holding her gaze, he brought his hands to the apex of her thighs, spread her sex open with his thumbs and leaned forward, licking up the length of her pussy.

Pleasure cracked through her like a whip and she cried out.

He did it again. And again. And again.

Her legs shook. She couldn't hold herself upright against the onslaught of feeling.

As she stumbled, Leo lifted her, carrying her the short distance to the bed, then placed her down. Spreading her legs wide, he settled between them, kissing, licking, sucking every part of her as her orgasm began to build, whirling from the edges of her skin to her core.

'Leo! Leo! Leo! Oh my god, Leo!' Her breath was jagged, her lungs labouring to draw in enough air as each flick of his tongue sent another shockwave through her. Her toes curled, her fingers flexed, her muscles tensing as her climax built towards its release.

Then Leo stopped and let out a frustrated yell.

Ella lifted her head from the mattress, her heart pounding. 'Leo?'

His gaze was fire as he showed her his index finger and thumb barely a millimetre apart. 'I'm *this* close to coming. You're just—' He broke off and shook his head, his eyes tightly closed. 'I—' Letting out a long breath, he dropped his forehead to her thigh. 'I love you so much I'm about to explode.'

She interlaced her fingers in his hair. 'Me too.'

Raising his head, he gave her a desperate look. 'I promise I'll put on a better performance next time. You're just so fucking hot and it's making me very, *very* uncool.'

A giggle burst out. 'You're my best, most fexy, fandsome, funny, fucking-hot—'

'Please don't add the word 'fast' to your list,' he muttered. 'I'll disgrace the family name.'

'Fantastically festive friend forever,' she continued. 'And I'm so fortunate to have you.'

'Don't forget "faithful",' he added. 'I'd quite like to spend the rest of my life loving you.'

Emotion fluttered like a butterfly in her heart. 'That sounds pretty perfect to me,' she replied softly.

There was a charged beat as they gazed at each other. A moment which contained in it the promise of an entire future of happiness together.

Then Leo inclined his head towards her breasts. 'I'm going back in, but I need your help.'

She trailed her fingers down to her nipples, maintaining eye contact as she rolled the tips between her fingers and thumbs, sharp pleasure shooting down to her clit.

'Fuck's sake,' Leo groaned. 'Could you please try to be a little less hot?'

She stuck out her tongue.

'Not helping,' he growled. 'Now all I can think about is kissing you.'

'Or perhaps me licking your cock?'

He let out another strangled yell, then head-butted the mattress between her thighs. 'Seriously?'

She laughed with joy. 'I love you.'

He raised his head. 'And I love you. Now I'm going to write those words with my tongue, and you're going to come. Okay?'

Her laugh became breathless. 'Okay.'

'Good.' His mouth lowered, and she twitched as he wrote 'I'.

She followed the words 'love' and 'you', but then he started again and her mind began to fracture, shockwaves juddering along every nerve. She lost track of anything except the heightening pleasure as her orgasm built in tighter and tighter circles.

'I love you,' she gasped. 'I love you. I love you.'

Lust burned bright in every cell, and love was the petrol being poured on the flames. Leo's tongue was fire and light, amplifying every sensation, every emotion inside her until she reached the point of no return. The moment when everything inside her exploded into blinding, pulsing, never-ending pleasure. Rocking her from the inside out. Taking her to heaven and beyond.

The waves kept coming. She was surfing the rolling edges of the universe in a perfect present, containing the totality of everything in an ever-unfolding moment of now.

I love you. I love you. I love you.

Ella was barely aware that Leo had moved, the pleasure still humming inside her like a choir of angels singing about orgasm-inducing chocolate.

But then his naked body was above hers, his forearms bracketing her head as he took her mouth in a blistering kiss.

She tilted her hips, finding the hard head of his shaft and pushing up onto it.

With a groan of surrender and release, Leo plunged his cock deep inside her.

Gasping at the intensity of the stretch, Ella clung to him. There was no other pleasure in heaven or on earth that could touch her like this. The raw and pure intimacy of him filling her body and soul.

His breath was ragged, his muscles tense and primed. Raising his head, he gazed at her, and her own breath stopped at the look in his eyes. She'd never felt so loved before. So cherished. So wanted. As if she were the very oxygen keeping him alive.

'I—' He stopped to suck in another breath, then held it, the tendons in his neck taut and thrumming with tension.

She stroked up and down the hard planes of his body, soothing him. 'I love you, too. It's okay.'

'But—'

She tightened her pelvic floor, squeezing his cock. 'It's okay.'

He made a strangled noise that was half whimper and half cry.

Scoring her nails down to his perfect backside, she splayed her fingers and tugged him closer to her. 'I want you to come.'

His expression was desperate now, as if hanging onto the edge of a cliff by his fingernails.

She guided his movements with her hips and her hands, encouraging him to take what he needed. Overwhelming emotion swelled inside her as she drowned in the intense blue of his eyes.

Then he thrust deep within her and it was as if lightning had struck her core. A sharp, brilliant bolt of pleasure that stole her breath. He snapped his hips again and a second crack of light shot through her.

A tiny part of her whispered that she couldn't come again. But then she fell into the feelings, knowing there was nothing more real than the sensations whipping inside her and the love between her and Leo that saturated her body, mind and soul.

They breathed as one, Ella's climax building with the inescapable power of a rocket preparing for launch. The earth-trembling roar of the engines as the fuel ignited. The pressure increasing until the point of no return.

His cock pumped quicker, stoking the fire within her until it was white hot. Her orgasm was hurtling towards her with unstoppable force, her limbs shaking, her breath frantic.

'Leo!' she gasped. 'I'm going to c—'

And then it hit. A thundering blast that rocketed her into the heart of a star. She was pure light and never-ending pleasure. Every cell shattered with a blinding sensation as the release rolled through her.

She held onto Leo for dear life as he tumbled into his own climax, his body wracked with shudders and her name on his lips. Love stung her eyes. He was so much part of her, she could no more untangle his heart from hers than she could walk on water.

'I love you. I love you,' he gasped, his breath still heaving.

'I love you too,' she whispered as tears ran down the side of her face.

Leo turned his head and kissed the tears away. 'Was it that bad?' he managed.

Ella huffed out a short laugh. 'Terrible. We're going to have to practise more.'

She felt his smile against her cheek. 'This task has just become more important than winning next year's Christmas quiz.'

'Wowsers. I didn't think there was anything more important than that.'

Leo raised his head, his gaze so full of love that her heart skipped a beat. 'Yes, there is,' he replied. 'You.'

Ella blinked rapidly, her jaw tight as she tried to stem her emotion.

'My beautiful Ella.' His fingers stroked her face. 'I'm going to love you so much, you're going to beg me to stop.'

She shook her head. 'Never.'

'Oh, Princess, you have no idea how insufferable I'm going to be. I'm going to moon after you in public like a lovesick puppy. I'm going to hold your hand during dinner and make sure you get the best bits of food. I'm going to serenade you under the moonlight and in the middle of Foxbrooke high street. I'm going to buy you so many flowers that even *Dad* will say I've gone too far. I'm going to write poetry praising your beauty. I—'

'Poetry?'

'Yep. I'll start small. Maybe with a haiku.'

She snorted.

'Ella, my princess. I love you with my whole heart. So there, says Prince Leo.' His face lit up. 'I'm a genius!'

'I'm impressed! There were even the right amount of syllables in each line.'

'I'm a poetry prodigy.' He cleared his throat. 'There once was a princess named Ella, who knew Leo, a charming young fella. They starred in a show, and true feelings did show. And at Christmas, they fell for each other.'

Laughter tumbled out. 'You're the best.'

He grinned. 'I'm the happiest. And the luckiest.'

She sighed contentedly. 'This is the best Christmas ever.'

'And it's still only December the twenty-second.'

'What do you fancy doing for the next three days?' she asked innocently.

Leo raised an eyebrow. 'Don't you mean to ask *who* I fancy doing?'

She let out another snort of laughter. 'Should we stick a "do not disturb" sign on the door handle as well as a sock?'

'Good idea.' He nuzzled her neck. 'And prepare yourself. I've got to give you twenty-one more orgasms by midnight.'

'Dear god. Is that even possible?'

Raising his head, he gave her a cocky grin. 'Shall we find out?'

Then he lowered his lips to hers and she let him sweep her into another ocean of bliss.

EPILOGUE

Christmas Day

No matter what time he got back from the Christmas Eve service, Leo always woke early on Christmas Day morning. The expectant thrill of excitement he'd felt as a child had never truly gone away, and this year there were enough butterflies in his stomach to pull Santa's sleigh.

The grey dawn light was muted as it peeked through the gap in the curtains, yet it was enough to illuminate the angel lying next to him. Love once again squeezed his heart as he gazed at Ella sleeping, her expression soft and peaceful, her dark hair meandering across the pillow like a winter stream cutting through snow.

How have I got so lucky?

Having Ella here, in bed with him, loving him maybe as much as he loved her, was the kind of luck that only happened once in a lifetime. Now there was no-one between them, no reason for his feelings to lie dormant; they'd woken like a hungry bear from hibernation finding themselves next to an all-you-can-eat buffet.

Ella stirred, then opened her eyes.

'Happy Christmas, Princess.'

She gave him a sleepy smile. 'Happy Christmas, Prince Leo,' she murmured. 'You really do love me, don't you?'

'One infinity per cent.'

'Even when I look like this?'

'The most beautiful woman in the universe?'

She snorted with laughter. 'Universe?'

'Yes. I need to account for all extraterrestrial life in my calculations.'

Grinning, she reached for his hand. 'How did I get so lucky?'

Leaning down, he brushed his lips over hers. 'I was just thinking the same thing.' He drew back and hopped off the bed.

'Where are you going?'

'I think the weather forecast was actually right this time,' he replied, then threw back the curtains.

Ella squealed with excitement. 'A white Christmas!' Leaping out of bed, she joined him at the window, circling her arms around his waist. 'It's so pretty.'

Leo twisted his head behind him to drop a kiss on her lips. 'Almost as much as you.'

They stood in a reverent silence, watching the soft flakes of snow dropping silently from the sky to land on the formal gardens behind the manor. The view was quiet and serene, but now Ella was awake, the nervous butterflies inside Leo's stomach were flapping around in a panic.

Too much, too soon? Will she think I'm crazy? Will she say—

'Shall we see what Santa brought us?' she said, interrupting his thoughts.

'First post or second?'

'Both?'

'Why not?'

Taking his hand, she pulled him to the door. Outside, hanging off the handle, were two stockings. One had the name 'Leo' stitched around the top, the other the word 'Ella'. Every Christmas Eve, each family member put a present inside everyone else's stocking, and part of the fun was guessing who had given each gift.

Ella carried them back to the bed. 'This is so exciting! And then we've got ours to open!'

'Uh-huh.' Leo forced a smile as he glanced at the stockings they'd made for each other at the end of the bed.

She took out the first wrapped gift. 'You know, this is the first time we've ever done this together.'

'Hmm.'

She glanced at him. 'You alright?'

Get a grip! 'Yep!' Taking his stocking, he upended it, shaking until every present dropped to the bedcovers.

'Leo!'

He grinned, then ripped the first present open. 'Look at this!'

'That's gorgeous.' Ella carefully peeled the sticky tape from her first gift and unwrapped it. 'I've got one too! What scent is yours?'

Leo turned the candle around to read the handwritten label. 'Blue cedar. What have you got?'

'Lavender. It smells amazing. Willow's so clever.'

'That she is. Are you going to be that slow opening all your presents?'

'Yes, I am.' She pulled out the next gift. 'Remember, the slower I go, the more pleasurable the experience is.' She smirked. 'I thought you didn't want to be known as Leo "fast and furious" Foxbrooke?'

He shot her a heated look as his cock twitched. 'For that remark, I'm going to keep you right on the edge of an orgasm tonight until you beg me to let you come.'

Her cheeks flushed. 'Promises, promises.'

He glanced at the bedside clock. 'I would torment you now, but there isn't enough time before my father makes his annual appearance. And today he's impervious to socks *and* locks.'

Ella giggled. 'Okay, I'll be as quick as I can, but in return, you have to take off every bit of sticky tape so we can recycle the paper.'

'Deal.' He ripped open the next package to reveal a rolled-up t-shirt.

'Ooh, I've got one too.' She opened it out and burst out laughing.

'What—oh my god, that's epic!'

He held his t-shirt up next to hers. His one said 'All I want for Christmas is you Ella', and hers read 'All I want for Christmas is you Leo'.

'This is now officially my favourite Christmas t-shirt,' she said. 'Who's it from?'

'No idea, but they're a legend.'

'We can wear them later and try to guess.'

He high-fived her. 'Plan.'

They finished opening every gift, then Ella made piles of the used tape and flattened wrapping paper. 'Now ours!' she said excitedly.

Leo nodded, his pulse suddenly quickening. This was it. No turning back now.

Ella pulled a thin rectangular package from the stocking he'd made for her. 'Ooh! Let me guess! Art supplies?'

'That's too easy. If you can guess *what* they are, then I'll be impressed.'

'Coloured pencils? Calligraphy pens?'

'My lips are sealed.'

She ran her fingernail along the edge of the paper. 'Where's the sticky tape?'

'I used Pritt Stick instead,' he replied with a grin. 'No excuse not to rip it now.'

She pulled a face. 'It feels like I'm hurting the paper if I do that.'

A laugh burst out of him. 'Seriously?'

Nodding, she gave him an embarrassed smile. 'I know it's bonkers, but I have to be utterly transparent about all of my foibles in case you change your mind about me.'

'They're not foibles, they're quirks.' He leaned in and kissed her. 'And they only make me love you more.'

She sighed happily. 'I don't think I could be any happier than I am right now.'

'You might be if you opened your presents?'

Carefully opening the gift, her face lit up at the set of brush pens. 'Ooh! Love them! Thank you! Now you have to open one from me.'

'Am I allowed to rip the paper?'

'Yes. Because I also used Pritt Stick so I didn't have to hunt for sticky tape amongst the debris.'

His heart flip-flopped in his chest. 'You're perfect.'

Her smile was luminous. 'I could say the same about you.'

They gazed at each other with dopey grins on their faces.

'Are we unbearably in love?' Ella asked.

'Definitely,' Leo replied. 'And the more Estelle makes retching noises later on, the more unbearable I'm going to be.'

She giggled. 'I can't wait.'

Leo gave her another kiss, then shook the contents of the

stocking she'd prepared for him onto the duvet. 'You didn't wrap the obligatory satsuma?' he asked when it rolled out last of all.

'Nature wrapped it.'

'True.'

As Leo ripped the paper off the rest of his gifts, his fingers trembled. Had he ever felt this nervous before? *No. Never.* His joy at what Ella had bought or made for him was tempered with anxiety at what he'd bought for her. And as she slowly drew each gift from her stocking, his pulse kept accelerating.

'Best gifts ever,' she declared as she pulled out the satsuma, immediately starting to peel it. 'Thank you! I love them!'

He swallowed. 'Have you got all of them out?'

She frowned. 'I think so. The satsuma's always last, isn't it?'

Leo attempted a nonchalant shrug. 'There might be one more.'

Lifting the stocking, she thrust her hand inside. 'I missed one!' She drew out a small wrapped package.

'Ella...' Leo began.

Shocked into stillness, she gazed at what was in her hand, then up at him, her eyes wide.

'Aren't you going to open it?'

She tore the paper away, ripping it to shreds, then stared at the box, the logo for Foxbrooke's jewellers on the lid.

'Ella—' he started again.

Flipping the lid, as if impatient to know exactly what might be inside, she gasped when she saw the ring.

'I know it might be too soon,' he said. 'But—'

'Yes.' Her eyes snapped to his.

'What? You *will*?'

'Yes,' she repeated.

'You'll *marry* me?'

'Yes! Oh, my god, yes!' Her hands shook. 'Yes, yes, yes!' She gazed at the ring again, blinking as if she couldn't quite believe it. 'Are you sure?'

Leo took the ring from the box and held her trembling fingers. 'I've never been more sure about anything. I want you for life, Ella Chamberlain, not just for Christmas.' He pushed the ring onto her finger.

'It's—oh, my god, it's so b-beautiful!' she stammered.

'It's a princess cut diamond.'

'I don't know whether to burst into tears or scream with excitement.'

'You could do both?'

She did, letting out a shriek that made Leo's ears ring, then promptly bursting into tears.

The door flew open and Arthur entered the room wearing a well-worn and slightly frayed Santa suit. 'What the bally hell's going on?' he cried, then his gaze fell to Ella's face. 'Did you find the mice?'

'The m-mice?' she replied. 'Have you lost them?'

'Er...'

Behind Ella, Leo mimed zipping his lips shut.

'No! Not at all, my dear.' He glanced at Leo. 'What on earth have you done to the poor girl? We're trying to keep her, not scare her away!'

Ella held out her hand to show him the ring. 'We're getting married!'

Arthur's jaw dropped, then he threw his hands in the air. 'Hurrah and Huzzah!' Grabbing a hunting horn from his belt, he blew it loudly. 'Happy bally Christmas!' He dashed back into the hall, then returned with two glasses. 'Buck's Fizz. I was just doing the rounds, waking everyone up.' He passed them the glasses. 'Congratulations my dears! When's the big day?'

Ella looked blankly at Leo.

'Dad, we've been engaged for less than a minute. We haven't got that far yet.'

'Okay, okay, well it's brekkie and family presents in an hour downstairs, then church at eleven! Maybe you could persuade Eveline to marry you today?'

Leo rolled his eyes. 'It takes at least a month to read the banns, Dad.'

'Well, you'd better get a move on then,' he replied. 'I want—'

'If you mention grandchildren one more time in this house,' Leo interrupted, 'we're all getting vasectomies.'

Arthur gasped and put his hands over his crotch. 'Blasphemy!'

Leo steered him towards the door. 'We'll see you downstairs in a bit.'

'Okay, okay,' he grumbled, then gave Ella a wave. 'Congratulations again, my dear! The family will be thrilled!'

Closing the door behind his father, Leo rejoined Ella on the bed and took her hands, pleasure rushing through him at the sight of the ring on her finger.

'They're all going to be as happy as I am that we're getting married,' he said. 'And I bet Mammy says, "About time", too.'

'You know, I even think *my* dad will be pleased.'

'He is.'

'Huh?'

'I asked his permission a couple of days ago and showed him the ring.'

'Oh, Leo, thank you,' she whispered, as her eyes shone with happy tears. 'Thank you,' she repeated.

Leo's heart overflowed and his own eyes pricked with emotion. 'Come here.' He took her into his arms. 'I love you. You're my everything.'

She held him tightly back. 'I love you too.'

'Best Christmas ever?'

'Definitely. Nothing can top this.'

'How about winning the Christmas quiz next year, then getting married on Christmas Day?'

Pulling her head back to gaze at him, Ella grinned. 'If you can wait that long?'

'I've already waited half a lifetime for you,' he said softly. 'Three hundred and sixty-four days isn't that much more.' He frowned. 'Although, saying it out loud, three hundred and sixty-four days sounds way too long.'

She smiled. 'I feel like we've got all the time in the world. As if my life is beginning again.'

'And I'm going to be by your side, every step of the way.'

He lowered his mouth to hers in a soulful kiss, and she kissed him back as if he was the source of all her happiness. Leo drank in her love, returning it tenfold. Ella was all his Christmases wrapped up into one. She was a perfect, magical gift, and he was going to spend the rest of his life loving and treasuring her.

THE END!

REVIEW CHRISTMAS OFF SCRIPT

WRITE A REVIEW & MAKE MY DAY!

Thank you so much for reading Christmas off Script! I hope you enjoyed reading it as much as I enjoyed writing it!

Even if just a few lines (or star rating), writing a review is the most amazing thing you can do! It helps people find my books, and lets them know what you loved about them.

You can review Christmas off Script at:
Apple
Amazon
Bookbub
Goodreads
Kobo
Barnes & Noble
Google Play
And any other storefront or platform you use!

And, if you want to share more about Christmas off Script on social media or your blog, please **help yourself to our library of graphics, elements and more by going to:**

www.eviealexanderauthor.com/christmas-off-script/

Thank you!

Evie

READ ONE NIGHT ONLY!

Next up is Connor and Avery's story!

ONE NIGHT ONLY
It was only ever meant to be one night...

After years playing a role that isn't truly her, lonely pop star Avery Taylor longs for a moment of freedom. A sizzling one-night stand with a stranger seems like the perfect escape – especially since he has no idea who she really is. But a year later, while recovering from an on-stage injury at Foxbrooke Manor, her nurse turns out to be the only man who's ever touched her soul.

Raised by celebrity parents who thrive on controversy, laid-back Connor Foxbrooke craves a drama-free life. Discovering his new patient is the mystery woman who rocked his world a year ago – and someone even more famous than his parents – is a shock, and he fears crossing a professional line will only lead to heartbreak.

But Avery's done playing it safe. If reclaiming control over her life means breaking a few rules, she's all in, starting with dismantling the walls Connor has built between them. Her plan? Challenge him to read the steamiest scenes from her favourite romance novels aloud to her. But as their passion ignites, time is ticking. Once Avery recovers, she'll return to her fast-paced life in the public eye – something Connor wants no part of. With their worlds so far apart, can they take a leap into the unknown and turn one night into forever?

One Night Only *is a second chance, forced proximity, standalone romantic comedy with a pop star lost in the glitter of stardom, and a cinnamon roll hero who's going to show her true love can be just as dazzling. A swoony romcom with no cheating or cliffhanger, but all the feels, scorching heat, and a guaranteed happy ending!*

Get One Night Only in print, audio, or eBook format from www.eviealexanderbooks.com

And have you checked out the **Kinloch series** yet? Laugh-out-loud steamy romcom that's heating up the Scottish Highlands!

Start with the multi-award-winning **Highland Games** (available in all formats) by going to:
www.eviealexanderbooks.com

NEWSLETTER SIGN-UP

Excited to read about Leo and Ella's magical Christmas Day wedding? Sign up to my newsletter to get their extended epilogue, plus so much more...

In my newsletter you get Evie news before anyone else, as well as exclusive content and goodies.

Newsletter subscribers are my extra special friends, and get everything from bonus epilogues, 19,000 words of deleted sex scenes from Highland and Hollywood Games, free stories, free audiobooks, extracts from my current work-in-progress, and exclusive offers and giveaways.

Sign up now!

www.eviealexanderauthor.com/subscribe

SEX INDEX
(AKA THE GOOD BITS)

There have been many great contributions to the world of literature. Gutenberg invented the printing press, Shakespeare invented romantic comedy, and J K Rowling invented Harry Potter. However, all of these achievements pale into insignificance compared to my contribution – the sex index.

Using this sex index, you can easily find the steamier moments from Christmas off Script. Enjoy...

Page 195 – Time for Cinderella to practice kissing with Prince ~~Charming~~ Humpalot

Page 218 – Best friends give the best orgasms

Page 238 – After a near-death experience, it's time to affirm life

Page 263 – That's a novel way to practice for the Christmas quiz...

Page 345 – Curtain down, clothes off!

And if that wasn't enough, don't forget I've got nineteen thousand words of super-hot deleted sex scenes from Highland

and Hollywood Games as well as Leo and Ella's extended epilogue available exclusively for newsletter subscribers.

If you want some extra action, then sign up to my newsletter today by going to:

www.eviealexanderauthor.com/subscribe/

ACKNOWLEDGMENTS

This book is dedicated to the ultimate Mr Christmas – my husband.

There is quite literally, no other human on this planet who loves the festive season more than he does. Christmas starts in March when he makes the Christmas puddings (note the plural) and continues throughout the year. In chapter three, when Leo details some of the things he and Ella make in each month, the info is lifted directly from my husband's calendar.

He has thousands of hours of Christmas music and films, a bookcase full of Christmas books, and would change our surname to Christmas tomorrow if I agreed to it.

He may not like romance novels (that's putting it politely), however he is unfailingly supportive of me and the best decision I ever made was to marry him.

I must also mention our daughter, Elway, who is equally Christmas-obsessed. She didn't arrive at Christmas, but she is a miracle all the same, and the best luck I've ever had.

Husband and daughter, I love you both to the ends of the multiverse and back.

Thanks as ever go to my fabulously-festive alpha reader, Pash Baker, to whom I write multiple Easter eggs, knowing that she is the only person in the world to recognise them as such. And my epic editing team - Margaret Amatt and Mike AF. Thank you to Matt Wellsted for designing this wonderful cover and Mark Karasick for taking such fabulous photos of me.

Thank you to my sensitivity readers, in particular the ever awesome Tori Ross.

My team at Emlin Press: Victoria, Mandy, and Liezl. Thank you for doing everything I can't, won't, or don't have time for. Thank you for tolerating my foul mouth, laughing at my unfunny jokes and sticking around.

And last, but by no means least, I want to thank my fabulous ARC team, the incredible online community of book lovers and, once again, YOU, the reader. Thank you for your continued support and for reading the fifth book in the Foxbrooke series. Each time you read my books, write me a review and recommend me in countless different ways, my heart gets a little fuller. Thank you!

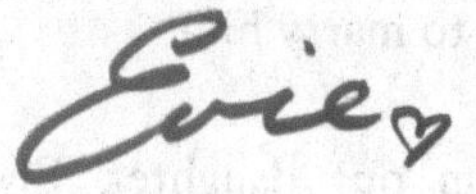

PS - I love, love, LOVE hearing from my readers, so please get in touch via email or social media to ask me anything or just tell me about your day!

hard truths. Can they find a future together, or will their love remain a Highland fling?

Tropes

Small Town, Dark Secrets, Bodyguard/Actress, Forced Proximity, Alpha-roll hero, Dating Game

MUSICAL GAMES

After lying to a Hollywood megastar, Sam needs Jamie to write an album with her in just ten days He's got the voice of an angel and the body of a god, but fame is the last thing on his mind. Will he help make her dreams come true?

Tropes

Small Town, Grumpy/Sunshine, Male Virgin, Cinnamon Roll Hero, Opposites Attract, Fish-out-of-Water, Forced Proximity

WEDDING GAMES

Rory and Zoe want to get married. Not easy when their mothers are mortal enemies and Rory's step-father is a Hollywood star with a death wish. Can they unravel the tangles in time to tie the knot, or is eloping the only answer? Get ready for Scotland's wedding of the year!

Tropes

Small Town, Grumpy/Sunshine, Opposites Attract, Soulmates, Fish-out-of-Water

CHRISTMAS GAMES

Having a baby's easy, right? Until wayward in-laws, an out-of-control cow and mad Santa get in the way. All Rory and Zoe want is a relaxing Christmas before their baby arrives, but straightforward is not their style...

Tropes

Small Town, Grumpy/Sunshine, Opposites Attract, Soulmates, Fish-

❧

THE FOXBROOKE SERIES

ONE NIGHT IN FOXBROOKE

When chef Ben 'Kenobi' Walker gets the call to help save a VIP dinner at Foxbrooke Manor, he doesn't expect to run into old flame Leia Perry. She's all grown up and even more attractive than when they were teenagers – but she hasn't forgotten what happened ten years ago, and she *definitely* hasn't forgiven him. Will one night give Ben the second chance he needs to prove himself and win back Leia's heart?

Tropes

Small Town, Second Chance, Return to Hometown, Enemies-to-Lovers, Bet, Brother's Best Friend, Work Colleagues, Forced Proximity, First Love, Reverse Grumpy-Sunshine, Opposites Attract

LOVE AD LIB

Shy and reserved Lord Henry Foxbrooke needs a fake girlfriend. Free-spirited actress Libby Fletcher needs a job. But when they arrive in Somerset for Henry's birthday celebrations, neither are prepared for their reception. As friendship blurs and faking it starts to feel a little too real, disaster strikes. Can Libby and Henry stick to the script, or has their entire act just bombed?

Tropes

Small Town, Fake Dating, Grumpy/Sunshine, Opposites Attract, One Bed, Different Worlds, Fish-out-of-Water

AN UNHOLY AFFAIR

Gorgeous Jack Newton has fallen in love with Eveline Shaw. But she's a female vicar dreaming of marriage and kids, and he's a male escort heading out of town. Can Jack show Eveline heaven and keep his secret safe, or are they both headed straight for hell?

Tropes

Small Town, Forbidden Love, Love at First Sight, Sworn off a Relationship, Priest, Different Worlds, Opposites Attract, Dark Secret

THE UPPER CRUSH

James Hunter-Savage is a cocky city boy who isn't used to anyone else taking the reins. Lady Estelle Foxbrooke is a fiery country girl who's about to show him who's boss. Can they learn to fight for love rather than with each other, or will their love hate relationship destroy everything they're working for?

Tropes

Small Town, Enemies-to-Lovers, Alpha Hero, Love/Hate, Playboy in Love, Different Worlds, Workplace Romance, Fake Dating

THE LOVE POSITION

Beautiful academic, Sophia Hunter-Savage, has run away to an ashram to reinvent herself. Hot yoga teacher, Isaac Hayward, has left town to avoid the only woman able to tempt him off the spiritual path.

But karma sucks.

Now Isaac's teaching Sophia and they're finding themselves in all kinds of unexpected positions. Will their forbidden love bring inner peace and happiness, or end in a tangled mess?

Tropes

Forbidden Love, Opposites Attract, Teacher/Student, Sworn off a Relationship, Forced Proximity, Love at First Sight, Different Worlds, Fish-out-of-Water

CHRISTMAS OFF SCRIPT

Best friends, Leo Foxbrooke and Ella Chamberlain, have never been single at the same time. Until now... Playing Cinderella and Prince Charming in the Christmas pantomime, their on-stage chemistry kindles an unexpected spark behind the scenes. Can they rewrite their friendship this festive season and finally unwrap true love?

Tropes

Small Town, Friends-to-Lovers, Best Friend's Ex, Oblivious to Love, Unrequited Love, Fake Relationship

ONE NIGHT ONLY

Pop star Avery Taylor craves a break from her public life, and a one-night stand with a stranger feels like the perfect escape. A year later, while recovering from an injury, she's stunned to find her nurse is Connor Foxbrooke, the man who touched her soul that night. Avery is ready to break the rules for love, but Connor, who values his quiet life, fears heartbreak. With Avery set to return to the spotlight as soon as she's recovered, can they bridge their worlds and turn their one night into forever?

Tropes

Second-Chance, Mistaken Identity, One Night Stand, Different Worlds, Opposites Attract, Injury, Forced Proximity, Fish-out-of-Water, Celebrity, Pop Star, Small Town

RIGHTING MR WRONG

Mooning a party of nuns is bad for anyone, but for TV star Aiden Wilder, it's catastrophic. Enter Willow Foxbrooke, a quiet PR worker who's tasked with saving his reputation through a fake relationship. As Willow teaches him how to recover his image, they start to fall for each other. But how can true love grow from something that was never real to begin with?

Tropes

Small Town, Fake Dating, Grumpy/Sunshine, Celebrity, Opposites Attract, Different Worlds, Fish-out-of-Water

UNDER THE INFLUENCER

Sunny Summer Foxbrooke's career as an Influencer is over. Now she's forced to work with grumpy Finn Oakley, the man who's avoided her for years. Will Finn finally return her love, or will she always just be his best friend's little sister?

Tropes

Brother's best friend, Grumpy/Sunshine, Beauty and the Beast, Age Gap, Unrequited Love, Rivals, Different Worlds, All Grown Up, Small Town

 measure

By Evie Alexander and Kelly Kay

EVIE & KELLY'S HOLIDAY DISASTERS SERIES

Evie and Kelly's Holiday Disasters are a series of hot and hilarious romantic comedies with interconnected characters, focusing on one holiday and one trope at a time.

CUPID CALAMITY

Featuring **Animal Attraction** & **Stupid Cupid**

Patrick and Sabina have ditched their blind dates for each other. Ben's fighting a crazed chimp for Laurie's love. Insta-love meets insta-disaster in these laugh-out-loud Valentine's day novellas.

COOKOUT CARNAGE

Featuring **Off With a Bang** & **Up in Smoke**

Cute farm boy Jonathan clings to a love ideal, blissfully ignoring what the universe has planned, while keeping track of his pet pig. Posh Brit follows his heart into the American Midwest in search of Sherilyn, his digital dream love.

CHRISTMAS CHAOS

Featuring **No way in a Manger** & **No Crib and No Bed**

In Scotland, Zoe and Rory attempt to have a civilised and respectable rite of passage, but straightforward is not their style. In Sonoma, Bax and Tabi attempt to throw a meaningful Christmas celebration. But there are too many people involved and it's nothing like they expect.

Get Evie's books in all formats as well as special offers, early releases, and exclusive deals direct from her website:

www.eviealexanderbooks.com

EMLIN
PRESS

ABOUT THE AUTHOR

Evie Alexander is a multi-award-winning author of sexy romantic comedies, blending snort-laugh humour and panty-melting chemistry into unputdownable stories that will steal your heart.

When she's not dreaming up swoony heroes and relatable heroines, Evie can be found in the beautiful West Country of the UK, where she lives with her ridiculously patient husband, miracle daughter, and two dogs who think they run the show.

eviealexanderbooks.com

www.eviealexanderauthor.com

[Instagram] instagram.com/eviealexanderauthor
[Facebook] facebook.com/eviealexanderauthor
[X] x.com/Evie_author
[BookBub] bookbub.com/authors/evie-alexander
[Amazon] amazon.com/Evie-Alexander/e/B08ZJGLP29?ref=sr_ntt_s-rch_lnk_1&qid=1630667484&sr=8-1
[Pinterest] pinterest.com/eviealexanderauthor

www.ingramcontent.com/pod-product-compliance
Lightning Source LLC
Chambersburg PA
CBHW011218190726
48287CB00008B/2657